Dragon Vein

BOOK TWO

BOOK TWO

BRIAN D.
ANDERSON

Dragonvein

Book Two

Copyright © Brian D. Anderson 2015

Published by Longfire Press

Books By Brian D. Anderson

The Godling Chronicles
The Sword of Truth
Of Gods and Elves
The Shadow of Gods
A Trial of Souls
Madness of the Fallen
The Reborn King

You can follow Brian D. Anderson @
http://briandandersonbooks.blogspot.com/
https://www.facebook.com/TheGodlingChronicles
https://twitter.com/GodlingChron

For my brother Hunter and his wife Sarah.

PROLOGUE

RENALD STARED AT the ripple on the water at the end of his line and spat a curse. "I know. I know," he muttered. "I'm wasting my time. You don't have to tell me."

He glared up at the grey, overcast sky, a deep frown on his face. The fish never bit on dull days like this. The lake was calm enough, and if the sun had been shining he was sure he would have caught a basket load by now.

"I don't care if I have salted pork in the shed," he continued. "I'm sick of bloody salted pork."

The rumble of a distant thunderhead warned him that the time for fishing was nearly over. If he didn't get home soon, he'd not only be eating salted pork and onions again, he'd be eating them while soaked to the skin.

Lifting the hook from the water, he stretched out a hand. "*Balik Gael.*"

The hunk of meat he was using as bait quivered and glowed yellow for a moment. Renald smiled briefly before dipping it back into the water.

"Shut up!" he barked. "I know what I'm doing." His arm waved through the air, striking out at some unseen nuisance. "It's not like *you're* helping me, you lazy little rat."

Only a few seconds later, the end of his pole began to dance. Renald stood up as fast as his old legs would allow. "You see?" he shouted excitedly. "I told you so."

The words were barely out of his mouth when the line went tight and the pole bent low. He jerked back with all of his strength. "I've got you now!"

As if in response to his claim, the fish pulled with renewed energy, dragging Renald closer and closer to the steep embankment.

"Oh no you don't," he growled, gritting his teeth. But the fish was too strong. Before he knew it, he had stumbled over the edge and was knee deep in the water. Once there, for a moment he managed to hold his ground, but then another massive tug from his prey yanked him sharply forward again and the pole was ripped completely away from his grasp. A split second later his feet slipped and he plunged head first into the bitterly cold lake.

For a second or two he simply lay there, floating face down. Then, feeling utterly defeated, he regained his feet and clawed his way back to shore. As he did so, a biting easterly wind sent chills shimmering through his body. He gazed down forlornly at his long, wiry grey beard and drenched clothes.

"Not a word," he grumbled. "Do you hear me? Not a damn word."

After squeezing as much of the water out of his beard as he could with his rapidly numbing fingers, he started for home. Today, the two-mile walk up the rocky hillside was made to feel far longer than usual by the persistent wind whipping about him. Soaking wet shoes did not help very much either.

Another rumble from the coming storm had him glancing over his shoulder. "Stop your laughing, you little rat," he snarled.

After finally cresting the hill, he could see that the storm was now only minutes behind him. Not that it mattered. He was already soaked. Each step that he took was accompanied by an unpleasant squishing sound, and he could already feel his toes pruning. He longed to take off his shoes, but knew that the sharp rocky ground would tear his bare feet to shreds in no time at all.

The first raindrop struck the top of his head when he was less than a quarter the way down the other side. He could see a thin line of smoke rising from his chimney – though the house itself was still hidden behind another, smaller hill.

"Well at least you lit a fire," he said. "But you won't be getting any of my dinner. You can bloody well find your own."

He quickened his pace as much as he dared. The rocks and gravel would make a fall very painful indeed. The scar tissue on his knees and elbows were a lingering testament to that.

By the time he reached the top of the small hill, the rain was coming down in earnest, and the frequent, uncomfortably close lightning strikes were unravelling his nerves.

His little stone cottage was now in view. It wasn't much. Though well-constructed, it was small...too small in his opinion. He had thought many times about expanding it, but his now old and frail body would never be able to stand up to the back-breaking work required.

As much as he longed to be inside, the void in his belly forced him around to the smoke house at the rear of the cottage. The aroma of meat sent a pang of hunger shooting through his belly. As quickly as he could manage, he retrieved a portion from a hook on the back wall and made his way over to the house porch.

A chair placed immediately outside the front door was inviting after his long and difficult walk. He plopped down into this and stripped off his shirt and shoes.

"I'm coming!" he shouted at the still closed door. "You want me to track water into the house?"

The muscles in his legs were aching, his feet shriveled and sore. He leaned back and took a long, deep breath. But it was a brief respite. He could not hang around outside in the cold for very much longer, especially in his present half-naked state. After a few seconds he heaved himself up and removed his trousers as well. Leaving all his wringing wet clothes draped over the porch railing, Renald stepped inside.

The warmth of the fire burning cheerfully in the hearth drew a long sigh of relief. He stood still for a moment, simply allowing the heat to wash over him.

The single room interior, if not spacious, was reasonably comfortable. His bed was pushed into the right rear corner, along with a small nightstand. Beside this was a wardrobe and two trunks in which he kept his clothing, plus a few other odds and ends. Also at the rear, on the left, was a small stove and some cupboards, though usually he would cook his meager meals in the fireplace. The circular dinner table was set dead center of the room with six chairs surrounding it – not that he had ever yet needed any more than one of these.

His collection of books had been shoved carelessly onto shelves situated between the two front windows. Aside from fishing, these were the only source of distraction he possessed. Sadly, he had read them all many times and could practically recite them verbatim.

His favorite spot was by the fire, where he would spend time in quiet contemplation while relaxing on his comfortable sofa. It was the one item of luxury he had brought with him. It had been in his family for generations and was so expertly crafted that it had never once needed repair.

"Where are you?" he demanded suddenly. But there was no reply.

With a shrug, he tossed the pork onto the table and found himself a fresh set of clothing. Once dried and dressed, he searched the cupboards beside the stove for the rest of his meal.

The water in the pot hanging over the fire was already beginning to steam. He scanned the room once again and frowned.

"Come out, damn you!" he called. "Or I really will eat it all myself."

In response to this, Renald heard a thump come from just outside the door. On opening it, he saw a very nice size lake trout lying on the porch just beyond the threshold. He shook his head and chuckled.

"All right. All Right. You little rat. You're forgiven…this time."

Picking up the fish, he took it inside and cleaned it, making sure to put the entrails and head in a bowl. Soon, the aroma of fish stew filled the house. He looked at the now forgotten piece of pork. Briefly, he considered taking it back out to the smoke house, but the ominous rumble of thunder instantly changed his mind. Instead, he cut off a large hunk and added it to the fish parts.

Once his meal was prepared, he sat at the table. "Are you coming?" he called out gruffly, placing the bowl of fish offal and pork on the floor beside him.

A few seconds later the sound of talons scraping on wood came from somewhere close to the fireplace. This was quickly followed by the appearance of a tiny white dragon. It skidded to a halt in front of the bowl and let out a high-pitched screech.

"It's about time," Renald groused.

The dragon looked down at the bowl, then back up.

"One fish," Renald told it. "You brought just one fish. Be thankful I gave you some pork."

The dragon sniffed loudly, then began devouring its meal. Renald also began eating, but despite his earlier hunger, soon found that he lacked the appetite to finish. The dragon was still slurping down bits of fish when Renald tossed the remainder of his own food onto the floor.

"Be sure you eat it all," he warned. "Or else we'll have ants."

The dragon needed no second invitation and quickly gobbled up the offering. Renald, meanwhile, cleared the table and took a seat on the sofa by the fire. A book lay on the cushion beside him, but he was in no state of mind for reading. A few moments later the dragon hopped onto his lap and curled up, a soft moan gurgling forth as it breathed. Renald stroked its head and smiled.

"You're sure in an affectionate mood," he remarked.

The dragon looked at him with sadness in its reptilian eyes that only Renald could understand.

"I miss him too," he said. "But he died to save us all."

The dragon buried its head in his lap and whined.

The old man sighed. "Let's just hope it was worth it."

CHAPTER ONE

ETHAN STEPPED QUICKLY to his left. Though the wooden sword in his hand was considerably lighter, it felt no less awkward to wield than his real one. He was doing his best to keep his attention focused on his opponent, but his thoughts were scattered and overflowing with instructions – keep your feet apart, shoulders straight, knees bent, grip firm, watch your enemy's feet, watch his eyes, watch his hands. How the hell was he meant to do all these things at the same time?

Markus grinned viciously, his own, longer wooden blade held high. "Are you just going to dance around? Move already. Or do you plan to kill the enemy by boring him to death?"

Ethan sniffed. "That only works once." He knew Markus was trying to goad him into attacking, but the soreness in his ribcage was a painful reminder that keeping a cool head was equally as important as skill. He took a step back while looking for an opening.

Markus frowned and shook his head. "Stupid," he murmured.

His sword shot forward, the tip striking against Ethan's forearm. In a flash, Markus followed this up by planting his knee firmly into his midsection. Ethan doubled over, his sword dropping to the floor. Before he could even start to recover from this, Markus had gripped him by the collar and threw him roughly to the ground.

The sound of girlish laughter mingled with Ethan's groans and gasps as he tried to regain some of the wind that had just been driven out of him.

"You won't last long like that," Kat teased. She was sitting on a bench a few yards away at the edge of the practice yard.

Ethan glared up at her, his face purple and clutching his stomach. Sitting beside Kat, a look of displeasure written plainly on his face, was Jonas.

"A mage has no business fooling about with swords," he said. "If your father was here he'd..."

"But his father isn't here," snapped Markus. "And he's not a mage yet, is he?" He pulled Ethan to his feet. "Are you all right?"

Ethan forced a smile. "I'm fine. You just knocked the breath out of me."

Markus had been instructing him for several weeks now, but only recently had they begun sparring. Jonas had been fierce in his opposition to all of this. He felt his time would be better spent studying his books and refining the few spells he had managed to learn.

"Are you ready to quit?" asked Markus.

Ethan shook his head defiantly. "Soldiers don't quit."

"Neither do fools," jabbed Jonas.

Markus slapped his friend fondly on the shoulder. "One more time then."

Ethan took a deep breath and moved into position.

"This time, try not to over-think things," Markus advised.

Ethan closed his eyes, imagining his next move.

"This is no time for prayer," laughed Kat.

Ethan's eyes popped open. He lunged hard left, bringing his sword up in a tight arc. Markus stepped easily away, increasing the distance that separated them. But this time Ethan did not hesitate. He immediately pressed in with a short stab, forcing Markus to parry and twist.

Encouraged by this success, Ethan brought his hilt up, aiming it for Markus' jaw. But Markus spun deftly away. The next instant his wooden blade crashed into Ethan's left arm, just above the elbow. Ethan sucked his teeth and backed away.

"Better," said Markus.

The sword fell from Ethan's hand as he rubbed his arm. "That'll leave a bruise for sure," he said ruefully.

"You're getting off easy," Markus responded. "I broke both my arms, my foot, and my nose twice when I was learning."

"This is absurd," hissed Jonas. "Every minute he spends here is a waste of time. He won't be fighting Shinzan with steel."

Markus cast Jonas a hard look. "Why do you even come? All you ever do is complain."

Jonas snorted. "I keep hoping that he'll eventually listen to me and stop this foolishness."

"But Markus is right," Ethan told him. "I need to know how to protect myself. Who knows how long it will be before I can use magic in a real fight."

Jonas glared at Ethan, then back to Markus. "Bah! Stubborn as your father." He threw up his hands and set off briskly toward the courtyard entrance, grumbling to himself all the way.

"I think you did fine," said Kat, smirking.

Ethan chuckled. "You just like watching Markus beat the shit out of me."

She cocked her head and batted her eyes. "That's not true." The corners of her mouth slowly turned up until the laughter she was holding in burst forth. "Okay. Maybe it's a *little* bit true."

The rapid stomping of boots outside the courtyard caught their attention. Ethan could see his guards had stopped a young dwarf boy. After a few short words, they allowed him to pass. He was clutching a folded parchment in his right hand and his face was flushed and his breathing heavy.

"What is it?" asked Markus.

The boy handed the parchment to Ethan. After reading it carefully, he dismissed the messenger.

"It's from King Ganix," he told the other two. "A courier has arrived with a message from Shinzan. King Halvar and the council are already gathering. He wants me to join them as soon as possible."

The mood suddenly became serious. For some time they had been waiting for a sign from Shinzan regarding his intentions, but the emperor had done nothing thus far. Even the smugglers, who by now Halvar had expected to stop coming, were still making all their scheduled deliveries. Aside from rumors of soldiers massing in the far north, everything was continuing as it had before.

Kat sighed and stretched. "Well, I'm going to Lady Thora's house. I promised Asta and Maile I'd visit today."

By the time they reached the edge of the courtyard, ten dwarf guards were already there to escort them back to the manor. Kat ran on ahead after a few blocks and vanished from sight.

The city was now quite a bit calmer than when Ethan had first returned. Most of the siege preparations were now complete, so there was little more for the population to do aside from carrying on with their usual daily tasks. Even so, morale remained high, and many greetings were called out as he and Markus passed by.

The beauty of the city never failed to touch Ethan's soul. The sheen of the buildings reflected the light of the street lamps perfectly, blending to multi-colored stone in a harmony of warm radiance. This was made even more pronounced by the thousands of magnificent frescos and breath-taking statues, all painstakingly situated to coordinate with their surroundings. On their many walks together, Ganix had pointed out where dwarves from various eras had left their distinct mark, each successive generation adding to the next, yet never overshadowing their predecessors. So vast was his knowledge that the old king could chronicle the history of his people simply by gazing at the construction of this fair city.

When they drew close to the king's manor, Ethan could see several council members hurrying inside. He also noted that the guard at the gate and door had been doubled. There was no doubt that the air was thick with tension.

Once inside, they spotted Jonas waiting near the door to the council chambers. His face was like stone, but his eyes betrayed his anxiety.

"I see that you've heard," said Markus. "Do you know what the message says?"

Jonas shook his head. "Only King Halvar and King Ganix have read it so far...and they certainly don't look as if they liked what it said."

Ethan let out a short laugh and gave him a toothy grin. "*Dear dwarves. Surrender or die.* I imagine it's something like that."

"This is no laughing matter," Jonas scolded. "I doubt a simple threat like that would rattle two dwarf kings. They look genuinely worried."

The tone of Jonas' voice wiped the smile from Ethan's face. The thought of either Halvar or Ganix showing fear was indeed disturbing. Without another word, he entered the chamber.

With the exception of his own chair at the near end, every other seat around the stone table was already occupied. While Ethan sat down, Jonas and Markus took up position standing against the wall by the door. Halvar and Ganix were at the far end of the table, talking in hushed whispers. Ethan could see at once that Jonas had been correct. Both kings looked tense and troubled. On looking up and spotting Ethan's arrival, Halvar nodded for the guard to shut the door.

After waiting a moment, he stood up – an open parchment in his hand. "Thank you for coming. As you are aware we received a message from Shinzan. I know you are all curious as to its content, so I won't delay." He cleared his throat and began to read.

"Greetings.

By now I am sure you will have wondered what my reaction to your blatant defiance of my rule will be. Many of you will undoubtedly fear my anger and dread the retribution I am capable of unleashing upon you for your recent acts of rebellion.

So let me set your minds at ease and say immediately that you need not fear me. I have no desire to invade your cities or harm your people. You have simply made an error of judgement, and for this you can be forgiven. I truly value the friendship of the dwarves, and would not see hundreds of years of peace destroyed by a momentary lapse in reason.

Among you is a human known as Ethan Dragonvein. You think to use him to undermine my power. You believe him to be the figure of hope spoken of in foolish elf prophecies. More than that, you actually believe he has the strength to challenge me. In all these things, you have been dangerously misled.

The truth is that I care nothing for this fledgling mage. He is no threat, and what limited power he may possess will not avail you in any way. My only concern is that you have endangered your people by challenging my *authority. And even though I am not eager to act against you, such a challenge cannot be tolerated.*

But it is not too late for you to make amends. Along with this letter I have sent a menax *crystal. Give this to young Dragonvein and convince him to accept the offer held within. Do so, and I give you my word that I will not harm your people in any way.*

As proof of my sincerity, up until now I have allowed your trade with the smugglers to continue. And once I have your favourable reply, you may continue to trade openly without fear or hindrance. I very much hope you will see the wisdom in my words and halt your journey down this dangerous path. As much as it pains me, should you persist, the horrors of the past most certainly will be repeated.

The Eternal Emperor

Shinzan"

The room remained silent as Halvar sat down again. Ganix placed a small wooden box on the table in front of him.

"It's a trick," said one of the elders. "It has to be."

Halvar rubbed his chin. "Of that, I am sure. But a trick meant to accomplish what? His armies have not come. And it is true that trade with the smugglers has continued unabated."

"What do you think, King Ganix?" asked the elder.

Ganix leaned back in his chair, his eyes fixed on the box. "I think that I would prefer an all-out battle rather than subterfuge and misdirection. This letter was meant to confuse us. I cannot reconcile in my mind that Shinzan wishes peace with the dwarves. That he has not arrived here already has concerned me for weeks. And when word does eventually come, it comes with a *menax* crystal."

"What is a *menax* crystal?" asked Ethan.

"A rare magical item," Ganix replied. "So rare in fact, that I have only ever seen *one*. And that was in a broken condition."

"What does it do?"

Ganix fingered the box. "It delivers messages...of a sort. But messages of a very personal nature. I'm not sure exactly how it works. My people lost the skill to make them long ago...even before Shinzan took power."

"You should leave it alone," warned Jonas. "It could be a trap."

Nods and murmurs of agreement echoed from the walls. Ganix and Halvar looked at one another, then to Ethan.

"I agree with Jonas," said Halvar. "It's too great a risk. Though King Ganix thinks otherwise."

Ganix took a long, cleansing breath. "Never have I heard of a *menax* crystal being used as a weapon. But it has been rumored that if one is used when damaged, it could trap the user's mind."

"For all you know, it might not even be a *menax*," Jonas countered. "Who knows what foul device Shinzan would send?"

"How does it work?" asked Ethan.

"It responds to touch," Ganix told him. "You simply hold it, and the message of the sender is then projected into your mind. It will only respond to the intended recipient, and only *they* can see and hear what is said."

"You mean I'll actually see Shinzan?"

Ganix nodded. "Possibly. If he wishes it. They were designed to send secrets and private messages during the war with the elves. If intercepted, there was no danger of valuable information falling into enemy hands." He picked up the box and passed it down the table to Ethan. Once there, Ganix folded his hands beneath his chin. "It is up to you," he said.

Jonas squeezed in beside Ethan and leaned forward. "If you would permit me?"

After a brief pause, Ethan slid the box in front of him. Jonas lifted the lid carefully. Inside was a simple oblong shaped, polished blue crystal – wholly unremarkable from its outward appearance. He touched it with the tip of his finger. Nothing. He gingerly picked it up and held it in his palm.

"Well?" asked Halvar.

Jonas pushed it around with his other hand. "It is apparently as King Ganix said. This is meant only for Ethan." He placed it back in the box. "But again I say that you should leave it alone."

Ethan stared at the crystal for a long moment. "Everyone should leave the room," he said finally. "If it *is* a trap, I don't want anyone else to get hurt."

Ethan felt a strong hand grip his shoulder. "I'll stay," said Markus.

"As will I," added King Ganix. Halvar opened his mouth to object, but a stern look told him that there would be no argument.

"Everyone else should go," announced Halvar.

"That means you, Jonas," said Ethan.

"I'll do no such thing," he protested.

Ethan smiled up at him. "If it is a trap, you'll need to find a way to release Lylinora."

"If you die, there will *be* no one to release her," he countered.

"Kat has talent," he said. "Maybe she can. And if not her, who other than you could find someone to do it?"

Jonas furled his brow and clenched his jaw, but said nothing. After letting out a loud and very expressive huff, he spun on his heels and marched away.

Once the room was clear, Markus and Ganix took a seat on either side of Ethan. Steeling his nerves, he picked up the crystal.

For a few seconds nothing happened. Then, gradually, he felt the crystal's surface grow warmer. A tiny vibration tickled his palm.

"Ah, you came."

The sudden voice from several yards away startled Ethan. He leapt up from his chair. Sitting at the opposite end of the chamber was a man dressed in a black silk shirt. His blond hair fell to his shoulders, and a smile accentuated his attractive features.

"What's wrong?" asked Markus.

Ethan pointed to the man. "Don't you see him?"

"They can't see me," he said. "Only you can."

"What does he look like?" asked Ganix.

Ethan described what he saw while the man waited patiently.

"You aren't what I expected," said the man. "Not much like your father at all."

"You knew my father? Who are you?"

He chuckled and shook his head. "And not very bright either. But I suppose a life on Earth may have limited your education." He paused and gave Ethan a long scrutinizing look, as if sizing him up. "But it's of little matter. To answer your question, I am Shinzan."

"Are you really here?"

"In a sense, yes," he replied. "These fools wouldn't know how a *menax* crystal really works. If they did, I doubt they would have been so eager to give it to you."

The implication behind these words caused Ethan's nerves to fray.

Shinzan held up a hand. "You needn't fear. I have no intention of harming you. But now that we are connected, it will be quite easy for me to find you whenever I need to."

"So this was all just a trick," Ethan retorted sharply.

"Not at all. But it was the only way to see you without the risk of you being killed."

"And why should you care about that?"

Shinzan smiled. "I have my reasons. What is important for you to know is that you cannot run. There is nowhere in Lumnia where I will be unable to find you. But don't worry. If you heed my words, none of that will matter."

"The letter you sent stated that you had an offer," Ethan said, his irritation and dismay with himself rising. He should have listened to Jonas. If there *really* was nowhere to hide and Shinzan could now locate him whenever he felt like it, he had endangered every one of his friends even more than before.

"Indeed I do," Shinzan replied. "My offer is this. Go home. Go back to Earth and leave this world to me. Do that, and I promise to leave you in peace."

Before Ethan could respond, Shinzan's face hardened. As it did so, a menacing shadow crept up from behind him. Within seconds, its darkness had enveloped the entire chamber.

When the Emperor spoke again, his voice was as harsh as his expression. "If you don't, I will kill every living soul in this rat hole of a mountain. I will slaughter them like sheep and bathe in their blood. And their deaths will be on your hands."

Ethan could feel the air growing colder – so cold that his breath was billowing out in fog like clouds. Fear gripped his heart, and he struggled to keep his voice from trembling. "I can't do that," he said. "Even if I wanted to, I'm not able."

The shadow remained for another long moment before finally receding. At the same time, the temperature gradually rose back to normal and the ice in Shinzan's eyes melted away. Within seconds, his expression was once again friendly and warm. "Of course you can," he said. "I can help you. But first you must come to me. I can open a portal to send you back."

Ethan burst out laughing. "Are you serious? You must think I'm *really* stupid."

"I think you care for your friends," he responded calmly. "I also think that by now you are well aware that I can and will make good on my promise."

His form began to fade. "The choice is yours. But choose quickly."

Once Shinzan had completely vanished, the crystal in Ethan's hand instantly turned to dust. He stared at the grains for a moment or two, then tossed them onto the floor.

"What did he say?" asked Markus.

Ethan remained silent for a few moments before telling them of his offer…and of the connection that Shinzan had now achieved.

"If he can find you anywhere, then that's definitely a problem," said Markus.

"Not yet," said Ganix. "But it will be once he leaves the mountain."

Ethan straightened his back. "No…it won't."

"What do you mean?" demanded Markus.

"I mean I'm going to accept his offer," he told him flatly.

Markus grabbed his shoulder and spun him around. "Are you crazy? He'll kill you."

"Probably. But if I don't, he'll come here and kill everyone."

"I'm not so sure," said Ganix. "Shinzan is not known for mercy or kindness. I think there must be more to this than we know. He could have come already, and yet he has not. He says that he cares nothing about you and that you are no threat, and yet he beckons you to him." He scratched his beard, absently twirling the wiry hairs with his fingers. "For now, I think you should do nothing."

"And if Shinzan comes?" asked Ethan.

"We still have the option of sealing the mountain," he replied. "But something tells me it won't come to that. No. Whatever his plan is, he wants you alive."

Ethan thought for a moment. "Then what do I do now?"

"First of all we need to free Lylinora," Ganix said. "Then…well, we'll figure that out when the time comes."

After giving Ethan a reassuring smile, he called King Halvar and the elders back into the chamber.

The reaction to Shinzan's message was mixed. Some suggested that Ethan should flee, while others felt that he should remain in the mountain. Halvar was conspicuously silent as he listened to the nervous bickering.

"It's clear that Ethan should not turn himself over to Shinzan," Jonas announced after a time. "That any of you would suggest he do such a thing…"

"No one is suggesting that," countered an elderly dwarf woman. "Only that he should flee…across the sea perhaps. To the Dragon Wastes."

"That would be the same as a death sentence," snapped Jonas furiously. "Yesterday you thought him to be the savior of your people. But now that Shinzan makes a few threats, you lose heart and want to abandon him. Have you no courage?"

"We will not abandon him," assured Halvar, breaking his silence. "Of that you can be certain. But we must take Shinzan's threat seriously. For now, Ethan must make every effort to free Lylinora. Once that is done, King Ganix will gain him passage across the sea to find the dragons. In the meantime I have already paid the smugglers vast amounts of gold and jewels to keep us informed. We should trust in our preparations…and hope that Shinzan is not yet ready to march."

His words were met with only mild enthusiasm from most. No one relished the idea of sealing the mountain, and Ethan was well aware that the stories of Shinzan's power and fury had been burned deep into their lore.

Regardless of the mood, Halvar rose and dismissed the council.

Ethan remained behind at Ganix's request, while Jonas lingered point-edly by the door. Ethan could tell that he was anxious to question him privately.

"We'll talk later," Ethan told him. "I promise."

Reluctantly, Jonas nodded and left.

"They are right to worry," said Ganix, once they were alone. "This move is surprising."

"Do you think Shinzan expects me to come?" Ethan asked.

"That's just it," he replied, "It is a ludicrous offer. Why would you trust him to keep his word? Why would *we*?"

Ethan sank into his chair and sighed. "I don't know. I mean...I'd go if I thought it would do any good. But if I did, there's nothing to stop him from just killing me on the spot."

"Then he'd simply need to wait for the right moment to move against us," added Ganix. He cocked his head, struck by a sudden thought. "Perhaps he stalls for time."

"Why would he need to do that?" asked Ethan doubtfully.

"I don't know," he admitted. "But he must surely be aware that we've now prepared for his coming. His army is massing, but not mov-ing. He waits and makes overtures of peace that he knows we would see as disingenuous. In fact, everything he has done causes us to delay further action and sends us into a state of confusion."

He met Ethan's eyes. "If I needed time...that's exactly what I would do."

There was a long silence. Ethan's mind was racing. He had no head for strategy, and the idea of trying to think in the same way as an all-powerful emperor was far more than he could handle.

"I know this is much to put on someone so young," Ganix said, clearly noticing Ethan's distress. "I was the same at your age. It takes time to learn to think as your enemy does."

Ethan gave him an embarrassed smile. "I know people think I'm something special. But the truth is that I'm just a baker's son from Brooklyn."

"Ah. But you were also a soldier."

"True. But not an officer. All I ever did was follow orders. There were better men who did the planning."

Ganix placed a hand fondly on Ethan's shoulder and gazed at him with a fatherly expression. "More experienced perhaps. But not better. You should be proud to have come so far. And I am confident that you will go further still." He started toward the door. "Come. Enough intrigue for now. We must continue with our efforts to free Lylinora."

The mention of her name snapped Ethan from his melancholy. Every night he had dreamed of what it would be like once she was free from her prison. Jonas had told him as much as he knew, though he admitted most of it was from the few times he had met her while travelling to her father's estate on business.

The last time was a year before Shinzan began his campaign to conquer Lumnia. By then, Lylinora was already a talented mage and a well-respected noble – known for her skill at healing. Her father, Lord Killian Jaymonte, had resisted quite a few overtures of marriage from the other houses. He insisted that Lylinora would marry for love, not political advantage. This had angered several prominent members of the Council of Volnar, but Lord Jaymonte didn't seem to care.

Jonas had also told him that Lylinora's father and his own had been quite close, and often expressed a wish that their two houses could be joined. Sadly, Ethan was only an infant at the time of their final meeting, making such a union all but impossible. But that was no longer the case.

He followed Ganix to the chamber where Lylinora had been kept for the past five hundred years. Ethan had already moved most of his belongings there, along with a more comfortable cot. Naturally, Kat hated this, and was constantly interrupting his studies. It had gotten to the point where Ethan had requested a guard be placed at the entrance. Not that this helped much. Given Kat's ability to remain unnoticed, she gained entry regardless. In fact, the presence of the guard only encouraged her to be increasingly spiteful with her practical jokes and tricks. Ethan would scarcely take a bite of food or sip of wine without closely examining it first.

As usual on arriving, a blanket had been thrown over Lylinora's crystal and his bedding was scattered about the floor.

Ganix chuckled. "I must say that I admire the girl's resolve. I had thought she would tire of such antics by now."

Ethan began to tidy up the mess. "Kat's as stubborn as an army mule. The Krauts wouldn't have lasted an hour against her."

"Yes," remarked Ganix. "The Krauts. They were the enemy you fought against on Earth, am I right?"

"Actually, their proper name is Germans. We just call them Krauts... or Jerry."

"Why?"

Ethan paused to think for a moment. "You know...I'm not really sure. We just did."

"We used to call the humans *heimskar* when I was young," Ganix told him, smirking. "It means stupid."

Ethan looked at the old king and frowned. "*Kraut* doesn't mean stupid."

"No? Well I'm sure that whatever it means, it's not meant to be flattering."

Ethan's hatred for his earthly enemy began to rise. "They're animals," he growled.

Ganix held up his hand. "No need to get upset. I know you will have good reason to think that way. But I wonder how you will refer to your new enemy. I'm sure that not every soldier you fought on Earth was evil. No more than all those in Lumnia who serve the Emperor are."

Ethan pondered his words for a moment. Maybe it wasn't all one-sided either? He had heard stories of captured Germans being executed. Men begging for their lives as US soldiers – the supposed good guys in the war – laughed and taunted them. He hadn't thought much of it at the time. The Krauts had been just as ruthless and cruel. Even more so. But Ganix was right. Not all of them would have been evil.

"I should not cloud your mind with this," Ganix continued. "War is a wicked thing. It can make monsters of us all. Better you stay focused on the task at hand."

Ethan nodded in agreement. But as he took his place in the center of the chamber, the old king's words were still eating at him. He had never considered the enemy as anything other than foul and deserving of death. He remembered the look of terror on the face of the Imperial soldier he had killed. Had he a wife? Children? Who missed him now that his life was snuffed out?

He closed his eyes and thought hard. Seven. He had killed seven men. Mostly from so far away that he couldn't make out their faces. But it didn't matter. They were dead anyway, and regardless of circumstances, he was the one who had taken their lives. He thought he'd come to terms with it, just as every soldier must. But something in what the king just said had hit home.

The sudden thump of the large, leather bound book being tossed onto the floor by his feet startled him. Ganix's normally kind demeanor was now hard and determined. Ethan sat down beside the book and opened it to a page near the end. At this point, it was very familiar. He must have read the same entry a thousand times by now.

"No warm up today?" he asked.

"No," replied Ganix. "From now on we will be working on one thing, and one thing only."

Ethan's shoulders sagged slightly with disappointment. Casting the few small spells he had so far managed to master was one of his favorite activities. Dragonfire was by far the most impressive, but it often took far too long to cast to be practical. He had also learned how to levitate small objects, and create tiny balls of flame that he would send crashing into the stone walls.

Ganix had been a great help to him during his studies. Though unable to wield human magic himself, he could understand many of its concepts, and had been instrumental in deciphering some of the book's more confusing passages.

Ethan looked at the text and concentrated. Even though he had it fully memorized, he could never get close to connecting with the power of the spell unless he could make a direct visual link with the words.

Slowly he began to rock back and forth. The words had to be spoken exactly, each syllable perfect. As he began reciting the spell he felt a warm rush of energy passing through him. With the other spells, this was a welcome sensation…but not with this one. The waves of heat continued to build in intensity until they felt as if they might push him over.

He reached the bottom of the page, but Ganix was ready for him and quickly turned to the next. Ethan was able to continue without pause all the way to the end of the spell.

Almost as soon as he finished, a blinding flash of white light erupted into existence. For a few seconds it was scattered and without form, but soon it merged into a tiny ball that hovered just a few inches above his head.

Ethan could feel his heart pounding with excitement. He had never gotten this far before. Reaching up, he touched the glowing ball with the tip of his right index finger. It was ice cold, and sparks of energy radiated out in minuscule flecks.

After hesitating for just a second, he wrapped his hand around the ball and squeezed. The light instantly penetrated his flesh, sending surge after surge of violent shocks coursing through his entire body. He jerked and gasped uncontrollably.

'Hold on to it!' he ordered himself.

But the pain increased with each passing second. He tried to stand up, but a fresh wave of power from the barely contained light pierced his flesh and shot down his arm. The pain was unimaginable. He let out a horrific scream.

Then everything went black.

CHAPTER TWO

E THAN COULD FEEL a cool rag gently wiping his brow. His limbs were numb, and for a moment panic gripped him as he realized that he could neither move nor open his eyes. Gradually however, sensation began returning. He let out a soft moan of relief, even though the numbness was now being replaced by extreme fatigue and soreness.

"Don't move." It was Kat's voice. "Ganix said that you are to stay in bed for today."

Ethan forced his eyes open. The chamber was barely lit, and even though Kat was sitting just beside him, he could see her only in silhouette.

He forced a smile. "So you came down here to take care of me?"

"Of course," she replied, sounding a bit offended. "Unless you'd rather Jonas do it."

"No, no. Thank you." He attempted to sit up, but Kat pressed her hand to his chest and eased him back down.

"What part of stay in bed for today didn't you understand?" she scolded.

It was clear she had no intention of allowing him to get up, so he settled back down in his cot, trying to ignore the aching in his muscles. After a brief silence, he asked: "Where is everyone?"

"Markus and Jonas left just a few minutes ago to eat," she told him. "King Ganix has also been here off and on to check on you. I expect he'll be back quite soon."

"How long have I been out?"

"Just a few hours. That's all."

A sharp spasm shot through Ethan's left leg, bringing a twisted frown to his face. He reached down to rub the painful limb, and in that moment realized that he was completely naked. With eyes popping wide, he pulled the blanket right up to his chin.

Kat laughed playfully while tugging at the corner of the blanket. "What's wrong?"

"Stop!" snapped Ethan. "That's not funny. Did you…I mean, how did I…?"

"Jonas undressed you, you big baby," she told him, still laughing. "I offered to help, but he wouldn't let me."

Ethan's eyes scanned around for his clothes. They were a few feet away, folded in the corner.

Kat followed his gaze. "Don't bother with those yet," she said. "Ganix told me he would need to treat you once you were awake. He said you'd be sore and tired."

"He's right about that," Ethan admitted.

She reached down and produced a small, orange colored mushroom. "Eat this. Ganix said to give it to you if he wasn't back and the pain was too much."

Ethan inspected the offering for a few seconds before popping it into his mouth.

Immediately, he grimaced in disgust. "That's revolting!" he exclaimed, pointing urgently to a pitcher of water on the floor beside Kat. Her laughter renewed as she handed the jug over.

"I've never tasted anything so disgusting!" he gasped between large gulps.

But disgusting or not, very quickly the pain in his muscles began easing. A short time later he was feeling light headed and finding it increasingly difficult to keep his eyes open.

As he drifted off he could feel Kat's hand resting on his brow. The last thing he saw before sleep took him completely was her sad brown eyes gazing down at him. He knew how she felt about him. Part of him even wished he could feel the same way about her. But none of that mattered. The fact remained that she was still little more than a child.

When he woke again he realized almost at once that the blanket covering him had been removed, though his rising panic soon subsided when he saw that he was now wearing a pair of soft cotton trousers and shirt. Kat was no longer there, but Jonas was sitting quietly on a nearby chair, reading and sipping a cup of wine.

Jonas noticed him stirring and immediately placed the book and cup on the floor. "How do you feel?" he asked.

Ethan took a moment. The soreness was gone and he was no longer tired. "Just hungry, I guess," he replied.

"Food is being brought," Jonas told him.

"So how long was I out this time?"

Jonas shrugged. "Not long. A day. Maybe a day and a half. That bloody mushroom was a bad idea. It was meant for dwarves, not humans."

Ethan sat up and stretched. "I suppose King Ganix told you what happened to me."

"Yes, of course he did."

Ethan had been expecting Jonas to scold him for putting himself in danger. But the old man continued to simply sit there, his face expressionless. Just then, a young dwarf boy arrived with a tray of porridge and fruit. Ethan thanked him and started into the meal without hesitation.

"I should try to release Lylinora again soon," he said after swallowing the last mouthful.

Jonas' face was still unreadable. "Should you? From what the king told me, your last attempt nearly killed you."

Ethan waved his hand dismissively. "I was fine. It just knocked the wind out of me."

Jonas huffed. "You should never underestimate what magic can do to you. I've read the spell. Even your father would have struggled with it."

"So you think I should just give up?"

"I don't know. I thought you might possibly be stronger by now.

But I can see I was allowing my fears to cloud my judgement. I should have persuaded you to stop long before this."

Ethan shot to his feet. "Stop? I can't stop."

Jonas remained unimpressed by his outburst. "Why not? Why would you continue to risk your life? You were lucky this once. But next time..."

"Next time will be different," Ethan insisted.

"Different how? Different in that you will succeed in killing yourself?" Jonas rose from his seat. "The simple fact is, you're not ready. And in truth, no one should expect you to be. Me in particular."

"King Ganix thinks I can do it," Ethan countered.

"King Ganix is a very wise dwarf," said Jonas. "But he is not a mage. He can't possibly know the toll such a spell takes on someone like you."

"What do you mean: *Someone like me?*"

"I only mean that you are untrained. In your father's time, you would never attempt this type of magic until you had been studying for many years."

"But I don't have many years," Ethan shot back. "Shinzan sure as hell isn't going to wait around until I am *properly trained.*" Anger seeped into his tone. "And for your information, I'm a whole lot stronger than you think."

"I have to admit that you've come far. But I still think this is too much for you." His eyes turned to Lylinora. "She is safe where she is for now."

"I need her," he protested. "I mean, *we* need her."

Jonas smiled warmly. "I know you think that you love her. But you don't. It's just infatuation. You haven't even spoken to her."

Ethan glared. "I'm not infatuated, and I *don't* love her. At least... not in the way you're saying. Is she beautiful? Yes. But she's also the only one in Lumnia who can teach me real magic. The elf prophecy says..."

"To hell with the elves," barked Jonas, cutting him short. "And to hell with their prophecy. They don't know the future. If they did, they wouldn't have been defeated."

Ethan threw up his hands. "It sounds to me like you think *we're* defeated."

"All I'm saying is that you're not ready yet. You need more time."

"There *is* no more time," he retorted quickly. "Or would you rather me just give up and turn myself over to Shinzan."

Jonas' face tightened. But before he could reply, the door flew open and Birger came running into the chamber. His expression was grave.

"There's been an attempt on King Halvar's life," the dwarf shouted before anyone could ask what was wrong.

Ethan felt a chill run down his spine. "Is he all right?"

Birger nodded grimly. "Yes. But three of his guards are slain."

"Who did it?" Jonas asked.

"We don't know yet," he replied, his fury barely contained. "King Halvar was attacked in his private chambers, but his guards fought the assassin off. All I know for certain is that, whoever it was, it was no dwarf."

Ethan started toward the door, but Birger caught his arm.

"The king has ordered that you stay here," he said. Seeing that Ethan was still determined, he added: "There are ten guards at the entrance. They won't let you through."

Grumbling with dissatisfaction, Ethan jerked himself free. "So where's Markus?"

"Helping in the search for the assassin," Birger told him. "He believes it was a Rakasa."

This news caused both Ethan and Jonas to stiffen.

"How did it get here?" demanded Jonas. "I thought no one could enter the mountain without your people knowing about it."

"So did I," said Birger, not even attempting to hide his concern. "Perhaps there is an entrance we are unaware of."

"Or perhaps one of your people has betrayed us," suggested Jonas.

Birger's eyes narrowed and he bristled with rage. "Watch your tongue. None of my people would ever do such a thing."

"Really?" scoffed Jonas. "So you think Shinzan knows your own mountain better than you do?"

Unable to come up with an immediate response to this suggestion, Birger simply glared angrily at Jonas for a few seconds longer. He then spun on his heels and stalked out.

"King Ganix will be here shortly," he called back. I suggest you keep such accusations to yourself when you see him."

"Do you really think a dwarf is involved?" asked Ethan once Birger was gone.

"I can't see another explanation," he replied solemnly. "Birger may not want to admit it, but I doubt anyone could get into the mountain, let alone the city itself, without help. And if that's the case, we'll need to decide quickly how we should react."

The pair of them waited for more than an hour before King Ganix arrived.

"The assassin has been killed," he announced. "I would have rather he be taken alive, but the beast was unwilling to give up."

"Was it a Rakasa?" asked Ethan.

Ganix nodded grimly. "We're still trying to figure out how it got into the city without our notice."

Ethan glanced over to Jonas, but he remained silent. "What do we do now?" he asked the king.

"That depends," Ganix replied. "I know that Jonas is opposed to you continuing your efforts. And part of me agrees with him. But I also believe Lylinora must be free if we are to have any chance of success. It will take years for you to learn sufficient magic alone...perhaps decades. We need her to help you *now*."

Ethan walked across to Lylinora's crystal prison and ran his finger over its smooth surface. He could feel the tingle of energy caressing his skin. She was safe here. He knew that to be true. But he also knew that she needed to be free. And, in spite of his denial, he did love her. The fact that he didn't really know her made no difference at all. He would never be whole until he knew one way or the other if she could love him in return.

Turning away, he retrieved the book of spells from the corner and settled down on the floor directly in front of the crystal. His determination was absolute as he opened the book to the appropriate page.

"This is foolish," objected a clearly startled Jonas. "You have only just recovered from the last attempt."

Ethan ignored him and continued to stare down at the words. As he heard Ganix walking over, he closed the book. "I don't need it this time," he said, handing it to the king.

Ganix took the book and backed away.

Ethan closed his eyes and concentrated. In the darkness of his mind, a pale figure appeared. It floated and rippled like the reflection of some ghostly spirit. Its face was almost clear enough to see. A feeling of familiarity struck him. He had seen this figure before. But when?

Say the words, it whispered to him. The voice was distinctly female, but distant and hollow. He wanted to say something in return, but before he could, the vision had vanished. Even so, Ethan was at once filled with renewed confidence. Without knowing why, the words of the complex spell suddenly made perfect sense to him. He almost started laughing. How simple it was. How did he not see it before? His body began to sway back and forth as he recited the incantation.

He felt the rush of energy penetrating his body as the magic began to build. This time there was no pain; quite the opposite in fact. It felt oh so soothing. The words flowed effortlessly from his lips. He could see them taking form as they commanded...no...persuaded the magic to weave into action. As before, a ball of white light formed just above his head. But this time, rather than reaching up, he held his hands out in front of him in a gesture of invitation. The light began to pulse, then slowly descended until it was hovering just above his outstretched palms. Ethan smiled, then closed his hands gently around the glowing ball. The light immediately began absorbing into his flesh, causing his entire body to shimmer with magical energy.

Rising to his feet, he placed his hands against the surface of Lylinora's crystal.

"I release you," he said almost inaudibly. An instant later, Ethan could feel the power draining away from his body. He took a few steps back.

"It's done," he said.

The words had barely passed his lips when the crystal began to melt away, as if made from ice rather than stone. In that moment he understood everything and his heart was filled to bursting.

Again he closed his eyes. The figure had returned, and this time he could see her clearly. It was a woman in her late forties, though still quite beautiful, with flaxen hair and kind green eyes. She was clad in a flowing white dress and her arms were open wide as she smiled lovingly.

'Who are you?' he asked inwardly.

He thought he should know her. Somewhere deep within his mind he knew the memory was there, but it was just out of reach. Then she began to fade. A pain stabbed at his chest, causing him to stagger back. The knowledge…the understanding of magic…that was fading as well. He cried out unintelligibly and fell to his knees. Moments later he felt hands on his shoulders holding him upright, but couldn't tell if it was Ganix or Jonas.

"No!" he screamed. "Please! Stay!" But she was gone.

Ethan opened his eyes. The crystal had dissolved to the point where the tip of Lylinora's nose was now exposed. Jonas was standing beside her. He looked at Ethan with a mixture of concern and elation.

"Can you stand?" asked Ganix.

Ethan tried to reply, but his tongue felt dry and swollen. As the king slipped his hand beneath his arm and lifted him up, his head began to spin. Ganix helped him over to his cot and eased him down.

"Is she alive?" Ethan managed to croak.

"I need help," shouted Jonas, before there was time for a reply.

King Ganix hurried over to him and took one of Lylinora's arms. A few seconds later the crystal was completely melted away. Lylinora's body went totally limp.

Ethan tried to stand, but was still far too dizzy. Instead, he deliberately rolled off the cot and onto the cold stone floor. "Lay her down here," he instructed.

Jonas and Ganix brought her over to the cot and placed her on her back as gently as possible. Once she was secure, Ganix helped Ethan into a seated position.

Jonas leaned in and placed his ear to her chest. "Her heart beats," he announced with a deep sigh of relief. He covered her with a blanket, then knelt beside Ethan. "You're a damn fool. You know that, don't you? But a lucky fool."

Ethan gazed at the unconscious form of Lylinora. His heart was a tempest of emotion. Although grateful that he had succeeded, the pain of his lost knowledge was tearing at his soul. Everything had been right there. He knew it all. But now it was as if it had never happened.

Ganix shouted for the guards and instructed them to bring a healer, as well as another cot for Ethan.

"I should have the guards take you back to your room," the king said. He chuckled as Ethan flashed him a defiant glare. "But I know very well that you would refuse to go."

"How did you do it?" asked Jonas. "How did you free her?"

Ethan gestured to a small flask in the corner before answering. Once Jonas had brought it over, he took a mouthful of water and swished it around, allowing it to sooth his dry tongue. He then recounted what had happened while casting the spell.

"I don't know who she was," he concluded. "But it was like she... she lent me all her knowledge of magic. I can't explain it any better than that."

Jonas looked at him thoughtfully for a long moment, then said: "Whoever she was, she has my gratitude."

"And mine too," added Ganix.

"I just wish I could have held on to all the things I learned," Ethan said. A little of his strength was beginning to return. He looked over to the cot. Lylinora's breathing was steady and her color was returning. "But it doesn't matter right now. As long as she's all right."

Jonas returned to her side to briefly feel her forehead. "As far as I can tell, she's fine," he said. "Only sleeping."

Ethan smiled and leaned back on his elbows.

The old king sat beside him. "You did it, lad. You actually did it."

Ethan looked at him sideways. "You sound surprised."

Ganix spread his hands. "I had my doubts. In truth, after the last time I was ready to move on without her."

"Move on to where?" Ethan asked.

"To find the dragons, of course," he replied. "But now that she is free, we should wait and see what develops."

A short time later the healer arrived, along with a soldier bearing a cot. Ethan was still weak and did not object when Ganix helped him to lie down.

Once the healer had finished examining Lylinora, she took a small flask from the satchel slung over her shoulder. "As far as I can tell, she's dehydrated and could use a hearty meal," she told the king. "Other than that, she appears to be in good health. Not that I'm an expert on humans."

After she and the soldier had departed, King Ganix turned to the others. "There is something we need to consider before she wakes. Lylinora is completely unaware of what has happened. As far as she knows, everything is as it was when she was first imprisoned."

"Surely her father told her what was happening," said Jonas.

"To my knowledge, her father imprisoned her against her will," Ganix explained. "Or at least that is the way the story was passed on to me."

Jonas reflected on this for a moment. "If that's the case, then I should be the one to tell her what has happened. She knows me. Better that such news comes from a familiar face rather than a stranger."

At that point, Markus came striding into the chamber. He stopped short and stared in utter disbelief the moment his eyes fell on Lylinora.

"You did it," he said, turning to Ethan.

Ethan grinned. "It looks like *everyone* was doubting me."

Markus gave him a lopsided smile. "Yeah. I guess it's still hard to imagine you as a mage."

"He's not," Jonas cut in. "Not yet. But now that she's free, he might very well become one."

"What news from King Halvar?" asked Ganix, briskly changing the subject.

Markus was still finding it hard to drag his eyes away from the sleeping girl. "Guards are scouring the city," he said. "They are searching for any other assassins who may have sneaked through. But I don't think they'll find anyone. Rakasa are usually lone killers."

"Any idea how it got in?" asked Ethan.

Markus' expression darkened. "Yes. That's why I'm here. There was a traitor."

King Ganix stiffened and his fists clenched. "Who was that?"

Markus hesitated.

"Who?" the king demanded.

"It was one of your escorts," he told him reluctantly. "A dwarf named Ferier."

Ganix's face turned red with fury. "Are you certain of this?"

Markus nodded. "He confessed just a few minutes ago."

"Where is he now?"

"He's being held in a room close to your chambers. King Halvar is waiting for you in his study."

Without another word to anyone, King Ganix stormed out of the room.

"I almost pity the dwarf who betrayed him," remarked Markus.

Jonas sighed. "I suspected treachery. Though I wish I had been wrong."

"I should join him," Markus said. "I have experience in interrogation." He turned to Ethan. "Will you be all right?"

Ethan waved his hand. "I'm fine. Just tired. You should go."

His friend took another long look at Lylinora and gave a soft chuckle. "You must be the luckiest son-of-a-bitch I've ever met." Still smiling, he then left the chamber.

Utterly fascinated, Ethan continued to watch as full color gradually returned to Lylinora's face. A few times he noticed her stir and thought she might waken.

Kat arrived a short while after Markus had departed.

"Lady Thora tried to keep me inside," she began as she walked over to where Ethan was lying. "She's such a worry wart. But I managed to sneak…"

Like Markus before her, she stopped short when catching sight of Lylinora. For a moment she simply stood there, her lips quivering. After flashing a quick glance at Ethan, she then turned and ran full speed from the room.

"Poor girl," said Jonas. "She really does care for you."

Ethan was now strong enough to sit up on his own. He sighed heavily. "I know. And I wish I could do something. But I can't."

"A pity she's not older," said Jonas. "As a companion she would complement you quite well. She actually reminds me of your mother in some ways."

Ethan knitted his brow. "Enough of that. There's no point in talking about it right now."

Jonas nodded. "Still, you should speak with her as soon as you are able. A kind word may go far to mend a broken heart."

Ethan couldn't help but smile at the almost fatherly role Jonas had taken on for himself in Kat's life. It was a far cry from the way he'd treated her when they first met. He genuinely cared, and showed her no small measure of consideration – even going so far as to speak with Lady Thora privately about the girl's future.

This thought was still passing through Ethan's mind when Lylinora let out a soft moan, then turned onto her side. He immediately struggled to his feet and stumbled over to her cot.

"You should get back," Jonas said. "There is no telling what will happen when she wakes."

Reluctantly, Ethan backed off a short distance.

Lylinora continued to shift and moan for several more minutes. Jonas knelt beside her throughout, holding her hand close to his chest. Eventually, her eyelids fluttered and then cracked open. Ethan could see that her lips were moving, but there was no sound forthcoming.

"Blue," whispered Ethan. When he saw Jonas look back at him questioningly, he said, "Her eyes. I've been wondering what color they were."

Jonas shook his head then turned back to Lylinora. She was still attempting to speak. "What is it, my dear?" he asked in his most comforting tone. "What can I do?"

After several more attempts, she was able to whisper a single word. "Father."

"Be still," said Jonas. "Everything will be all right."

"Father," she repeated, this time a touch more loudly.

"He's not here," he explained.

She looked up at Jonas pleadingly. "W...W...W...Where?"

"Rest for now," said Jonas. "I'll explain everything later."

Ethan could see the confusion and fear in her eyes. Desperately wanting to help, he took a pace forward, but a warning glance from Jonas halted him.

Lylinora reached up and touched the old man's face. "J…Jonas? How…when?" Tears began streaming down her cheeks.

"Please, sleep. I promise all will be well."

For several seconds Lylinora struggled to sit up, then collapsed into unconsciousness.

She remained still for another twenty minutes before stirring again. This time, Jonas had a cup of water at the ready. When she opened her eyes, he lifted her head gently and helped her to take a few small sips. After a brief cough and a sputter she took a much longer drink, this time clutching desperately at the cup until it was completely drained.

"More," she said, heaving her breath.

"You are dehydrated," Jonas told her. "Too much too soon is not good for you."

With a sudden and surprising display of strength, she gave Jonas a hard shove. "More!"

Jonas fell back, landing ungainly on his backside. He immediately scrambled to his feet but kept his distance. "Please, My Lady. Be calm."

The fire in her eyes was very evident. Ethan was impressed by how quickly she was recovering. She leaned up onto her elbows. "Where is my father?" she demanded. "Where is King Vidar?"

"What do you remember?" asked Jonas.

"I asked you a question, servant." Her voice, though not loud, had become steel. "Lord Dragonvein may tolerate your insolence, but *I* won't." By now she had managed to fully sit up. Her eyes turned to Ethan for a split second, then fixed back on Jonas.

The old man hesitated for a painfully long moment and then lowered his eyes. "Both your father and King Vidar are dead, My Lady."

Her eyes shot wide and her mouth fell agape. For a full minute she did not utter a word.

"I'm sorry," Jonas said in a half-whisper. "I truly am."

She eventually spoke. "That can't be true. I just saw them. You must be…you must…"

Her words began to stumble as she finally began to take in her surroundings. Panic rose and her hands trembled. "How did I...where...?"

Jonas drew a deep breath. "I don't know how to say this gently, My Lady," he began. "The truth is, a very long time has passed since last you saw your father."

He took a cautious small step toward her. "Much has changed."

"How long?" Tears were now flowing freely down her face.

Jonas sucked in another, even deeper breath. "Five-hundred years."

The effect of this revelation was instantaneous. Lylinora scrambled from the cot and backed away until she was hard up against the wall. "Liar!" she screamed. "That cannot be."

"I wish it was not so," said Jonas. "But it is. Your father sealed you away and left you in the care of the dwarves." He took another wary step closer.

Her face was by now completely stricken with terror. "No! That's not true. You lie! You'd be dead too."

A flash of yellow light erupted just in front of Jonas. Before he could move he was encircled by a ring of fire that blazed up to his waist.

"Tell me the truth," Lylinora demanded. "Or I'll roast you alive."

"Please, My Lady!" he begged. "If you will just calm down and listen to me."

His pleading drew no response. The fire began to intensify and the stench of singed hair was soon filling the chamber.

"Stop!" cried Ethan. "He's telling the truth." He started toward Jonas, but another ring of fire sprang to life around him.

"And who are you?" hissed Lylinora. "Another snake here to deceive me?"

"No," he insisted. "My name is Ethan Dragonvein. I am the son of Praxis."

Lylinora glared. "You think I'm a fool? The son of Praxis is an infant...and his name is not Ethan. It's Weslyn." Both circles grew taller and hotter. "One more chance...then you both die."

Ethan was becoming desperate. "I swear to you. I'm not lying. I was the one who released you from the crystal."

But his words only filled her with renewed rage. "*And* you claim to be a mage. If that is so, then save yourself. That is, if you really are the son of Praxis Dragonvein."

The circle of fire continued to grow taller still until it was well above his head. After reaching this height, it gradually began to close in. Ethan could feel the flesh on his arms and cheeks beginning to burn. Crying out, he covered his face with his hands and fell to his knees. But this offered no protection at all. The pain only intensified. Very soon, he would be roasted alive.

Then, with a loud sucking huff, the flames vanished.

Ethan removed his hands. The cool air of the cavern felt like a healing spring. He looked over to where Lylinora had been standing. She was now flat on her back, unconscious. Looming over her with a thick book gripped in both hands was Kat. She was scowling down at the helpless woman as if debating whether or not to strike her again.

"Are you two all right?" she asked.

Jonas' face was bright red and his clothes were smoldering in several places. Even so, he gave a sharp nod.

"I'm fine too," replied Ethan. "Thanks."

"I knew she'd be a bitch," said Kat. "But no one ever listens to me."

Ethan struggled to his feet. The stinging of his skin was fairly mild at the moment, but he knew that it would get much worse later on. "She was just scared," he told Kat. "It's not her fault."

It was not the smartest thing to say. Kat threw the book at his head, missing by only a few inches. "Scared hell!" she exclaimed. "She didn't look scared when she was about to kill you."

"Help me move her over to the cot," said Jonas.

Ethan obeyed. Once there, Jonas examined where Kat had struck her.

"She'll have a headache," he said. "But I don't think she's badly hurt."

"Then I should have hit her harder," Kat grumbled, her arms crossed and a look of contempt written plainly across her face.

"We need to figure out what to do," said Ethan. "When she wakes up she'll..."

"Kat," said Jonas, cutting him off. "Go and get King Ganix."

Still staring hatefully at Lylinora, she made no reply.

"Kat!" barked Jonas. "Hurry."

After a brief scowl, and still without a word, she turned and left, slamming the door behind her.

"What do we do if she wakes up?" asked Ethan.

Jonas shrugged. "Hope that she doesn't kill us."

Nearly ten minutes passed. By now, Ethan was growing increasingly nervous. Lylinora had stirred several times, but thankfully hadn't yet woken.

When the door finally did open again, it was King Ganix who appeared. His expression was strained and his shoulders were slumped. In his right hand he held a book which Ethan recognized as the journal written by King Vidar.

"The girl has told me what happened," Ganix said. "You two should leave. I will speak with Lylinora when she regains consciousness."

"What of the traitor?" asked Jonas.

"That matter has become…complicated. But for now there is nothing to be done about it. Markus will tell you what happened. He's waiting for you in your chambers."

He took a chair from the wall and placed it beside the cot. "Now go."

"But, Your Highness," Jonas protested. "I should be here too. She knows me."

"And she almost killed you in spite of that," he replied flatly. He looked to Ethan and saw the concern on his face and smiled reassuringly. "I'll be fine. I doubt she'll attack me."

"And if she does?" asked Jonas

He reached into the folds of his robe and produced a short green rod. "If she does, I can protect myself far better than either of you."

Jonas took another long look at Lylinora before nodding his agreement. "You're right, of course. But please…be gentle."

"I will," he promised

Jonas followed Ethan from the chamber and together they climbed the ladder leading up to the manor. Once at the top, they were met by Kat. The sheer intensity of activity here was startling. The attempt on King Halvar's life, along with the revelation that there was a traitor in their midst, had everyone on edge and scurrying about in a thousand different directions. The guards at the entrance who escorted all three of them to Ethan's room, never allowed their hands to stray from the hilt of their weapons.

Just as Ganix had said, Markus was there waiting for them. He was seated at the small table in the corner, a bottle of dwarf whiskey in his hand. Ethan could hear the guards standing just outside the door talking nervously. The words *'murder'* and *'doomed'* reached him quite clearly through the thick timbers.

"They are right to be afraid," said Markus, also listening. "Ganix's escort did not betray us willingly."

The other three quickly took seats at the table. Within moments, in an action entirely uncharacteristic of him, Jonas snatched the bottle from Markus' hand and turned it up to his mouth.

"Careful, old man," Markus warned. "That stuff is stronger than what you're used to."

Jonas suppressed a cough and wiped his mouth on his sleeve. "I think I *need* something strong right now." He offered the bottle to Ethan, who politely refused.

"Yeah, it looks like you might," Markus agreed, noticing the redness of their skins.

"What do you mean, the escort didn't betray us *willingly?*" Ethan asked, eager to be brought up to date.

Markus frowned. "I mean that he was under some sort of magical influence. He remembers everything clearly - how he helped the Rakasa through the gates, and telling him all about the layout of the manor. And yet, as soon as the beast was dead, he confessed to it all without any persuasion whatsoever. Apparently, he was under a spell or curse... something like that. But after the Rakasa died, the spell was broken and the escort immediately became his normal self again."

Jonas rubbed his chin and took another, much smaller drink. "Does anyone know *how* he was cursed? Or more importantly, *when?*"

"Not exactly," answered Markus. "But it was before King Ganix arrived in the city. At least, that's what we think."

Jonas nodded. "Good."

"Why is that good?" asked Kat.

"Because it means he was not influenced by someone already among us," Jonas told her.

"But it also means that Shinzan has plans," added Markus. "Plans that have been in motion far longer than we'd hoped."

This consideration brought on a long and somber silence.

Breaking the dark mood, Kat reached over to snatch the whiskey bottle from Jonas. But before she could raise it to her mouth, Jonas grabbed it back.

"Wine is one thing, young lady," he scolded. "But this is *not* something a girl your age should be drinking."

Kat frowned. "You're no fun at all."

Jonas leveled his gaze. "You are certainly right about that."

"Tell me what happened with Lylinora," said Markus. "I gather from the way Ganix tore ass out of his room that it didn't go quite the way you thought it would."

Ethan recounted most of the events, though Kat interrupted, insisting that she tell how she snuck up and hit Lylinora, thereby saving both Jonas and Ethan from being burned to cinders.

"So she's not exactly the delicate flower you were hoping for then, Ethan," teased Markus.

"She was afraid," he shot back. "That's all."

"Hopefully, King Ganix will be able to reason with her," said Jonas.

Ethan lowered his eyes. "I guess we'll know soon enough."

CHAPTER THREE

HOURS TICKED BY, and still there was no word from Ganix. At one point Lady Thora came in looking very displeased and began scolding Kat for sneaking away. But after discovering that the girl had saved the lives of both Ethan and Jonas, she was unable to mask her approval.

"Brave and foolish," she said. "So much like my own daughter. Come now. Asta won't stop whining about your promise to play with her today."

"Go on," urged Jonas. "I promise I'll let you know if anything happens."

Reluctantly, Kat left. But not before Making Jonas repeat his promise.

It was nearly time for supper when King Ganix at last entered. He looked exhausted and plopped heavily into a chair across the room from the table. "She'll be fine," he announced before anyone could ask. "She just needs some time alone to take it all in."

"Did she attack you?" asked Ethan.

"No," Ganix replied. "She was hesitant to attack a dwarf, and I was able to convince her of my good intentions. Once she had read the journal of King Vidar, she was able to accept what has happened – though far from easily. The poor girl has lost everything she knew."

"Can we see her?" asked Jonas.

"Not yet. Give her a day to come to terms with things." He pointed to the half empty bottle of whiskey, which Ethan quickly handed him.

Ganix held the bottle under his nose and smiled. "Made by the Lugnar family. Where did you find this?"

"King Halvar gave it to me," Markus said.

Ganix raised an eyebrow. "A fine gift to be sure. And rare."

"You're welcome to what's left," offered Markus.

He smiled broadly and took a long drink. "Ah. Nothing quite like it."

"Are you sure it's wise to leave Lylinora alone?" asked Jonas. "Don't you think I should at least see her?"

Ganix took another drink. "Not yet. Though she did ask me to convey her apologies for what she did."

"How much did you tell her?" asked Ethan.

"As much as I could," he replied.

"Did she mention me?" Ethan pressed. As the words came out, he realized how childish and love sick he sounded.

Ganix chuckled. "She did indeed."

There was a long pause.

"Well?"

"She said that you look nothing like your father."

Ethan's shoulders sagged.

This revelation drew a hearty laugh from Markus. "Sorry, Ethan. I guess it's not love at first sight after all."

Ethan's face turn bright red. "That's not what I meant. I just...I was just wondering if she..."

"She knows who you are, lad," assured Ganix. "And she knows it was you who freed her. And I'm sure she is grateful. But as I said, for now we should leave her alone."

"There's still the matter of the dwarf who betrayed you," noted Jonas. "He might not be the only one who was compromised."

Ganix's mood instantly darkened. "Yes, that's very true. And until I find out how Ferier was cursed, we must take extra precautions. He has been a part of my personal guard for many years and would never have betrayed me willingly. If he can be made to do so, then there is no telling who else might have been corrupted."

"What will you do with him?" asked Jonas.

Ganix lowered his head. "He must be imprisoned. At least until we can be sure the spell has been lifted."

"I'm sorry," said Jonas.

Ganix nodded. "As am I. He has been a loyal friend for many years. But too much is at stake to risk that he is still under Shinzan's control."

Markus then took up the conversation to recount how they had tracked down the Rakasa. He made a point of saying how well the dwarf fighters had handled themselves.

"For what they lack in sheer speed, they more than make up for in cunning," he said. "I don't think the creature was prepared to be outmatched."

"In the forest or a human city, the Rakasa may hold an advantage," explained Ganix. "But within our own walls, no one could escape us without using powerful magic." His voice carried noticeable pride.

A short time later a messenger came to summon Ganix for a meeting with King Halvar. Soon after that, both Markus and Jonas decided that they'd had enough excitement for the day and retired to their chambers.

It took a long time for Ethan to relax enough for sleep. He thought about taking a walk, but the idea of being followed by guards was not appealing. Better to be alone in his room than have his every step hounded, he felt. Eventually, he changed into his bed clothes and laid down.

For more than an hour he stared at the ceiling, a vision of Lylinora's anger and fear as she threatened to burn him alive boring into his mind. He had certainly been hoping for a far tenderer greeting than that. The idyllic fantasy of her falling into his arms once she discovered it was he who had released her was now well and truly shattered. Not that it was ever real to begin with. Jonas had constantly warned him that she might not be receptive to a romantic situation, and that he should not be building up hopes for one. In response, he consistently denied that he even held any such hopes. But both of them knew it was a lie.

As he drifted, he could hear her voice screaming at him in terror. But it was soon replaced by another, all too familiar call – the dragons.

"Come to us," they beckoned. "Time is running out."

Ethan desperately wished he could reply. So many questions. And in spite of everything he had learned about his past and his family, he was still no closer to the answers he needed. Shinzan was out there... waiting. But for what?

A cool breeze warned him that the door to his room had opened. For a moment he thought it was just an illusion brought on by being on the edge of sleep. But the hard clack of the door closing again sharpened his awareness. Someone was definitely in the room.

As slowly as he could, he reached beneath his pillow and felt for the small dagger he kept hidden there. When Markus had first suggested this precaution he'd thought it excessive. Not any longer. His hand wrapped around the cold hilt, but he did not dare make a move until first having a good idea of where the intruder was standing.

In spite of straining his ears to the maximum, only a few random sounds coming from the hall outside reached him. He cracked open his eyes. After a few seconds he was able to make out a silhouette standing absolutely motionless just a short distance inside the door. It was close enough for Ethan to think that he might be able to leap from the bed and surprise his attacker.

He held his breath and tensed. One...two...three.

Jerking the dagger free, he rolled his feet quickly to the floor. The moment they made contact, he burst forward. But fast as he was, he'd barely taken two paces when a stream of green light ignited and wrapped itself around his legs and torso. Before he could even cry out in alarm, it lifted him a foot into the air and began to contract. Ethan struggled, but the pressure only intensified. As the dagger fell from his hand, sparks danced from the encasing light in a series of sharp pops and sizzles. He twisted and tried to call for help, but was like a rat caught by a giant snake.

"Be still, Dragonvein," called a soft and distinctly female voice.

His eyes had been dazzled to near blindness by the light. All he could see was a blurred shape of someone with an arm extended toward him – the apparent source of the attack. He could feel consciousness leaving him. Then, as quickly as it appeared, the light vanished and he dropped hard down onto his knees. Coughing and gasping, he clutched at his throat and chest while searching for breath.

"I didn't mean to hurt you," the voice continued. "I'm sorry if I did."

Ethan felt two delicate hands on his shoulders. He looked up. It was Lylinora. She was now dressed in a white cotton robe tied at the waist by a blue sash. Her hair was pulled back in a loose ponytail that allowed it to spill over her shoulders. She met his eyes with a look of concern.

Ethan tried to speak, but for the moment he could only continue gasping for more air. Yet even through his distress and pain, he still felt thrilled by the mere touch of her fingers.

"Can you stand?" she asked.

Ethan nodded, then struggled unsteadily to his feet. Lylinora took his hand and led him to the plush chair near the breakfast table. Satisfied that he was settled, she sat facing him.

"I – I'm fine," he managed to gasp out with only a small cough.

"I had not intended on waking you," she said. "I should have waited."

Ethan shook his head and held up his hand. "No!" His tone was a touch too eager. "I'm glad you're here. I was worried."

"Worried? Why?"

He did his best not to sound like some kid with a crush. Choose your words carefully, he warned himself. "King Ganix told us you were upset."

Lylinora narrowed her eyes. "Is that really why?"

She paused, but Ethan said nothing.

"Yes. I was upset," she affirmed. "I still am. I have a right to be. My world is gone and all of my family are dead. And if that alone was not hard enough to accept, I discover that the one to blame for this now rules over all of Lumnia. So yes. In truth, I am *very* upset."

"I'm sorry," said Ethan. "I understand."

"Possibly you do." She leaned back and folded her hands in her lap. "King Ganix tells me that you've been watching over me."

Ethan felt heat rushing to his cheeks. "I was trying to free you."

"Is that why you slept down there?" she asked. "To free me?"

"It was just easier that way," he lied. "I've been trying to learn magic. It seemed like a better place to do it."

"And that is what the young girl will say when I speak to her? You know. The one who hit me with the book?"

"Kat? She…she was just protecting us," Ethan explained. "She didn't mean to hurt you."

"Don't misunderstand. I'm grateful. Otherwise I would have likely killed both you and Jonas. But such daring and courage usually comes from love. And King Ganix has said enough for me to suspect that it wasn't Jonas she was protecting."

Ethan was unsure how to reply.

She waved her hand and smiled. "It doesn't matter. I'm sorry if I've embarrassed you."

"You didn't embarrass me," he replied unconvincingly. "Kat has feelings for me. But she's too young."

Lylinora raised an eyebrow. "Is she? And how old are you?"

"Eighteen."

"And you harbor no feelings for her at all?" Her tone was probing.

"I care about her. But I don't love her…not in *that* way."

Lylinora nodded with a satisfied grin. "This is good. With things as they are, you cannot afford to make unwise choices."

Ethan furled his brow. "I don't understand."

"You will soon enough."

Lylinora rose to her feet. Her movements were graceful and her demeanor not at all like someone who was feeling the deep pain of loss. Instead, she appeared resolute and fueled by a fierce conviction. "We shall speak more in the morning," she said.

Her imminent departure had Ethan rising quickly up out of his chair. "Don't go yet!" he pleaded. "There are so many questions I want to ask you."

"They'll have to wait," she said firmly, making her way to the door. "But don't worry. If what King Ganix told me is true, we'll be spending plenty of time together."

He could only watch as she left the room. What was that all about, he wondered? It didn't make sense. It was almost as if she was saying that they would be...

He shook his head, cursing himself for being stupid. She was probably just curious about him and nothing more.

He got back into bed and closed his eyes, his heart pounding as he thought about her. How beautiful she was. How graceful. Even the call of the dragons was now dull and distant to him. Only with a tremendous effort was he able to push her from his thoughts and allow himself to sleep.

*

A hard knock at the door startled him awake. Before he could respond, Markus came striding into the room, a broad grin on his face.

"Rise and shine, mate. Are you going to sleep all morning?"

Ethan rubbed his eyes and yawned. "Why are you so chipper?"

Markus opened Ethan's wardrobe and fetched him some clothing. "Looks like we might just be getting the hell out of here." He tossed a shirt and trousers onto the bed. "King Ganix is out gathering supplies, and King Halvar is waiting for us...with Lylinora."

At the mention of her name, Ethan instantly snatched up the clothes and began to change. "Already? What time is it?"

"Early," Markus replied. "At least, I think it is. Who the hell can tell down here? Jonas is already on his way. When he heard Lylinora was up and about, the old boy nearly jumped for joy."

The rumble in Ethan's stomach as he finished dressing reminded him that he had not eaten for some time. On his way to the door, he spotted the dagger he had dropped. Markus gave him a curious look when he paused to pick it up and put it back under his pillow.

"Lylinora came here last night," he explained.

Markus cocked his head and smirked. "A beautiful woman comes into your bedroom in the middle of the night...and you pull a dagger on her?"

"She surprised me. I thought it was an intruder."

"What did she want?" he asked.

Ethan told him about the encounter.

"Interesting," Markus mused. A wry grin crept up from the corners of his mouth. "Though if I were you, I wouldn't mention any of this to Kat."

Ethan couldn't help but laugh.

The guards outside led them through the manor and up to a spacious room on the third floor with a long wooden table placed in the center. The walls were bare, and there was no carpet or rugs. Ethan assumed it was a room not often used.

At the head of the table sat King Halvar, with Lylinora beside him. Ethan stopped short the moment he saw her. She was still wearing the same white robe and sash, but her hair now fell loosely down her back, held out of her face by two delicate silver combs. He scanned the room for Jonas, but the old man was nowhere to be seen.

The pair, engaged in deep conversation, scarcely noticed their arrival. "It's too dangerous," Halvar growled to Lylinora. "I won't risk the lives of my people on this."

"And if you are killed?" she countered. "What good will that do for them?"

"Did we interrupt?" asked Markus.

For a tense moment the king and Lylinora remained with locked eyes. Halvar then snorted and leaned back in his chair.

Lylinora looked up at Ethan. She gave him just a slight nod before transferring her attention to Markus. Her eyes lingered on him for several seconds.

Markus bowed and introduced himself.

"I know who you are," she replied. "But I was not informed you were in need of healing."

Markus appeared confused for a moment. He then touched the scars on his face. "Healing? No, My Lady. Old wounds. Nothing more."

Ethan glanced over to his friend, afraid that Lylinora might have embarrassed or offended him. But he seemed unconcerned.

"That much I can tell," she said. "But why suffer the discomfort?"

Markus smiled. "There is no discomfort, I assure you. Unless you mean the discomfort my appearance causes to others. But there is nothing I can do about that."

Lylinora scowled and shook her head. "What a barbaric time this is. See me later. I'll show you what can be done."

He waved his hand dismissively. "There really is no need."

In spite of this casual response, Ethan definitely saw something in his friend's expression change. Hope? Excitement? Fear? Perhaps all of these things. He couldn't tell for sure.

"I insist," Lylinora replied. Her tone stated that there was to be no further discussion on the matter, prompting a brief silence.

Ethan and Markus both took a seat. "Where's Jonas?" Ethan asked.

"He'll be returning shortly," said Halvar.

"Should we wait for him?"

Lylinora sniffed. "For your servant? Certainly not."

Ethan was unsure what she meant. Instinctively, he was put off by her attitude. After all, he was just a baker's son from Brooklyn, and his mother had taught him to never look down on people.

Lylinora laughed softly, sensing his displeasure. "My father always said that Lord Dragonvein allowed Jonas to be overly familiar with him. But take my advice; do not make the same mistake. I only spoke with Jonas briefly and could soon see that he is not telling all he knows. He is here to serve you, and has no right to keep secrets."

"He's not really my servant," Ethan contended. "He was my father's, that's all." Being at odds with Lylinora made him feel distinctly uncomfortable. Nonetheless, he pressed on. "If Jonas has secrets, then that's his own business."

"He serves the House of Dragonvein," she said with an air of superiority that further unnerved him. "As did his father and his grandfather before him. He is bound to you by both oath and blood. That he has never made this clear to you is shameful. If he were mine, I'd have him whipped."

Ethan stiffened. "I'm not having anyone whipped."

His hands were trembling. Would she really do such a thing? He didn't want to think so, but her eyes told him that she would. She looked at him as if to scold him for his ignorance.

"Enough of this useless banter," Halvar interjected. "We have important matters to discuss."

"Indeed," Lylinora agreed, focusing her attention on the king. "How long until things are prepared?"

"What things?" asked Ethan, suddenly feeling like a child seated at the adult table.

"King Ganix feels it's time for you to find the dragons," Halvar explained. "Now that Lylinora is free, there is nothing holding you here. The assassination attempt on me was only the beginning. Though the beginning of what, I do not know. But we both believe that the longer you wait, the more perilous our situation becomes. Shinzan is no fool. Everything he does has a specific purpose."

"But why try to kill you?" Ethan asked. "Why not come after me?"

"I think that he wants you alive. Perhaps he believes he can corrupt you, or use you in some other way."

"Which is why we should move quickly," added Lylinora.

"Or maybe that's what he wants," Markus suggested. "To drive Ethan out into the open where he's vulnerable. To make us act before we have time to think things through."

"You have a point," agreed Halvar. "But even if that's the case, we have one key advantage. Shinzan has no way of knowing about Lylinora."

"I may not be as powerful as my father," she said. "Or yours, Ethan. But I should tip the balance in our favor. At least for a little while."

"At minimum, it will give you a better chance to escape," Halvar added.

At this point, Jonas entered the room with Kat at his side. He bowed low, but she merely took a seat beside Ethan, her eyes shooting daggers at Lylinora throughout. Jonas took the seat beside her, which drew a huff of displeasure from Lylinora.

"If my presence is unwanted, My Lady," began Jonas.

"You may stay." Her voice was impassive. "Though I would ask for you to remain silent."

Ethan was on the point of protesting when Kat spoke first.

"Pretentious bitch," she muttered.

Lylinora's eyes flashed with anger. "Mind your tongue, girl. Just because you are Lord Dragonvein's pet, it does not give you the right to speak to your betters."

Kat sprang to her feet, but Ethan caught her arm and pulled her back down.

"Be very careful," warned Lylinora. "You caught me unawares before." She held out her palm, causing a blue orb of light to appear. "Next time you will not be so fortunate."

"You just better be glad I didn't have my knife," Kat spat back at her.

Lylinora was unimpressed. The orb blinked out and she folded her hands on the table. "The girl has spirit. I see why you keep her around. But she could use some…refinement."

"I like her just the way she is," Ethan snapped back. "And I wish you would be just a bit more polite to my friends."

He was slowly growing to dislike this woman. Anger born out of disappointment was building. If Lylinora's attitude was anything to go by, the way he had so stupidly envisioned her could not have been more wrong.

Kat gave him a sweet smile, then shot her adversary another disdainful sneer.

Lylinora flashed an innocent smile in return. "I meant no offence. Please pardon my ignorance. I am unaccustomed to low company."

Ethan could see Kat's fists balled up at her sides. Jonas, on the other hand, was unruffled.

So too was Markus. "Our ways are crude and direct," he said calmly. "But these are qualities you may find to be an advantage where we are going."

She gave a slight nod. "I'm sure you are right. And to that point, King Ganix has informed me that we are to gain passage on a smugglers' vessel. Is that correct?"

"That is so," Halvar confirmed. "It's the best way for you all to travel unnoticed. You'll head up the coast and leave ship when drawing close to the secret Island of Borgen. There is a hidden boat on the mainland that will take you across to the island itself. From there, King Ganix will transport you across the sea to the Dragon Wastes."

"And how will he do that?" asked Markus.

"He says he has a way," Halvar replied. "But he hasn't shared it with me. I know many of his best craftsmen work there, so I imagine there's a ship of some sort."

"And who will be going?" asked Ethan.

"I am!" Kat said immediately.

Ethan chuckled. "I doubt I could leave you behind, even if I tried." His words drew an exasperated sigh from Lylinora...which he ignored.

"Jonas and Markus will both go," said Halvar. "Birger has also volunteered. We think it best to keep the party small, so King Ganix will leave his escort here. And in light of recent events, that is probably for the best."

"I disagree with bringing the child along," said Lylinora. "She will be an unnecessary burden."

"She's coming," snapped Ethan. This drew a soft mutter of approval from Kat.

Lylinora tilted her head slightly and nodded. "As you wish, My Lord Dragonvein."

"Until then you should keep quiet about your departure," Halvar stated.

"And what of the matter we discussed before?" Lylinora asked him.

His jaw clenched. "I told you. I'm not risking harm to my people?"

"What are you talking about?" asked Ethan.

Lylinora sighed. "As you know, the dwarf who aided the Rakasa was cursed. Unfortunately, if anyone else is afflicted in the same way, I don't possess the proper skills to remove the curse with any degree of safety. And even if I did, it would take years to check every dwarf individually. Therefore, I have suggested a way to protect the king, but he has so far refused to cooperate."

"How?" asked Ethan.

"By erecting a barrier around his home that will strip all spirit magic from whoever enters. The curse Shinzan used bonded itself to Ferier's spiritual essence. Traditional healing is not right for such a thing. If I try, it could kill him."

Ethan's faced twisted into a confused frown. He glanced over to Jonas and noticed the old man's mouth twitch. He clearly understood her intention.

"But better a servant dead rather than his lord," she continued. "Wouldn't you agree, Jonas?"

A stone faced Jonas nodded. "Much better, My Lady."

"If I erect a barrier, it would cleanse anyone who walks through his doors."

"And kill them if they are cursed," Halvar cried out, throwing up his hands.

"Not necessarily," she countered. "It would be painful to be sure. But some may survive. If they are strong enough."

Halvar's expression was unyielding. "Some? Does life mean so little to you that you risk it thoughtlessly?"

"It is not thoughtless." Her voice never rose and her smile never faltered. "How can it be, when I am thinking most seriously about your well-being, Your Highness? Surely your life is important enough to warrant such precautions."

Ethan was finding it difficult to understand that this was the same woman who, only hours earlier, had discovered that everyone she knew was long dead. How could he feel anything for such an insensitive person? But the truth of the matter was, in spite of it all, he still did. And he was beginning to despise himself for it.

"Might I make a suggestion?" Markus chipped in. "Why not examine the King's guard, the council, and anyone else who resides in the manor. See if any are affected. After that you can erect your barrier and forbid entry to anyone else."

Lylinora nodded approvingly. "Not bad for a brutish sell-sword."

"I have my moments, My Lady," Markus responded. If he was bothered by her arrogant demeanor, he certainly wasn't showing it.

Halvar remained silent for several seconds before speaking. "I'll consider it. How long would it take you?"

"It depends on the number of staff," she replied. "At least two days I should think. Perhaps three."

"I'll give you an answer by tonight then," he said. "For now, I think we have spoken enough." He looked to Markus. "King Ganix will want to speak with you about travel outside the mountain. You have by far the most experience, and he will want your advice."

Markus bowed. "I'll see him as soon as possible."

Halvar rose. Ethan had expected a longer meeting, but it was clear that the king had talked as much as he was willing to do so for now.

As they filed out, Lylinora whispered something into Markus' ear. He nodded and allowed her to pass in front. Kat's eyes never left her rival; fury etched on every inch of her face. She jostled herself in front of Ethan and slowed her pace. Jonas stayed back as well.

With the exception of Lylinora who was returning to the underground chamber, the guards escorted everyone else to Ethan's room. Markus stayed there for only a moment before excusing himself by saying that he had some errands to run.

"I should have beaten her bloody," snarled Kat, once Markus was gone.

"You don't mean that," Ethan told her.

"The hell I don't," she shot back. "Little Miss High and Mighty can kiss my ass as far as I'm concerned."

"Don't judge her too harshly," said Jonas. "She is from a different time. And she's still coping with the loss of her entire family."

"She didn't look too upset to me," said Kat.

Ethan couldn't help agreeing, but decided not to say so.

"People deal with pain in their own way," Jonas pointed out.

"What was she like when you knew her?" asked Ethan.

"Much as you see her now," he replied. "Only a little less outspoken. Her mother was a true noble and made certain Lylinora understood her place in the world."

"So she was a bitch then, and she's a bitch now," remarked Kat.

Jonas frowned. "You shouldn't say that. She may cling to certain ideals, but when I knew her, she was considered to be one of the kindest and most generous nobles ever to grace Lumnia. She spent a fortune seeing to the welfare of those who lived on her family's lands, and she healed the sick regardless of their status without any thought of payment or thanks." He planted his hands on his hips. "So save your judgmental attitude for someone else, young lady."

"I'll say what I like," Kat snapped back. "Ethan agrees with me. Don't you?"

Ethan shrugged. "I don't know what to think. I will say she's certainly different from how I imagined she'd be."

Kat huffed. "You just don't want to say it because you're..." She stopped short and shook her head. "You're a moron. That's what you are. How can you love someone like that?"

"I never said I loved her," Ethan responded rather too quickly.

Kat's face was red and her lips trembled. "You didn't have to."

He wanted to argue with her, but he knew she was right.

In spite of everything he had seen and heard, he did still love Lylinora.

CHAPTER FOUR

MARKUS LOOKED OVER his shoulder at the door to Ethan's room. The guards there had barely given him a second glance. I suppose I'm not important enough to follow around, he thought, smiling. Satisfied that no one would see where he was going, he started toward the chamber where Lylinora was waiting.

The dwarves watching the entrance stepped aside the moment they saw him. Clearly she had left word that he would be coming. While descending the ladder he began to feel ripples of anxiety, though he was unsure as to why.

Upon stepping into the chamber, he saw Lylinora sitting in a chair beside a small table. She was reading one of the books Ethan had been studying.

"How could he expect to learn anything from this?" she said without looking up. "Everything in here is theory. Nothing practical at all. It's a miracle he was able to free me."

She gestured to a chair that had been placed across from her. Markus sat down and waited while she continued to thumb through the pages. After a few minutes she placed the book on the table and sighed. "I really do have my work cut out for me, don't I?"

"I'm not sure what you mean, My Lady," he replied.

Lylinora scrutinized him for a moment. "Do I make you nervous?"

"No, My Lady."

A tiny smile formed at the corners of her lips. "You may call me Nora when we are alone."

Markus nodded. "As you wish, Nora."

"You are friends with Lord Dragonvein, yes?"

"Yes," he affirmed. "Good friends."

"Then I can assume that you know his likes, dislikes, things of that nature?"

"I suppose I know him better than most."

Lylinora stood to retrieve a bottle of wine and two glasses from the corner. After filling both glasses, she handed one to Markus. "In that case, I need your help."

"My help?"

"Yes." She sat back down and took a sip from her drink. "I need to know how best to deal with Lord Dragonvein."

Markus furled his brow. "What do you mean by *'deal'* with him?"

She held up her hand and laughed. "Nothing sinister, I assure you. I only wish to know how best to help us get along."

"Ethan's a good natured person. You shouldn't have trouble making friends with him."

"Yes, but I need us to be more than friends." She took another sip of wine. "I need him to be...how should I say it...committed."

Markus suppressed a laugh. "Committed? You mean romantically?"

"Possibly. Yes. At some point. But for now, I just need him to trust me. If we are to have any hope for success, I must take on the role of teacher. One for which I am not entirely suited."

"Why not?"

"I was little more than an apprentice when I came here," she explained. "To Lord Dragonvein, my powers will appear miraculous. But compared to his father...or mine, I am nothing. Still, there is no one else to instruct him. And the path is not an easy one."

Markus took note of the ever so subtle change in her tone when she mentioned her father. "If you really want him to trust you, then you need to open up. Tell him how you feel."

"But I don't feel anything for him," she replied. "He is a handsome young man, but..."

Markus chuckled. "That's not what I'm saying. Please don't be offended, but you come across as being somewhat callous and cold, and frankly…more than a bit arrogant."

"Is that so?" Her expression was reserved and her tone even, but her hands were now folded tightly in her lap.

Markus paused. "If I have offended you…"

Lylinora lowered her head. "You didn't. I want you to speak candidly. Please continue."

"Ethan is a very open person. He shares his deepest feelings with those close to him. If you really want him to trust you, you need to share your feelings too."

She slowly stood and walked over to the small alcove where she had been kept for so long. "Such things are…difficult for me. My talents in magic are strongest in the healing arts." She looked over her shoulder and forced a smile. "I don't expect that to mean anything to you. The mages are gone. All but me."

"And Ethan," he added.

"Ethan may very well become a powerful mage…one day. But for now he knows less than I did at the age of five. You say I should open myself to him. But you don't understand why that is difficult for someone like me. Mages who learn to heal the body must touch the spirit of those they heal. When this happens you are faced with the unfiltered pain of that person. Not just the physical; everything. You think me cold and unfeeling. But I feel far more deeply than you can fathom."

Markus nodded with sudden understanding. "So you push it away."

"Yes," she affirmed. "If I didn't, I would go mad. The pain and suffering of the people I've healed has never left me. I still experience it as keenly as the moment I first touched them."

"Then why do it? Why put yourself through something like that?"

"Because I was needed," she explained. "Mages have a responsibility to those they are charged to protect. Shinzan was wreaking havoc throughout Lumnia - there were so many sick and wounded begging for help, and I couldn't turn even a single one of them away." She let out a soft laugh. "My father begged me to stop. He could see how it was affecting me. But I…I couldn't."

Markus felt a sudden urge to comfort her. To wrap her in his arms and tell her that he understood. The pain he himself chose to hide from the world was often unbearable. But for Lylinora…she had been forced to shoulder the burdens of countless people like him. It was a miracle she had been able to even think about continuing.

With a sigh, she turned to fully face him. Her smile was now bright and cheerful. "Thank you, Markus. Your advice has been most helpful."

He was bitterly regretting his earlier words. She was far from callous and cold. He could see that clearly now. "I think that if you told him about what happened…."

"No!" she said, cutting him short. "And I would ask that you do not mention it again."

"Of course."

"Now, I would like to show you my appreciation."

"For what?"

"For your council, of course," she said.

She glided across the room with effortless grace and took hold of Markus' hands. He stood absolutely still, a confused look on his face.

"Close your eyes," she told him.

Without thinking, Markus did as instructed. Then he felt the soft touch of her slender fingers on his cheeks. Instantly, his eyes opened again and his hands shot up, grabbing her wrists.

"No," he said. "You shouldn't."

She looked at him like a mother scolding a disobedient child. "You will release me at once." Her tone was stern and measured. "You may be a friend to Lord Dragonvein, but I am still a noble lady of high birth."

Markus lowered his eyes, though his grip on her wrists remained. "I understand, My Lady. Even so, I can't allow you to do this."

"You have no choice in the matter," she said, this time more forcefully. "You attract far too much attention looking as you do. Besides, I would like to see your outer-self match what is inside of you."

Markus looked up. "I'm afraid it already does."

Her laughter was like chimes in the wind. She pulled her hands free and pushed Markus' arms to his side. "Nonsense."

"Please," he whispered. "No."

Her laughter ceased and her expression softened. "Tell me why."

"I don't want you to...to know..."

She pressed her finger to his lips. "Your secrets will be safe. I will not be able to know them unless you allow it."

"But you said..."

"I will know your pain. But not what caused it."

"I would not want that either," he said.

"Don't worry. Healing scars does not require as much as healing wounds. I will only need to touch your spirit ever so slightly. I'll be fine. I promise."

Markus could feel his heart beating in his ears. He wanted to refuse. But he couldn't. He closed his eyes again and felt her gentle touch. At first it was warm and soothing. Then, slowly, the heat increased until it bordered on being painful. The air filled with a strange sweet scent that reminded him of lilacs. After only a few seconds the heat began to recede and he felt her remove her hands. The absence of her touch was oddly disturbing.

As he opened his eyes he could see that tears were streaming down Lylinora's face. Her lips trembled and her arms were hugging her torso.

"I'm...I'm so sorry," she said in a half-whisper. "I had no idea."

Before Markus could even speak, she fell to her knees and began weeping openly. He knelt down and placed his hands gently on her shoulders. His heart ached from the pain he knew he had caused her.

"Are you all right?" he asked.

Lylinora did not answer for a long moment. Then she looked up at Markus and cupped his face in her hands.

"Forgive me," was all he could say.

She gazed into his eyes, her expression a mixture of sorrow and longing, then pulled his face to hers and kissed him – at first in a gentle and tender way. But as her tears soaked his skin, the kiss became deeper and ever more passionate. Her hands slid around his neck. Markus could feel her breasts pressing against his chest. He pulled her harder to him, his manhood swelling and his desire burning fiercely. The heat radiating from her body sent his mind reeling.

For a moment their lips parted and he looked again into her eyes. There were no more tears, only yearning and lust. The absence of her mouth was more than he could bear. He tightened his hold around her waist. In response, she rubbed her hips hard up against his, moaning softly.

The invitation was clear. He eased Lylinora to the floor, running his hand over her shoulder and parting the top of her robe before raising himself up to gaze down at her. Her flesh was flawless; her breasts perfectly shaped. Touching her nipple he felt it instantly harden and she craned back her neck, eyes shut, lips parted and breathing rapidly. This sent even more violent waves of passion coursing through him. Never had his manhood ached and throbbed with such desire. Never before had he wanted a woman so completely. He gently moved his hand downward, the cloth of her robe falling away to either side as his fingers traced the curve of her stomach.

When his touch was mere inches away from her most intimate place, Lylinora's eyes suddenly popped wide open. She grabbed him firmly by the wrist, preventing any further movement. He looked at her with utter confusion. His mouth opened to speak, but no words would at first come out.

Her voice was almost inaudible. "No," she whispered. "I can't do this."

His hand was now trembling and his heart pounding like a blacksmith's hammer. "I – I don't understand," he stammered.

"I can't do this," she repeated, this time more forcefully.

She closed her robe with her free hand and shifted from beneath Markus.

"Did I do something wrong?" he asked. "I didn't mean to…"

Scrambling to her feet, she began straightening her robe. "You should go."

He stood and took a step toward her, but she quickly backed away.

"What's the matter?" he asked. The warmth of her body still lingered on his flesh and feelings of desperation and panic filled his chest.

"I said go!" she snapped. "Go now!"

Markus stared at her pleadingly for a desperate long moment, but she refused to meet his eyes. Finally, she turned away from him completely.

Only with tremendous effort was he able to tear his eyes away and start toward the exit.

"Say nothing of this to Lord Dragonvein," she called after him.

He paused briefly in his step, but made no reply.

While making his way dejectedly to his own room, feelings of guilt began to set in. *Why did I do that,* he kept asking himself? *What was I thinking?* Only when he was a few yards away from his door did he notice that the dwarves he passed were looking at him strangely. It was like a red rag to a bull. He wanted to lash out at them. He wanted to lash out at anyone, if only to forget what a bloody fool he had been.

Once inside his room, he found a bottle of wine and slumped heavily into a chair opposite the dresser. With every emotion from humiliation to rage and regret battling for space inside his head, he downed nearly half the bottle in a single gulp. It was only then that he caught sight of his reflection in the dresser mirror.

The bottle slipped from his grasp and shattered on the stone tile floor.

Gingerly he touched his cheeks. His scars…they were gone. Every single one of them. Staring back at him was someone he didn't know. Or at least, had not known for a very long time. He could barely recognize the boy he had once been in the man he was now seeing.

Tears streamed down his face as he slid from his chair and wept into his hands. After a few minutes he regained a small portion of his composure and crawled onto the edge of his bed. The torrent of emotions raged in his heart like a cyclone, sending him into fits of anger one moment, then unfathomable sorrow the next. Finally, anger won out. He rose and found another bottle of wine, draining it nearly dry in a single gulp. He would not allow his feelings to rule him. Not Specter.

CHAPTER FIVE

E THAN KNOCKED ON Markus' door, but there was no answer. He was certain that he had heard him go in earlier. He tried the knob, but it was locked.

"Markus?" he called out. "Are you all right? I thought I heard glass breaking."

After a long silence, Markus finally responded. "I'm fine. I just need to be alone for a while."

Ethan frowned. He could hear in his friend's voice that something was seriously bothering him. "Are you sure?" he asked.

"Yes, damn it!" he shouted back. "Just leave me alone."

"O...Okay." Ethan lingered for a few seconds longer, but it was pointless so he returned to his room. Whatever was bothering Markus, he obviously had no intention of sharing it.

Jonas came by a while later. He had located King Ganix, who was still busy making preparations for their departure.

"You should be pleased to know that things are well in hand," Jonas told him. "We'll be well supplied and carrying enough gold to bribe a bloody king if needs be."

"Did he tell you how we'll be getting to the Dragon Wastes?" Ethan asked.

"When I asked him that, he just smiled and held a finger to the side of his nose."

"I suppose it will have to be a surprise then," said Ethan.

Jonas scowled. "I don't like surprises."

Ethan considered out loud if he should visit Lylinora, but Jonas said he had tried earlier and was told by the guards most firmly that she was not receiving anyone at present.

Seems like everyone is having problems today, Ethan thought. A short time later Jonas excused himself so that he could return to help King Ganix.

Ethan spent the rest of the day reading quietly, deciding to take his meals in his room rather than the main dining hall. He had just finished dinner when an exhausted looking Kat arrived.

"Maile and Asta are acting like it's the last time we'll ever play together," she complained as she flung herself onto Ethan's bed. "I should never have told them I was leaving."

He laughed. "You might wish you weren't."

She leapt up and planted her hands firmly on her hips. "Don't *you* start. I've had to listen to Lady Thora ranting on about me leaving every time we're in the same room together. You know, she even asked King Halvar to make me stay? And when that didn't work, she went to King Ganix."

She regarded Ethan suspiciously. "She hasn't come to you, has she?"

"No," he said. "Not yet."

"If she does, you had better not…"

"Don't worry," he said, cutting her off. "I promised that you could come, and I meant it."

"You'd better," she warned. "You need me."

Ethan cocked his head. "Is that so? For what exactly?"

"For one thing, to make sure that witch keeps her hands off you," she replied.

"If you're talking about Lylinora, you haven't got much to worry about. I don't think she's interested in me. At least, not in that way."

Kat sniffed. "She'd better not be. Like I told you. You have to wait for me to get older."

Having stated that, she grinned impishly and danced from the room.

Ethan shook his head and gave a soft chuckle. He had enjoyed seeing the change in the girl since she'd started spending time with Lady

Thora and her granddaughters. In some ways, it was as if she had recovered a bit of the childhood she'd been denied. And though he knew she was in fact quite serious about wanting him to wait for her until she was older, there was now much more trust and understanding in their friendship.

After reading for a bit longer, he felt his eyes growing heavy. It was still rather early, but he decided to sleep anyway so as to be well rested for the coming day.

It normally took him at least a half hour to settle his mind sufficiently to doze off, but on this occasion his body felt uncharacteristically drained. Even the ever-present call of the dragons was but a mere whisper that evening, and within minutes sleep had taken him.

His dreams were wild and unintelligible. A mass of swirling colors and unfamiliar images appeared, constantly shifting and changing before he could make any sense of them.

"Lord Dragonvein," called a soft feminine voice. It came from just beyond his sight. "See me."

With a loud gasp, Ethan suddenly found himself sitting bolt upright in the bed. Something had awakened him. The shock from being pulled so abruptly from his dream had his heart racing.

"Did I startle you?" It was the sweet voice of Lylinora.

"Yes," he replied. "I mean…no."

At first, he could make out only her silhouette against the light creeping in from beneath the door. As his eyes slowly began to adjust, his jaw suddenly went slack. It was definitely Lylinora standing there – but she was completely naked. Even in the dark, he could tell that her eyes were firmly fixed on him.

"What are you doing?" he finally managed to croak.

She made no reply, instead merely advancing with graceful steps to the side of the bed. Ethan tried to scramble from beneath the blanket, but she placed her hand on his chest and gently pushed him back down.

He couldn't take his eyes off her. She was perfect. Her breasts, her stomach, her hips, everything…perfect. He reached out to touch her face, but she took his hand and kissed the tips of his fingers.

"Be still." Her voice was soft, yet commanding.

As if carried on a cushion of air, she slid into the bed and straddled Ethan's torso. He could feel his manhood engorging as the heat from her loins hovered tantalizingly just above him.

She leaned down and kissed his forehead. "Sleep," she whispered. "This is just a dream."

He struggled to keep his eyes open, though the harder he tried, the more difficult it became. He wanted to cry out, but his voice was gone. Then, the blackness irresistibly closed in.

"Ethan."

"Lylinora," he replied.

"Ethan." This time the voice was accompanied by a pair of strong hands shaking him roughly awake.

He opened his eyes, blinking several times until his vision cleared. He saw Markus standing over him, a large smirk on his face.

Ethan sat up instantly. "Your face...your scars! They're gone."

Markus touched his cheeks and stroked his chin with obvious satisfaction. "Are they? I hadn't really noticed." He had shaved his beard, and though older, now resembled the man Ethan knew before coming to Lumnia.

Ethan slid from the bed and took a lingering look at his friend. "My god! She did it." He wrapped his arms around Markus, nearly lifting him off the ground.

"Take it easy," he laughed. "Do you want to crack my ribs?"

Ethan set him down and took another long look. "I can't believe it. Is this why you wanted to be alone last night?"

Markus paused for a second before nodding. "It was just a bit much to take in all at once. Sorry about that."

"It's fine. I understand. Is that what she wanted with you yesterday?"

"That - and to ask me some questions about you."

"Really?" The vision of Lylinora's body in the dim light was still fresh in Ethan's mind. But had it been a dream? He couldn't tell. Part of him knew that it must have been. And yet he could still feel her on top of him, kissing his forehead. He could even remember the sweet scent of her perfume.

"What did she want to know?" he asked.

Markus shrugged. "Nothing much. Just what kind of person you are. Your likes and dislikes. Stuff like that."

"Maybe it *was* real," Ethan muttered, mostly to himself.

Markus picked up on it anyway. "Maybe what was real?" he asked.

"Oh nothing. It was probably just a dream."

"Tell me," he urged.

Ethan felt suddenly embarrassed and uncomfortable. "Really...it was nothing."

"Was it about Lylinora?" he pressed, smiling. "I heard you call out her name in your sleep."

Ethan lowered his eyes. "Yeah. It was." He walked to the dresser and began rummaging for a change of clothes. "I dreamed that she came to my room last night."

"Is that right?" His voice took on an odd tone. "What happened?"

"What difference does it make? It was just a dream."

"Humor me."

Ethan recounted the details as he dressed. Once he was done, he noticed that Markus' eyes had become narrow and his jaw tight.

"What's wrong?" he asked.

Markus shook his head and his smile returned. "Nothing. Come on. We're having breakfast with King Ganix and King Halvar this morning."

Ethan studied his face; something was still bothering him. Though, with his scars now healed, it was hard to imagine what his friend's problem might be. Had Lylinora perhaps said or done something to trouble him?

Markus didn't give him a chance to ask anything further. He opened the door and gestured for Ethan to follow.

They soon arrived at a small parlor with a round table and several chairs situated in the far corner. Already seated there were Halvar, Ganix, and Jonas. Ethan felt a stab of disappointment on seeing that Lylinora was not with them. A meal of porridge, fruit, and sweet wine had already been set out.

After bowing, Ethan and Markus both took their seats.

"I have reconsidered, and have now agreed to allow Lady Lylinora to erect a barrier around my manor," Halvar informed them. "After she has cleared all the staff and the elders, you will be departing immediately."

"How long will that be?" asked Markus.

"Two days," replied Halvar. "It should then take you four more to arrive at the rendezvous point where you'll meet the smugglers."

"We'll be ready," Markus said.

Ganix had just begun to explain their route through the mountains when Lylinora arrived.

Ethan sprang to his feet rather too eagerly. "Good morning," he said.

She nodded politely and sat down. A servant hurriedly brought her a plate. "I've already begun checking your house staff for signs of a curse," she informed Halvar. "They're all quite cooperative and well-trained."

Halvar nodded. "Thank you. Many have served my house their entire lives."

"Might I say that you did a wonderful job in healing Markus, My Lady," remarked Jonas.

"Yes," agreed Ganix. "I almost didn't recognize him earlier this morning." "It was nothing," she said. "I was the least I could do for the best friend of Lord Dragonvein." She gave Ethan a tiny smile.

Markus cleared his throat. "Yes. Thank you."

Lylinora's eyes never left Ethan. "As I told you yesterday. You should not mention it again."

"As you wish...My Lady."

Ethan felt that Markus' tone was unusually abrasive. But this was driven from his thoughts as Lylinora's gaze captured him.

"And how did you sleep, My Lord?" she asked.

Ethan shifted in his seat. "Fine. Just fine."

"He had strange dreams," Markus blurted out.

She raised an eyebrow. "Is that so? Please, do tell. Some mages can foretell the future through their dreams."

"Yeah," said Markus. "I bet he'd like that."

Ethan shot Markus an angry glance. "I'd rather not talk about it, if you don't mind."

A sneer formed on Markus' face. He sharply pushed back his chair and rose to his feet. "If you'll excuse me, I have things to do before we leave."

"Wait a minute," said Ethan. "I'll go with you."

But Markus gave no indication of having heard him and did not even break stride. Ethan stared after him for a moment before turning back to the others.

"He'll be fine," assured Lylinora. "Healing can be an emotional experience."

As soon as she had finished eating, Lylinora also chose to leave. Ethan hurried to catch up with her in the hallway. The words he wanted to say were on the tip of his tongue, but the moment she turned to look at him, the sensual memory of her closeness made him unable to speak.

"Is there something you wanted?" she asked. When Ethan didn't reply, she reached out and took hold of his hands.

The warmth of her touch sent his heart racing madly. He wanted to ask her about the previous night, but instead found himself saying: "I was wondering when you plan to begin teaching me magic?"

"We can do so later today if you wish," she replied, at the same time pulling his hands up against her breasts and slightly bowing her head. "And it will be my pleasure to do so."

After a second or two of silence from Ethan, she eased his hands away and released them. "For a moment, I thought you were going to tell me all about this dream of yours."

"No," he said, unable to meet her eyes. "It's…it's kind of hard to explain. Besides, I can barely remember any of it."

"What a pity," she sighed, turning away. "Never mind. I'll be attending to the house staff until dinner time, but you can join me after that for your first lesson if you wish."

After flashing him a quick smile over her shoulder, she continued on her way back to her chamber.

*

From around a corner back along the corridor, Markus had been watching throughout as the pair of them spoke. Anger that he was unable to contain flared when he saw Lylinora pressing Ethan's hands to her breasts. She *had* gone to his room. He was sure of it.

He wanted to scream – or shout – or hit something. But most of all he just wanted her to explain why. Why had she acted as if she had wanted him? Then, after luring him in so far, why had she stopped so suddenly? And why had she gone to Ethan's bed only a few hours later?

When Ethan first told him about his 'dream', he'd suspected that the boy was lying. How could he *not* remember being with a woman like that? Even with his current anger raging, his own desire for her was burning as fiercely as ever. But after the way Ethan had gone on to describe things, he'd come to accept that she had most likely used some sort of magic on him. But why would she want him to forget?

For a wild moment he had considered dashing across and confronting them both. Somehow, he managed to curb the instinct. Such a rash move would only cause more problems. He couldn't help feeling angry and jealous, but Ethan had done nothing wrong. And if Lylinora wanted him instead…so be it.

"I can't force you to care for me," he muttered under his breath.

With that, he drew back and hurried away before either of them might catch sight of him.

*

Lylinora took a long cleansing breath while on her way back to the chamber. At least Ethan was still behaving politely, she considered. It could be worse.

Her thoughts then drifted to Markus. Even with his scars, he had been a powerful figure of a man. Without them, he was more than powerful…he was almost regal. But the pain in his heart was immense. How could he bear it?

Quickly, she drove such matters from her mind. There was nothing to be done. Her destiny was clear, and it did not include the love of a roguish swordsman.

The cooler air of the cavern felt nice on her skin. The dwarf city was dry and far too warm for her taste. King Halvar had offered her a room in the main part of the manor, but for some reason she felt more comfortable down here.

"We need to talk," said a voice from the far end of the chamber. It was Kat. She was sitting cross-legged in a chair.

Lylinora did not display any great surprise. "You're really quite good at that," she remarked. "How did you learn it?"

"If you're talking about the way I can vanish and reappear, I learned it on my own," Kat said. She pointed to an empty chair just in front of her.

"Impressive," Lylinora said, ignoring the request to sit. Instead, she poured herself a cup of wine. "I'd offer you some, but aren't you a bit too young for wine?"

Kat sniffed. "If you're trying to make me angry..."

Lylinora held up her hand. "Not at all. I was just thinking that I wasn't allowed wine until I was twelve years old."

"I'm thirteen," she stated, chin held high.

"Ah. Well, you shouldn't worry, my dear. Some girls develop late."

Kat's face turned crimson. "And some girls can't keep their legs together," she retorted.

This made Lylinora pause. "What are you trying to say?"

"I saw you go into Ethan's room last night," Kat told her. "And I saw Markus leaving here before that with his scars healed. Then, just a minute ago, he was watching you flirt with Ethan in the hallway."

"And?" Lylinora retrieved another cup and filled it.

"I know the look on a man's face when he's heartbroken. Markus had that look."

Lylinora crossed the room and handed the wine to Kat before sitting. "How would you know about things like that?"

"Men are easy," she replied. "I've seen it when they fall in love with a whore. They think they'll be able to save them. But they're always wrong."

"Are you calling me a whore?" Lylinora's tone took on a dangerous quality.

Kat shrugged. "Only if the shoe fits."

"You're playing a perilous game, little girl. I could kill you here and now, and no one would ever find out what happened." A blue light glowed in her eyes for a few seconds, then dimmed.

"I'm not afraid of you," Kat said, her voice firm.

Lylinora smiled and allowed her posture to relax. "No. I can see that. Which is why I am going to be completely honest with you."

"So you did fuck Markus?"

"No," she said. "I did not...*fuck* Markus."

Kat looked at her incredulously. "I thought you were going to be honest."

"I *am* being honest. Though you can certainly choose to think otherwise. I don't care." Lylinora gave a sharp nod. "Like I said, I did not sleep with Markus. As for Ethan...yes, I did. Though he doesn't remember much about it."

Kat huffed a laugh to disguise her jealousy. "That bad, was it? I know some girls who could give you a lesson or two."

"I'm sure you do," she said with a forced smile. "But the reason he doesn't remember is that I cast a spell to make him forget. In his mind, it was all a dream."

"Why would you do that?"

"I have my reasons. And I do not care to share them with you."

"Well, I'm sure Ethan would like to know about it."

Lylinora folded her hands in her lap and leaned forward. "But you won't tell him, my dear."

"More threats?"

Lylinora shook her head. "This is not a threat. This is a fact. Because if you tell him, I'll simply deny it."

"Ethan will believe me," Kat snapped back.

"Really? What makes you so sure of that? Ethan is in love with *me*, not you. Why wouldn't he think you're simply lying in order to drive us apart?"

"First of all, he's *not* in love with you. Lust or infatuation maybe. Though I don't expect you to know the difference. And second, he'll believe me because he's my friend."

Lylinora waved her hand dismissively. "Lust, love...it doesn't matter. What does matter is that he wants me. And he wants me enough to believe whatever I say. If you tell him any of this, all that will happen is you make yourself look like a jealous fool, and I appear the innocent victim of your anger."

She paused to give a smile. "But even that is not the main reason why you'll keep quiet."

Kat sneered. "So tell me what is?"

Lylinora's smile broadened. "Because you love him, and you hope one day to have him for yourself. Of course, I cannot allow this to happen. He is far too important to waste his life on you, my dear."

Kat didn't even bother to try and deny her feelings. Although struggling to remain calm, the smug look on Lylinora's face was sending surges of rage racing through her.

"I know that my words insult you," her tormentor continued. "But there is no other way to put it. I am the last living mage in Lumnia, and he is the son of Praxis Dragonvein, the most powerful mage of his time. It is our duty to restore our kind."

Kat laughed scornfully. "That's what this is all about? Bringing back the mages? You really think Ethan cares about that?"

"No," she admitted. "Not yet. But he will in time. Gradually, he will come to understand the importance of our kind. The importance of the good that mages do for the world. Once he sees this, there will be no other choice for him but to be with me."

Kat's hands trembled. She knew Lylinora was right. Yet her feelings for Ethan would not allow her to accept the situation. "I can use magic," she offered weakly. "At least a little."

"Indeed you can. And that's precisely the point I'm making. I am the only one who can teach you to develop that skill. But if you say anything, or if you try to come between us, I will refuse to do so. Any hope you may have of gaining Ethan's affections will then be gone forever. Not that there is much hope to begin with. It will be many years before you are old enough for him…at least in his eyes."

With that, Lylinora stood. Though not exceptionally tall, her posture gave her an imposing appearance. "And as long as you love him, you will continue clinging to that hope."

Kat could only glare, her tiny fists clenched. A single tear fell forlornly down her cheek.

Lylinora drained her cup and turned toward the exit. "You can stay here until you collect yourself. But you will stay gone from my sight until we depart. Am I understood?"

Without bothering to wait for a reply, she left the room, tossing the cup into a corner as she moved along.

Hugging her knees to her chest, Kat remained absolutely motionless for several minutes. Eventually, her head lifted and her voice was filled with resolve as she softly swore an oath.

"I won't let you have him," she repeated over and over. "I won't – I won't."

CHAPTER SIX

LYLINORA'S CHECKING OF the elders and house staff was completed sooner than anticipated. To everyone's great relief, none of them had been afflicted by a curse. And though King Halvar remained apprehensive over the installation of the barrier, he took solace in the fact that when the announcement about it was eventually made, there had not been a single voice of protest raised. In fact, most of his subjects were simply relieved that their king was now protected.

During the previous two evenings, Ethan had joined Lylinora for his first lessons. He found her to be a patient and understanding teacher, which allowed him to master several minor spells such as conjuring flaming arrows and creating reflective surfaces in rough stone. She also taught him a faster, more efficient way to cast *dragonfire*.

"You have a natural talent," she told him at the end of their second lesson. "You'll be worthy of the title *mage* sooner than I thought. You are definitely your father's son." Eager to please, Ethan vowed to work even harder. This resolve was helped along considerably by her overtly flirtatious nature with him.

During this period of preparation, it had occurred to him several times that he had not seen anything of Markus or Kat, but dismissed this as unimportant. Markus was most likely busy making preparations for the journey, while Kat was surely spending most of her remaining time with Lady Thora and her granddaughters.

On the morning of their departure, Jonas and Birger came to his room. Ethan's excitement had been building, and he was now more than ready to get under way.

"The others will be waiting for us ahead," Birger told him. "King Ganix didn't want any fanfare, so he, Markus, Lylinora and Kat have already departed the manor. King Halvar sends his apologies for not seeing you off, but he's extremely busy at the moment."

The dwarf led them through a seldom used exit, then to a small side gate. Outside, Ethan was surprised to see several hundred dwarves lined up in the street, their numbers stretching all the way up to the main entrance of the king's residence.

"What are they doing?" he asked Birger.

"They've requested that King Halvar allow them to walk through the barrier," he replied.

"Why?" asked Jonas. "If they're cursed, it could kill them."

"No one wants to live with Shinzan's curse inside them," Birger explained. "Better to die."

Jonas nodded solemnly. "Yes. I suppose I can understand that."

They wound their way through the streets to the edge of the city. Ethan spotted Markus sitting on a stool outside the very last building, fiddling with a dagger. He looked up and waved them over. From around the corner, the rest of their party then appeared. Lylinora smiled warmly at Ethan, but Kat scarcely gave him a glance.

Several identical looking packs had been set out along the wall. King Ganix tossed one to each of them before shouldering his own.

"No time for pleasantries, I'm afraid," he said. "I want to be well on our way before anyone realizes we're gone."

Birger led them all to a tunnel directly opposite the main city gate. Before passing through, Ethan took a long look back. A sigh slipped out. Such beauty and magnificence was definitely worth fighting for, he told himself.

They pressed on, with Birger remaining in the lead and Markus guarding their rear. Ethan was finding his pack relatively light considering its bulk. He had offered to help with preparations, but Jonas had assured him that all was in order. Of course, this meant that he now had no idea as to what he might be carrying.

They walked on in silence for several hours before stopping to rest and eat. Kat and Markus sat away from the others, while Jonas made a point of not speaking to anyone unless spoken to first. Ethan assumed that this was so not to incur Lylinora's anger. He was still uncomfortable with the way she treated those she perceived as low born or servants, but his yearning to please her quickly overcame any impulse to raise the subject between them.

While they ate, Lylinora flashed him a succession of smiles, and several times reached across to lightly touch his knee. On one of these occasions, he happened to glance over at Markus and thought he caught a hint of irritation flash across his friend's face. But the dim glow of the rajni stone they used to light their way, made him uncertain about this. Even so, he knew for sure that something was bothering him. Kat as well. Her normal spirited jabs and teasing remarks had been replaced by what Ethan could only describe as sulkiness.

After the break, they marched on for a further three hours before stopping to bed down for the night. Lylinora beckoned Ethan to follow her a bit further down the tunnel. "We should continue with our lessons while traveling," she told him.

They walked until just beyond earshot of the rest, then sat on the ground facing each other. Ethan closed his eyes and began drawing in deep cleansing breaths exactly as Lylinora had shown him. After a moment or two, he heard the sound of footfalls hurrying up behind him.

"You promised to teach me too," said Kat.

Lylinora frowned. "I will. But I had intended to begin with you once we have boarded the ship."

"Why wait?" she asked, grinning innocently. "You don't mind, do you, Ethan?"

"Of course not."

"She needs individual instruction," said Lylinora. "You are already too far ahead of her."

"I'll just watch then," Kat suggested.

"I don't think that's a good idea," Lylinora countered.

"She won't get in the way, I'm sure," Ethan said.

Lylinora let out an exasperated breath. "Very well. But if she becomes a distraction, she will have to go."

After nodding in agreement, Ethan patted the ground alongside him. Kat quickly settled in, her smile never once fading.

The lesson was shorter than usual – only one hour – and Lylinora was clearly bothered by Kat's presence throughout. Just before they headed back to the others, Kat drew her aside.

"Tell me, is this right?" she asked, holding out her right palm. In her most authoritative tone of voice she commanded: "*Inisia!*"

Instantly, a streak of blue flame erupted, shooting into the rock directly above their heads.

Lylinora raised an eyebrow. "I'm impressed. You've managed to get it right on your very first attempt."

Ethan wrapped his arm around Kat's shoulder and gave her a fond squeeze. "That's much better than *I* did. It took me four tries before I got it."

Kat smiled up at him, but her smile soon vanished when she saw the frown on Lylinora's face. "Thank you," was all she said before pulling away from him.

The remainder of the journey through the mountain passed fairly uneventfully. Loud rumbling calls that sounded uncomfortably close, reached them on a few occasions, but Birger quickly explained that these were only coming from adult trolls. Apparently, their feeding grounds were not so far away from the path they were on. Ethan sighed with relief when the dwarf added that this ensured there would be no young trolls nearby to threaten them.

The lessons continued well, with Kat doing as she was told and keeping quiet. Even so, to Lylinora's surprise, after each session was over the young girl was able to cast almost every spell that had been shown to Ethan without having practiced it at all.

"You'll be a fine mage one day," Lylinora admitted at the end of their final lesson before arriving at the mountain exit. "But don't expect it to always come so easily. These are just trifles. *Real* magic requires both strength and discipline. And you can guess which one of these I think you lack."

Ethan was shocked when Kat did not respond to this obvious insult. Also, he had noticed that she would often look away when Lylinora scolded her. He tried asking Lylinora if something had happened between them, but she simply shrugged and poked his ribs playfully – a ploy which was always sufficient to distract him from making further inquiries.

It was well after nightfall when they finally reached the exit. Here, a narrow path would take them down the remaining several hundred feet of the mountain. Millions of stars were splashed vividly across the vast expanse of sky, unobstructed by even a wisp of cloud.

Birger shuddered at the sight and took a moment to steady himself. "I have never liked it out here in the open," he told the others.

Ethan slapped him on the back. "Sorry, but you'll have to get used to it."

"Wait until he gets on board the ship," said Markus. This was the first light-hearted comment he had made in several days.

Ethan laughed. "I puked my guts out the first time."

"I'll be fine," said Birger, clearly not amused.

They ventured the rest of the way down the mountain. Shadows of a dense forest ahead gave the atmosphere an ominous feel. Ethan sniffed the air and detected a faint hint of salt mixed in with the earthy smell of trees and grass. The sea was not far away. He listened for the crashing of the waves, but all that reached his ears was the chirping of insects and the rustle of small animals scurrying through the undergrowth.

All at once he felt exposed and vulnerable. Behind him, the mountain was looking more and more like a safe haven, giving him a sudden sympathy for Birger's unease.

They stopped just at the edge of the forest to make camp. Markus advised against building a fire in case there were enemies about. "We should sleep in a circle," he instructed everyone. "And keep your weapons ready."

Once settled, they ate some dried fruit and a piece of what the dwarves referred to as *krilin,* a hard brown disc made from vegetable paste. It had a gritty texture and bitter taste that Ethan cared little for. But it was no worse than the food they had served at the base in

England. And it was certainly better than the rations he had been forced to eat while in France.

With the meal over, Ganix addressed the group. "When we meet with the smugglers, there are a few things you must remember," he began. "Firstly, as far as you are concerned, I am *not* a king. Do not under any circumstances call me Your Highness, or say anything else that might suggest who I really am. I'm simply Ganix, a lowly metal worker. Secondly, do not ever allow the crew to see you using magic. Keep your lessons quiet and within your own cabin. And lastly, if we are attacked or boarded by the Empire, do nothing until I say so. Does everyone understand?"

They all nodded.

"Good," he said. "We should be boarding the ship tomorrow. The smugglers will be waiting for us a few miles north of here just after sunrise."

Before settling down, Markus decided to check the surrounding area. Ethan offered to accompany him, but this was refused.

"I need to be alone," Markus told him.

Ethan frowned. "What's wrong? You've been acting very strange these last few days."

He flashed a forced smile. "I guess I'm not used to being so damn handsome. It takes some getting used to."

Reluctantly, Ethan accepted his explanation. Lylinora had said that the healing process could be a very emotional experience. Perhaps it took a greater toll than he realized.

He was just settling into his bedroll when Lylinora spoke to him. "I think it's time to attend to you," she said.

He sat up, unsure what she meant.

"King Ganix mentioned that Shinzan might be tracking your movements," she explained.

Ethan had all but forgotten about this. The reminder caused him to frown. "Yes. At least, that's what he claimed he would be able to do."

Kneeling beside him, Lylinora took hold of his hands. She muttered a few words and almost immediately he felt a tingling sensation rush up his arms and all the way through his body.

She let out a quiet laugh. "Such simple magic from someone so powerful. I expected more." She released her hold. "It's done."

"You realize this may rouse Shinzan's suspicions," noted the watching Ganix.

"Better that than the alternative," she responded.

"Agreed."

Ethan tried to stay up until Markus returned, but after more than an hour of waiting he eventually drifted off. Lylinora had laid her blanket just behind his, and he could hear her humming softly. The melody was both moving, and a bit sad. The last thing he remembered before sleep consumed him was a vision of his mother back on Earth. Did he miss her? Or did he just feel pity for the sad and lonely life to which fate had now condemned her? With so many other things competing for room in his overcrowded mind, it was sometimes hard to know what his true feelings were.

It felt like just a few minutes had passed when a stiff north wind and the rumbling of thunder far off to the south woke him. With the morning sun breaching the horizon, King Ganix and Jonas were already awake and almost ready to go. Birger, Kat and Lylinora however, still slumbered peacefully on. As for Markus, he was nowhere to be seen. His bedroll looked untouched, but before Ethan could ask anyone about this, his friend appeared from out of the forest. He didn't look tired, just depressed. That was the only way Ethan could see it.

The king called for everyone to wake. Jonas then distributed some *krilin* and water.

"I hope they have better fare aboard the ship," complained Lylinora. "I don't know how long I can survive on this."

Ganix laughed. "It's not *that* bad, is it?"

Her face twisted as she took a bite and then hurriedly washed it down. "How your people eat this, I can't fathom."

"Ours is a life of practicality," the king replied. "*Krilin* doesn't spoil for months, and small portions will keep an adult dwarf strong for days."

"I just hope they have meat," Ethan chipped in. "I'd kill for a steak right now."

Both Birger and Ganix shuddered.

"Disgusting," murmured Birger. "Eating dead flesh is for animals."

Once on their way again, Markus took over the lead. He was far more familiar with the threats outside of the mountain, and smugglers were not to be trusted. Ethan followed him closely.

"I forget sometimes that you were a soldier," Birger said to Ethan.

"There are times I wish I *could* forget," he replied.

"Did you see much death and battle?" asked Lylinora.

"Me and Markus both did," he told her. "The Germans were tough as nails."

"Yeah," agreed Markus. "But we were tougher."

Ethan grinned and nodded. "Damn right we were. They couldn't match the 101st."

After a brief pause, he added by way of explanation: "The 101st Airborne was the name of our division. Best of the best. Ain't that right, Markus?"

Markus grinned back, but the smile was fleeting. When his eyes briefly met with Lylinora's a moment later, it faded instantly. "We should be quiet," he said brusquely. "I'd rather that no one know that we're approaching."

They continued for a short time longer. Markus quite suddenly then motioned for a halt and silence. Ethan heard it a second later. Voices - three men, just beyond a thick patch of brush.

He, Markus and Birger all drew their weapons.

"The rest of you stay here until I call," Markus whispered.

The three of them crept silently closer until they were able to clearly hear the men's conversation.

"Bloody dwarves," one of them was saying. "What the hell are we doing? We've already delivered their goods."

"I told you," replied another. "We're taking on passengers."

"What kind of passengers?" asked the first.

"The kind that pay," he replied irritably. "So just shut your fucking mouth and stop complaining."

Ethan could make out that the smugglers were waiting for them in a small clearing, but from his current position he could only catch glimpses of the men themselves. Without a word, Birger then stepped forward into the open. Markus and Ethan quickly followed him. There was a clattering of steel as the startled men drew their weapons.

All three of them were dressed in worn shirts and tattered pants. Their faces were weathered and burned bronze from life at sea and long days in the hot sun. Two were thin, wiry individuals of average height, the third shorter and much thicker set.

"Peace," said Birger.

The men looked at each other for a long, tense moment.

"You're the passengers?" one of the thin smugglers eventually asked.

"We are," confirmed Birger. "The rest of us are just over there." He flicked a hand in the direction of the others.

The stout man sneered. "Since when do dwarves pal around with humans?"

"That's not your concern, now is it?" said Birger.

"Not as long as you have gold," he agreed.

Birger put away his weapon. Ethan, Markus and the smugglers cautiously did the same.

"Then suppose you bring your friends over," said the thin smuggler on the left. "I want to get back. These woods make me nervous. Too many places to hide around here."

Birger nodded to Markus, who called for the rest to come forward. The moment Lylinora appeared, all three smugglers grinned brutishly.

"Well, well, well," the stout smuggler leered. "The captain didn't mention this one. Who do you belong to lassie? Not to any of these fellows, I hope."

"I belong to myself," snapped Lylinora. "And you'd do well to remember that."

The man let out a hideous laugh. "Spirited little wench, ain't she fellas? Well, my pretty, we'll see who you belong to before this trip is done."

His words sparked an explosion of anger in Ethan. He reached for his sword, but had scarcely touched the hilt when Markus sprang forward in a blur of motion. His right fist smashed into the smuggler's jaw, sending him hard down on his back. Before anyone could speak, he had straddled the man and was pressing a small dagger to his throat.

"Stay back, or he's a dead man," he shouted to the others.

The two other smugglers gripped the hilts of their swords, but did as Markus told them.

Ethan moved forward, but a warning glance from his friend halted him in his tracks.

Satisfied that no one was about to cause a problem, Markus bent down, his eyes fixed on the smuggler. "Do I have your attention?" he demanded.

The smuggler glared defiantly for a moment, but wisely nodded after Markus pressed the knife tip into the fleshy part of his neck, raising an immediate trickle of blood.

"I want you to listen to me very carefully," Markus told him. His tone was measured and unemotional, but his eyes were ablaze. "If you ever speak to her again. If you look in her direction. If you so much as see her in your dreams, I'll cut off your balls and ram them all the way down your miserable throat. This is not a threat. This is a cold, hard, indisputable fact. Are we clear?"

After the man nodded a second time, Markus looked up at his crew mates. "That goes for the two of you as well." He lifted the blade and stood. "Now take us to your fucking ship."

The man scrambled to his feet and joined his comrades. All three drew their weapons.

"You'll pay for that, dog!" the stout one shouted.

Ganix stepped quickly forward. "Wait! This is not necessary." Reaching into the pouch on his belt, he pulled out a handful of gold ingots. The mere sight of them was enough to make the smugglers hesitate.

"I'm sorry for my friend," the king continued. "I'm afraid he's a bit overprotective of the Lady." He thrust the ingots forward. "Here. Take these."

The men faltered, their eyes darting from the gold to Markus, who was stone faced but otherwise apparently relaxed. After putting away the dagger, he allowed his hand to rest casually on the hilt of his sword.

"Take them. Or you can explain to your captain why you insulted the woman who supplied the gold for this trip," Ganix concluded.

The stout man reached out and snatched the gold. "Just keep that one away from me," he snarled, pointing to Markus.

As the smugglers moved a short distance away to divvy up the ingots, Markus turned and smiled at Lylinora. But rather than receiving a look of appreciation, she stared at him furiously.

"What were you thinking?" she hissed. "You could have lost us the ship. Then what would we do?"

Markus was taken aback. "I didn't want them…"

She cut him short. "Didn't want them what? Insulting me? Ogling me?" She drew a deep breath. "Allow me to explain something to you. I am *not* your lady. And you are *not* my protector. The only reason you are here at all is because of Lord Dragonvein. So please get that into your thick head."

Markus lowered his eyes. "I apologize."

Ethan blinked. He had never seen Markus so submissive. First of all Kat, and now this. "Don't be angry with him," he said to Lylinora. "I was about to do the same thing."

She peeled her gaze away from Markus and looked at Ethan. At once, her expression softened. "You shouldn't worry about me. I've dealt with rogues like this before. I'll be fine."

"Move it if you're coming with us," shouted the stout smuggler.

Ganix and Birger led the way, followed by Lylinora. She brushed her shoulder against Ethan as she passed.

Markus huffed and shook his head. "It must be nice."

"What do you mean?" asked Ethan.

"Nothing," he replied. "Forget it."

"You better be glad that Markus was the one who hit him," said Kat, smirking. "That guy would have probably beat the crap out of you."

This raised a laugh from Markus.

"She's right you know," added Jonas. "You shouldn't be fighting unless it's absolutely necessary. You're too important right now to risk your life needlessly."

Ethan scowled. He hated being treated like some small child who was unable to take care of himself. But deep inside he knew Jonas was right. He had to make it across the sea to the dragons. The feeling of urgency was growing stronger each day. And each night he felt more and more as if time was slipping through his fingers. The dragons' call was becoming ever more desperate. Almost to the point of pleading.

After a few miles, the trees began to thin and Ethan could hear the sound of waves carrying on the wind. Then he caught sight of the sea and stopped short, almost causing Kat to bump into him. Rather than the often somber looking dark bluish green of the Atlantic, the water here was a sparkling baby blue that reflected the sun so brilliantly that he had to shield his eyes. Pure white foam capped the relentless series of waves as they pounded the beach of bright yellow sand.

A small row boat was waiting, and a few hundred yards off shore he could see their ship anchored. It reminded Ethan of the schooners he had watched in the New York Harbor as a boy. Three masts rose from a deck that, even from a distance, he could see was sleek and narrow. It was a ship built for speed rather than comfort. Good for a smugglers' vessel, he guessed.

"It will take two trips to carry you *and* your gear," said a thin smuggler.

Ethan didn't like this idea one bit. Noticing his apprehension, Ganix gave his arm a light squeeze. He reached into his pouch, produced another three gold ingots, and tossed them to the man.

"I think you'll find that we can fit everything into one trip," he said

The man snorted. "Fine. But someone else can take the bloody oars."

Chapter Seven

ACHING BADLY FROM the hard rowing, Ethan rubbed his shoulders while watching the others climb the rope ladder to the ship's deck. To his relief, rather than having to carry their packs up on their backs, these had already been hauled on board in a net. Only he and Lylinora were now left to climb.

"Don't worry," she whispered, smiling seductively while stepping onto the ladder. "I'll take care of your aches and pains later."

His heart raced as he tried to imagine exactly what she meant by this. The dream he'd had of her coming to his bedroom passed slowly through his mind.

The sound of Markus' voice snapped him out of his reverie. "Come on. Move it."

With a jolt, Ethan realized that Lylinora was already at the top. The burning in his shoulders grew much worse as he clambered up, and he was more than grateful for Markus' extended hand helping him the final few feet and over the rail.

No sooner was he on board than Ethan felt the motion of the ship throwing him off balance. While grabbing hold of the side to steady himself, he noticed that Ganix, Jonas, and Birger were doing exactly the same thing, though Markus, Kat, and Lylinora seemed to be having no problem, and were already busy sorting out their packs.

The loud barking of orders and bursts of harsh laughter from thirty or more men scattered across the deck going about their various tasks dulled the sounds of the ocean in Ethan's ears. He spotted a door at the rear of the ship just below the main wheel that had been propped open. Through here, men were constantly squeezing in and out as fast as their legs could carry them.

Looks of curiosity and suspicion came from all directions as the crew began taking note of the new arrivals. Dwarves were a rare sight to them. And as for a beautiful woman…such a presence was sufficient to draw forth a whole multitude of lustful stares.

A tall, black bearded man with grizzled features and oily, shoulder length hair moved toward them, his long leather coat flapping loosely in the breeze. Around the waist of his black trousers was strapped a wicked looking curved blade. When just a few yards away, he stopped to scrutinize Ethan and the others.

"Who here is named Ganix?" he demanded. His voice was deep and gruff.

"I'm Ganix," the king replied, bowing low. "Do I have the pleasure of addressing the captain of this fine vessel?"

The man huffed and spat. "Keep your pleasantries to yourself, dwarf. I'll have the rest of my gold, then you'll have my name."

"Of course," said Ganix. He stumbled over to his pack, twice nearly falling before managing to retrieve a small box. He held this out. "Here is your payment. I think you'll find it to be more than adequate."

The man took the box, eyeing it warily before raising the lid. However, after looking briefly inside, a broad grin crept upon his face. "I'm Captain Jeridia. My ship is yours."

He let out a high pitched whistle and three sailors immediately ran to his side. "Find these fine people accommodations and a good meal." He looked at Ganix, then to Birger. "I'm not sure what dwarves eat, but you're welcome to share what we have."

"I'm sure we can find something to our liking," said Ganix.

"I could do with some meat," Ethan blurted out.

The captain glanced down at the box. "I have smoked pork and some lamb in my personal stores. I'll see that you have it."

Ethan's mouth watered at the prospect.

Two sailors picked up everyone's packs, while the third one led them through the open door and into the ship's interior.

"The women will stay in the first mate's cabin," he told them. "The rest of you will need to bunk in the cargo hold."

As they moved along, Ethan noted the location of the galley, as well as what looked like a crew area where several tables were placed. The first mate's quarters turned out to be alongside the captain's cabin at the very rear of the ship. Lylinora gave him a tiny smile as she entered. Kat did not look at all pleased while following her, but said nothing.

The smugglers must have completed most of their deliveries, because once down in the main cargo hold Ethan noted that it was relatively empty at present. They were taken to a raised platform at the bow that was covered with empty sacks and a few crates.

Birger grumbled. "Smells like filth."

"Best we can do," said the lead sailor. "This ain't no pleasure vessel, after all."

"It will do nicely," Ganix assured him.

The other two sailors tossed the remaining packs onto the platform. All three then hurried back to their duties.

"How long must we suffer this?" asked Birger. He was beginning to look distinctly pale.

Ganix cracked a smile. "A rough, strong miner like you should be able to endure."

Birger swallowed hard. "This is no place for a dwarf. Give me a tunnel any day."

"Come with me," Markus told him. "You need some fresh air before you vomit all over yourself."

At first Birger shook his head, but a moment later his hand shot up to cover his mouth and he nodded furiously.

Both Ethan and King Ganix burst into laughter. Jonas however, was also looking rather pale. "I think I'll go with you," he said.

After the three had gone, the remaining pair cleared away the sacks and crates.

"Poor Birger," remarked Ganix, still grinning.

"The ocean doesn't seem to bother you," Ethan said.

"It did the first time," he admitted. "And to be honest, I'm still not exactly fond of the sea."

"Me either," said Ethan. He went on to tell the king of his voyage from America to England.

"Do you miss it?" asked Ganix. "Earth, I mean."

Ethan shrugged. "I did when I first got here. But to tell you the truth, the longer I'm in Lumnia, the more it feels like my home." He thought for a moment, picturing the world he had departed. "When I left, almost the whole world was at war with itself. And now that I'm here, I find things are just the same."

"But *here,* the fate of that war rests squarely on your shoulders," said Ganix.

"True." Ethan hesitated before adding: "I can't explain it, but I know this is where I belong."

Ganix locked eyes with him. "That feeling wouldn't have anything to do with a certain young woman, would it?"

Ethan blushed. "It's not just that."

"Be careful with her. I sense she has her own agenda."

"What do you mean?"

"Nothing evil or harmful," he explained. "But with mages…and nobles, not everything is always as it appears. As a noble myself, I should know." He squeezed Ethan's shoulder. "I just don't want to see you getting hurt."

"I'll be careful," he promised. But in spite of the king's words, he couldn't make himself believe that Lylinora was deceiving him in any way. Her feelings were genuine. They must be.

Ganix nodded. "I can see the recklessness of a young heart in you. Just know that if you need my council, I'm here to give it."

"Thank you."

They both unpacked a blanket and a small pillow, along with a few other odds and ends. Ethan had no idea what purpose half of the things inside his pack were meant for. Also, annoyingly, several mementos he had picked up from the dwarves were missing. Next time, I'll pack my own equipment, he promised himself.

The rapid ringing of a bell suddenly sounded from above. A few minutes later Kat arrived bearing a sour expression.

"Lylinora wants to see you," she told Ethan.

"What is it between you two?" he asked.

"Nothing," she replied. "I just don't like her."

"Hell, I know that. But you act...I don't know...like you're afraid of her."

Kat straightened her back. "I'm not afraid. It's just...I...I want to learn magic. And she's the only one who can teach me."

"I'll teach you if you'd rather," he offered.

She laughed sarcastically. "You? I pick it up twice as easy as you do already."

"Yes, but at least you wouldn't have to be around Lylinora. I'll teach you whatever she teaches me."

Kat shook her head. "Thanks anyway, but I'd rather learn from her."

Ethan shrugged. "Suit yourself."

Kat plopped down on Ethan's blanket and rolled over. "You better go or she'll be mad at you."

Somehow, Ethan doubted that. Lylinora never seemed to be unhappy with him...even when she had good reason to be.

He set off back to the first mate's quarters. The sailors he passed on the way regarded him with clear suspicion, and some even with out-right dislike. He wondered if their attitude was simply because he was a stranger, or perhaps due to the fact that he traveled with dwarves. Either way, he decided that he would have to stay very much on his guard until they reached their destination.

Lylinora answered immediately when he knocked. She was wearing just a soft cotton robe and a pair of slippers. Her hair was now untied and hanging loosely, tumbling down over her shoulders and back. The cabin itself was small and sparsely furnished. A single bed was to his left, and a small desk stood in the far right corner. A seaman's chest plus a rickety dresser and an upright wooden chair completed the décor.

"It's a bit tight in here," Ethan observed.

She picked up a brush from the dresser and sat on the bed. "I don't mind. At least, not when you're here." She smiled at him and began slowly brushing her hair.

Even such ordinary tasks appeared seductive to Ethan. Her eyes twinkled in the dim light of the brass lantern hanging from the ceiling. Tiny beads of perspiration glistened on her chest.

He sat down beside her. "Kat said you wanted to see me."

"I just wanted to relieve the pain in your shoulders," she replied. "As promised."

Only then did he notice that the dull aching was still there. "I'm all right. Really."

"Nonsense." She set the brush down and placed her hands on his arms. Instantly, he felt the heat of her touch. Within seconds, the pain was gone completely.

"There. Isn't that better?"

He rolled his shoulders and nodded. "Amazing. I wish I could do that."

Lylinora tilted her head and crinkled her nose. "I doubt you'll be very good at healing. You're more like your father. Elemental magic and conjuring. But I can try to teach you, if you would like."

She resumed brushing her hair, humming softly all the while. Ethan was unsure if he should stay or go. Her gaze was still fixed on him, and the sweet sound of her voice was incredibly soothing. In a moment of sudden abandon, he leaned in to kiss her.

With a small gasp and eyes wide with shock, she jerked back away from him. Ethan was instantly mortified at what he had done. How could he have been so stupid? He leapt up and covered his face. "Oh my God!" he gasped. "I'm so sorry. I shouldn't have…"

Cheeks burning, he started to leave.

"Ethan! Wait!"

He froze just as his hand was reaching for the doorknob. He heard the floor plank behind him creak, then felt her hands on the small of his back. "I'm so embarrassed," he mumbled. "I thought you…I should go."

Taking hold of his arm, she gently turned him around. "No. I'm the one who should feel embarrassed. My actions caused this. I made you think I was ready for something I'm not."

She placed her hands on his face. "But if you are patient with me…I will be."

Much as he wanted to, Ethan was unable to meet her direct gaze. "Of course," he said meekly. "As long as it takes."

Without another word and with head lowered, he hurried from the cabin. The cold pressure in his chest was making the narrow hallways of the ship feel like a prison. He needed to get up onto the deck outside.

"What was I thinking?" he growled. "What a moron!"

"Who's a moron?"

Looking up, Ethan saw Markus emerging from the galley door only a couple of paces ahead.

"*I'm* a moron," he said.

"You're only just figuring that out?" his friend teased. But he could see that Ethan was in no mood for jovial banter. "I'll come up on deck with you," he offered.

When they stepped outside, the ship's sails were already unfurled and they were now heading steadily away from the shore. Birger was midship, his head hanging over the side. Markus chuckled at the sight, but soon noticed that Ethan was not sharing his amusement. His smile fading, he led him up a ladder to a catwalk a few yards behind the main wheel. The captain was there and nodded a greeting.

"What's wrong?" Markus asked after moving them out of earshot.

Ethan leaned against the railing and closed his eyes. He could still see the look of shock on Lylinora's face. "I just made a complete fool of myself," he admitted.

"How's that?"

Ethan told him what had happened.

Markus' face became unreadable. For a second he looked as if he would say something, but then instead turned to stare out at the ocean.

"I should have known," Ethan muttered through clenched teeth after a moment or two of silence.

"Known what?"

"That she wouldn't want someone like me."

Markus looked at him sideways. "Actually, I'm amazed that she turned you down. She's done nothing but flirt with you for days."

"I know. Well, that's what I thought she was doing. But I guess I was wrong about that."

Markus shook his head. "You weren't wrong, I'm sure of it. If you ask me, I think she's playing games with you."

"Maybe," said Ethan. "But I still can't help feeling like I did something wrong."

"You didn't. I promise." He flashed a toothy smile and put his arm around Ethan's shoulder. "You're a bloody boy scout. You couldn't do anything wrong if you wanted to."

His words made Ethan feel a touch better. "Thanks," he said.

"Don't you go worrying yourself about Lylinora," Markus continued. "She'll come around. I'd put a sack of gold on it." With that, he gave Ethan a hearty slap on the back and strode away.

"Where are you going?" Ethan called out, just as his friend reached the ladder.

"Nowhere special," he replied. "Just taking a look around."

*

Markus waited until he was certain that Ethan hadn't followed him before pounding on the cabin door.

Lylinora answered. Her face darkened the moment she saw him.

"What do you want?" she demanded.

"Can I come in?"

After letting out a heavy sigh, she backed away and allowed him to pass.

Markus regarded her for a long moment, then took a seat on the edge of the bed. Lylinora turned the chair away from the dresser, picked up a hair brush, and sat down facing him.

She began running the brush through her hair. "I am busy, so please tell me quickly what it is you want, Markus."

"What I want…*Nora*, is for you to stop playing games."

"I'm sure I don't know what you mean."

"Yes you do," he shot back. "You know good and damn well."

"If you're referring to what happened between us…"

"I'm referring to Ethan."

Her brushing paused for a moment. "What about Ethan?"

"You need to stop playing around with his feelings. He doesn't deserve it."

"What goes on between Lord Dragonvein and myself is none of your affair. So you need to curb your jealousy and stop meddling in things that are beyond you."

"*Ethan* is my best friend, so that certainly does make it my business," he retorted sharply.

Though she opened her mouth to respond, he pressed on regardless. "I appreciate what you did to heal me. I can also accept that you don't want me. Yes, I admit I was jealous for a while; I *thought* we had connected. But I was wrong, and this has nothing to do with the way I feel about you. This is about Ethan. You lead him on, then spurn him. You act like you're practically ready to rip off his clothes, and when he tries to get close, you make him feel like he's done something wrong."

"Is that what he told you?" she asked.

Markus shook his head. "Not at all. He told me that he had made a fool of himself. In fact, he didn't place any blame on you whatsoever. In his eyes, you're perfect. But I know better. You're just a selfish schemer, blind to anything but your own agenda. You plan to get whatever it is you want and to hell with anyone you hurt along the way."

She swung around in her chair to place the brush on the dresser. Her face was expressionless when she turned back. "Are you quite finished now?"

"Not quite. You may not have feelings for me, and I can take that. I've dealt with heartache before. But something tells me you don't have any feelings for Ethan either. And if that's the case, what you are doing to him is wrong."

Markus noticed that her head was now bowed and her hands folded on her lap. "When you healed me, you said that it can be an emotional experience; that you would touch my spirit and share my pain. It was too much for you. I get that. It's too much for *me* sometimes. But I felt *your* pain too. Don't ask me how, I just did. I know that you miss your father and mother. I know how hard it was for you to discover that everything you once knew is now gone. I know, because *I* lost everything too."

He paused, but she remained silent, her gaze still directed downwards. "Oh yes, you can hide your pain...just like me. You can make everyone believe that you are able to handle what has happened to you. But I know you better than you think. And that's why I know you are toying with Ethan's heart. There is no way you can feel for him with the same passion he feels for you. You're in too much pain to be capable of that."

He rose to his feet. "I won't let you hurt him. Hurt me all you want if it makes you happy. But either commit to Ethan, or leave him alone. He deserves better."

Having delivered his thoughts, Markus turned abruptly away. But he was only halfway to the cabin door when he heard soft sobs coming from behind. Almost instantly, he regretted his hard words. In spite of his anger, he did still care for Lylinora. More deeply than he wanted to admit. What they had shared during his healing continued to haunt him. Going back, he placed a comforting hand on her shoulder.

The effect was instantaneous.

Lylinora sprang up, her arms spread out wide. "Don't touch me!" she screamed. Her cheeks were soaked in tears - her hands clenched so tightly that her knuckles were white.

Before Markus could even blink, he found himself enveloped by a green light. He struggled to move, but was firmly trapped.

"You think you know me?" she sneered. "You think you can fathom the responsibility that I have been burdened with? And then you dare to question me?" Rage dripped from her every word. "I care nothing for you. You hear me? Nothing! And if I want to toy with Ethan, I'll toy with him. I don't care that he is your friend. He is far more important than that. He is the future of my kind. And if you ever try to interfere with me again..."

Markus was finding it virtually impossible to breathe. She was standing almost nose to nose with him, her face twisted into a dreadful combination of pain and fury. But even now – though she was using her magic to hold him powerless, he could feel only pity for her. She truly believed what she was saying. Suddenly, it all made sense.

She held him there for a few more seconds before releasing the spell. Markus crumbled to his knees, coughing and gasping for air.

"You... you... really think you'll... be... able... to live...like this?" he croaked.

"I will do what I must," she replied. "Now get the hell out!"

He struggled to his feet and stumbled to the door. "It won't work you know. He'll see through you eventually. He's not as naïve as you think."

"And why should that bother you?" Though she tried hard to contain it, there was a small quiver to her voice now. "Didn't you come here to stop me?"

"I...I just don't want to see you end up alone," Markus told her. "Especially after what you have lost." He opened the door and stepped slowly through it.

She said nothing more, but as he pulled it shut behind him he could hear the sound of her weeping once again.

This time, he left her to it.

CHAPTER EIGHT

ONCE THE EMBARRASSMENT of his impulsive attempt to kiss Lylinora had eased, Ethan began to rather enjoy being on board the smugglers' ship. The crew's initial shock of seeing the dwarves on their vessel did not last for long either. Within a day or two they were relaxed enough to speak casually with Ethan, spending time to teach him a bit about being a sailor and even including him in a few of their drinking sessions. The latter quickly drew stern lectures from the ever cautious Jonas about how too much wine can often produce a dangerously loose tongue.

Markus spent most of his time below deck. He and Birger could frequently be heard honing their fighting skills, which, quite apart from the obvious benefits, also had the practical effect of ensuring that the crew knew their group of passengers were far from defenseless. Ethan joined in with their practice from time to time, but mostly he dedicated himself to Lylinora's lessons. Her cramped quarters made it impossible to do very much in the way of casting aggressive spells, but he was learning quite a lot about the nature of magic.

"All magic is essentially the same," she told him. "It is the mage that changes it. Each one has certain natural endowments given to them at birth. I, for example, have a talent for healing and altering nature."

"Altering nature?" Ethan asked.

"Yes. I have a particular understanding for things that grow and the power they possess. An especially useful skill when you need to feed hungry people."

"But I've seen you use fire as a weapon."

"Of course. But that is not where my true strength lies. Your father could create a sea of flames that could stretch for miles. I can't do that. But I can make a field of apples ripen overnight, or heal a body with less than a single breath of life remaining. And that's just the beginning."

"You said I take after my father. What does that mean exactly?"

Lylinora shrugged. "That remains to be seen. Praxis Dragonvein was tremendously powerful. As was your mother. Though *her* talents were far more like mine. You have the gift for elemental magic – that much is clear. But we'll have to wait a little before discovering whether you possess your father's skill as a conjurer. We can't learn that here. It's too dangerous."

"Too dangerous?"

Lylinora smiled sweetly. "You wouldn't want to unleash fire breathing wolves on board this small vessel, would you?"

"No. I guess not."

The idea of creating such spectacular magic excited Ethan enormously and found himself more impatient than ever for them to reach their destination.

Kat joined them for most of the lessons, As usual, she remained silent throughout, though Ethan could see she had not missed a single word. He had a strong feeling she would easily master almost anything Lylinora could teach.

King Ganix chose to stay below most of the time, even taking his meals in the cargo hold.

"It's better I stay out of sight," he said when Ethan mentioned he was becoming concerned that he was alone too much. "The crew have all but forgotten I'm down here. And if I could, I would have them forget I ever was."

It was early one morning, two weeks into the journey, when Ethan felt himself being roughly shaken awake. Instinctively, he reached for his dagger, but stopped on seeing Kat.

He rubbed his eyes and yawned. "What time is it?"

"You have to get up," she said, the urgency in her voice clear.

"What's wrong?"

"An Imperial patrol ship has been sighted on the horizon."

Ethan immediately woke Markus and the others. Before they even had time to throw on their clothes and weapons, the captain arrived, a worried expression on his face.

"The dwarves should stay out of sight in the hold," he said. "The rest of you come on up top with me and do exactly as I say."

Ethan looked to Ganix, who gave him a reassuring nod.

Once on deck, Ethan saw immediately that the crew was frightened. Furtive whispers suggesting that the passengers should be killed and thrown overboard clearly reached his ears.

"Be ready," Markus told Ethan.

Looking calm, Jonas casually walked over to the railing and stared at the horizon. Ethan could see the white sails to the east.

"Are you sure it's Imperials?" he asked the captain.

"It's them all right," Jeridia replied darkly. "And from the look of it, they've already seen us. Now we have to wait and see if they want to come on board."

"And if they do?" asked Markus.

"Then I can either try to outrun them, or do nothing and hope they let us go."

"*Can* you outrun them?" asked Ethan.

"Not likely," he replied. "That's a patrol vessel, not a warship. If it were close to dusk I could probably lose them in the night, but..." He pointed to the sun that was only just breaking the horizon.

Just then Ethan spotted Lylinora approaching. Markus merely gave her a curt nod before moving away with Kat to join Jonas.

"Don't worry," said Lylinora. "If it comes down to it, we *will* get away."

She gestured for him to follow her to the starboard railing a few yards away from the others. Once there, she closed her eyes for a moment and whispered: *"Jiora"*. Her gaze then concentrated on the approaching ship.

"There are at least twenty soldiers apart from the crew," she informed Ethan. "But I see no heavy weapons on the deck. Just bows. Though they might have some dwarf weapons of course."

He recalled the spell of enhanced sight she had been teaching him recently. Maybe he could see these things too?

"*Jiora*," he said.

Nothing happened, producing a grunt of frustration. Ethan repeated the word several more times before finally giving up.

Lylinora was watching him closely. "Slow your mind," she told him. "Magic isn't something you can force out. It's a companion, not a slave."

He closed his eyes, took a deep breath, and did his best to clear all thoughts from his head. Once prepared, he tried again.

"*Jiora.*"

On opening his eyes, at first everything appeared the same as before. But only for a moment. The distant ship then rushed in toward him at a startling speed, causing him to jump back in alarm.

"Be calm." Lylinora smiled. "I know it's unnerving at first."

Ethan could only stand there, slack jawed and amazed by what he was seeing. It was as if he was now looking through powerful binoculars, only much, much clearer. He could see the men on the Imperial vessel working the ship's rigging and scurrying about.

He reached out his hand. "It feels like I could actually touch them if I wanted to."

"In time you'll be able to hear them too. But for now you've done well."

Fascinated, Ethan continued watching until he felt Lylinora's hand touch his arm. The moment he looked away from the ship, the spell was broken and his eyesight instantly reverted back to normal again.

Very soon it became apparent that the Imperial ship had indeed spotted them, and was now changing course to intercept.

Markus approached them. His eyes settled on Lylinora. "You and Kat should return to your cabin. It will raise less suspicion if you both appear afraid and are cowering below deck."

Lylinora regarded him with a stony expression before answering. "Yes. You're right."

She called for Kat, and the two of them returned to their quarters.

"You didn't say anything to her, did you?" Ethan asked, once they were gone.

Markus tapped the hilt of his sword anxiously. "Why do you ask?"

"It's just that she seems...different."

"How do you mean?"

"She's a bit more reserved. Not as...I don't know...not as flirty, I guess."

Markus gave him a sideways grin. "And I suppose you wish she still was."

Ethan shrugged. "No. Not really. Not unless she means it. I've already made an ass out of myself once when I got it wrong. I don't want *that* to happen again. Ever."

"I wouldn't worry, mate. It'll work itself out."

Ethan dearly wanted that to be true. Following Lylinora's rejection, it had taken all of his courage to face her again. That she was able to act as if nothing had happened in order to spare him further humiliation only made his feelings for her stronger.

For what felt like an eternity they watched the Imperial ship until it was less than one-hundred yards off their starboard bow. A trumpet sounded, causing a hush to fall over the deck.

"Raise the red flag!" the captain shouted. "And keep your wits about you."

Slowly, the patrol ship maneuvered alongside. After a series of ropes had been thrown over and made secure, a long wooden plank was lowered, bridging the two vessels. Twenty soldiers charged across with weapons drawn. They immediately set about herding everyone to the center of the deck.

With the entire crew contained and disarmed, a tall man with close-cropped dark hair strode across the plank. He was wearing a long black coat bearing six red chevrons on the sleeve. After dropping nimbly onto the deck, his dark eyes carefully surveyed the scene.

"Search below," he ordered in a surprisingly pleasant, yet still commanding voice.

Six soldiers broke away to do as instructed. As they did so, Captain Jeridia's voice thundered across the deck.

"What the devil is the meaning of this?" he demanded, descending from his position behind the main wheel. As soon as he reached the deck, two soldiers blocked his path.

The man in the long coat waved the soldiers aside. "You are Captain Jeridia, yes?"

"I am," he said proudly.

"And I am Captain Garon Marvdra." He gave a long sweeping bow. "I appreciate you not forcing me to chase you. It would have been such a bother."

"So why have you boarded my ship?" Jeridia challenged. If he was afraid, he was showing no sign of it. "We have done nothing wrong."

Marvdra laughed. "A renowned smuggler and thief such as yourself is always worthy of notice. And when I heard that your vessel was spotted heading in my direction, I just couldn't resist the opportunity to meet you."

Jeridia scowled angrily. "And now we've met. Kindly let us be on our way."

"In time, perhaps. We shall see."

While this exchange was going on, Ethan had been staring nervously at the door leading below. Moments later he saw Kat and Lylinora emerge with two soldiers at their backs. They both had their heads hung low as they were taken over to Marvdra.

"What have we here?" he asked.

"Passengers," replied Jeridia. "No law against that, is there?"

"Certainly not," Marvdra replied. He lifted Lylinora's chin. "Especially one so lovely. But it begs the question: Why is a smuggler taking on passengers?"

"Gold. Why else?"

Marvdra turned his attention to Kat. "And aren't you just the sweetest thing," he said, squeezing her arm lightly. "A bit underfed though." He shot an admonishing look in Jeridia's direction. "You really *must* take better care of your guests, Captain. Or perhaps they would prefer to come with us. I would be most pleased to assist you ladies in finding more…suitable transportation."

"Thank you," said Lylinora. "But I think we will remain here."

"Nonsense. I have a dear friend who would love to have such elegant company aboard his vessel."

She was saved from having to respond further by a shout from a soldier emerging from below decks. "Captain! We've found dwarves!"

Behind him appeared Birger and King Ganix. Ethan's heart sank.

Ganix walked the deck with head held high and shoulders straight. In contrast, Birger glowered and grunted as the soldier at his back shoved them forward.

Marvdra clicked his tongue. "My dear, Jeridia. You are aware that dealing with dwarves is illegal?" He let out an exaggerated sigh. "I fear that this complicates matters."

"Be ready," Markus whispered into Ethan's ear.

"My Lord," said Ganix, bowing. "Captain Jeridia is not at fault. He..."

Marvdra's hand shot up. His eyes now looked dangerous and accusing. "Silence dwarf. I did not give you permission to speak." He turned to Lylinora. "I hope you are not involved with this pair. That would be most unfortunate."

"They're not," said Ganix. "They didn't even know that we..."

Marvdra threw back his coat to reveal a long thin sword with a heavily bejeweled gold hilt. In an instant, he had the blade unsheathed and was stepping menacingly forward. In response, Birger jerked Ganix back by the collar and placed himself in the Imperial captain's path.

Marvdra halted. The fire in his eyes cooled and a tiny smile formed at the corners of his mouth. "Your father, is he? Or your lord perhaps? Whatever he is to you, I take it you are willing to die in order to protect him."

Birger glared unyieldingly, but said nothing.

Chuckling quietly, Marvdra turned his back. But only for a moment. He spun back around, this time with the sword fully raised. "Then let me help you perform your duty," he snapped, plunging the blade deep into the defiant dwarf's chest.

Birger let out a loud gasp, both his hands clutching at the steel.

"No!" shouted Ganix.

Ethan started forward, but Markus held his arm tight.

There was no restraining Kat however. Before Lylinora could do anything to stop her, she rushed to Birger's side. He was still on his feet, though held up only by Marvdra's grip on the still embedded sword. Blood dribbled from his chest, and from the corners of his mouth. He smiled weakly at Kat.

With a savage grin, Marvdra jerked his sword free, at last allowing Birger to collapse onto the deck.

Kat's face was contorted with rage. "You bastard!" she screamed. With fingers extended like claws ready to tear his eyes out, she made ready to leap at Marvdra. This time though, Lylinora was prepared and able to wrap restraining arms around her. Kat struggled wildly to free herself, but after a few moments went limp and began weeping uncontrollably.

"So you *do* know the dwarves," remarked Marvdra, his pleasant, conversational tone never faltering. "Now I am *truly* dismayed. I was so hoping that the two of you were telling the truth."

Ethan's rage was boiling. Markus eased his way in front of him. "Not until I say so," he whispered. His face was like stone; his hands rock steady.

Marvdra retrieved a cloth from his pocket and proceeded to wipe the blood from his blade. "I'm afraid, my dear Captain Jeridia, that you are in a spot of trouble. Harboring dwarves is a serious offence. One that I simply cannot overlook."

Jeridia cast an eye around. The soldiers had the entire deck surrounded. "What do you intend to do with us?" he asked.

"That all depends," Marvdra replied. "First, I will take the women aboard my ship. Then I will ask them a few questions. If they answer to my satisfaction, I just might decide *not* to set fire to your ship and fill anyone who jumps overboard with arrows. If they do not, I shudder to think what might happen to you…and to them."

Ethan saw Lylinora glance over at him. Her face was twisted and her lips trembled. Kat was still weeping in her arms.

"Take them," ordered Marvdra. "And kill the other dwarf."

Markus nudged Ethan. "Be ready now. We kill their captain first."

Reaching into his sleeve, he produced a dagger. "Stay behind me until you can get hold of a sword."

A soldier had already ripped Kat from Lylinora's arms and was starting to drag her toward the plank. Markus took a step forward, but just as he was about to strike at the nearest soldier, Lylinora spoke. Her loud and confident voice carried all over the deck.

"There is something you should know, Captain."

He gave a short, mocking laugh. "And what might that be?"

"I don't like answering questions."

As she spoke, Lylinora's arms spread wide and her eyes began to glow a brilliant red, radiating huge waves of energy.

The change in Marvdra was instant. Uncertainty and fear suddenly gripped him. "What in the name of...?" he began.

The man's words were cut violently short by the jagged spears of white light that flew from Lylinora's hands and shot directly into his mouth. All the time uttering a series of weird choking sounds, he staggered back and forth in erratic patterns until eventually falling heavily onto his back. Once down, he continued to writhe around on the deck for a short while longer, as if wrestling with invisible demons. Then, after one final agonized cry and violent jerk, he became still and silent. Throughout it all, the soldiers, as well as all the smugglers, could do nothing but watch, every one of them paralyzed with terror.

Seizing this opportunity, Markus and Ethan burst forward. In a single deft movement, Markus slashed the throat of the nearest soldier while Ethan kicked another in the back, sending him sprawling. In a flash, he snatched up the dying first soldier's dropped sword.

"There's no need," Lylinora called over to them, a wicked grin on her face. "I can handle this lot...easily."

By now, some of the soldiers had recovered from the initial shock sufficiently to begin creeping nervously toward her. All of the smugglers, including Captain Jeridia, remained horror stricken and paralyzed.

Closing her fists, Lylinora yelled: *"Dao Gaat Sustesvo"*. Her voice boomed and echoed, startling the soldiers so badly that they stopped dead in their tracks.

By now, Kat had run to King Ganix. He folded her protectively within his arms.

In response to Lylinora's words, a whirl of black smoke rose from the deck planking a few feet in front of her. Sparks of blue energy spewed out from the column in all directions, exploding with sharp cracks as they hit the ground. The whirling mass rapidly picked up both speed and size until it had formed the shape of a miniature cyclone approximately the height and breadth of a man. Then, all at once, it froze still. Only the creaking of the ship and the heavy pants of terrified men could now be heard.

Lylinora's grin vanished. "You should run, fools."

It was a pointless warning. Before anyone could make the smallest move to escape, half a dozen bolts of lightning shot forth from the stilled column, each one striking a soldier in the center of his chest. Their eyes flashed wide and they were dead even before they fell. With the stench of scorched flesh now mingling disgustingly with the fresh smell of ozone, the tempest resumed spinning, throwing out bolt after bolt into the ranks of their foes and stalking anyone who held a threatening sword.

Ethan could only watch in horror and awe as fifteen men were killed within just a few seconds. The remaining four cast away their weapons and fell face down, begging to be spared. But Lylinora was not inclined to be merciful. The tempest paused only briefly before striking these soldiers too. The job done, the dark spell became calm until Lylinora clapped her hands hard together. Instantly, it vanished.

There was a long silence. Kat then broke free from Ganix and knelt beside Birger.

"Can you help him?" she pleaded.

Lylinora took a moment to survey the aftermath before joining Kat beside the body. She placed her hand over the dwarf's forehead and took a deep breath. "I'm sorry," she said after a few seconds. "He is beyond my aid."

Seizing hold of Birger's hand, Kat broke down into a flood of tears. Ganix knelt beside her, muttering softly with closed eyes.

After witnessing the carnage, sailors on board the Imperial vessel had already cast aside the plank and cut the ropes in a mad scramble to get away from the smuggler's ship.

Ethan looked around for Jonas and spotted him standing amongst the smugglers still gathered in the center of the deck. As his eyes settled on the old man, Lylinora arrived at his side.

"Are you all right?" she asked.

"Fine," he replied, though that was not exactly the truth. He was unsure what to do next. They were exposed, and must now deal with a frightened captain and crew.

As so often in the past, it was Markus who provided the first positive action. He approached the captain, who was still more or less frozen with fear.

"Have your men throw the bodies over the side," he ordered.

When Jeridia didn't move, he slapped the man's face. "Do you hear me?"

The captain finally snapped out of his trance, blinking several times. "Yes…yes…of course…" He turned to the crew. "Do as he says. Throw the bodies over."

While his order was being carried out, Lylinora placed a hand gently on Ganix's shoulder. "Is there some ritual or rite which needs to be observed for Birger?"

Ganix shook his head. "None that could be performed here. I would ask only that his body be burned. Not cast aside as food for the sea creatures. Also, I would like to clean his wound and change his clothes."

"Of course."

Jeridia approached them. "My…My Lady," he began. "What of the Imperial ship? They'll return with many reinforcements unless…."

By now the Imperial ship was fifty yards away, its sails already snapped full. With an unconcerned air, Lylinora held up her right hand and began rubbing her thumb and forefinger together, at the same time whispering almost inaudibly. After more than a full minute, she turned away with a smile of satisfaction.

"You needn't concern yourself about that any longer," she told the captain.

No sooner had she spoken than smoke began rising from the enemy ship. Within a minute it was totally engulfed in flames. The screams of the dying carried clearly across the water as men desperately jumped into its depths to avoid being roasted.

"We should be well away from here before anyone notices they are missing," Lylinora remarked. She winked at Ethan and moved close to whisper into his ear. "Just imagine what you will be able to do one day."

She then tenderly took hold of Kat's arms and lifted her to her feet. "Come, my dear. Allow Ganix to prepare Birger for his journey. Go to the cabin. I'll be along shortly."

Ethan was happy to see her treating Kat with such kindness. "You should go with her," he said. "We'll clean up the mess."

Lylinora nodded and followed Kat below. A moment later, Markus helped Ganix carry Birger's body to the galley.

"What now?" Ethan asked Jonas.

"Now we deal with our smuggler friends," he replied.

"That may not be so easy."

Jonas shrugged. "After Lylinora's display, I seriously doubt they'll give us much trouble."

It seemed like his judgement was probably correct. Once all the bodies had been disposed of, the crew quickly gathered together in a tight group around the center mast, whispering amongst themselves while eyeing Ethan and Jonas. But it was with suspicion and fear rather than hostility.

When Ganix and Markus returned, Jeridia called all four of them to the bow. Some of his former authority now appeared to have returned.

"What the devil have you gotten me into?" he demanded. "Who is that witch? And why is she here?"

"Her identity is none of your business," Jonas warned. "Best you keep your curiosity at bay. All you need to know is that we still intend for you to honor our agreement."

"Are you insane?" the captain shouted. After a quick glance at the crew, he then lowered his voice. "I'll not transport the likes of her."

Markus burst out laughing and threw an arm around Jeridia's shoulder. "Then I suggest you tell her that yourself. Let's go. This is something I'd very much like to see."

Ever the peacemaker, Ganix moved quickly to calm the situation. "Come now," he said. "There is no reason for this to be unpleasant. It is not Captain Jeridia's fault that we were boarded. In truth, we have been less than forthcoming. But the fact remains, we will not be leaving this ship until we arrive at our destination. You can certainly profit handsomely from this, captain. And you have my word of honor that you will."

Jeridia stepped away from Markus and cast his gaze around the group in a long, hard look. After heaving a heavy moan, he threw up his hands in surrender. "Very well. As I seem to have little choice in the matter, I suppose I should at least pick some gold out of this pile of shit. You head below. I need to speak to my crew alone."

He lowered his head and rubbed the bridge of his nose. "They are not going to like this. Not one little bit."

CHAPTER NINE

ETHAN WRAPPED A comforting arm around Kat as they watched Markus and King Ganix gently lay Birger down on the ship's deck. The king had found a well-made shirt and trousers to dress the body in, and the fallen dwarf's axe had been placed ceremoniously across his chest.

Jonas and Lylinora were standing a few feet away, their heads slightly bowed. The crew had cleared the deck for the funeral gathering, partly by request, but mostly because no one wanted to be near Lylinora anyway. They now regarded her as some kind of devil. One sailor had actually shit himself when she passed by him in the hallway.

The sun was slowly sinking into the horizon, turning the sky all around it into a vivid shade of violet threaded with wisps of orange and red. The gentle swells of the sea sparkled and shimmered in the fading light, and for a short and solemn period, only the calling of the sea birds and the creaking of the ship's timbers could be heard.

Markus bowed to the king, then took up position beside Ethan. Ganix stared down at Birger's body with misty eyes. He drew a long, deep breath before speaking.

"I am so sorry, my friend," he began. "I know you would have rather rested beneath the mountain. As you told me: This is no place for a dwarf."

He turned to face the others before continuing.

"Birger was by far the most important dwarf to live in more than five-hundred years. At least, that is how I shall remember him. Not because he was the one who found Ethan Dragonvein and brought him to us. No. Perhaps even more important than that, it is because he was the first amongst us to understand how true friendships are made - through trust and through understanding.

"I can promise you that Birger did not befriend any of you without a great deal of effort. But he possessed a pure heart. And a pure heart allows you to accomplish things that others deem impossible. It was through his example that we have a chance to drive out the darkness that has plagued this world for far too long. The bonds he formed with all of you taught us that our fears, our hatred, and our prejudice, are not insurmountable obstacles. They are tests. Tests of our character. Tests of our worthiness to exist. Tests that Birger passed even before those who wear a crown were able.

"In my life I have known many others - the strong, the wise, and the brilliant. But among them all, Birger proved to be the one who left me with the deepest regret. I mourn the fact that I did not have the chance to know him better. I can also see this same regret in the eyes of his new friends who stand here on this day. So even in death, Birger reminds us of what our hearts should never forget. We are here…together. And in his absence, we realize how precious a thing that is."

Tears were now running freely down Ganix's cheeks, soaking into his beard. "I ask you all to never forget what this noble dwarf has done. And to keep his memory fresh in your hearts."

With his speech over, he nodded to Ethan, who took up position beside the king. After taking a moment to bow to Birger, he began his own tribute to the fallen dwarf.

"I asked King Ganix to allow me to speak because I thought it would be the proper thing to do. I spent the better part of the day going over what I would say. I tried recalling everything I knew about Birger – the stories he told me and the times we spent together. But nothing I can say will be enough to explain the loss I'm feeling right now. I didn't know him long. I didn't get years with him. Just a few short months. But I didn't need years to know that he was everything King Ganix has said…and a whole lot more. I wish I could say something to make everyone feel better. I really do. But right now, all I have in my heart is anger. Our enemy has taken so much from so many. And now he has taken a dear and trusted friend."

The set of his mouth firmed. "Even though I was taught that vengeance is wrong, vengeance for this terrible crime is what I most surely want. Would Birger approve? I'd like to think he would. To tell you the truth, right or wrong doesn't matter very much to me now. Shinzan *will* pay. This is the promise I make...to Birger, to all of you, and to myself."

A brief silence followed. Ganix then placed his hand on Ethan's shoulder. "I cannot say for certain whether or not Birger would approve of your anger. But I do know that he would most surely understand it."

Ethan returned to his place with the others. Lylinora then stepped forward and bowed to the king. "I am ready," she said.

Ganix nodded and pulled a short, green rod from his sleeve. At the same time Lylinora raised both her arms, levitating Birger's body several feet off the deck. It hung motionless in mid-air for a moment, then drifted beyond the ship's railing, stopping when about thirty yards out over the water. Once it was there, the king raised the rod. Great streaks of fire burst forth from it, completely engulfing Birger's body. Ganix kept the fire coming for more than five minutes. Finally, when the rod ceased to glow and the fire was gone, not a trace of Birger's body or his weapon remained.

Ganix threw the spent rod into the sea and bowed his head. "Thank you, Lady Lylinora."

"It was my honor to help," she replied solemnly.

The king looked up, stifling his tears. "Come. It is our tradition to drink in remembrance of fallen comrades. The captain was kind enough to provide us with some wine."

"We have the same tradition on Earth," Ethan told him.

They all went below to the main cargo hold where several bottles awaited them. They drank until just before dawn, each of them taking turns recalling their fondest memories of Birger. Tears flowed as abundantly as the wine throughout. Kat seemed particularly affected by what had happened. Ethan thought to comfort her, but she stayed close to Lylinora. Surprisingly, Lylinora didn't seem to mind, even allowing the young girl to rest her head on her shoulder for long periods.

Ethan wanted his anger to subside, but the memory of the callous way in which Birger had been slain only added fuel to the rage. Are they all evil, he wondered? Maybe not. But those who were, made it very easy to hate his enemy.

The next morning after breakfast, he found Lylinora up on deck with Kat.

"As there is no further need to hide my identity as a mage, I've decided that we will have our lessons out here," she said.

"Do you think that's a good idea?" Ethan asked. "The crew…"

"To hell with the crew," snapped Kat. "They're a bunch of cowards as far as I'm concerned."

"Now what did we talk about, young lady?" scolded Lylinora.

Kat folded her arms, pouting. "You're right. I'm sorry."

"As I was saying," Lylinora continued. "The lessons will be on deck. But they will take place at night when most of the crew are asleep. And from now on, Kat will be participating."

Ethan raised an eyebrow. "Really? Why the change of heart?"

"The girl needs to be able to protect herself," she replied. "If I hadn't been here, those men would have dragged her to their ship and…" Her lip curled. "I don't want to imagine what they would have done to her. In spite of Kat's shortcomings, she has a natural talent. And after seeing how men of this age treat women, I regard it as my duty to train her."

That night, the three of them gathered below the center mast. For more than three hours Lylinora drilled them on defensive spells – some intended simply to incapacitate, others designed to kill. Ethan was pleased to see that Lylinora was now far more accepting of Kat. And he understood her feelings. Having leapt to Kat's rescue himself shortly after arriving in Lumnia, he was equally appalled by the barbarity he had witnessed. Lylinora was right. Women were treated very badly here; a situation he knew she intended to one day change.

A few days later, Captain Jeridia came down into the hold to speak with them.

"I'm afraid we must stop in Port Hull," he announced.

"Why exactly?" asked Markus.

"I could tell you that supplies are low," he replied. "But the truth is, I am barely containing a mutiny. The lady's display of magic has shattered some of the men's reason. I need to rid myself of them before things get out of hand."

Markus frowned. "How many are complaining?"

"Six. No more. We'll simply allow them to leave the ship and move on. The delay will be brief, I promise."

Ganix thought for a moment. "Perhaps it's not a terrible idea. We could probably do with some fresh information. Besides, a mutiny would be most inconvenient."

"I want to know which men are causing trouble," Markus said. "Can they be trusted to hold their tongues?"

Jeridia regarded Markus and shook his head. "You have the bearing of a dangerous man. Those who will be leaving are simply afraid. They do not deserve to die."

"I didn't say they did," Markus retorted. "I wish only to speak with them and offer gold in exchange for their silence."

"Be that as it may," said Jeridia. "I will not reveal them to you. I have already quelled the situation by promising to make port and let them go. That will have to be enough for you."

Markus smiled broadly. "Very well, Captain. I respect your decision."

"When will we arrive?" asked Ethan.

"In two days," Jeridia replied. Before walking away, he added: "I advise that you stay aboard while we are there. Port Hull can be a dangerous place."

"You realize we can't allow them to just leave, don't you?" Markus said, as soon as the captain was out of earshot.

"You can't just kill them," Ethan protested. "They didn't do anything wrong."

"Even so, Markus is right," said Jonas. "If they talk, Shinzan could learn about Lylinora. The empire certainly has eyes and ears among the smugglers."

"But Markus said he'd pay them to keep quiet," said Ethan.

"I lied," his friend responded. "Unfortunately for me, the captain knew it. One benefit my scars gave me was hiding what I was thinking. I suppose I'll need to be more careful in the future."

"What do you think, Your Highness?" asked Jonas.

The king rubbed his beard and looked down at his lap. "I need to speak to Markus...alone."

Ethan tried to divine what Ganix was thinking, but his expression was unreadable. He then felt Jonas touch his arm. After a brief meeting of eyes, he followed the old man out of the hold.

"What do you think he'll do?" Ethan asked.

Jonas shrugged. "Who can tell?"

They went into the galley to eat. Several crew members were still finishing their meal, but the sight of the two passengers ensured that any food remaining in their bowls was quickly gobbled up. Soon, the pair were completely alone.

Ethan stared at his bowl of stew, stirring it absently with his spoon. "It makes me wonder," he remarked.

"Wonder what?" asked Jonas.

"Suppose Shinzan is defeated. And suppose the mages return in the way Lylinora wants. How will people react? Will they even want us?"

"Of course they will," Jonas assured him. "The mages were protectors of the people. They were feared, yes. But also loved."

"All I see is the fear."

"You'll look at things differently in time. The more you learn, and realize how much good you can do, the more you'll understand how much this world needs you and your kind."

Ethan sighed. "Maybe. I hope you're right."

Just as they were completing their meal, Kat arrived. She plopped herself down beside Ethan.

"Lylinora has gone to talk with King Ganix," she said. "So I thought we could work on some spells together."

"Did she say what he wanted?" Ethan asked.

Kat shook her head. "No. Markus showed up at the door and said they needed her to come down to the hold. That's all. She didn't look too happy about it. But I think that's only because she doesn't like Markus very much."

After Kat had finished eating, the two of them went to her cabin. They practiced levitating objects for a while, throwing them back and forth to each other like a game. Kat had written down every spell and incantation Lylinora had taught them, so after a time they decided to review some of the more difficult spells. One of these enabled them to confine a foe inside a coil of magical energy. Ethan remembered experiencing this spell first hand when Lylinora had come to his room late at night. He shuddered on realizing how easily she could have crushed the life from him.

When Lylinora returned, her expression was grave. But it softened the moment she saw Ethan.

"I'm pleased to see you two working," she said.

"It was Kat's idea," Ethan said. "*She* deserves the credit."

Lylinora nodded approvingly. "Perhaps you have more discipline than I thought."

"What did King Ganix want?" Ethan asked, trying not to sound suspicious.

Lylinora flicked her hand. "Oh, nothing much. He just wanted to know if I could do something to prevent the men leaving the ship from talking."

"And can you?"

"Perhaps. Memory spells are tricky though. They don't always work."

"Sometimes they do," Kat chipped in.

Lylinora shot her a stern look. "Don't you have anything else to do?"

Kat gathered up the parchments on which she had copied the spells. She opened her mouth, but shut it again when Lylinora's stare hardened. "I'll be in the hold," she finally said.

Ethan chuckled after Kat left. "You've taken a real interest in her."

Lylinora sat at the dresser and began brushing her hair. "She needs to learn. And there is no one else to teach her. It's a pity she didn't grow up in a different time. She would have made quite the mage."

"She still might."

Lylinora glanced over her shoulder to smile at him. "True. If we have the time."

"Why wouldn't we?"

"*Your* training is far more important," she explained. "Once we get to learning more complex magic, I'll need to focus my attention on you, and you alone." She gave him a suggestive wink. "I hope you don't mind."

Lylinora had been far more restrained lately, and this renewed flirtation sent Ethan's heart racing for a moment or two. But visions of her shocked expression when he'd tried to kiss her soon snapped him back to reality.

"I should go," he said, trying not to sound excited.

Lylinora put the brush down and swung around to face him. "No. Stay and talk with me."

Ethan stood up and took a step toward the door. "I really should find Markus."

She gave a light-hearted laugh. "For a soldier, you scare very easily." Rising to her feet, she draped her arms around his neck. "Do you remember what I told you?"

Beads of sweat formed on Ethan's brow. He could feel the warmth of her breath on his face. The sweet scent of her perfume and the seductive tone in her voice stoked his desire until it was all but beyond his control.

She leaned in to put her lips next to his ear. "I said I wasn't ready. But that I *would be*."

Her teeth began softly nibbling at his earlobe. His hands trembled, but still he kept them down at his sides. "I remember," he said, his voice a croaky whisper.

Her lips crept closer to his mouth, hovering just above his cheek. "Well, I'm almost ready now."

She kissed him softly, her tongue parting his lips, searching until it had found his. Ethan could feel the hardness of his manhood pressing against her as the kiss became ever more passionate. Tentatively, he placed his hands on her hips. Then, unable to stop himself any longer, he slipped his arms all the way around, crushing her against him.

When the kiss ended he was nearly mad with carnal hunger. "I love you," he whispered.

Lylinora took a small step back. For a terrifying moment Ethan thought he had once again made a fool of himself and upset her. But then he saw that her smile was still in place.

She took hold of his hands. "Not yet. But soon."

With that, she turned and settled down in front of the dresser once again. After picking up the brush, she cast a glance back at him. "You really should sit down," she suggested.

It took Ethan a moment to realize that the bulge in his trousers was all too noticeable. Crimson faced, he quickly dropped down onto the edge of the bed and crossed his arms over his lap.

Lylinora looked at him with thinly disguised amusement. "Impressive, by the way. Most impressive."

This only furthered his embarrassment. More than a minute passed, during which time Lylinora casually continued humming and brushing her hair. Eventually, he felt able to stand up once again.

"I should go," he said.

"Off to find Markus?" she teased.

Ethan left the cabin without replying and returned to the cargo hold where King Ganix and Markus were talking quietly.

"You look flushed," Ganix observed.

He gave a vague shrug and sat down. "Never mind that. What are you two planning?"

Markus looked at him innocently. "Nothing. Nothing at all."

"You know, you're right about your new face," Ethan told him. "You have a much harder time hiding it when you're lying now."

"Better that you're not involved," Ganix interjected quickly.

"Why? Because I'm just a kid?"

"Not at all," the king replied. "I would not insult you so, nor do I see you that way. It's merely that you already have enough to concentrate on."

Ethan scowled. "You're going to kill those men, aren't you?"

Ganix leveled his gaze. "Yes, we are."

"You're too much of a bloody boy scout to be a part of this," added Markus. He spread his hands. "I love you, Ethan, but it's true. You need to keep your mind on learning magic. Let *me* handle the dirty work."

"I don't like being lied to," Ethan snapped back. "And I'm *not* a fucking boy scout anymore."

Ganix rested his hand fondly on Ethan's shoulder. "Markus is right.

There are some tasks for which you are not suited. Assassination is one of them. Believe me when I tell you that I don't like it either. But there is too much at stake. We only wanted to spare your conscience the additional burden."

"Then why tell Lylinora?" he demanded.

"She doesn't know," said Markus. "All King Ganix asked her to do was keep you busy when we arrive at Port Hull. She thinks it's to keep you from wandering off and getting into trouble."

While listening to this, a disquieting thought flashed through Ethan's mind. Everything that had just happened between them in the cabin - had it been merely to distract him? He quickly dismissed the idea. She wouldn't do such a thing. Besides, she had only been asked to keep him on board. She could achieve that easily enough without resorting to...*to that.*

"Ethan, there is something you will need to soon learn," said Ganix. "Sometimes there must be sacrifices. And more often than not it involves doing things we find distasteful. One day you will be forced to make difficult decisions. People will die, and you will bear the burden of responsibility. But that day has not yet come. Be grateful."

While looking at Ganix's strained expression and bent posture, Ethan suddenly understood. They were right not to include him. He wasn't ready. The thought of being the cause of such a cold and ruthless act, regardless of how necessary, was revolting. I guess I *am* still a boy scout, he thought.

"I *am* grateful," he told them. "And don't worry. I'll stay out of the way."

Markus smiled. "And so you know, I don't think you're a kid. Just a good man."

It was well after dark, two days later, when they reached Port Hull. In the run up to their arrival, Lylinora became increasingly flirtatious whenever they were alone together. She had kissed him in the same highly arousing way on three separate occasions. Each time afterwards, it took more than an hour before Ethan could hold any kind of clear thought in his head.

Port Hull was not a very impressive sight. Ten or so ships were currently docked, most of which resembled Captain Jeridia's vessel. Beyond this, the lights of the town twinkled. It wasn't exceptionally large – no more than eight square blocks in any direction, and when they drew close enough, Ethan saw that the buildings were mostly dilapidated shacks. With the sounds of rough laughter and music carrying over the water, drunken men could be seen stumbling about everywhere. As the crew tied off, prostitutes immediately began making a beeline for the ship.

Lylinora joined Ethan by the railing. "Disgusting," she remarked.

"Didn't they have prostitutes in your time?" he asked.

"Of course they did. It was disgusting then, too. Women shouldn't sell themselves."

A minute later, Kat bounded up. "Ah, whores on parade," she remarked brightly.

"That's not funny," snapped Lylinora. "They should be pitied."

"Have you ever met one?" Kat asked her, smirking. "Most of them would slit your throat rather than look at you. And the men who own them are even worse."

Lylinora's face contorted. "Own? You're saying they're..."

"Slaves," said Kat, completing her sentence. "Or close to it. There's not actual ownership. Not like in the east. But seeing as how they can never leave, it's pretty much the same thing."

With the ship's bell sounding, the captain called for his crew to gather at the center mast. All but six men complied. These outsiders, huddled together in their own small group, glared at their former crew mates with fury in their eyes. Not that they remained like this for very long. The instant they noticed Lylinora approaching, they scrambled down the gang plank as fast as they could. Paying not even a flicker of attention to the enticing calls of the prostitutes, they pushed their way past and sped on down the dock toward town.

Ethan spotted Markus emerging from below. The captain took note of him as well, but turned away and began addressing the crew.

"No one is allowed off the ship unless they're with me," Jeridia announced. The shouts of discontent this raised became more stifled when he added: "I'll be giving each man an extra gold coin this trip, so stop your complaining."

Ethan continued to track Markus as he strolled casually from the ship and quickly vanished into the now large gathering of prostitutes and merchants converging on their vessel.

"Where do you suppose he's going?" asked Kat.

Ethan shrugged. "Who knows? As long as he's back before we leave, what does it matter?"

"Come," said Lylinora. "We should go to the cabin for a lesson. The sight of this turns my stomach."

Ethan nodded and gave her a smile. "Good idea."

CHAPTER TEN

MARKUS TOOK A long look at the parchment he had eventually *'persuaded'* Captain Jeridia to supply him with. He'd been forced to play a little rough with the man during their private talk, but the threat of 'bad things to come', together with an offer of extra gold, had worked well enough in the end. And the information he now had would make his task much easier.

While navigating his way through the crowded streets, he breathed a long sigh of contentment. It felt good. Hard as it was to admit, he could never completely leave behind the man he had been for such a large part of his life...Specter.

Specter was cunning. He was patient. He was calculating. And most of all, he was deadly. How many people had fallen to his blade? For sure, far too many to count. Some never even knew they had been killed until the instant their eyes closed forever.

He would do his best to make it quick and painless this time. But the thought of blood flowing as his blade slid across exposed flesh was irresistible. For him, seeing the fear and desperation in his victim's eyes could be more satisfying than the embrace of a beautiful woman. He thought of Lylinora. Well, most women.

Focus, he scolded himself. She's not for you. But the men listed on the paper were; they were his. He allowed the excitement of the coming kill to soak in, giving his mind clarity.

Four of them would stay together. The other two would go off in different directions through the town. But he knew how to find them all. And how it would be done.

He approached the tavern where the first target was reckoned to be. Inside, dozens of sailors were drinking and laughing. A flautist and a singer were in the far corner playing an upbeat melody to which people were dancing and singing along.

While approaching the bar, he noticed that he was drawing a few indifferent glances. This was an odd feeling. In the past, his scars had usually kept people from looking directly at him. He smiled inwardly. He was just an average guy now, out for a good time. Nothing to mark him out.

He ordered a mug of ale and leaned back on the bar. Sitting at a table close by, alone for the time being, was the man he sought. Markus reached into his shirt and felt the cold handle of the small dagger. He could do it easily enough from here. But the man had his back turned. He wanted to see his face first. He wanted to watch the light leave his eyes.

A dark haired prostitute sauntered up to the bar beside him. "Hey there, gorgeous," she said, draping her arms over his neck. "Haven't seen you before."

For a moment, Markus was taken aback. With the scars on his face, women had never been prone to approaching him. Not even whores.

"Not interested," he told her. The stink of the men she had already been with hung in the air, causing a frown to form. He pushed her away. "I'm waiting for a friend."

"Suit yourself, honey," she said, seemingly unaffected by the rejection. "But if you change your mind, I'll be here all night."

Markus switched his attention back to his target. Turn around, damn it, he thought. He was beginning to lose patience. Another first. Several women came up to the man, but he shook his head and waved them away. After a few more minutes, a tall, dark skinned youth entered and took a seat at the same table. Very soon, the pair were engaged in deep conversation. Markus scowled. How much longer would he have to wait to see his victim's face?

"Don't be stupid," he muttered. "Just get it done."

At that moment a brawl broke out in the area immediately in front of the musicians. For a short period, just about everyone's gaze was focused on this. It was an opportunity too good to pass up. In a fluid motion, Markus drew the blade and hurled it. The man gave a sharp jerk as the point struck home, burying itself deep into the back of his neck. Markus took note of the young companion's confused expression and smiled to himself. That'll have to do me for now, he thought. By the time his victim slumped face down onto the table, Markus had already passed through the door and was back on the street.

He followed the directions on the parchment to a small hovel near the edge of town. Most of the street lamps were either out or missing, so moving through the shadows was fairly easy. Only a few drunkards and beggars were about, and none bothered to look at him.

Creeping around to the rear of the dwelling, he squatted down beneath a window. He could hear two men talking in hushed tones, though it was impossible to make out what they were saying. Markus cursed himself for having taken so much time over the first man. Now this one was likely telling the tale of how Lylinora had killed the Imperial soldiers. And in doing so he had unwittingly sentenced his companion to death as well.

He raised his head just enough to peer inside. There was only one room, and the men were seated a few feet beyond the window at a table near the hearth. Both had swords at their sides.

After a moment's thought, Markus crawled to the rear door. Once there, he reached into his belt and pulled out another dagger. This one was longer and ill-suited for throwing. Using the tip of the blade, he began scratching softly on the wood.

In this position, the men's voices carried to him a little better. "Do you hear that?" he heard one of them ask.

Markus persisted with the scratching.

"Yeah, I hear it," replied the other.

"What the hell is it?"

Markus heard the sound of swords being drawn.

"It sounds like…I don't know. But it's coming from outside."

There was the scraping of chairs being pushed back. Seconds later, the door flew open.

The instant it did, Markus sprang into the attack. Faster than the eye could follow, his blade thrust out. The leading man's eyes shot wide. With blood already spurting from the deadly wound to his throat, his sword fell to the floor. In a continuous movement, Markus pulled the dagger free and shoved the body away to his right.

The second man, only a few feet behind, had no time to react. Markus was already on him. Again, his dagger strike to the neck was nothing more than a blur. And equally deadly. The second victim stood there motionless for several seconds, his face contorted in terror and utter disbelief of what had just happened to him.

Yes, thought Markus. That's what I wanted to see.

At last the stricken man crumpled to his knees, then rolled over completely. In a kind of grotesque duet, the two men gurgled and gasped simultaneously until the life had drained from both of their bodies. Markus looked on throughout, only shifting his gaze when they had stopped moving all together. Satisfied, he cleaned his blade on the first man's shirt.

He closed his eyes. *This* is what he really was. *This* is what Ethan and the others could never understand. And no matter how hard he tried, Specter would always show himself...eventually. This was the darkness he didn't want Lylinora to see. It wasn't a darkness brought on by past deeds and regret. It was something that was still very much alive inside of him.

He looked at the parchment once again. Four at once. A challenge. But one he was more than prepared for. Reaching into his pocket, he felt the small box within. If his information was accurate, *this* would do the trick.

On his way back to the center of town, he passed the tavern where he had claimed the first life. Several men were talking out front. Markus slowed long enough to hear that the conversation was about the murder of the sailor. No one knew how it could have happened without a single person noticing. He had to restrain himself from laughing.

The last four sailors on his list were supposed to be in a gambling den only a few blocks away from the tavern. Pulling his hood up over his head, he pressed on.

There were four large, tough looking men guarding the front of the two story establishment. Markus watched from across the street for several minutes as dozens of people came and went. He sniffed the air. The putrid stench of the smugglers' town brought memories flooding back. Bad memories...yet at the same time, good ones. Places like this was where he had learned to kill. Where he had honed his skills. And where, in the end, he had sold his soul.

A tall, lean man in a red shirt and tan trousers stopped on the walkway beside him. "There's no need my friend," he said quietly. "It's already been taken care of."

Markus jumped back, his hand shooting to the hilt of his dagger. "Move on," he hissed.

The newcomer smiled, but made no effort to do as instructed. His sandy blond hair and green eyes gave him an unimposing appearance. However, his confident voice and fluid movements told a different story. Markus knew at once that he was genuinely dangerous.

"I said move on," he repeated, taking a menacing step forward.

"I heard you the first time...Specter."

So great was his surprise, Markus' jaw fell slack.

The man chuckled. "No need to fear."

He quickly recovered his wits. "Tell me who you are and how you know me," he demanded. "If you don't, I swear you'll die right here and now."

"A threat not to be taken lightly, to be sure," the man said. His gaze returned to the gambling den. "My name is Gault. And who *doesn't* know the great Specter...even sporting such a handsome face. How did you manage that, by the way?" Markus' glare produced only a shrug. "Little matter. I'm sure you're much happier without those dreadful scars."

"You have until the count of three to tell me how you know me and why you're here."

Gault held up his index finger. "One..." His middle finger followed suit. "Two...."

At this crucial point, four men burst from the gambling den door, each one clutching at his throat and wheezing desperately.

"Ah, just in time," Gault remarked.

Markus looked closer at the dying men. These were the four he had come to kill.

"How…?" he began, but fell silent as, in rapid succession, each of the men collapsed in the street with vast quantities of blood issuing from both mouth and nose. After only a few seconds, all four of them had become still.

"Messy, but effective," observed Gault.

Markus' patience snapped. Grabbing Gault by the collar, he shoved him hard into the wall of the building just behind them. "Who the hell are you?" he demanded.

The man's satisfied smiled did not fade for a moment. "I've already told you who I am. But I think what you really want to know is how I knew about your mission to kill those men. And probably, who sent me. Am I right?"

"If you think I won't kill you right here in front of everyone…"

"I know you would," Gault replied. "But surely you don't think I came to you unprepared. At this moment there are six bows trained at your back. The moment I die, you will join me."

Markus scanned the area, but could see no one.

"Oh, believe me when I tell you they are there," Gault continued. "So why don't you release me? We can take a stroll together. I have something to tell you that you may find interesting."

Markus tightened his grip; his desire to throttle the man was almost overwhelming. Nonetheless, he weighed his options. Even if there were six bows trained on him, he could still possibly strike and move away in time. But Gault, knowing as he did of Specter's reputation, would be aware of this. Yet he remained supremely confident. This suggested that maybe he had more than just the bows for protection. With a snarl, Markus released his hold.

"Wise decision," Gault told him. "Now come. Let us make our way back to your ship. Your work here is done."

Markus shook his head. "Oh no! You said you had something to tell me. So tell me and be gone."

A sigh fell from Gault's mouth. "Very well. If you're going to be difficult. I was sent to make you an offer regarding your young friend."

His words raised a sneer. "So, you're Shinzan's puppet. Then you have nothing to say that I want to hear."

"I have no allegiance to Shinzan," he retorted. "Certainly no more than *you* ever did. I am simply in his employ. He wishes to offer you a life. A real life. One of wealth and comfort. Your own kingdom if you wish it."

Markus chuckled. "You waste your time. I'm not going to betray my friend for gold and land. Tell your *employer* he can go fuck himself."

Gault folded his hands and nodded. "Yes. I thought that's what you would say. I even told the Emperor as much. I know you well."

"You know me well?" Markus mocked. "How do you, *know me well?*"

"The Urazi have been watching you for a very long time."

The word Urazi sent a chill running down Markus' spine. Much as he tried to conceal his reaction, something must have shown.

"I see you've heard of us," smiled Gault. "That's good. We would have recruited you long ago, but we didn't think you'd be willing to bend to our will. After all, you've caused the Hareesh no end of difficulty. Don't get me wrong. Your results are undeniable – even if your methods do need a bit of refinement. If we had a few dozen like you, we'd soon be more powerful than Shinzan himself."

He waved his hand. "But that's neither here nor there. Shinzan offers you far more than land and gold. He also offers you all the time in the world to spend it." He rubbed his chin thoughtfully. "What were his exact words…ah, yes. *I will bestow upon him a kingdom and with it, immortality. He will be beholden to no one – free to rule as he sees fit until the end of time.*"

He paused for a second to let the words sink in. "A generous offer, is it not?"

"It is. So why wouldn't you try to collect it yourself?" Markus demanded.

"That's not how things are done in the Urazi. I was sent here to deliver a message and return with your reply. Nothing more."

"And if I say no?"

"Then the Emperor will undoubtedly be displeased. But if you're wondering about your own safety, you needn't be concerned. I was given orders not to kill you. And frankly, I would not see the great Specter die in the streets of Port Hull. Such a disgusting place. You deserve a better death."

Coming from the Urazi, Markus couldn't help but feel honored by such a compliment. "Then I shall not waste any more of your time," he said. "Tell Shinzan…"

Gault held up his hand, smiling. "I know. To go fuck himself."

Markus grinned involuntarily. "Exactly." He turned and set off back toward the ship.

Gault called after him. "You'll forgive me if I word your response a bit more…diplomatically."

With each step, the anxiety in Markus' chest grew. He wanted to run. But even in a place like Port Hull, so many bodies would cause a stir, and the sight of a man running through the streets would draw far too much attention.

By the time he reached the ship, his anxiety had developed into full blown paranoia. How the hell had Gault known to be here? Was there an agent of the Empire on board?

The captain was standing on deck, directing his men as they lowered crates of supplies through a trapdoor in the planking.

"We need to cast off now," Markus told him, without any preamble.

"There is only one more crate to be loaded," Jeridia replied. "Once it's aboard…"

"We leave now," barked Markus.

"This is still my ship," he shot back. "We leave when I say so."

Markus very pointedly placed his hand on the hilt of his dagger. "Unless you want your first mate to get an immediate promotion, you'll do as I say."

The two men locked eyes, but the battle of wills lasted only a few seconds.

"Cast off!" the captain shouted.

Markus spun on his heels and headed immediately to Lylinora's room. After banging hard several times, Ethan answered. Beyond his young friend he could see Kat and Lylinora sitting on the bed, poring over several pieces of parchment.

"We're leaving now," Markus announced. "All of you, come down to the hold." Without giving time for a response, he turned sharply away and left.

He found Jonas and Ganix reading quietly on their bedrolls. On seeing his severe expression, they quickly put down their books and sat up straight. He took a seat just as the motion of the ship told him they were casting off.

"What's happened?" asked Jonas.

Markus said nothing until the others arrived a few moments later. He then told everyone about his encounter with Gault. The word Urazi caused all but Ethan to stiffen.

"What's the Urazi?" he asked.

"A myth," replied Markus. "Or that's what most people think."

"More like a nightmare," corrected Jonas.

"They are a society of assassins," Markus continued. "Older than the five kingdoms. Some say they formed when humans first discovered magic. No one knows for sure. But one thing is certain; they are deadly. Once given a contract, they do not fail...regardless of the cost."

"You think this Gault fellow was truly one of them?" asked Ganix.

Markus shrugged. "I suppose he could have been lying. But I don't think so."

"Urazi or no, he knew we were here," said Lylinora. "We need to know how he came by this information."

"I was thinking perhaps one of the crew," Markus offered.

"But how would he have got word to Shinzan?" asked Ethan.

"There are ways," said Lylinora.

"Can you detect if there is a *sending rod* on board?" Markus asked Ganix.

"There isn't," he assured him. He held up his hand and touched a thin silver ring on his little finger. "If there was dwarf craft here, this would have told me so."

"I'll need to examine the crew anyway," said Lylinora.

Jonas frowned. "However this man Gault found us, we need to know his method before we get to Borgen."

"I think we should consider changing our original plan," Markus stated.

Ganix leaned back and scratched his beard. "First of all, let Lylinora see if the crew is compromised. We'll determine our next move from there."

Markus stood up. "Very well. I'll inform the captain."

As he turned to leave, Ethan called after him. "Are you all right?" he asked.

The darkness of earlier was still there inside of Markus. It felt like an old familiar friend, overcoming even the fear of encountering the Urazi.

He looked over his shoulder and smiled. "Yes. Never felt better."

CHAPTER ELEVEN

CAPTAIN JERIDIA WAS far from happy when Markus spoke to him about the situation. Even so, he had no intention whatsoever of objecting directly to Lylinora, so in the end reluctantly agreed to her examining his crew.

The crew was equally unhappy at first. It wasn't until several of the men reported that all she did was hold their hand for a few seconds that their fear subsided. In the end, she found nothing suspicious in any of them.

"Perhaps the enemy was simply watching the exits from the mountain and saw us leave," Markus suggested, once all the examinations were completed. "Given our course, it wouldn't be hard to figure we might stop in Port Hull. And remember, the Imperial ship that Lylinora destroyed had warning we were coming their way."

"But that doesn't explain how they knew about the men you were targeting," Jonas pointed out. "The decision to kill them was made a mere two days in advance, and only a handful of people were ever aware of your intentions."

Ethan felt uneasy thinking about Markus using his skills as a cold blooded killer. He quickly waved his hand. "There's no point worrying about all that now. It could be just a coincidence."

"When it comes to the Urazi, there's no such thing," Markus told him. "Gault was definitely expecting to meet up with me in Port Hull." He smiled at his friend. "You're right though. There's no point in worrying about things we can't control. If someone is contacting the Empire, we'll find them eventually."

After three more days of searching and careful observation, King Ganix was fully satisfied that there was no one aboard who had passed on information. He summoned their group to the hold on the morning of the fourth day.

"I've decided we will go directly to Borgen," he announced.

Ethan noticed Markus' expression grow tense. It took him a moment to realize why. When he did, the objection flew out.

"You can't do that," he said fiercely.

"We have no choice," Ganix told him. "If we're spotted coming ashore, we might never make it any further."

"I'll take that chance."

"I don't understand," Kat chipped in. "Why do you care, Ethan? It would be quicker straight there, right?"

They looked at one another, waiting for someone to explain the situation to her.

"The crew can't be allowed to know the location of Borgen," Ethan said. "But if they take us all the way there, then they will."

Realization washed over Kat's face. "So you plan to kill them? All of them?"

"We have no other choice," said Markus. His eyes were cold and distant.

"I won't do it," yelled Ethan. "You hear me? To hell with all of you. I won't fucking do it."

Lylinora placed her hand on his shoulder. "We have to."

Ethan looked at her, horror-struck. "You can't seriously agree with them. There's more than thirty men here. And the captain has done nothing but help us."

"The captain would slit our throats and throw our bodies overboard if he could," Markus countered. "His loyalty is based on his fear of Lylinora. Nothing more."

Ethan shot to his feet. Kat stood beside him. "I won't be a part of this," he stated. "And if you tell the captain to take us to Borgen, I'll tell him why he shouldn't. I don't care how scared he is of Lylinora, he won't go willingly to his death."

Having spoken his mind, he spun around and stalked away with Kat hard on his heels. Just as he reached the stairs leading to the next level, he paused to look back at the others. "And if you think I won't do it, just try me."

After making his way to the deck, he gazed at the horizon. It was one thing to kill six men who would almost certainly betray them. It was quite another to plan the massacre of an entire crew. He had socialized with some of these men and got to know them quite well in the days before Lylinora had terrified them with her destruction of the Imperial ship.

"Would you really tell the captain?" a voice said.

Ethan hadn't noticed Kat was still with him. "Damn right I would," he responded.

She took hold of his arm and rested her head on his shoulder. "Good."

Ethan allowed his own head to rest on top of Kat's. "I can't help it. There's only so far I can go."

They stood there together like this for nearly an hour, only moving when hearing the bell announcing that lunch was ready.

Lylinora was waiting for them in the galley. "The others have agreed to keep to the original plan after all," she told them as soon as they'd sat down. "So you can stop worrying about the crew."

Ethan took a quick glance around the room. No one else was close enough to overhear their quiet talk. "But you think I'm wrong, don't you?"

Lylinora nodded. "Yes. But I *can* understand why you feel the way you do."

"Well, I *can't* understand you. How can you agree with such a thing?"

"That is what separates us," she replied, forcing a weak smile. "And perhaps that's a good thing."

A young boy, no older than twelve, brought them each a bowl of stew and a cup of water. Several sailors came in, though none dared to sit at the same table as Lylinora.

Ethan could see the fear in the boy's eyes as he hurried back to assist the cook. A distressing question then formed in his mind. What kind of monster was capable of killing an innocent child?

The thought lingered painfully with him. During the final few days until they reached the drop off point, he kept very much to himself. Even when Lylinora invited him to join her for a quiet dinner in her quarters, he politely refused.

They were due to leave the ship just before sunset, and neither the crew nor Captain Jeridia made any effort to disguise their relief at seeing their passengers depart. They all gathered on the deck with their belongings while the small landing craft was being prepared for them. Ethan looked to the shore. A thin stretch of beach led directly into thick trees and brush.

Ganix was also studying the terrain, a heavy frown on his face. "I have one final request," he eventually said to the captain. "I ask that Markus be allowed to go ashore first in order to scout the area. If all is well, the rest of us will follow immediately."

The captain scowled, and for a moment it appeared that he might deny the request. But a stern look from Lylinora soon changed his mind. "Just so long as he's quick about it, I suppose," he muttered.

"I'll go too," said Ethan.

Ganix shook his head. "Better that you stay."

"I wasn't asking permission," he shot back.

"Please, Ethan," said Lylinora. "Stay here."

"I said I'm going." He checked his sword.

Markus merely looked at him, then gave a sharp nod.

As the pair of them climbed down the rope ladder, Ethan could see the worried expressions of his friends. Kat was wringing her hands, though she did manage to force a smile. He smiled back at her, adding a confident wink for good luck.

Once in the boat, Markus took the oars. "You need to ease up on everyone," he said. "You've been angry for days now."

Ethan kept his eyes fixed on the shore. "I have good reason to be."

"No," he corrected. "You really don't. This is war. And people die. Sometimes in horrible ways. You're 101st Airborne. You know this. Hell…you've seen it."

"Mass murder isn't war, Markus. That's what the goddamn Nazi's do. Not us."

Markus grunted. "If you keep trying to play by the rules, you're going to get a lot of people killed. Good people. People who truly don't deserve to die. Not like the scum on that ship."

"Better to die a man than to become an animal," Ethan responded.

His words were met with a hollow laugh. "Tell that to the mothers of the people you'll be sending to their graves. Tell it to their children."

Markus stopped rowing and said nothing further until Ethan was forced to look him in the eye. "You'd better wise up. Shinzan is playing for keeps. You need to play that way too if you want to win. So either do it, or get the hell out of the bloody game."

Ethan shifted his gaze back to the approaching beach and lapsed into silence. His mind was going around in circles. Was Markus right? And even if he was, could he ever force himself to accept the same harsh attitudes? He didn't think so. But then, he could look at his friend and see what a life of hardship was capable of doing to a man. Even without the scars, he could still see the darkness in Markus' eyes.

Once ashore, they pulled the boat up the beach for a few yards and drew their swords. Ethan strained his ears, but the rumble of the surf overcame everything.

Markus led the way. Creeping to the edge of the tree line, he got down on one knee. "Stay a few yards behind me," he instructed.

They had only moved a short distance into the woods when Ethan caught the smell of body odor and stale wine. A moment later, gruff voices sounded off to his left. He looked at Markus, who quickly took up position behind the closest tree and signaled for Ethan to do the same thing further back. He silently mouthed the words: *Get ready.* Three men then came into view. Ethan's heart sank on seeing the Imperial crest emblazoned on their breastplates.

For the moment they hadn't been spotted. But he knew there was little chance of them both avoiding detection when the soldiers got closer. He tried to control his breathing and readied himself to charge.

The very instant the first soldier sensed danger, Markus leapt into the attack, swinging his blade high and completely severing the man's arm at the elbow. At the same time, Ethan burst into a dead run to join the fray. The two remaining soldiers hastily backed up a pace and drew their weapons. With his incapacitated first opponent no longer a threat, Markus thrust low at the second soldier's gullet. The blade pierced his armor, but inflicted only a slight wound, allowing him to fight on. With Markus still occupied, the third soldier moved in to attack him on his exposed left side.

A horrified Ethan could see that his friend would not be able to avoid the coming strike. And although closing fast, he was just that bit too far away to stop it from being delivered. Anguish tore at his soul. From somewhere deep within him a terrible cry escaped, shattering the air with the violence of its intensity. It was half a warning shout - half a feral war cry. Driven forward by the sheer force of his desperation, it speared across the rapidly reducing gap separating him from the others like a sonic missile.

For a critical moment, petrified by the ear-shattering sound, the third soldier delayed his strike. It was long enough. He glanced over just in time to see Ethan's sword swinging down on him. The adrenaline charged blow struck the man violently across the chest, renting his breast plate almost completely apart and sending him sprawling. He lay writhing on the ground, moaning and gasping, blood spurting in short gushes from his wound in time with the beating of his heart.

With nothing to distract him, Markus quickly dispatched the second soldier with a series of precise blows, the final one removing his head from his shoulders.

The first man to fall was still crying out in agony, searching frantically for his severed arm.

"Back to the boat!" Markus shouted.

Ethan ran headlong toward the beach. No sooner had they reached the boat than they heard aggressive shouts coming from their right. Six more soldiers were running down the shoreline at them, swords drawn. They pushed the boat through the clinging sand with all of their strength, but it was obvious they wouldn't be able to get it into the water in time.

"Go without me," shouted Markus. "I'll hold them off."

Ethan ignored him and readied himself for the assault.

"I said go! Or we'll both die!"

Ethan knew he was right. There were too many. But he also knew he couldn't abandon his friend. The soldiers were mere seconds away. There was only one thing left to try. Dropping his sword, he raised both hands in the air. His voice boomed out with unnatural depth and volume.

"*Alevi Drago!*"

The sheer force of his words halted the soldiers' advance. A wave of heat then blew forth, forcing them to shield their faces and sending them stumbling backwards.

"*Alevi Drago!*" Ethan repeated. This time his voice was so loud that the sand at his feet rippled.

A ball of white flame manifested directly above his head and flew toward the soldiers. It stopped, suspended in mid-air, just before reaching them. With a vicious grin, Ethan turned to Markus, who could only gaze in silence, stunned and slack-jawed at what was happening.

"You should look away now," he said. "It's about to get bright."

Heeding the warning, Markus tore his attention away from the scene and shielded his eyes.

Ethan felt no pity for the terrified men as they began fleeing. The flame expanded and intensified until it took on the form of a giant dragon with wings spanning thirty feet across and measuring at least twice that distance from head to tail. The soldiers had made it only fifty yards down the beach when he sent the flaming beast upon them. Hellish fire from its gigantic jaws rained down, roasting their flesh the instant it made contact. The creature gave a thunderous roar, completely drowning out the dying men's screams of agony. Then, in almost no time at all, it was over. In another blinding flash, the dragon vanished. Nothing was left but small heaps of twisted metal and scattered ashes. The sand sparkled in the sun; melted into glass from the unimaginable heat.

Ethan touched Markus on the shoulder. "*Now* we can go."

Markus looked at him in awe for a moment and then quietly chuckled. "I think we're about even now."

Smiling and shaking his head, Ethan held up two fingers. This time Markus let out a hearty laugh and slapped him on the back. "Okay. So it's my turn to owe you for a change."

When they reached the ship, Ethan could see Lylinora and Jonas grinning from ear to ear. Ganix was a little more restrained, merely nodding his approval.

Kat ran up and threw her arms around him the moment he stepped on board. "That was amazing," she cried. Her embrace lasted for several seconds before she eased back. "We thought you two were dead for sure."

"So you saw what happened?" asked Ethan.

"Oh, do you mean that enormous flaming dragon?" she mocked. "Yes. Of course we saw it. Heard it too. Scared the hell out of the crew."

"Impressive," added Lylinora. "Using magic in battle isn't easy."

"At first I was only able to create hot air," Ethan explained. "But that frightened the soldiers long enough for me to concentrate and try again."

Ganix touched his arm. "Come. Now that we know that these shores are patrolled, we must decide what to do next."

Ethan's elation instantly evaporated. He knew what the king was thinking, and at once his expression darkened. While crossing the deck he glanced up at the captain standing behind the main wheel. Fear was etched deeply into Jeridia's face. Perhaps even deeper than what could be seen on most of the crew's.

By the time they reached the cargo hold, a deep fatigue was seeping into Ethan's muscles. Lylinora sat beside him and placed her hands on his forehead.

"You're weakened," she said. "I can tell. Powerful magic does that."

He felt a rush of energy pass into him. At once, the fatigue vanished. He nodded his appreciation.

"You know what must be done," Ganix told him. "There is now no other choice. If this ship approaches Borgen, my people *will* kill everyone on board."

"You could stop them," Ethan said. "You're the king aren't you?"

"I am. But I *won't* stop them. If the location of Borgen is discovered, years of work will be lost. Along with more than three-hundred lives."

"Why is Borgen so important?" asked Kat. "What's there?"

"Things beyond your wildest imaginings," Ganix replied. "It is where we keep all that is left of my people's former glory. There are wonders which, in time, could change the face of Lumnia. They may even be the difference between victory and defeat."

Lylinora leaned forward until she was directly meeting Ethan's eyes. "If King Ganix is right, then this is a small sacrifice to make."

Ethan averted his gaze, this time from anger rather than any attempt to hide his feelings. "I don't care. I won't allow this slaughter."

"You didn't mind roasting those soldiers," remarked Markus. "In fact, I think you enjoyed it."

"That was different," he shot back. "They were going to kill us. These men here mean us no harm. *That* makes it murder. And I'm *not* a murderer."

"Well I am," Markus said. "Many times over. And I can promise you that I'm not alone. I bet most of the crew are as well. We're talking about smugglers...not a ship full of innocent children."

Ethan thoughts turned to the young boy in the galley. "I don't care. I won't let you do it."

"Could you erase their memories?" Kat asked Lylinora.

She flashed the young girl a warning glance. "No. It doesn't work like that."

"*What* doesn't?" asked Ethan.

"I know a spell that can alter a person's perception," she explained. "But it only works when the person is either asleep or almost asleep. And it isn't completely reliable."

"You could take them prisoner," Ethan suggested, now becoming desperate in his search for a solution.

"And keep them where?" Ganix asked. "Borgen? That's not possible.

There are barely enough supplies for the people already there." He sighed. "No. I'm afraid the reality is clear. If we don't do this deed, then we must leave the ship immediately. And that means we will almost certainly be captured or killed, and our purpose exposed."

Ethan snorted. "You saw what I just did. We can fight the soldiers off."

"Don't get overconfident," Lylinora warned him. "You managed to cast one spell in battle. But make no mistake, there are ways to kill a mage."

"If the enemy has dwarf weapons, then you might not fare as well," added Ganix. "Even sheer numbers could be enough to stop you."

"You could also draw Shinzan right to you," said Jonas.

Ethan fumed. At that moment he loathed every one of them. Even Lylinora. Not because of the brutal nature of what they wanted to do. But because he knew they were right. He looked at them one by one, hoping for someone to say something to alter this course. Only Kat regarded him with any degree of sympathy.

His shoulders sagged; he was defeated. "Can you at least spare the boy who works in the galley?" he asked weakly.

Ganix gave a labored sigh. "Very well. I'll find room for him somewhere on the island."

Ethan couldn't bear to look at any of them for a moment longer. He rose to his feet and left the cargo hold. Ganix followed him up on deck soon after to inform the captain that they would be changing course. He watched the abhorrent scene from a short distance away. The dwarf king handed the captain more gold for his troubles – gold that Ethan knew the man would never have a hope of spending.

He'd expected Kat to join him. She was the only one who seemed to understand his feelings over what was soon to happen. But it was Lylinora who appeared. He could smell her perfume, even before he saw her approaching. But no longer did his heart pound wildly. And when she leaned against the rail beside him, he inched away from her.

"I do not see the same revulsion in your eyes when you look at Markus," she remarked.

Ethan said nothing for a long moment. It was true. He saw Markus differently. The darkness within his friend made his attitude almost a forgone conclusion. "I suppose I held you to a higher standard," he eventually responded. Glancing over, he could see that his words had stung her.

"I'm sorry," she replied. "Truly. But this is not the first time I've been faced with this choice. Nor will it be the last time for *you*."

"When were you faced with it?" he asked, his tone incredulous.

Her eyes grew distant. "It was shortly before my father and I fled from our home. Shinzan's army was almost at our door, and we knew for certain that everyone in the house would be subjected to terrible torture. So my father told me what had to be done." She faced Ethan. "I reacted much like you did. I had known some of those people for my entire life. My father waited until I agreed…then killed every soul who lived under our roof."

"But you were saving them from torture," contended Ethan. "What we plan to do now isn't the same thing at all."

Lylinora huffed a laugh. "That's what I told myself. But there was more to it. I just couldn't say it out loud." She drew a deep breath. "Those people knew where we were going. They knew our plan to take refuge with the dwarves. And they died for it." A tear slowly rolled down her cheek.

The revulsion and anger in Ethan gradually gave way to pity. "I'm sorry," he said.

Lylinora shook her head. "Don't be. Though I didn't know it at the time, it was important that I survived. My father only did what had to be done to protect hope for the future."

"And to protect his daughter," Ethan added. He took her hand as they stared at the shoreline. "I can't help the way I feel about all this. And I'm not sure I can make it right inside. But I'll try not to take things out on you and the others from now on."

She leaned her head on his shoulder. "I hope you can never make it right," she said. "Because it's not. It's a very long way from that."

CHAPTER TWELVE

GANIX INSTRUCTED THE captain to steer well away from shore so not to be seen by passing merchant ships. Or, more importantly, Imperial patrols.

The remaining two days of the journey saw Ethan become increasingly depressed and withdrawn. Although managing to keep his promise about not taking his anger out on the others, he found solitude to be the only salve for the pain he was feeling. Not even Kat could shake him from his melancholy. The crew, now as terrified of him as they were of Lylinora after seeing his display on the beach, were a constant reminder that he was not strong enough to save them. Even overhearing them talking of the men they had killed and the unwilling women they had ravaged did nothing to lessen his sense of guilt.

By the time they were due to arrive, his nerves were stretched to the limit. The wind had all but died, and an unnatural fog that lingered just above the water had set in. Only the creaking of timbers and anxious whispers of the frightened crew could be heard as he and the others gathered their belongings on deck.

Ethan didn't know exactly how the slaughter would be done. He didn't *want* to know. But he knew it would happen soon. He peered into the fog, but could see only a few yards beyond the bow.

Ganix was standing beside Captain Jeridia at the main wheel. After an hour, a small globe in the king's hand begin to pulse with green light. The captain rang the ship's bell, signaling the crew to drop anchor. As the landing boat was lowered into the water, Ganix nodded to Lylinora.

She sat cross-legged on the deck and began chanting softly.

"What's she doing?" Jeridia demanded.

"Just lifting the fog," the king replied. "Nothing to be concerned about."

Ethan could hear the lie in Ganix's voice, causing his anger to resurface. Lylinora continued with her chanting for several more minutes. Soon, Ethan noticed that the crew was becoming disoriented. Some stumbled and fell onto the deck, unable to rise. Others walked around in circles, mumbling incoherently.

Beads of sweat formed on Lylinora's brow as she started slowly swaying from side to side in time with the motion of the ship.

The captain was the very last to lose his senses. Panic-stricken, he bolted toward the stern railing, but fell to his knees a few feet before reaching it.

With the entire crew sprawled out unconscious on the deck, something locked inside of Ethan finally found its release. A primal scream flew from his mouth, after which he began pounding the center mast repeatedly with his fists. He felt a hand touch his shoulder. It was Jonas.

"Come," the old man said. "Let Markus finish this."

Ethan looked at him with tear filled eyes. "Finish it?"

"They're only sleeping," he explained. "Lylinora refused to kill them with magic."

Ethan regarded Lylinora for a moment. Kat was at her side, helping her over to the ladder going down to the landing craft. Her face was somber and she looked as if she hadn't slept in days.

"She'll be fine," Jonas said. "The spell has taken a lot out of her. She just needs some rest."

Ethan nodded. Having spent hours worrying about the matter, he was now greatly relieved to know that it would not be Lylinora who killed these men. If she had taken it upon herself, he wasn't sure he'd ever be able to feel the same way about her again. He spotted Markus standing at the bow, his aspect dispassionate and calm. This would not be the first time he'd killed helpless men. But Ethan had always held onto the hope that his dear friend would never have to do so any more. That hope was now gone.

"What about the boy?" Ethan asked. "We agreed that he'd be spared."

"Markus will bring him," said Ganix. "You have my word."

Ethan climbed down into the boat. Lylinora had her head resting in Kat's lap, her eyes shut. Once everyone but Markus was on board, they waited in solemn silence. Ethan tried not to imagine the carnage that was occurring up on the deck at that very moment. But ghastly images flashed through his mind anyway, causing him to shudder with disgust and regret.

*

Markus waited until the others were all in the boat before starting his deadly work. And for this particular task, he knew he was well suited.

He took a moment to survey the main deck, taking note of where each unconscious man was, then headed below. On checking the main cargo hold he found a smuggler lying close beside where they had slept.

"Probably looking to see if we'd left behind anything of value," he mused.

While sliding cold steel across the man's throat he heard the familiar gush of air, followed by a faint gurgle. He almost sighed with satisfaction.

That's right, Specter. This is what you really are, isn't it?

Markus shook his head and waved his hand as if shooing away a fly.

You can fool the others, but you know what's in your heart. Don't you? You can pretend to be Markus all you want. You can pretend you're the man Ethan wants you to be. But deep down...

He looked at his blood soaked blade, then made his way back to the upper decks.

"Better go front to back," he softly advised himself. "Or I'll track blood everywhere."

Or the others will see the blood on your boots. They'll look into your soulless eyes and know how much you enjoyed it.

"Shut up," he grumbled, continuing with his work. "Just shut the hell up."

You're off your game, Specter. Killing sleeping sailors is not a challenge. You had better be glad Gault spared you in Port Hull.

"He didn't spare me," Markus responded. "I spared him."

If that's what you need to tell yourself, so be it. But we both know better. Ethan has turned you into a coward. A weak, worthless coward. Him... and the girl, Lylinora.

"That's enough," he snapped. "I'm tired of you."

He took a mental note of how many smugglers he'd so far killed. Six. The next sailor he came to was old and grizzled. The man stared vacantly up at him through one eye that was still open. Markus' anger began boiling over. This was no way to kill. No way for men to die.

That's right. Let a farmer slaughter helpless cattle. Men should be given a fighting chance. Not that they have one when Specter comes calling. It's all his fault. He's the one who wants you to change. He has taken your courage. He has taken your life. And he's taken her.

Markus plunged the dagger hard down into the open eye. The body jerked and convulsed for a few seconds before becoming still. "Ethan's my friend," he growled. "And she was never mine to begin with."

She wants you, and you know it. But you're too weak to do anything about it. How could she love a pathetic boy like Ethan? Tell me! How? You're twice the man he'll ever be. You're Specter!

"You're wrong. I'm Markus."

Is that so? Would Markus slaughter these men? Would Markus have the stomach for such a thing? Look at the blood. Look at it!

Unable to resist, he watched as blood spilled from the dead man's eye socket and pooled around his head. A malevolent grin crept up at the corners of his mouth.

Have you ever seen anything so beautiful?

Markus shook his head violently. "I won't let you do this to me!"

He reached the galley. The young boy he was supposed to spare and bring with him was crumpled in the corner. He sat on his heels beside the youngster.

Prove that you're still the man I know you are. No one will need to know. You can say he woke up and attacked you.

Markus grabbed the boy's hair and lifted his head.

That's it. Do it. You've killed far younger. You know you want to.

He placed the tip of his blade directly above the boy's heart. All he had to do was lean forward. Just apply a little bit of pressure. His blade was sharp and he knew exactly where to put it. It would be so easy.

"Markus?"

He spun around to see Lylinora standing in the doorway.

"What are you doing here?" he demanded.

"Ethan was getting worried. I didn't want him seeing…" She paused to eye him suspiciously. "Isn't that the boy we're taking with us?"

He nodded. "I was about to bring him up."

Her eyes drifted to the bloody dagger in his hand. "Then you should hurry." With that, she turned briskly away and left.

Lifting the boy easily onto his shoulder, Markus carried him to the top deck. After securing him to a rope and lowering him down to the others waiting in the boat, he then quickly set about completing his gruesome task.

The moment he was done and in the boat, Lylinora started whispering a spell, the effect of which was almost instantaneous. Markus had rowed them for only a few yards when the big ship began to burn. Seeing the scowl on Ethan's face as his friend watched the flames intensify, he tried to force a smile and think of something to make himself feel better. But a white hot rage was steadily growing in his chest.

The voice persisted.

You can't keep me away forever…Specter.

CHAPTER THIRTEEN

AFTER HALF AN hour of rowing, the fog lifted. Ethan strained his eyes, but could see nothing apart from the rhythmic rise and fall of the swells and a few sea birds darting in and out of the water.

"Are we in the right place?" he asked Ganix.

The king smiled, his eyes twinkling with excitement. "We're almost there. You'll see."

A few minutes later, the light in front of them began to ripple and distort. Everyone but Ganix began to scramble to the rear of the boat.

"There is nothing to fear," he chuckled. "See?"

A moment later the air cleared and an island appeared in the near distance ahead. The rocky shore spanned approximately a mile across, with lush trees scattered over a tall hill that was situated in the exact center. As they drew closer, Ethan spotted several colorful birds flitting from branch to branch in search of food. The haunting cry of some hidden animal carried on the waves.

Ganix could see Ethan's unease. "It's just a tree *manlilu*," he said. "They're big and loud, but quite harmless."

"How did you manage to hide this place?" asked Jonas.

"The fog and cloak were already here when we found it," Ganix explained. "Left by my ancestors long ago. I'm not sure how it works, but it keeps us hidden and safe."

"It's astounding," remarked Lylinora. "And without magic?"

Ganix shrugged. "Not exactly. There's magic involved. Of sorts."

He directed Markus to row to the eastern shore where the rocks gave way to fine yellow sand. Ethan jumped out the moment he felt the boat scrape bottom and began heaving the craft onto the beach. Markus and Jonas moved quickly to help him. While securing the boat to a protruding rock, Ethan spotted something sitting in the trees.

It looked like a monkey he had seen when his father took him to the Bronx Zoo. It had snow white fur, pink eyes, and an almost human face, though flatter and with pitch black skin. It gripped a long branch in one hand, and its furry tail was wrapped around another. Ethan guessed it would be about two feet tall, though considerably thinner than a man.

"Is that a tree *manlilu*?" he asked.

Ganix glanced up and nodded. "A baby. The adults are shy and keep mostly out of sight, though you might see one if we're here long enough."

"Where are your people?" asked Markus.

"They'll be along," he replied. "Once they confirm that I'm with you, then they'll reveal themselves."

As soon as the boat was unloaded, Markus and Ethan gathered some wood from the edge of the tree line and built a small fire. Once that was burning nicely, Kat curled up against Ethan and covered herself with a blanket from her pack.

"What about the cabin boy?" asked Jonas.

The youngster was still unconscious, though beginning to stir.

"I'll keep him asleep for the time being," replied Lylinora.

"It's getting cold," Kat complained. "I've always hated being this far north."

Markus nodded. "I've never enjoyed it much either."

"You two complain like spoiled children," Lylinora sniffed. "I love the cold. My father and I would hike for miles through the snow every winter."

"An easy thing to do when you can stay warm with magic," scoffed Markus.

"We never used it," she replied proudly. "My father didn't believe in employing magic for every little task. We built our own fire and made shelters from blocks of snow."

"Doesn't sound like much fun to me," remarked Kat.

"How would you know? Did you even know your father?"

"I'll have you know that I'm a princess," Kat snapped.

Lylinora laughed. "Yes. I'm sure."

"Actually, she is," Ethan chipped in.

"I'm sure that's what she told you. But do you have any proof?"

Kat folded her arms and huffed. "I don't care what you think. At least I don't have to trick someone…" A stern warning look from Lylinora stopped her short. After a brief pause, she said instead: "You still believe me, don't you, Ethan?"

"Of course I do," he replied.

Satisfied, she stuck her tongue out at Lylinora and cuddled closer to him.

It wasn't until the sun was hanging low in the sky that they heard the rustle of footfalls approaching through the trees. Markus instinctively reached for his sword, but Ganix grabbed him and stayed his hand. A moment later, a lone dwarf appeared.

He was wearing a white one piece jumpsuit under a hard leather apron. His salt and pepper hair was close cropped and neatly tended. But what struck Ethan most about him was, even though obviously an adult, he had grown no beard.

The dwarf bowed low. "I am Fralgar, my king. And I am pleased to receive you." He cast a suspicious eye over the rest of the group. "But we did not expect visitors."

Ganix bowed in return and introduced the others.

On hearing the name Dragonvein, Fralgar raised an eyebrow. "Truly, Your Highness? A child of the Dragonvein family? Here, in Lumnia? I thought they had been wiped out."

"I'm the last," Ethan told him.

Fralgar nodded and shifted his gaze to the unconscious boy. "Is he injured?"

"No," replied the king. "But he will be staying here from now on."

Fralgar did not bother trying to hide his displeasure. "That would not be wise, Your Highness."

"Until we can trust him not to reveal the location of this island, he stays," Ganix stated firmly. "I'll explain once we are inside."

Fralgar bowed once again. "Of course, Your Highness. Please forgive my manners. We are quite isolated here…as you well know."

Ganix smiled warmly. "No need to apologize. Lead on."

After dousing the fire, Markus threw the boy over his shoulder. Together with the others, he followed Fralgar through the tree line onto a well-worn trail that twisted and turned its way deep into the forest and up the massive hill.

Roughly halfway to the top, Fralgar gestured for everyone to stay where they were while he continued on alone for another fifty yards. Here, he reached down and lifted a small lid buried in the ground. Ethan thought he could hear him talking to someone, but couldn't be sure. A few seconds later, the dwarf beckoned them all to come.

Just as they drew near, the ground immediately ahead of them suddenly opened up. Ethan took a startled leap as two doors slid back, screeching and groaning in protest until a broad staircase leading deep into the island's interior was revealed. There was a familiar ringing sound as their boots struck the metal stairs. Together with the steel handrail on either side, it reminded him of the ship that had carried him to England.

The stairs ended at a long and bare hallway that was lit by strips of luminescent crystals along the ceiling. They walked for more than ten minutes before coming to a fork, where they took the right hand path. This passage had metal doors on either side at regular intervals. After a while they encountered more dwarves, all of them wearing similar one-piece garments. They eyed the passing group of strangers with no small measure of surprise. Like their guide, all of the men were clean shaven.

"I must warn you, Your Highness," Fralgar said. "Rakaal is in a foul mood today."

Ganix snorted. "When is he not?"

"Not often," he laughed. "But today is a particularly bad day. We thought we had the *suldaat* problem worked out. But it was a dead end."

Ganix heaved a sigh. "Wonderful."

After several more turns, they halted in front of a door where two thickly muscled dwarves were standing. This pair, like nearly all the adult male dwarfs Ethan had encountered in Elyfoss, did wear beards, along with hand axes on their belts.

"Guard the human child," Fralgar instructed them. "If he wakes, keep him here until you receive word from the king." He unlocked the door and pointed for Markus to enter.

Inside was a small wooden desk, a cabinet and a bed. Markus laid the boy down on the latter.

"Try not to frighten him," Ganix told the two guards before departing. "When he wakes up, he won't know where he is."

For the next five minutes, Fralgar led them down another series of hallways. By this point Ethan was completely lost. Each passage looked identical and seemed to go on indefinitely.

Finally, they came to a double door, outside of which Fralgar halted. "He's in there, Your Highness," he said.

Ganix took a moment before moving on. "Here we go," he muttered to himself.

His demeanor put Ethan's nerves on edge. He wondered who could rattle the king so much. As the door swung wide he could see a large room with six long tables on either side and a single one in the center that very nearly spanned the entire fifty feet to the rear wall. Bits of strangely shaped metal were scattered everywhere, along with unfamiliar tools and various implements. On the walls were charts and chalkboards covered in odd drawings and what looked to be calculations. A workshop, he thought.

Several dwarves were standing by the tables going about their work. Some seemed to be merely tinkering, while others were writing furiously on parchment or the chalkboards.

"Everyone out!" bellowed a deep gruff voice that came from the far end of the center table.

Everyone immediately stopped what they were doing and hurried from the room. Once they were all gone, a thin dwarf with stringy grey hair that fell down over his shoulders came stalking toward them. He was old. How old Ethan couldn't accurately tell, but older than King Ganix for sure, even though he moved quite nimbly. His blue eyes were focused intently on the king, and the deep lines on his wrinkled face were twisted into a fearsome scowl.

"Five years!" he bellowed. "Five bloody years since you've been here. And when you do show up, you bring a pack of bloody humans with you. What happened? Were there no other dwarves willing to suffer your intolerable company? Or perhaps they feared that you'd bore them to death."

"Mind your tongue, Rakaal." Ganix's tone was equally forceful, though not quite as loud. "I'm still your king, and you *will* show me due respect."

Rakaal halted a few feet away from Ganix and planted his hands on his hips. "King? Ha! If you were a proper king like Halvar, and ruled a proper city, I wouldn't be in the state I'm in."

"Then perhaps you should leave here and join him," suggested Ganix. "Halvar is widely known to tolerate fools and braggarts. I'm sure you'd fit right in." He took a step forward.

Not to be outdone, Rakaal moved in a pace as well. "Leave here? Are you insane? You must be. Or have you been at the whiskey again." He glanced over to Ethan and the others. "He drinks too much, you know. He doesn't want to admit it, but he does."

"Only when I'm forced to share your insufferable company," Ganix shot back.

"Did he tell you about the ships that travel amongst the stars?" he mocked. "He loves that one. Or is that little bit of history still a secret? No! What am I saying? You aren't dwarves. He wouldn't mind telling you."

"You know perfectly well why that's not spoken of amongst our people," Ganix said. "And I'll remind you to watch what you say in front of strangers."

"Strangers? Is that what they are? I see no dwarf escort. You expect me to believe that you travel with strangers?"

Ganix glared. "Truly, you are still the same arrogant bastard you always were."

"And you are still the same self-righteous, pompous ass. Just with a crown on your fool head."

By now the two dwarves were nose-to-nose. For a long tense moment they locked eyes, fists clenched. Ethan could hear a low growl coming from each of them. Then, slowly, the growls turned into chuckles. Seconds later the two dwarves threw their arms around one another and began laughing boisterously. Instantly, all tension subsided.

"Where the hell have you been you old trickster?" Rakaal asked. "I was beginning to think you'd forgotten all about me."

Ganix released Rakaal, stepped back a pace, and smiled. "Forget *you*? How could I? You're my cousin."

"Only a *distant* cousin, thank the ancestors," said Rakaal, grinning. "But it *has* been too long." He turned and started back toward the rear of the room. "Come. You and your companions can sit and tell me the reason for your visit."

He settled into a chair at the far end of the table and gestured for the others to do the same. Once everyone was seated, Ganix made the introductions.

"So that's why you're here," Rakaal said, frowning. "Two mages have appeared, and one of them a Dragonvein."

"There's more to it than that," Ganix told him. "Much more."

Rakaal let out a high pitched whistle that brought a young girl scurrying in. "Bring us food and wine," he ordered. "Then prepare a room for our guests."

The girl bowed and hurried away. Rakaal shoved aside various pieces of metal and papers until there was space for everyone to eat. A few minutes later, three dwarf men entered bearing wine, together with fruit and nuts. One tray even had some fish on it.

Ganix's top lip curled as he looked at the fish. "When did you start eating this bile?"

Rakaal shrugged. "It's not that bad, really. Supplies have been scarce of late. We've had to make do with what's available."

"I'm sorry," Ganix said, suddenly contrite. "It's been difficult to get you what you need. I've tried, I swear."

Rakaal waved a hand. "I know you have. And I know Shinzan doesn't make it easy."

Once the wine was poured, Ganix told him what had so far transpired, and of his group's intentions. Rakaal listened patiently for close to an hour without any outward sign of emotion. When the king was finished, Rakaal stood and turned his back.

"Hearing about the death of Birger grieves me deeply," he said. "I knew his father. But I am grateful he saved you."

"Can you help us?" Ganix asked.

"The ship is in working order, so there should not be a problem," Rakaal replied. "It can carry your friends to the Dragon Wastes if they wish it. But I would ask that *you* stay here with me."

Ganix rose and placed a fond hand on his shoulder. "I cannot stay. But I will not be going to the Dragon Wastes either."

This news came as a surprise to Ethan. Looking around, he could see that his friends were equally taken aback.

"I need to evacuate my city and take the people to Elyfoss," Ganix continued. "My kingdom is not nearly so well-fortified. We could not hold out for long against a determined assault."

Rakaal turned to face him, his expression grim. "Then you'll have to march in the open. You realize that? In the *open*. With women and children and elders. How will you survive?"

"The humans will be too startled to stop us," said Ganix.

"Forget the humans," Rakaal said. "What about the elves? You will need to travel straight through elf lands to get there. They may leave a small party of dwarves alone. But you can't seriously think they'll ignore tens of thousands stomping through their territory."

"There is no other way," said Ganix. "Better to risk a fight with the elves than wait for Shinzan to come and slaughter us."

Rakaal gave him a desperate look that lasted for several seconds. He then lowered his head and sighed. "You're right, of course. You have to get them out."

"Enough of this dark talk," Ganix said briskly. "I hear you're having trouble with the *suldaat*."

Rakaal threw up his hands. "Bah! Whoever built those bloody things was a demon. Every time I think we've got one working, it catches on fire and falls apart."

"What's a *suldaat*?" asked Ethan.

Ganix laughed. "A true wonder. Well, it would be if Rakaal could get them to work."

This criticism drew an irritated glance from his fellow dwarf. "I'll get the bloody things working. You'll see. Just give me time."

A young girl entered the room. "The boy is awake," she told Ganix.

After dismissing the girl, the king turned back to his cousin. "We have much to discuss. But that can wait until morning. First, I must attend to our captive. And I'm sure my friends are tired."

With that, he hurried off, leaving Rakaal to show the others to their room.

The accommodations could hardly be described as luxurious. To both left and right, bunk beds were attached to the wall, while at the rear a door led through to a small bathroom. Near the entrance stood a metal table and six chairs. Other than that, the room was bare.

"Men and women room together here," Rakaal informed them. "I hope you don't mind."

Ethan looked to Kat and Lylinora.

"It will be fine," Lylinora answered, though there was a hint of a frown on her face as she looked from Markus to Jonas.

Rakaal gave them a slight bow. "Please remain in your rooms until I've had the opportunity to speak with my people. You are the first humans to visit here, and I don't want anything unfortunate to happen." Without waiting for a reply, he hurried out.

Kat leapt onto one of the top bunks and kicked off her boots. "Have any of you ever seen a place like this?" she asked.

Ethan settled down on the bunk beneath her. "What do you mean?"

"Everything here is made of metal," she pointed out, lowering her head over the edge of the bed so that she was looking at Ethan upside down. "Not a splinter of wood in the place. Even in the mountain they had *some* wood."

"That's not what I find odd," Jonas joined in. "Have you noticed the construction? All the tables, chairs, doors - everything I've seen here so far - was built for someone considerably taller than your average dwarf."

Ethan hadn't really noticed this aspect. But now he had cause to think. When in Elyfoss, he was constantly being forced to duck into rooms. And his feet had hung some way off the end of his cot. "You're right," he said. "But surely it was the dwarves who built this place."

"If they didn't, I can't imagine who did," said Jonas. "This is like no human design I've ever seen."

"Actually, it reminds me a bit of how the Navy makes things," said Markus. He sat on the bed directly across the room from Ethan. "Like on the ship that took us to England. Remember, Ethan?"

"I was thinking the same thing," he replied. "But that doesn't explain why everything here has been made too big for dwarves."

"I wouldn't worry yourself over it," said Lylinora. "We have other matters to occupy our minds."

"Yeah," agreed Kat. "For one thing, I'm sure as hell not using the same bathroom as the men."

This produced a round of laughter from everyone. They each found a bed and stretched out. A short time later, King Ganix arrived.

"The boy will be fine," he told them. "Rakaal has agreed to keep him here until he's sure he can't lead anyone to the island. Meanwhile, they will find a use for him."

This eased Ethan's mind. He mentioned to the king how they had noticed the odd size of everything.

"That's a mystery to me as well," he replied. "I know for sure it was the dwarves who built this place. But why they built it for people of human proportions, I couldn't say. One of the many puzzles I may never solve."

"When do we leave?" asked Lylinora.

"Rakaal is having your ship made ready to depart," Ganix replied. "So I would say twenty-four hours at the most." He opened the door. "I still have business to attend to. But tomorrow I will show you why we guard this place so jealously."

"Something just occurred to me," Ethan said shortly after Ganix had left. "I don't know a damn thing about piloting a boat. Do any of you?"

They all looked searchingly at one another.

"Let's assume that Ganix has also thought of that," said Markus. "I'm more worried about how we find the dragons when we get there. As I understand it, the Wastes are vast. Do we even know where we're going?"

Ethan smiled. Even now he could hear the dragon's call. "I can find them," he assured his friend. "You can bet on that."

They each took turns bathing and changing – with Lylinora and Kat naturally going first – then decided to turn in for the night.

This time, Ethan's nightmares returned with renewed intensity. Visions of blood and death swirled around in a violent tempest as dragons tumbled from the sky, consumed by a raging black fire. He tried to force himself awake, but each time he felt consciousness returning, an invisible hand pulled him back in.

When he woke, he was drenched in sweat. The first thing he saw was Markus sitting up in bed regarding him curiously.

"More bad dreams?" he asked.

Ethan could still hear the screams of the dying tearing through his mind. "I thought they were gone for good," he said. "Ever since I started learning magic, even that bloody voice calling in my head hasn't been so loud. But now...now it's worse than ever."

"You'll get used to it," Markus said. "When I was a slave in the mines, I had nightmares every time I closed my eyes." He cracked a weak smile. "Of course, then I'd open them again and things got even worse."

His words send a pang of guilt through Ethan. It was easy to forget that his best friend had lived a life of slavery, death, and murder... all because of him. He seemed so different now from the embittered Specter he'd first met. And yet, from time to time, something would flash over Markus' face. An inexplicable fury. Usually, it was gone before Ethan fully realized he had seen it. But there were a few times when it was clearly visible. He couldn't tell what brought on these flashes of rage, and was afraid to ask. Markus looked to be at peace with himself most of the time and he would not want to risk changing that with unwelcome questions.

The door cracked open, allowing King Ganix to peek inside. "Are you awake yet?"

"Just me and Markus," Ethan answered.

"Me too," added Kat from above.

Markus climbed from his bed to shake Jonas awake. The old man yawned and stretched, his joints cracking loudly in protest.

"Wake up Lylinora," Markus instructed Kat. "We'll wait outside while the two of you dress."

Lylinora looked fatigued when she exited the room. This was in stark contrast to Kat, who bounced around with a smile on her face, bumping playfully into Markus and Jonas.

Ganix led them to a small office where Rakaal had breakfast waiting. Once they'd eaten, they were then taken down a series of halls until arriving at a large double door. Rakaal stopped outside this and turned to regard the visitors.

"Beyond this door you will see things that only a few dwarves are even aware exist," he announced ceremoniously. "King Ganix has assured me that each of you holds his uttermost confidence and trust. I don't expect that to mean much to a human. But to me, there can be no higher endorsement."

His little speech brought a smile to Ganix's face. "And you say *I'm* pompous," he joked. "Just open the door and get on with it."

Chuckling quietly, Rakaal ushered them inside. They found themselves on a long raised walkway overlooking the rest of the interior. Ethan was immediately struck by the sheer size of the place. It was vast, measuring at least six hundred feet from side to side, and twice that from front to back. Above was a flat ceiling with what looked like massive doors embedded into it at regular intervals. Immense light fixtures were hanging from either side.

Below, lined up in row after row on the floor, were innumerable varieties of machinery. Some of these resembled vehicles, but most Ethan couldn't even begin to identify from a distance.

"This, my friends, is the true craft of the dwarves," said Ganix.

Ethan and the others were awestruck by the sheer scale of what they were seeing.

"What *are* these?" gasped Jonas.

"Some of them we understand," replied Rakaal. "Others…well… frankly, we have no idea. What we do know is that they were built by our ancestors thousands, maybe tens of thousands of years ago. No one is sure exactly when."

"So you weren't joking yesterday about your people building ships that travel the stars," remarked Kat.

"I told Ethan that story back in Elyfoss," Ganix chipped in. "But no. Rakaal wasn't joking. And this in my mind, proves it."

Rakaal moved toward a flight of stairs leading to the ground level. "Let's take a closer look, shall we?"

They followed him down to a row of strange looking devices, each about ten feet long and fitted with what looked like a seat and hand controls on the top middle section. The metal exterior that completely encased the inner workings was a deep red color striped with veins of silver.

"*This* is a flying machine," Rakaal announced proudly.

Ethan moved closer and ran his fingers over the surface. It was surprisingly warm to the touch. "How do you know?" he asked.

"Because I made one fly," he replied. This grabbed everyone's attention. He gave a slightly embarrassed smile. "Well, in truth I got it to hover for a few seconds before it burst into flames. There are nearly one-hundred and fifty of them all together...if I can ever get them to work properly."

Ethan noticed that some of the flying machines were made from a different material. He touched one and this time felt the familiar cold of tempered steel.

"Ah, yes," said Rakaal. "Some are made from metals that can be found here in Lumnia. The others are different. Whatever they're made from, it's so hard and strong that our best tools can barely scratch it."

"My guess is that they're older," added Ganix. "Perhaps the builders ran out of material and started using whatever they could find here."

"Put some wheels on it and you have yourself a motorcycle," noted Markus.

Ethan nodded. "Amazing."

"Indeed," agreed Lylinora. "How long have you known of this place?"

"My father found it," replied Rakaal. "He found clues to its location in some ancient books a few years before I was born."

"So does that mean you've spent your whole life here?" asked Jonas.

"Most of it, yes."

Rakaal beckoned them to follow. For more than three hours he led them down row after row of various devices, freely admitting that he didn't understand most of the older ones.

"We can't even get inside them to see how they operate," he explained.

The newer devices were a different story. There was everything from construction tools, to transports, weapons, and even small household items used to prepare food.

"But how much of this stuff here actually works?" Lylinora asked.

Rakaal gave an embarrassed frown. "None of it. We can't get any of them to function for more than a few seconds. Then boom! They either catch fire or explode."

"Then what good are they," she asked.

His back stiffened. "If we succeed, we will have weapons and tools that can bring down the Empire. Is that not a worthy enterprise?"

Lylinora shook her head dubiously. "You think a bunch of old trinkets can defeat Shinzan?"

"One of these *old trinkets*, as you call them, is going to take you to the Dragon Wastes," he retorted.

"I thought you said nothing worked," Kat pointed out.

"Nothing in *this* room," he said. "But we have had *some* success. We have managed to power four sea going vessels."

"Powered with what?" asked Markus.

"Magic, of course," he replied. "What else?"

"You'll see for yourself when we show you the ship," added Ganix.

They continued with the tour for another hour before going back to their room where a meal was waiting for them.

Rakaal excused himself, not forgetting to give Lylinora a contemptuous glance on his way out. Ganix remained and joined them for lunch.

"As much as I hate to admit it, you're not wrong," he said to Lylinora. "Unless we can make these things work, they are little more than interesting trinkets. But if Rakaal and the others succeed, we may just have the power to free ourselves from Shinzan's yoke."

Lylinora lowered her eyes. "I didn't mean to offend him, Your Highness. But dwarves already make mighty weapons, and they have had little effect against his power. Why should these be any different?"

"They may not be," the king admitted. "But being that you are the only trained mage in existence, it's not as if we have other tools at our disposal."

"Even if there was a thousand mages," said Markus. "Didn't Shinzan already wipe you out once?"

Lylinora's eyes burned. "We were taken by surprise."

Jonas cleared his throat, but when Lylinora looked at him, he folded his hands on the table and remained silent.

At that moment, the entire room began to shake violently. This was accompanied by the harsh scraping of metal and a series a deep booms. The disturbance lasted for only a few seconds, but it was long enough to have everyone apart from Ganix on their feet and scrambling under the table.

The king threw his head back in laughter. "It's all right. Nothing is wrong."

"What the hell was that?" demanded Jonas.

"The machine which powers this place can be…temperamental," he told them.

Lylinora stood and straightened her dress. "Machine?"

Ganix helped Jonas to his feet. "Yes. The lights, hot water, plumbing, even the concealing cloak and fog – everything is powered by a great machine."

"I thought it ran on magic," said Kat.

"It *seems* like magic," Ganix replied. "But it's not. At least, not in the way we understand it. The best we can tell is that it somehow draws its power from the sea. Beyond that, we really don't know how it works."

"It's a power plant!" exclaimed Markus. "There's a big one at Niagara Falls back on Earth. It's powered by the current of the river. I bet your machine works the same way."

Ganix cocked his head. "The river current you say? That's interesting. I must pass this information on to Rakaal."

Ethan was beginning to understand why King Ganix had kept the true history of his people secret. If they did in fact once travel the stars, it would be hugely demoralizing to see these wonders and know that you were now no better than a child playing with your father's tools.

Apparently, Lylinora was having a similar thought. She looked as if she were trying to measure her words and waited several seconds before speaking. "Do you think it's wise to meddle with the things here?" she eventually asked. "Perhaps they would be best left alone. Rakaal has told us that everything you try to repair ends up either exploding or in flames. Suppose you touch something far more powerful than a flying machine?"

"It is a concern," Ganix conceded. "But if we can recover even a small portion of our knowledge, imagine what the world would become."

Ethan lowered his head and frowned.

"You have an opinion, Ethan?" Ganix asked.

He shrugged. "It's just that I remember the story you told me. How your people used their technology to rule. How you treated the humans and elves so badly back then. So now, I can't help but wonder: What if you succeed in regaining that knowledge?"

For a moment, Ganix stared at Ethan blank-faced. A warm smile then gradually appeared. "You continue to amaze me with your insight, Ethan Dragonvein. And I suppose that what you suggest is a danger. But I hope that wise dwarves...those like Birger...will be the ones who guide us into the future. If so, we can avoid the mistakes of the past."

Markus leaned back in his chair and stretched. "We're getting a little ahead of ourselves, aren't we? Let's kill Shinzan first. Then we can worry about dwarf machines."

A few minutes later, Rakaal came into the room. There was a glint of excitement in his old eyes.

"There *is* one more thing I would like you to see before I show you the ship that will be taking you to the Dragon Wastes," he announced.

Chapter Fourteen

SHINZAN LEANED BACK in his throne, his hands steepled beneath his chin, and regarded the scene. The dozens of finely dressed men and women scattered throughout the spacious hall consciously avoided eye contact with their Emperor. They knew better. Catching his attention rarely ended well. The craftier of them would skirt the edges of the room and duck behind pillars whenever the Emperor's gaze wandered in their direction. But this was only a brief delay. In time, all of them would feel the bitter kiss of Shinzan's lips. They would experience the exquisite pain of his touch. No one was safe for long.

The delicate sounds of the musicians reverberated perfectly off the vaulted ceiling. Though there were only six players, the acoustics made it sound as if they were twice that in number. Even so, no one was dancing. Shinzan considered ordering those in attendance to do so, but dismissed the idea. Better to leave them free to plot and jostle for position. That was far more entertaining.

The two naked women at his feet ran their nimble fingers up his inner thighs. He smiled down at them. Once they had been noble women of worth and status. Now they were gifts given for his pleasure by families desperate to gain his favor. The pretty blond kneeling at his left was once the wife of a Ralmarian lord, given away on the very evening of her wedding. When she came to him, she had not even changed out of her ceremonial gown. What was her name? Ah, yes. Varia.

He smiled down at her. "Varia, my sweet. After tonight you shall entertain the guards. Once they are satisfied, I will return you to your husband. Does that please you?"

Varia lowered her head in submission. "Yes, Your Majesty. Thank you."

"It might take you several days to get around to them all. At last count there were…"

He paused to scratch his head. "Three-hundred, I think. Give or take a dozen. But I'm certain your husband will be happy upon your return."

"Yes, Your Majesty. I'm sure he will be." Tears began to well in her eyes.

It was the little spites, the tiny pinpricks, that he enjoyed most of all. Varia would return to a husband unable to accept what she had done – regardless of the fact that it was beyond her control. Shinzan would send the man a letter describing her time with him in lurid detail. Then, when he shunned her, Varia would come back. This time willingly. Within a year, she would not remember having ever been anywhere else. Shinzan chuckled at the thought.

The red haired beauty on his right had been brought to him by her own father. Even when told of the perverse nature of her duties, he still allowed her to stay. Shinzan had forgotten her name entirely. Whore. That was what she responded to now. My little whore. Shinzan always made sure her father was kept well informed as to her condition and activities.

He reached down and stroked her hair. In response, she leaned her head on his leg, smiling.

"I was thinking of sending you home as well," he told her.

In an instant, her smile changed to a look of desperation. "No, Your Majesty. Please don't send me away. I'll be good. I promise. I'll…I'll…"

He placed his finger over her lips. "Quiet now. I only thought that you might want to go home to see your family. Don't you miss them?"

She looked confused. "I don't know who you mean, Your Majesty. I have no family. I've been here. Always. Please don't send me away."

Shinzan clicked his tongue. This one was completely broken. He noticed the terrified expression on Varia's face as she witnessed the spectacle. And when she looked up at him, she knew. This was her future. Tears streamed down her cheeks and her body quivered from sobs.

Breaking these women was certainly one of his favorite distractions. He had broken men in the same way, but found them to generally be weaker in will and consequently far less entertaining. Nothing could compare in strength to a woman of character and determination. Several had even resisted enough to attack him. With *them*, he had been merciful. A quick, painless death. But the two who were now at his feet did not possess such strength. A pity.

The massive double doors to the hall eased slowly open to reveal Mrulo, a short, fat, shrew of a man. He ran up to the Emperor as fast as his squat little legs could carry him – though in truth it was more like a rapid shuffle than a run. Sweat was already pouring down his rosy round cheeks and he was panting wildly. When just a few feet in front of the throne, he dropped to his knees.

"You are sweating on my floor," scolded Shinzan. "Get on your feet and tell me why you have interrupted my party."

Heaving himself up, Mrulo bowed. "My apologies, Your Majesty. Lord Drakion has arrived and wishes to see you."

Shinzan regarded the man. He may be short, fat, and stupid. But there was never fear in his eyes. Not a glint. "Send him in," he commanded.

Mrulo backed away and started out.

"And you can take Varia with you," Shinzan called out. "When you are done with her, send her to the guard barracks."

A wide grin of anticipation split Mrulo's face. "Thank you, Your Majesty."

Varia's tears flowed anew on hearing this. Nonetheless, she stood and bowed to Shinzan, then took hold of the servant's chubby little hand.

Shinzan chuckled. Mrulo's penchant for pain and bondage was well known among the women in the palace, something which in the past had often caused serious injury, and once even death.

Shinzan cleared his throat. "Oh, and Mrulo. Do see to it that she is still in…working condition before you deliver her."

He nodded vigorously. "Yes, Your Majesty."

Varia let out a soft cry as the grinning man jerked her forward.

A few minutes later, a tall, lean man dressed in a bright red cape, black ruffled shirt and black trousers entered. His thick locks of auburn hair fell well below his shoulders, bouncing freely with each stride he took. At his side hung a gold hilted sword sheathed in an elegantly jeweled scabbard. His features were thin and angular, and his ruddy complexion contrasted sharply with his ice blue eyes.

He stopped a few feet away from Shinzan to give a sweeping bow. "Thank you for seeing me, Your Majesty."

Shinzan frowned. "I did not expect you, Lord Drakion. Why have you left Ralmaria without permission?"

"The army is ready to march, Sire." His tone was confident, in spite of Shinzan's displeasure. "I come for weapons."

"Do you not have enough already?"

"No, Sire. Not if we are to fight the dwarves. We have mostly steel and bows. Only a few men possess dwarf weapons. *They* on the other hand, will certainly possess many."

Shinzan's eyes bored into Drakion. "Is your leadership and skill not sufficient? Do you expect me to deplete the defenses here? And what shall I do if the palace comes under attack?"

This was a ludicrous question. No one would be fool enough to attack Shinzan in his own palace. Still, he waited for an answer.

"If you wish it, Your Majesty, I will carry out my orders without dwarf weapons. And I will prevail. Though I must tell you that our losses will be great."

Shinzan remained silent for several seconds. Lord Drakion was an effective leader. And his tactical skills were second only to Hronso. He waved a hand. "Very well. You shall have what you need. But do not fail me."

Drakion bowed. "Thank you, Your Majesty."

"Speaking of failure," Shinzan added offhandedly. "What word of King Halvar?"

"I can only assume he lives," Drakion replied. "The Rakasa never returned."

"Even so, he may have been killed after succeeding in his mission."

"Perhaps, Sire. But I doubt it. Halvar is well loved by his people. His death would surely have lured them out of the mountain in search of vengeance."

Shinzan nodded approvingly. "An astute observation, Lord Drakion. Which is why I sanctioned the plan when you offered it. I am disappointed that it failed, however."

Drakion shifted nervously.

"But I do not blame you," Shinzan continued. "The Rakasa had very little chance to begin with."

Drakion visibly relaxed, though a slight frown lingered. "I have also received word that one of our patrol ships is missing and believed destroyed. Admiral Grysjin thinks it to be the work of smugglers."

"And what do *you* think?"

"I think smugglers wouldn't have the courage to attack an Imperial patrol. In my opinion it was either dwarves or..." He hesitated.

"Or what?"

Drakion carefully averted his eyes before speaking further. "I have heard rumors that a mage has returned. It could have been responsible."

"And did you tell this to the admiral?" asked Shinzan, smiling.

"I did, Sire. He...he did not agree with me. He said that I was delusional."

Shinzan's smile grew broader. "Then you should be pleased to learn that the admiral has been relieved of his command. I expect his head any day now. And you should be further pleased to know that you were right. A mage *was* responsible. And there is not one of them...but two."

Drakion's eyes grew wide. "Shall I send - ?"

"They are not for you to worry about," Shinzan cut in. "I have everything under control."

"If it's not overly presumptuous, Sire. How do you know all this?"

Shinzan beckoned his commander closer. With nervous steps, Drakion did as instructed. Shinzan then leaned across to whisper in his ear.

"I know, because there is a traitor amongst them."

CHAPTER FIFTEEN

WITH EACH STEP he took, Rakaal appeared ever more excited while leading them through the labyrinth of broad corridors.

"I've always thought it a shame that more dwarves didn't take an interest in mechanical devices," he remarked to Ganix. "Too much time is spent fooling around with bloody magic. If only you'd send me a few more sharp minds I could..."

"Let's not rehash this," the king interrupted. "You know good and well that you already have some of our brightest minds working here." He glanced over at Ethan. "My cousin thinks we should abandon magic entirely and rediscover our past."

"And why not?" snapped Rakaal. "What has meddling with magic ever achieved? Nothing, that's what. If our people truly did once travel the stars, then shouldn't it be our goal to achieve such accomplishments again?"

"Yes, and that's exactly why you are here, my friend," said Ganix. He reached out and gave the older man's shoulder a fond squeeze. "But I doubt our ancestors achieved flight overnight. It will take time. More time than either of us have on this troubled world, I imagine."

Rakaal sniffed sourly. "Speak for yourself. I'll see these machines functioning again. Mark my words."

Ganix chuckled. "I hope you're right."

They entered a room similar to that in which they had first met Rakaal. Tables lined the walls, with a larger one running all the way down the center. Various cogs and unidentifiable parts were scattered everywhere. But at the rear stood something that immediately caught everyone's eye.

A massive metal man.

Made of gleaming silver metal, the figure stood seven feet tall and was twice as broad as a normal human. At the joints, the metal separated to reveal a thin black mesh, and its oval shaped head bore vertical slits where eyes should be.

"This is a *suldaat*," Rakaal announced proudly.

Ethan scratched his head. "A mechanical man?"

"You have these in your world?" asked Ganix.

Ethan shook his head. "No. Nothing remotely like this. Does it work?"

"Not yet," replied Rakaal. "We can make them walk, but they have no mind."

"How many do you have?" asked Jonas.

"About a thousand. And like the other devices, some of these are made from metals we are familiar with, while others are crafted from the unidentifiable material of old." Rakaal ran his finger lovingly over its breast plate. Can you imagine what an army of these could do?"

Everyone took a long moment to stare in awe. It was Lylinora who eventually broke the silence.

"I can see why you work so hard," she said. "But the fact remains that, unless they function, we must look to the tools we already have."

Rakaal frowned at her. "Take you no joy in the beauty of the unknown? Can you not look at what my people created and see beyond your own needs and wants?"

"It is beautiful," she admitted. "But time doesn't care about beauty. Time is our enemy. Let's defeat *that*, then by the spirits, I'll gaze at every hunk of steel you possess for as long as you desire."

Rakaal threw up his hands. "You only wish to see things that will help you here and now? Is that it? Then you shall." He stalked back toward the door.

Ethan ran his hands over the cold metal of the *suldaat*. "This world gets stranger and stranger," he muttered. He noticed Markus still staring at it as well. "Imagine what the Krauts would have thought about these," he grinned.

Markus smiled back. "They'd have shit themselves for sure. Hell, I almost did when I saw it. Who could make such a thing?"

"I keep trying to picture them walking," remarked Kat, staring uncomfortably at the metallic man. "It's frightening to think about."

Their brief reflection was broken by Rakaal giving a sharp whistle from the doorway and waving impatiently for everyone to follow him. He led them through another corridor and down a long flight of steps which ended in a tall archway. Ethan could taste the salt air as they passed beneath it. Seconds later, he heard the echo of waves crashing against rocks.

Beyond the archway was a massive, sea water filled cavern – several hundred feet across and tall enough to accommodate a four story building. The mouth opened up to the ocean facing east.

Four vessels were docked, two on either side of the enclosure. They reminded Ethan of the power boats he had seen in Hudson Bay during the summer months, but forged from a red metal rather than crafted from wood. They were longer and sleeker too – sixty feet long at least, and only about twenty feet wide.

"No sails?" asked Lylinora. This time she looked genuinely impressed.

Rakaal cast her a sideways glance. "No sails."

They descended a long stairway which took them to the main dock, then on to the boat sitting nearest the mouth of the cave. Rakaal led them up the gang plank to the forward deck where several dwarves were busy making preparations for their journey.

Atop the cabin was a small wheelhouse, and toward the stern another open deck area lined on either side with cushioned benches. Rakaal waited until all the dwarves had disembarked before ushering the group up a short ladder to the wheelhouse.

Here, a line of three chairs had been bolted to the floor, the central one positioned directly behind the wheel. In front of this was a long control panel packed with an intimidating array of knobs, dials, and gauges. Ethan felt his anxiety rising. He didn't recognize anything here, and was certain that no one else in his group did either. Even the symbols marking the gauges were unfamiliar.

Seeing his disquiet, Rakaal placed a hand on his shoulder. "Don't worry. You won't need to know most of this. Hell, we don't understand half of it ourselves."

"Do you at least know how the thing runs?" Ethan asked.

"Of course," he replied. Reaching into his pocket, Rakaal produced a green rod about six inches in length and twice as thick as a man's thumb. "This is what powers it. And we've loaded the hold with enough of them to keep you going for months."

He waved the others in closer. "It's really quite easy. The wheel steers you. That's simple enough for anyone to understand." He then touched a silver lever on the panel. "This is the throttle. The further you push it forward, the faster you'll go. And this black button here is what starts and stops the engine. That's really all you need to know. All these other gauges tell you the engine temperature, fuel levels…things like that. But one power rod will last for a full week, and I'll show you how to replace them."

Satisfied that everyone understood, he took them below to inspect the cabin. Just beyond the door was a small area to prepare meals and a sink, while benches on either side unfolded to allow for two people sleeping on each. A door further in revealed another bed, as well as a small lavatory.

"Keep your fresh water usage to a minimum," Rakaal warned. "What comes from the sink is pure and good to drink. But there's only enough to sustain you for two or three weeks."

"This will be a smelly trip then," said Kat.

"Oh, I think not," countered Lylinora. "I intend to stay clean. And I'll not be surrounded by unwashed brutes. Purifying sea water is a simple matter."

"Bloody magic," Rakaal grumbled under his breath.

After showing them how to change the fuel rods and a few other basic operations, he escorted them back to their room. Once there, he spoke privately with Ganix for a short time before leaving. The king then asked everyone to gather around the table.

"That went better than I expected," he remarked. "Rakaal detests magic, and the idea of helping anyone who uses it bothers him."

"But don't all those devices you showed us also run on magic?" asked Jonas.

"Of course," replied Ganix, smiling. "Just don't point that out to Rakaal. He hates to be reminded."

"Whatever powers them, it's certainly proof that your people once possessed great skill," said Jonas. "A pity that most of that knowledge is now lost."

Lylinora sniffed. "It's all so unnatural. Metal soldiers and flying machines. Have you ever considered there is a reason your people no longer use such things? That perhaps the knowledge was not lost... but abandoned."

"It's possible," Ganix admitted. "But I do not see what was hidden away here as being unnatural. Rakaal wishes to restore the devices made by our ancestors. And I admit, I would like that as well. But even more importantly, when I look at the magnificent craft used to fashion these treasures, I see hope for my people. Hope that we can aspire to be more than we are today. To be more than we ever dared to dream. Perhaps we can, in time, even return to the stars. Sometimes I wonder if that is where we truly belong."

He paused to wave a hand dismissively. "But this is a conversation we must put aside for another time. You will be departing soon, and this may be our last chance to speak of more pressing matters. As you already know, I will be leaving to lead my people south to Elyfoss."

"Won't Shinzan try to stop you?" asked Markus.

"Indeed he might. But we have little choice. My kingdom is far less secure than King Halvar's. Even without Shinzan leading it, a determined attack on us could well succeed given time." Ganix reached into the folds of his robe and handed Ethan a small blue stone. "Once you have finished your business with the dragons, this will lead you to me. Just hold the stone in your hand and concentrate. It will tell you where I am."

For a while they continued to talk of practical issues – routes, provisions, and anything else they might need. Ethan got the impression that King Ganix was not optimistic about his chances of making it all the way to the relative safety of Elyfoss without a fight. Such things, he imagined, weighed heavily on a ruler's mind.

The conversation then turned to more pleasant matters. Time slipped by with ease, and before they knew it, a messenger had arrived to tell them that all was ready and they could depart at any time.

Everyone gathered their belongings and followed King Ganix back down to the dock. Ethan could feel a combination of excitement and dread rapidly building. The call of the dragons would soon now be answered.

Rakaal was waiting for them at the gangplank, a sullen scowl on his face.

"You have no idea what parting with this boat is doing to him," whispered Ganix when drawing close.

As if in response, Rakaal barred their way and planted his fists on his hips. "I expect this to be returned...and in the same condition," he growled.

Ethan bowed low. "You will get it back, I promise. And thank you for all you've done. We couldn't have managed without your help."

Rakaal stared at him silently for a moment, then turned to Ganix. "I hope you know what you're doing," he muttered before stalking away.

Ganix embraced each one of them in turn. "I wish you luck," he said.

"And good luck to *you*," responded Markus. "I think we'll be needing it.

Once they were all on board, Ganix pulled the gangplank free while two other dwarves untied the boat and tossed the ropes onto the deck.

Taking up position behind the wheel, Markus pushed the start button. Ethan was expecting to hear a roaring grumble come from the engine, but to his surprise there was only a low-pitched hum and virtually no vibration.

He stayed in the wheelhouse with his friend while the rest settled on the benches at the rear of the deck. Cautiously, Markus eased the silver lever forward a fraction of an inch, but even this was sufficient to make the craft lurch forward quite dramatically. Knowing that none of the others would have experienced such sudden power before, Ethan glanced over his shoulder to see what effect this had had on them. Lylinora was looking most unsettled and clutching hold grimly to the railing with both hands. Contrastingly, Kat was grinning from ear to ear and steadying herself with just one hand, while Jonas was holding on steadfastly to the edge of the bench.

Markus steered to the cavern mouth and gave Ethan a smile. "Not bad, eh? I wonder how fast she'll go."

"Unless you want to make Lylinora really angry, I'd wait for a while before finding out," Ethan suggested.

Once beyond the cavern, Markus eased the throttle a little further forward. Again the boat instantly picked up speed. Though the water was relatively calm, the bow still bounced playfully on the small swells. They were already surpassing the speed any sailing vessel could hope to achieve, even in the most favorable of conditions.

"That's enough," shouted Lylinora. "The *spirits* only know what will happen if you go too fast in this abomination."

"Relax, My Lady," he laughed. "Enjoy yourself for a change."

Barely were the words out of his mouth when he leapt forward, yelping in pain. Frantically he began beating at the seat of his pants where a small flame had erupted. Ethan could hear Kat laughing hysterically.

"Do *not* tell me to relax," Lylinora warned, glaring furiously at him.

Markus glared back, but said nothing in reply.

"Take the wheel," he brusquely told Ethan before storming off down the ladder and disappearing into the cabin below. Ethan could not suppress a laugh as he caught sight of the singed hole in his friend's pants.

He glanced back at the island that was already shrinking into the distance. All at once, it vanished completely and they were passing through the protective curtain of fog. Not that this lasted for very long. At their current speed they were out of it in less than five minutes. By the time Markus returned wearing a fresh pair of trousers, they were well away.

"With your permission, My Lady," he called sourly. "I would like to hurry us along."

Lylinora seemed rather pleased with herself and was fiddling with a stray piece of cloth that had come loose from her dress. "That will be fine," she told him. "But not too fast. Understood?" She held up her index finger, causing a tiny ball of fire to appear just above it. "I don't imagine you have an unlimited supply of clothes with you."

Hissing a curse, Markus urged the boat faster, but only until hearing Lylinora ominously clear her throat. With a smile on his face, Ethan slapped him on the back and left to join the others.

"An amazing craft," remarked Jonas. "I never imagined traveling so swiftly. Just think what one could do with a whole fleet of these."

Lylinora sniffed. "I prefer not to."

"What bothers you so much about dwarf technology?" Ethan asked her.

"You should know," she replied. "King Ganix told you the story. They used their machines to practically enslave humankind. I would not see history repeated."

"Some people say the same thing about magic," remarked Kat. "There are stories of how the mages ruled through cruelty and fear."

"That's not true and you know it," Lylinora snapped. "It *is* true however that dwarves abused their power."

"I don't think King Ganix or King Halvar would do anything like that," Ethan said.

"And will they live forever?" she countered. "What of those who come after them? Will they be as kind and wise?"

Ethan shrugged. "I don't know. Maybe it's just that I'm used to having machines around me. Where I grew up, they're everywhere. And we don't have any magic at all."

Lylinora shuddered. "It sounds like a dreadful place."

"Not really," he said. "I mean, Bay Ridge isn't much to look at, but upstate is nice. And the New York skyline at night is really something to see."

"I think I'd prefer not to see it at all, thank you," Lylinora said, waving a dismissive hand. "And once you've discovered the true beauty of magic, I doubt you'll look back on Earth quite so fondly."

Jonas nodded in agreement. "From what little I saw of it, I would not choose to return."

"All you saw was a bombed out town," Ethan told him. "It's not like that everywhere."

Kat jumped up and slid in beside him. "Well, *I* want to see it. If they have things like this boat on Earth, I wouldn't ever want to come back here. Promise that you'll take me if you get the chance."

Ethan smiled. "Sure thing. But I wouldn't count on us ever finding a way of getting there. Not from what I've been told, anyway."

"Still, you never know," she said. "Just remember that you promised."

The day continued without incident, and it didn't take long for both Lylinora and Jonas to become more at ease. Soon, everyone bar Lylinora was vying to take a turn at steering the boat. As Rakaal had said, operation was simple and direct, though Ethan couldn't help but wonder what they might do if the engine were to suddenly develop a fault.

The first night was pleasant enough. The food provided for them left much to be desired, but they ate on deck and talked happily about simple matters and times past. It was decided they take turns at the helm in four hour shifts.

Ethan was grateful to be first. The cacophony of pleading dragon voices in his head was becoming unbearable, and the solitude of the ocean at night helped to calm his mind.

I'm coming, damn it, he thought. Leave me alone!

But they did not heed him. Once his shift ended and he was on his bed, the voices grew even louder and more urgent. By morning, he had managed to get only a little sleep.

The first week at sea passed more or less uneventfully. Lylinora purified and heated water for bathing each night, and spent the mornings instructing Kat and Ethan. Jonas and Markus did their best to keep themselves occupied as well, but the cramped conditions did occasionally cause tempers to flare between them.

By the second week even Lylinora didn't object when Markus pushed the vessel to go faster, though at night it was agreed they should slow down considerably. In the darkness, they had already passed uncomfortably close to several small islands without seeing them until they were almost directly off the bow.

It was during Ethan's shift on the tenth night when Lylinora joined him at the wheel. Since leaving the island, their conversation had been sparse and more formal than usual. He attributed this to the lack of privacy on board, so was glad to at last have a few minutes alone with her. She was dressed in a soft blue cotton robe, and had her hair tied loosely back. With the moonlight reflecting off the waves to give her skin a soft glow and her eyes a sparkle, Ethan found himself transfixed by her beauty.

"Do you really miss your old world?" she asked.

"Sometimes," he admitted. "But not always."

"I can't imagine living in a place without magic. How ugly it would be to spend your life surrounded by machines."

Ethan smiled. Without thinking, he draped his arm around her shoulders. In response, she leaned closer. "You're not exactly surrounded," he told her. "And some of them are useful. There are cars to take you where you want to go. Airplanes that can fly you anywhere. All sorts of things."

She shuddered and pulled her robe tight around her. "I just can't imagine it. Humans weren't meant to live that way."

Ethan was about to point out that Earth was in fact the place from where all humans on Lumnia originated, when a sharp pinging sound against the metal wall of the wheelhouse trapped the words in his throat. Instinctively, he pulled Lylinora behind him and peered out of the window. But there was nothing to see apart from the moonlight dancing on the ocean.

Just as he was relaxing a little, another loud ping, this time just inches away from the window, had him tense again. Signaling for Lylinora to stay where she was, he began creeping down the ladder to the forward deck.

"Are you armed?" she asked.

Ethan shook his head.

"Then you should be the one up here hiding," she said playfully. "Anyway, we're hundreds of miles from shore. Nothing can harm us out here."

Ethan cast his eyes over the deck and spotted two small pieces of what appeared to be shattered bone just below the wheelhouse window. He knelt to examine them. Each one was as thin as a nail and just as sharp at the tip. Cautiously, he reached down to pick one up. As he did so, a searing pain shot through his upper body and he let out a hissing cry. Protruding from his chest, just below his left collarbone, was another of the missiles. It had penetrated nearly an inch into his flesh, and blood was already seeping from the wound.

"Get back," he shouted to Lylinora, who had started to follow him.

But she ignored his warning and hurried down the ladder to his side. The moment she arrived, Ethan felt himself struck again, this time in the leg.

Lylinora threw out her right hand, sending a flash of light exploding over the port side. The water below erupted into dozens of tiny splashes. Meanwhile, ignoring his pain, Ethan hobbled over to the cabin door.

"Everyone up!" he shouted. "We're being attacked."

Lylinora kept the light blazing over the water, but nothing unusual showed itself. She waited until Ethan was inside the cabin before following.

Markus was already on his feet, sword in hand. Jonas was still rubbing his eyes while trying to regain his senses.

"Look to his wounds," Lylinora instructed Markus. "I'll check on Kat."

Ethan hopped onto the bed, wincing with every movement. The tiny projectiles felt as if they were digging in deeper by the second.

Markus rushed to his side. "What the hell happened?"

"I don't know," he replied. "Something attacked us from out of the darkness. Got me twice before I could make it inside."

Markus examined the wound. "It looks like some sort of dart," he said, gingerly touching the end. "Made from fish bone, I think." He tried to pull it free, but Ethan let out a cry of pain.

Kat burst in, hair tangled and clutching a dagger. Lylinora, looking considerably calmer, followed her.

"Have you ever seen anything like this?" Markus asked.

"*Sirean*," said Jonas under his breath.

Markus cast him a jeering glance. "There's no such thing."

"Then what do you suppose did this?" he shot back.

Markus had no reply.

Lylinora knelt beside Ethan. "I'll try to numb the pain, but it will still hurt a bit," she warned. The tips of her fingers glowed as she gripped the dart protruding from his shoulder. In a single swift movement, she pulled it free.

Ethan let out a stifled grunt. "Damn! It feels like you ripped out a pound of meat."

She grinned at him. "Mages don't whine and complain."

"I'm not..."

He cut off and sucked sharply through his teeth as she pulled the second dart free.

Closing her eyes, Lylinora then placed a hand over each of his wounds. Ethan felt a cold tingle shoot through his entire body. Within seconds, the bleeding had stopped and the pain was gone.

"What's confusing me is why anyone would attack with such ineffective weapons?" Markus said.

"They felt pretty effective to me," Ethan countered sourly. He examined his injured leg. Only a light pink area revealed that there had been any wound at all.

Lylinora stood up. "He's right. You would need to be struck by dozens, if not hundreds of them, to pose any real threat. It would be different if the darts were poisoned, but they aren't."

"Well, whatever the case, we can't just sit here," Ethan pointed out. "I'm getting us the hell out of here." He pushed himself up off the bed and approached the cabin door.

At once, both Lylinora and Markus were at his back. Kat also attempted to rise, but Jonas grabbed her arm, holding her fast.

"Oh no you don't, young lady," he said. "I'm not going out there. And I won't be left here alone. Besides, if the worst happens, some of us need to remain uninjured."

The look in Jonas' eyes denied her any argument. After letting out a loud huff, she plopped down hard on the chair with arms folded tightly across her chest.

Ethan smiled inwardly at the scene before easing the door open and taking a cautious step outside.

"What do you see?" called Markus.

Ethan surveyed the area. "Nothing so far." He moved around to the ladder.

The moment he set foot on the first rung, he heard Markus cry out and glanced across to see his friend clutching his right arm. An instant later, pings and sharp cracks filled the air as dozens of tiny darts zipped in from the darkness. Markus quickly shoved Lylinora behind him, while Ethan scrambled up to the wheelhouse.

He was struck three times – twice in the leg and once in the back – while climbing. Spasms of pain ran through him, very nearly causing him to lose his footing.

"Get back inside," Markus shouted to Lylinora.

Ignoring his instruction, she raised her arms skyward. "Enough of this nonsense."

A ball of blue light exploded overhead, firing dozens of lightning streaks into the ocean. The barrage of missiles instantly ceased. Even so, the lightning continued for a full minute before stopping. The blue light then turned to white, illuminating everything for a hundred yards. Lylinora stepped past Markus to look out over the water.

Ethan was in the wheelhouse, ready to push the throttle forward if necessary. "Are they gone?" he called.

After a brief silence, Markus pointed over the rail. "There! Do you see that?"

Floating and bobbing in the swells was a small creature no more than three feet in length. Lylinora waved her hand and whispered almost inaudibly. The figure slowly rose from the water and drifted onto the deck.

Ethan could barely believe his eyes as details of the creature became clearer. From the look on their faces, neither could Markus and Lylinora.

It had arms and hands just as any human might, though with pale blue skin and fleshy webbing between its fingers. The narrow head, which crested into a ridge just above its brow, featured close set eyes and a nose that was little more than a small bump with a tiny slit on either side. The creature's thin mouth hung half open, revealing a vicious looking set of jagged teeth, while lower down, its lean torso tapered away into a fishlike fin. Across its chest, a dark area of burned flesh still smoldered where the lightning bolt had struck.

"Is it dead?" ask Ethan.

Markus approached the figure cautiously and poked it with his boot. "I think so."

Lylinora's eyes darted back to the ocean several times. "We should leave at once. Throw it overboard."

With an expression of utter distaste, Markus picked up the body and did as she asked. "I guess Jonas was right," he said, turning back toward the cabin. "The *sirean* are real."

Ethan pushed the throttle, sending the boat swiftly forward. At his feet was a broken dart. He picked it up and examined it closely. Markus' observation began to repeat relentlessly in his head. Why would they attack with such ineffective weapons? It didn't make sense.

Lylinora came up to heal his wounds a short time later, but proved to be in no mood for conversation. Clearly the encounter had shaken her more than Ethan would have thought. He was still thinking on this when Jonas arrived to relieve him at the wheel.

"I wish they had not been so quick to dispose of the body," the old man remarked sourly. "I would have very much liked to see a *sirean* up close."

"It was...unusual," said Ethan. "No doubt about that."

"Markus said it was no longer than three feet long."

Ethan nodded an agreement.

"Strange. I'd always heard they were as large as a man," Jonas said. "A pity it had to die." Heaving a sigh, he took over the wheel.

Ethan frowned. Something was wrong - something just didn't fit. Whatever it was, he felt as if the answer was tantalizingly close, on the very edge of his mind.

Still puzzling over this, he said goodnight to Jonas and went inside.

CHAPTER SIXTEEN

A S THE DAYS progressed, Ethan could feel their destination growing ever nearer. By now, the call of the dragons was a constant, ever-demanding rumble in his mind. So intense had it become, he was barely able to concentrate on even the simplest matter, and only able to sleep for a few hours at a time.

So far, the *sirean* had not returned, but both Lylinora and Jonas continued to keep a watchful eye. And when they were forced to stop in order to change the fuel rod, Lylinora stood on the bow, hands glowing red – ready to unleash her deadly magic upon them should they seize this opportunity to attack.

It was almost three weeks since departing Borgen when they caught their first glimpse of the Dragon Wastes. Markus was at the wheel, and immediately called Ethan up from the cabin.

"Now what?" he asked.

Ethan stared long and hard at the distant shoreline. Mile after mile of rocky terrain in both directions was broken only by the occasional short stretch of beach, giving no indication whatsoever as to which part of the vast coast they should be making for. Eventually, he shut his eyes and listened to the dragon's call.

"Head south," he replied after a few moments.

"How far?"

Ethan shrugged. "I'll know when we get there."

He stayed by the wheel with Markus while the others gathered their belongings and changed into suitable clothing. As the sun touched the horizon, Markus slowed the boat to a crawl.

"I'm no sailor," he said. "But even *I* know better than to travel this close to shore at night."

"He's right," called Jonas from the deck. "We can't risk hitting a rock or running aground."

Ethan remained silent while continuing his careful watch. Slowly, a smile crept upon his lips. "We're here," he announced. His hand shot out, pointing to a small outcropping of rock.

Markus and the other strained their eyes, at first seeing nothing. Then, as they eased closer, a small wooden dock that blended almost perfectly with the hue of the stone could be made out.

"I don't suppose it was dragons who built that," remarked Jonas.

"Yeah. I thought no one lived here," said Kat.

Ethan spread his hands. "I don't know. But I suppose we'll find out soon enough."

Markus continued to steer the boat in, scraping the hull against the side of the dock and crushing several of its planks. While Lylinora treated him to a withering look of scorn for his clumsiness, Ethan leapt off and secured the vessel.

A well-trodden path at the end of the dock led up a hill and over a low ridge. The terrain all around was barren and uninviting, without even a single blade of grass – only rocky ground and a few, long dead trees. Not even insects buzzed about. It was as if the land had been completely robbed of all life.

"How far is it from here?" asked Lylinora.

Ethan gazed at the top of the ridge. The dragon's call was now rattling in his head so loudly that it felt like steel talons were trying to claw their way out of his skull.

"I'm not sure," he replied. "A mile. A hundred miles. I wish I knew."

After briefly jumping back on board to retrieve his sword and his pack, he took the lead with

Markus at his back. Everyone else had an uneasy air about them as they followed up the path. Kat stayed close to Lylinora, while

Jonas walked just behind them, his hand resting tensely on the hilt of his blade.

Just as they reached the top, Ethan came to a sudden halt, a look of utter astonishment on his face. The transformation was incredible. Spread before him now was a vast expanse of rolling hills covered in lush grass and peppered with a myriad of multi-colored wild flowers. The stale, dusty air was immediately driven away by their sweet fragrance. Tall trees, each one bearing a different type of delicious looking fruit, lined a well-trodden path that vanished between two hills.

"What the hell?" gasped Markus.

"Indeed," agreed Jonas, coming up to join them. "Not at all what one would expect of the Dragon Wastes."

Lylinora walked just off the path and knelt to place her hand on the grass. "Magic," she whispered after a few seconds. "Powerful magic lives here."

Ethan joined her and mirrored her actions, but could feel nothing. "Can you tell where it's coming from?"

"From me," an unknown voice answered from behind.

Ethan shot up, his hand flying to his sword. Markus shoved Kat and Jonas to his back and did the same.

Standing only a few yards away was an old man clad in a tattered brown robe and worn leather shoes. Bent of posture, and with a wiry ashen beard more than a foot in length, his gaze was fixed firmly on Ethan. His unkempt silver hair fell down his back in tangled knots, and his countenance, deeply carved with the lines of many years, was grim. Ethan shifted nervously under the intensity of the stranger's piercing, emerald green eyes.

"Put away your weapons," he ordered in a humorless tone. "They'll do you no good here."

Lylinora stepped forward, her hands glowing red. But before she could speak, the old man flicked his right index finger as if casually dismissing something of no consequence. Lylinora was instantly pushed several feet back and the glow around her hands was extinguished.

"That will be quite enough out of you, young lady," he scolded. "Too much of your mother in you, I see."

Slack jawed, Lylinora stared down at her hands in disbelief.

Markus took a step forward, but Ethan caught his arm. "Who are you?" he demanded.

The old man regarded him for a long moment and then grunted. "Nothing at all like your father. Ah well, that may be for the best." He looked over his shoulder. "I see the dwarves were kind enough to furnish you with a vessel."

"I asked you a question," pressed Ethan.

"So you did," he replied. "And I have not yet answered." His gaze shifted to Jonas. "And you...what's wrong with your sight? Don't you recognize me?"

Jonas crept forward, eyes narrowed. After a few seconds, he stiffened. "It can't be. It's impossible."

"Who is he?" asked Ethan.

His question was ignored. Jonas' gaze remained fixed on the newcomer. "Renald?" he asked in an awed whisper. "Is that really you?"

The old man snorted. "What's left of me. But I see the years have not affected you. Bloody portal magic, I suppose. Well, come on then. Let's get going."

"I'm not going anywhere until I get some answers," Ethan told him.

"Ethan," said Jonas. "This is your uncle – Renald Dragonvein."

Ethan's eyes shot wide. "My uncle?"

"Yes, your uncle," Renald repeated irritably, pushing past him and starting down the path. After a few yards he stopped and turned. "And unless you enjoy that incessant voice rattling around in your head, boy, I suggest you keep up."

Lylinora was still unable to move or speak. Kat, standing beside her, had a mystified expression on her face.

Ethan placed a hand on Lylinora's shoulder. "Are you all right?"

His touch sparked a reaction. She blinked several times and clenched her fists. "He shouldn't be able to do that." She looked up fearfully at Renald, who had already started hobbling away. "No one can cut a mage off from magic like that. We should get back to the boat."

"Jonas says he's my uncle," Ethan responded. "I think we should go with him." It was unsettling for him to see Lylinora so disturbed and afraid, but he knew he must continue. "If you want, you can wait on the boat. I'll come get you when I'm sure it's safe."

After thinking for a moment, she shook her head. "No. If you go, I go too."

Ethan gave her a reassuring smile and led the way onward. They had walked no more than a few steps when Lylinora gripped his hand tightly.

"Stay close to me," she said.

"I promise."

It didn't take long for them to catch up with Renald, though he all but ignored their presence. After rounding the next hill, a small cabin came into view. It was sturdily built with a spacious porch across the front. Off to the side and further back stood two lesser structures – the aroma of meat clearly identifying one of these as a smoke house.

Renald opened the front door and gestured for them to enter. "Leave your things on the porch. It will be cramped enough inside without all your junk making it worse."

He pointed to the small dining table, then tottered over to the stove. "I haven't had guests in some time. So it will take a while for a meal to be ready."

"We have food if that helps," offered Jonas.

Renald ignored the offer. Instead, he looked away from everyone, scratching his chin. "I know it's rude," he muttered. "But you can't expect me to cook for so many people." He waved his hand irritably, as if swatting an invisible fly. "Fine. I'll do it."

The entire party looked at one another, unsure what to make of this odd behavior.

"Excuse me," said Ethan. "But who are you talking to?"

Renald gave him a sideways glance, then with a flick of his wrist, lit the stove with a spark of magical flame. "Jonas, fetch me some water. There's a well in the shed beside the smoke house." He nodded to a large pot in the corner. "Purify it if you don't mind. You still remember how, don't you?"

Jonas hesitated only briefly. "Yes. Of course, My Lord."

"And hurry back," said Renald. "We have much to discuss."

"We do indeed," agreed Lylinora, a sharp edge to her voice. "For example: How were you able to block my use of magic?"

Renald sniffed. "Young people. You learn to make a bloody fireball and you think you're already a mage. Your father was far too indulgent with you. Letting you wander off, playing and frolicking when you should have been studying. And as for your mother...well...let's just say that she wasn't exactly the brightest of mages."

Lylinora's face reddened. "Mind what you say about my mother, old man."

"I'll say what I please," he shot back. "Do you even know *how* I took your power?" He waited for several seconds before answering his own question. "Wards, my dear. Simple wards."

Lylinora knitted her brow. "That's not possible. No ward can do that."

"Wards can do many things," he said. "They have kept this land fertile. They keep the foul beasts who roam the wastelands at bay. And they tell me that one among you is in contact with Shinzan at this very moment."

This announcement caused the entire party to stir.

"Who?" asked Ethan skeptically.

"We'll get to that later," he replied, as if unconcerned by the matter. "First of all we need to get that voice out of your head." He gave a high-pitched whistle. "Come on out, you old rat. It's time." His words were met by silence. "I don't care," he continued. "He can't learn anything if that bloody voice is thundering away all the time."

After another long pause, a sharp clicking sound came from the porch outside. Renald opened the door. At his feet stood a tiny dragon, almost identical in size and shape to the one Ethan had seen before, only this time it was white with black spines. It took a step inside and regarded Ethan, growling menacingly.

"It's beautiful," gasped Kat.

"*It* is a *she*," corrected Renald. "And she has a name."

"Maytra," said Ethan in a half whisper, before Renald could continue.

"Can you hear her?" asked Lylinora.

Ethan nodded slowly. Tears were welling in his eyes and his hands began to tremble. He slid from his chair and knelt, extending his hand.

Maytra glanced up at Renald, who nodded his approval. Slowly, she approached Ethan, still growling and hissing. Ethan extended his arm further, but in a flash she snapped her jaws, clamping down on his thumb. Before he could react, she released him and backed away. Blood was dripping from the wound, but Ethan gave no immediate reaction other than to lower his head. Then, after a few moments, he began to weep, his falling tears mingling freely with his blood on the floor. Soon, great sobs were shaking his entire body.

"What's wrong?" asked Markus.

"Give him a moment," said Renald. He bent down to stroke Maytra's head. "I know that was hard. You can go now." The tiny dragon let out a screech, then scurried from the house, taking flight as she passed the threshold.

"Why is she so small?" asked Kat.

"She was cursed as a hatchling by Shinzan," Renald explained. "Along with Jafari, her mate."

Lylinora moved to join Ethan, but was halted by a stern look from Renald. It was more than five minutes before Ethan finally stood up and returned to his seat.

Renald sat in the empty chair across from him and took a long breath. "I think you'll find that your powers have now returned," he told Lylinora.

At once, she reached out for Ethan's injured hand, but he pulled abruptly away, holding it to his chest. She touched his shoulder. "What's wrong?" she asked.

"I killed him," Ethan said. His voice was tormented and distant. "And now she's all alone."

"Who's alone?"

Ethan looked up to meet her gaze. "Maytra. Her mate was the dragon who came to save me in the forest from Hronso."

"The effects will subside shortly," Renald told him. "Right now, you're just feeling what Maytra feels. Her rage; her pain. The irreplaceable loss.

She opened herself up to you so that you could block out the call of the dragons. You should now allow Lylinora to heal you."

Ethan nodded and held out his hand. After the wound had been closed, he laid his head on the table and continued weeping.

Realizing that he had been gone far too long, Markus asked, "Where's Jonas?"

Renald's face tightened. "Gone for now."

Markus rose sharply from his chair. "What do you mean, 'gone'?"

This was enough to shake Ethan from his sorrow. He too shot Renald an accusing stare.

"He lives," the old man added. "But I cannot have him near when we discuss sensitive matters. It's bad enough that you have brought him here."

"What the hell are you talking about?" demanded Kat.

Renald raised an eyebrow. "You speak this way to your elders?"

She drew her dagger and joined Markus. "I'll do more than just talk if you don't tell me where Jonas is."

Renald sneered. "You bring a traitor to my home, and then think to threaten me?"

"Jonas is no traitor," snapped Markus. "An old pain in the ass, maybe. But he's not a spy."

"He may not know it," Renald countered. "But he is most definitely under Shinzan's control. I knew it the moment he stepped through my wards. I'm just not sure to what extent."

"I checked for any sign of influence before we left Elyfoss," Lylinora objected. "I wouldn't have missed it."

Her claim drew a mocking laugh from Renald. "You think much of your abilities. Even so, I assure you that I am not mistaken. And for now you must trust that he is unharmed."

"Show him to me," demanded Ethan. All trace of sorrow was now gone from his eyes, replaced by a steadily building anger. "Show me, or I'll leave right now."

Renald leaned forward to scrutinize Ethan closely before responding. "Stubborn. That much at least you have in common with Praxis." He pushed back his chair. "Very well. Come with me." The others began to rise, but he held up his hand. "Only Ethan. His word that Jonas is unharmed will need to suffice all of you."

Markus began to object, but Ethan waved him off. "I'll be fine."

"If you're not back in five minutes, I'm coming after you," Markus stated.

Ethan gave him a nod and a smile before following Renald outside. They rounded the house and approached the building beside the smoke house.

"You're friends are devoted," remarked Renald. "A good quality. Though they are not the type of people I would have expected."

"And what *would* you expect?"

Renald laughed softly. "For certain, not a rogue, a fledgling mage, and a child." He opened the door and gestured for Ethan to enter.

Ethan stopped short the moment he was inside. There stood Jonas, eyes closed, hands hanging loosely at his sides, and completely motionless. Ethan moved closer to touch him on the arm. His skin felt like stone, and there was no movement in his chest to indicate he was breathing.

"What did you do to him?" he growled.

"I simply suspended him. And rest assured, in spite of appearances, he lives."

Ethan turned to face the old man. "If I find out you're lying…" He allowed the implied threat to hang in the air.

Unmoved, Renald exited the building and started back to the house. "I want you to know that I was fond of Jonas. It gave me no pleasure to do this."

"And you're certain that he's been sending information to Shinzan?"

"Absolutely," he replied. "But like I said, he may not be aware of it."

"Can you help him?"

Renald paused just as they reached the porch. "I don't know. I will try." He waved a hand. "But there are more important things than Jonas to deal with at present. For now we must attend to *you*. There is much to do, and very little time."

Ethan scowled, hating the thought of Jonas being held against his will and with an uncertain fate hanging over him. Yet what could he say?

Difficult as it was to believe that Jonas had somehow been bewitched, Renald did not appear to be attempting any sort of deception.

The others were already on their feet when they stepped back inside. "Jonas is…" Ethan began. "Well…he's not hurt."

"I cast a suspension spell on him," Renald explained as he took a seat at the table. He looked at Lylinora. "I'm sure that even with your limited training you are familiar with these. Though I doubt you could cast one."

Lylinora puffed up, her eyes furiously boring into the old man. "I'll have you know that both my mother and father trained me very well."

He gave her a scoffing grin. "If you say so. I suppose we'll see soon enough."

Once everyone was reseated, Renald leaned back in his chair and closed his eyes. The sharp cry of Maytra outside penetrated the walls.

"She's still quite upset," he said. "It may be some time before she allows you to touch her again."

Ethan nodded slowly as he once again began to feel the tiny dragon's immense sorrow. He scratched his thumb where she had bitten him. "You said that we were running out of time."

Renald's eyes cracked open. "True. And even with you now here, there is still very little hope."

He leaned his elbows on the table. "You require years of instruction. And I am too old to be of much use." His hand shot up, silencing the barrage of questions rising on the tip of Ethan's tongue. "Before you assault me with your ignorance, I would hear everything that has happened. Leave out no detail."

For the next several hours, Ethan told his story. Renald listened patiently with hands folded and chin resting on his chest. Only the growling of Markus' stomach forced a pause in the telling. Renald left the house and returned a few minutes later with a portion of smoked ham. After a quick meal, Ethan continued.

He noticed a frown on the old man's face at the mention of the dwarves, and a look of anger when he spoke of General Hronso. But it was the story of their encounter with the *sirean* that really produced a reaction. Renald leapt from his chair, face awash with fury.

"Why would you do that?" he shouted, throwing his hands up in the air. "Why would you attack them?"

"Attack them?" repeated Lylinora. "*They* attacked us."

"Idiot girl! They were just children. How could they possibly have harmed you?" He began pacing the floor rapidly, rubbing at his temples. "You have no idea what you've done."

Ethan could see the pained expression on Lylinora's face. He was about to speak, but Kat came to her defense first.

"Lylinora was only protecting us," she insisted. "She did the right thing."

Renald spun around to face the young girl. "She killed a child. One who was merely having a bit of fun. If they wanted to seriously harm you, why would they have thrown darts used only to hunt seagulls?"

"I...I didn't know." Soft sobs were creeping into Lylinora's voice, though her expression was unchanged.

Renald took a breath and sat back down. "Calm yourself. I do not think you acted out of cruelty. The fault rests with those who taught you."

This did little to salve her guilt. "I would have never harmed a child. Not intentionally. No one in living memory has seen a *sirean*. Most thought they were a legend. How was I to know?"

Ethan recalled feeling that something was wrong about the encounter. Now it was clear. The attack was nothing more than mischief. Harmless by their way of thinking. "There's nothing to do now," he said, attempting to move on. "What's done is done."

"Killing a *sirean* child will most surely spur retribution from the parents," Renald told him. "If they know where you are, you will not be allowed to leave this place alive." His brow creased in thought, then he shrugged. "But as you said: what's done is done. I'll go to the shore tomorrow and see if you were followed. From there we can know what actions, if any, need to be taken."

An uncomfortable hush fell over the room.

"What about the dragons?" said Kat, breaking the silence. "Ethan came here because of them. Where are they?"

"Ethan will meet them soon enough, child," he replied. "After I have dealt with the *sirean*, he and I must depart. And before you ask - no, you cannot go with us."

Kat folded her arms across her chest. "And why not?"

"Because I'm not sure how they would react," he answered flatly. "Dragons do not care for strangers. Your presence might easily upset them, and believe me when I tell you that you do *not* want to upset a dragon."

By then it was long after dusk. Renald stretched and yawned.

"How have you survived for so long?" asked Markus.

Renald pinched the bridge of his nose. "I'll answer this question. But then I need to rest. I haven't used so much magic in more than two-hundred years. It has taken a toll on these old bones."

Ethan was clearly disappointed, but he nodded with understanding. Kat was already rubbing her eyes wearily.

Renald looked over to Lylinora, who was still obviously disturbed. "Clear your mind of troubles for now. I was overly harsh. I'll deal with the *sirean*. You have more important tasks to focus on." He motioned to Kat. "Like teaching this young one magic."

Lylinora frowned. "But I thought now that you are with us you'd be –"

"I'll be instructing you, and to a lesser degree, Ethan," he said, cutting her short. "But I have neither the strength nor the will to take on one so young as an apprentice. It would likely kill me if I tried." He waved his hand. "But now to your question, Markus, so I may rest."

He drew a long breath. "I came here just after the fall of the Council of Volnar. Praxis had asked me to go with him and the others still left alive to challenge Shinzan. I knew it was hopeless, so I refused. Shinzan's power is way beyond what we could understand. Its very essence is unlike anything I have even heard of. The things he is capable of, made most mages seem as children.

"Shinzan had already destroyed most of the dragons by the time I arrived here. The lands were a vast smoldering waste, and the few who had managed to survive were in hiding. It was only through my connection to them as a Dragonvein that I was able to make contact. I was still young and strong back then, so I built my home and cleansed the land surrounding it.

"I would have been content to live out my natural life here and allow the mages to pass into the depths of history. But the remaining dragons would not allow that to happen. They knew of the elf prophecy. And they knew that I was still needed. So through them I have lingered on; kept alive for century upon century by their power. And now that Ethan is here, my time is nearly at hand."

He pushed back his chair. "So there is your answer. I live because the dragons willed it to be. More than that, I don't have the strength to tell right now." He heaved himself up. "But no matter. Being that you will be staying here for some time, there will be ample opportunity for answers later on. For now, find yourself a spot on the floor to sleep."

Ethan watched as he hobbled over to his bed and unceremoniously threw himself down. In seconds, the old man's breathing was deep and regular.

"Are you certain Jonas is all right?" asked Kat.

Before Ethan could answer, Lylinora spoke. "The spell he describes is harmless."

"But do you really believe him?" Kat persisted. "If Jonas has a spell on him, you would have detected it, right?"

Lylinora first glanced to Ethan, then spread her hands. "Perhaps not. I remember my father talking about Renald Dragonvein. He was a powerful mage. Almost as powerful as Praxis himself. He turned down a seat on the Council of Volnar because he said he couldn't stand the politics. But my mother thought it was because he was too close to the elves. The rumor was that he had even lived among them for a time."

This revelation caused Markus to stiffen. "How could a human live among elves?"

"I said it was a rumor," she pointed out. "It may not be true. Although from what I've seen so far, I wouldn't doubt it." Anger was seeping into her voice as she glanced over at Renald's sleeping form. "He's a crude, brute of a man compared to your father, Ethan. It's a wonder that they were brothers."

Her words had an immediate effect on him. Only now did it fully strike him that Renald was indeed a blood relative. All his life he had wondered about his true family. And now…an uncle. Although a mean, cantankerous old bastard, he was probably the best Ethan could hope for.

"I want you to be careful tomorrow," Markus told him. "I don't care if he *is* your uncle. He didn't blink an eye before imprisoning Jonas. There's no telling what he's capable of."

The mention of Jonas cast a gloom over the party, bringing all conversation to a temporary halt as people reflected. It *had* seemed odd that the Emperor was able to follow their every move. And though Ethan was confident that Jonas would never consciously betray him, if his uncle's claim was true, it would explain a great deal.

"Could you free him, Lylinora?" asked Kat.

She thought for a moment before replying. "I doubt it. At least, not here. If it's the dragons that are enhancing Renald's power then I can't know how strong the spell is. And even if I tried to do something, I might end up accidentally hurting Jonas instead. Possibly even killing him if it's the wards Renald has cast."

"What are *wards* exactly?" asked Ethan.

"Barriers," she replied. "Safeguards against harmful magic. I used a simple form of one to protect King Halvar. But as far as I know, it's been a very long time since most mages bothered to learn the art of true ward making."

"Why is that?"

"There hadn't been a war between mages in centuries," she explained. "The Council of Volnar had all but eliminated the possibility. But long ago, before the council was formed, there was a great deal of fighting among our kind. In those days, wards kept a mage's home safe from his foes. Some were said to be very powerful, even preventing physical attacks."

"From the look of it, they work pretty well," remarked Markus.

Lylinora nodded. "It would seem."

At this point, Kat jumped up from her chair and grabbed Ethan by the hand. "I want you to show me where he's keeping Jonas," she told him. When Ethan hesitated, her eyes took on a pleading quality. "Please! I'll be able to sleep much better if I can see he's all right."

Knowing how close the pair had become, Ethan reluctantly agreed.

It was as he feared though; seeing Jonas only made her mood worse. The sight of his frozen form caused her tiny hands to clench tight until her knuckles turned white. All the way back to the house, Ethan could hear her muttering furiously under her breath.

Lylinora was already on the couch, and Markus was busy unpacking his bedroll. They found an empty area near to the fireplace and did their best to get comfortable.

Ethan stared at the ceiling, a faint smile on his face. Though his mind was filled to bursting with questions, the voices in his head were now silent. Very quickly he began to drift. The hard, unyielding wood floor was not to his liking, though without the constant desperate call of the dragons raking at his mind, it didn't matter so much.

I'll sleep outside on the grass tomorrow night, was his final thought before drifting off completely.

*

A gentle touch on her arm woke Lylinora. Her eyes peeled open to see Renald standing over her, a grave expression etched deeply into the lines of his face.

"Come with me," he whispered.

She sat up. The others were still sleeping soundly. "Where are we going?"

"To see the *sirean*," he replied.

Lylinora's heart froze. "Did they follow us?"

"That's what we're going to find out."

She rose and followed Renald outside. The sun was only just breaking the horizon, and a cool southerly breeze caused her to shiver. Once they were well away from the house he stopped and turned to face her.

"If they are here, regardless of what happens, you are to do nothing," he told her sternly. "If it is needed, I will protect you. Do *not* use your magic. Understand?"

"Do you think they'll attack?"

"I don't know," he replied. "But if they do, *I* will handle it."

Lylinora lowered her eyes. She had already made one tragic mistake from sheer ignorance. And as much as she disliked Renald, she was not prepared to make another. "I'll trust you," she told him.

He chuckled. "I seriously doubt that. You've far too much of your mother in you. *She* never trusted me." He shook his head, smiling, before setting off once again toward the shore.

"You knew my mother well?" she asked.

This drew a hearty laugh from the old man. "Knew her? I almost married her."

Lylinora's eyes shot wide. "That's a lie."

He gave her a sideways glance. "Why would I lie about that? I was betrothed to your mother when I was thirteen years old. But sadly, neither of us wanted the union. She was too…aristocratic for me, and I too unsophisticated for her. Thank the spirits that your father and I were friends at the time. Otherwise, *I* might have been your father."

Lylinora sniffed. "It's funny that my mother never mentioned this."

"Not at all," he corrected, clearly amused by her unease. "It was not something either of us would care to remember, let alone talk about. When we refused to marry, it caused quite a stir. Almost to the point of a war between our families. Fortunately, your father was deeply in love with her and managed to persuade her family that he was the better choice of husbands."

Lylinora tried to envisage the situation. The Dragonvein family was one of the wealthiest and noblest in all of Lumnia, and to cast aside a betrothal would have been a dreadful insult. Her father's lips must have dripped honey for mere words to have had such an impact. Particularly on his mother's family. They were strict traditionalists and took such matters very seriously indeed.

"I'll tell you the story in full one day if you would care to hear it," Renald promised. "Your father was really quite courageous."

This brought a smile to her face. "I would. Most definitely I would."

They continued on until catching sight of the dock. Their boat was still safely secured there, and from outward appearances, untouched.

Renald veered right toward a narrow span of beach where waves lapped lazily onto the shore. He stopped just as he reached the water's edge.

Lylinora looked out, but could see nothing aside from the gentle swells and a few seagulls. "Are they...?" she began.

His hand shot up to silence her. "Say nothing. And do not move." He gave out a series of sharp clicks. After only a few seconds, the water stirred a hundred yards out.

A head popped up from the sea. Its face, though broader, was similar to that of the young one Lylinora had seen before, while its flesh was a burnt orange color peppered with coin sized spots of both black and red. As the *sirean* slowly rose higher, she saw crisscrossed over its muscular torso two black straps, both of which held a multitude of the same tiny white darts with which the children had assaulted them. The creature tensed, flexing its powerful chest and toned arms. In its right hand it held a long bone knife – poised and ready.

In response to its appearance, Renald spread his arms wide, palms upturned, and walked into the ocean, stopping when the water was up to his thighs. The *sirean* regarded him for a long moment before tucking the knife away behind its back and spreading its arms likewise.

The calm water immediately around Renald was suddenly transformed into a churning tempest of foam. From out of this bubbling mass, his body elevated until only his feet were touching the surface. Without making even the smallest movement, he glided toward the *sirean*, stopping only a few feet away.

From the corner of her eye, Lylinora caught sight of a second *sirean* watching Renald intently. This one was clearly female. Far more slender in frame and bare breasted, she had long, jet black braids and was armed with a bone tipped spear. Very soon another one appeared. Then another, and yet another. In almost no time at all, more than a hundred of the creatures had surrounded the old mage.

She tried to hear what Renald was saying, but the wind muffled the sound. She cursed the fact that he had told her not to use magic, otherwise she could have easily heard what was being said. Not that this would have been guaranteed to help her, of course. There was a very good chance she wouldn't be able to understand the language they were speaking anyway.

Twenty minutes passed. The conversation then abruptly ceased. Renald bowed low, after which the *sirean* gave a curt nod in return and drew his knife. Lylinora's tension rose sharply, particularly when she saw Renald pull open his robe to bare his chest at the now distinctly hostile looking creature. With thin lips twisted into a snarl, its hand shot out, thrusting the blade deep into Renald's exposed flesh. Incredibly, Renald did not flinch a muscle. After a few moments, the *sirean* withdrew his blade and backed away.

Closing his robe, Renald bowed once again and started back to the shore, his head downcast and his face dire. The *sirean* watched him go for a part of the way, then, after letting out an ear-piercing scream that was clearly an escape for all the anger and anguish bottled up inside, it plunged back into the depths. In a massive flurry of movement, all the others followed suit, their numbers churning the water's surface to a boiling white foam.

When reaching the shore, Renald dropped to his knees, gasping for air. Lylinora was instantly at his side.

"I'll be fine," he said, waving her off. "Though I need a few moments. When beyond my wards, even small amounts of magic take a great toll."

Ignoring his weak efforts to push her away, she helped him to his feet. "What happened out there?"

"You are safe. The *sirean* will not hinder you."

"What did you say to them?"

"That is my business," he replied. "You needn't concern yourself."

Lylinora scrutinized him for a moment longer. "You're hiding something. And before you deny it, remember who my mother was."

Renald regarded her as if she was an unruly child. Then, gradually, he began laughing. "She *was* quite adept at seeing the truth of matters," he admitted.

He placed his hand on her shoulder and allowed her to assist him back toward the house. "Of course, I still won't tell you what transpired.

But I am being truthful when I say that you have nothing to fear from the *sirean*. Let's just say that we came to an understanding."

"How did you learn to speak to them?"

"Years of practice," he replied. "They spend much of their time on these shores. And I've had plenty of time to learn."

It was well into the morning when they arrived back at the house, and the earlier chill had given way to the heat of the rising sun.

Ethan and the others were still sleeping, though Markus was twisting and mumbling, his face contorted into various fearful and angry expressions.

"I need to sleep for a while," whispered Renald. "Wake me in two hours."

"I will," Lylinora promised, helping him over to the bed. His eyes closed the moment his head touched the pillow, and a few seconds later his steady breathing told her that he had already fallen asleep.

She sat on the sofa watching the old man slumber with the same question revolving around and around in her head. What bargain had he made with the *sirean*? What had he been able to offer that could convince a grieving parent to forgo vengeance for the death of their child?

No answer came readily to mind.

CHAPTER SEVENTEEN

ETHAN CRACKED HIS eyes open. For the first time in weeks his sleep had not been plagued by nightmares. His back was a touch stiff from the cold hard floor, but that aside, he was feeling refreshed and excited.

He glanced around the room. There was no sign of Renald, but Markus was sitting at the table with Kat – both of them looking exhausted in spite of having slept for quite a long time. Lylinora was reading quietly on the sofa. She smiled up at him and pointed to the table where a plate of berries and a bowl of steaming porridge waited.

Ethan crossed the room and took his seat. "Where's he disappeared to?" he asked, nodding toward Renald's disheveled bed.

Markus shrugged. "Search me. He was gone before I woke up."

"He'll be back soon," Lylinora said. "He's gathering some fruit for your journey."

In fact, Ethan was just finishing his meal when Renald appeared. In his arms was a small basket of apples and what reminded Ethan of peaches – though they were a touch bigger and bright yellow in color.

"You needn't take much with you," the old man said.

"How long will we be gone?" Ethan asked.

"A day. Perhaps two. Or at least, that's my hope. Dealings with dragons can be tricky."

Ethan gathered a few things from his pack outside and tucked them into his bedroll. While he was doing this, Renald stuffed several pieces of the freshly picked fruit into a small satchel, which he then attached to the rope belt holding his robe together.

As they departed, the others followed them out onto the porch. Kat threw her arms around Ethan, only letting go when Markus tugged on her shoulder. Lylinora's farewell was rather more personal. After draping her arms seductively over his shoulders, she brushed her lips over his ear.

"Stay safe," she whispered.

Ethan's heart pounded at her touch. Temporarily oblivious to the fact that he had an audience, he held her close. "I will," he promised, kissing her lightly and allowing the contact to linger for several seconds before backing away.

Kat's reaction was almost instantaneous. Red faced and with lips pressed firmly together, she spun on her heels and stomped back inside the house, slamming the door behind her. A sharp pang of guilt shot through Ethan. He should have known better. Such open displays of affection only served to hurt the poor girl's feelings. Surprisingly, Markus also appeared to be a little put out by his actions. There was no customary approving smile from his friend. Rather, his expression was stern, and for a brief moment almost held a sour quality.

"*Just* like your bloody mother," huffed Renald, glaring at Lylinora. He started off toward the path, mumbling and shaking his head.

Ethan gave her a final smile before hurrying after him.

"You should be careful with that one," the old man said after about a quarter mile.

Ethan grinned. He could still feel the impression of Lylinora's lips, and smell the lingering scent of her perfume. "And why is that?" he asked.

"The women in her family are known to be…how should I put it…cunning. They rarely act without purpose. And never give their hearts easily."

Ethan's grin quickly changed to a deep frown. "Are you saying she's just pretending?"

"No. She may very well see in you all that she could want in a mate. Though it occurs to me that she has very little choice in the matter. I mean, who else is there?"

His words did not sit well with Ethan. The idea that Lylinora had only become close to him from lack of options rather than genuine affection was a sharp blow to his pride.

"What can you tell me about my father?" he asked, choosing to change the subject.

"What's to tell?" Renald replied. "He was strong, bold, and often foolish. That's not to say he was stupid. But he acted too swiftly and emotionally."

"Did you get along?"

Renald shrugged. "As well as brothers do, I suppose. We had different ideas regarding magic and how to wield it. And in a mage family, that can cause quite a bit of tension."

"How did you disagree?"

"If I explained it, you wouldn't understand. Not until you've learned more. Praxis was the true embodiment of strength. His use of magic reflected that." He cast a sideways glance at Ethan. "It is your mother who you should seek to emulate. Illyrian was a truly gifted mage, intuitive in ways that your father couldn't comprehend. Where he would send a firestorm to destroy the enemy, she would make them forget why they were fighting in the first place."

As they continued walking, Ethan noticed a small herd of sheep and a few cattle wandering the grassy slopes, as well as a well-tended vegetable garden. He kept up an almost non-stop barrage of questions about both his parents. It soon became clear that Renald had genuine affection for his brother, but even more for Lady Illyrian.

"I'm surprised that you know so little," his uncle remarked. "Jonas should have told you at least some of this."

"Jonas doesn't seem to want to say much," explained Ethan. "He pretends not to know, but I think he does."

"He does indeed," said Renald. "Jonas was quite close to Praxis. Much more so than is usual in a master and servant relationship. Your mother, on the other hand, he did not care for."

Ethan's surprise showed on his face. "Why?" he asked.

"I doubt it was anything personal. But her family was not exactly amongst the most highly regarded. Not that they were of low character.

But they were mostly healers and mystics – caring more for others than for themselves."

"You mean healers weren't well thought of?"

"Healers, yes. Mystics….not so much."

"So what's a mystic exactly?"

"They center their talents on the world around them. Guiding people according to the will of Lumnia."

Ethan furled his brow. "You mean like a fortune-teller?"

Renald laughed. "Most definitely *not* like a bloody fortune-teller. It's a voice. A will. A consciousness. Mystics can hear its call and feel its intent. It guides them. And in turn, they can then guide others."

"Like when I hear the dragon's voice in my head."

"In a way, yes. But this is infinite in its depth and wisdom. The elves understand it. Before Shinzan came, it was what guided their every move. It gave them the power of foresight."

"But didn't the humans and the dwarves defeat them?"

Renald frowned. "If you know a day ahead of time that a man will attack you with a sword, but all you have to fight back with is a stick, knowing what's coming doesn't save you. Elves were not equipped to make war with such people."

"The ones I saw seemed pretty damn capable," he countered. "Everyone I've met so far is scared to death of them."

"That's because everyone you have met so far is an idiot. Elves are not sinister or warlike. And in spite of what you might have been told, they were never the aggressors."

Ethan thought on this. Markus clearly would disagree, having suffered at their hands. But he also remembered how they had allowed him and his friends to live when traveling through the forest on their way to Elyfoss.

"Lylinora told us there was a rumor you lived among them," he said.

"For a time," the old man confirmed. "Though it took almost three years to convince them to permit it."

"Why did you want to?"

"To learn," he replied flatly. "Humans wield magic. Dwarves forge it. But elves…they feel it - deep within their spirit. They are connected to

Lumnia in ways that you and I can scarcely imagine. I wanted to understand that."

"And did you? Understand it, I mean."

Renald sighed. "Sadly no. I had hoped my connection with the dragons would help. But alas, I could never learn to see as an elf does. In the end I gave up and returned home."

At that moment they crested a low rise. Here, the abundant grass and vegetation abruptly ceased. Before them lay a vast expanse of broken earth and jagged rocks. Unlike the shores, not even a few dead trees could be seen to suggest that there had ever been life in this desolate place. Stretching across the horizon was a line of jagged peaks looking uncannily like the shattered grin of a feral beast. Even the air was suddenly changed. It was dry and carrying a hint of sulfur on the almost non-existent breeze.

"This is what Shinzan's power can do," said Renald. "This is what we must prevent."

Ethan was horror-struck at the sight. "He did this with magic?"

"Yes. He scoured this place of all life without a thought or hint of remorse."

"How long did it take him?"

"He hunted the dragons for more than five years before giving up the chase." His tone was a mixture of fury and anguish.

"Aren't you afraid he'll return?"

"No. It's unlikely he'll venture far from his palace any time soon. And none of his minions possess anything like the power it takes to challenge a dragon."

They walked on for another two hours before resting. Ethan could see the fatigue building in Renald with each passing minute. The landscape was unchanging and brutal. He asked where they were going, but received only irritated grunts in reply.

Five hundred years, Ethan thought. How could anyone live alone for so long?

By late afternoon he was growing increasingly concerned that Renald would not be able to walk for much further. On several occasions the old man had halted, his legs wobbling and his face pale. But when Ethan tried to assist him he was pushed away with a strength surprising in one so old.

"It's difficult being so far from my home," Renald explained when finally realizing that Ethan was not going to give up on his attempts to help. "The power that sustains me is centered there. The greater the distance I am away from it, the weaker I become. But it's not important. We're nearly there now."

He pointed off to the northwest. Ethan strained his eyes, but as yet could see nothing. Not even when they veered off the main trail to follow a barely visible path. But then, after they had walked along this for a few minutes, the top of a narrow canyon came into view. The path took them to the very edge of a sheer rock precipice that plunged down more than one hundred feet. Carved into its face was a walkway that zig-zagged all the way to the bottom.

Far below on the canyon floor was a circle of six, tall black pillars, each one crowned with a massive orb. Two orbs were white, two black, one crimson, and one blue. Set within the center of these was an octagonal dais carved from the same black stone as the pillars.

"From here you go alone," said Renald. As if to emphasize his point, he sat down, joints cracking and moaning with relief at finally being able to rest.

"What do I do?" asked Ethan.

"I have no idea," he replied, reaching into his satchel and retrieving an apple. "I suppose you'll find out when you get down there."

Ethan stared into the canyon for a few moments. Something was strangely familiar about this place. Despite its ominous appearance, he felt no fear. In fact, as he took his first step down the canyon wall, a sense of elation washed through him.

The way down was narrow, warning him to be cautious. But so great was his excitement, it took no small effort to restrain himself from bursting into a run.

When he reached the bottom, a low rumbling sound emanated from deep within the earth, shaking the ground beneath Ethan's feet and compelling him to stop. It continued to rise in volume for more than a minute, echoing off the towering rock walls as if the canyon itself was the maw of a great beast poised to snap shut.

Then, as suddenly as it had begun, the rumbling ceased. Ethan approached the pillars with determined strides. The dragons were near. He could feel them – their eyes were watching his every move.

As he walked between the pillars, another, far quieter sound reached him. At first he thought it was distant thunder coming from high above. He looked up but the sky was clear blue, with not even a wisp of cloud to be seen. Then he realized that it was not thunder he was hearing. It was the sound of breathing - immeasurably deep and labored breathing, as though the source was struggling desperately for each gasp of air. He climbed upon the dais and stood in the center, trying to ascertain where it was coming from. He scrutinized the pillars one by one. Then it dawned on him. Looking even closer, he could now see the circumference of each stone expand and contract at regular intervals.

"They're alive," he whispered.

He moved toward the pillar topped with the blue orb, but after only a few steps his legs inexplicably lost all strength and he fell to his knees. Worse still, no matter how hard he tried to stand up again, his legs refused to support him. With no other means of movement available, he crawled back to the center of the dais. Instantly, his strength returned.

Panic was now starting to creep in. Trapped. But why? Surely the dragons didn't bring him all this way simply to make him a prisoner. Gazing up the side of the canyon, he called out to Renald. His voice echoed repeatedly, but there was no response. He called again.

Barely had the echoes of his second call faded when a wall of fire shot skyward, completely surrounding the dais in a hellish inferno. With the sudden heat threatening to roast him alive, all Ethan could do was curl up into a ball and shield his face as much as possible. As he lay there, even above the loud roar of the flames, he heard the booming thud of something massive landing on the stone floor of the canyon.

His flesh was bubbling into tiny blisters, the pain covering him like a swarm of angry wasps. Then, just when he felt he could stand no more, a soft feminine voice whispered into his ear.

"Dragonvein."

He peeked out from behind his hands. No one was there.

"Dragonvein," it repeated. "We need you."

"Please, make it stop," was all he could manage to say.

But the heat only intensified.

"Coward!" thundered a different voice, this one masculine and coarse.

"No!" cried Ethan. "I'm not."

He felt a slender hand touch his shoulder. "We are here. And we believe in you. Show them. Show them who you are."

This voice was kind and compassionate. It reminded him of his mother when he was a small boy. He could see her kindly face looking down at him with the love and affection that only a mother can give. It bolstered his courage.

"Let go of your fears, young Dragonvein," the voice continued. "We are here. Our power is yours. Use it. Save yourself. Save *us*."

Inspired by these words to shut out the pain, Ethan removed his hands from his face. By now, the wall of fire had closed in to the very edge of the dais. But that no longer mattered. He reached out, although whether it was actually with his hand or just in his mind, he couldn't be certain. Whichever it was, there was no mistaking the ball of light that blinked into existence just above his palm. At once, his flesh cooled and the blisters subsided. This was not magic. Not in the way he had come to understand it. No. This was something else. Something far more intimate.

Suddenly filled with confidence, he stepped down from the dais and into the flames. The ball of light expanded to wrap itself protectively around him. Moments later, with a great sucking of air, the flames vanished. More than that, the pillars were now gone, replaced by the very creatures he had come seeking. The dragons.

In general form, they were all similar to the dragon that had come to his aid on the mountain when fleeing Elyfoss, though with slight variations in size. Two were white, two black, one crimson, and one sapphire blue. Each was in a position that corresponded to the color of the orb that had rested atop the pillar.

Ethan's eyes focused on the black dragon directly in front of him.

Though the one next to it was virtually identical, he knew that this was the one who had come to save him. He bowed his head in a gesture of thanks. The mammoth creature blew out a huff of steaming hot air and lowered its head.

"I'm impressed," came a voice from the dais.

Ethan turned. There stood a young woman in her early twenties wearing a plain tan skirt and white cotton blouse. Her straight auburn hair was clipped neatly at her shoulders, perfectly framing the delicate features of her face. She gave him a welcoming smile and beckoned for him to come closer.

He hesitated for a moment. Not out of fear, but out of awe. He knew her. He was sure of it. He even knew her name.

"Heather," he said, as much to himself as to her.

"Yes, my dearest," she replied. "I am so very happy to see you at last."

Her voice was musical, yet bore a certain authority that told him she was a person of great importance. And though attractive, she possessed something far more than mere physical beauty. It radiated from her spirit and descended upon everything around her.

Ethan was drawn to her in a way he had never experienced before. It was love. Pure love. As effortless and natural as the love a child has for its mother, though even this seemed an inadequate way to describe what he was now experiencing. Even after having emerged from a raging inferno and being surrounded by dragons, all he could see was Heather's face. They were connected to each other. He knew this for certain. He could feel it deep within his heart.

"Are...are you real?" he asked.

She laughed softly. "Of course I am. Do I not look real?"

He gave a flushed smile and scrambled up to stand in front of her. Her skin was flawless ivory, and her movements ethereal as she folded her hands across her waist.

"Do you know who I am?" she asked.

Ethan struggled to contain an impulse to reach out and touch her hand. "Yes. Your name is Heather."

"It is indeed," she affirmed. "Though I was called Ariki in the old language. But regardless of that, my name is not *who* I am."

A cold spear stabbed at his heart when he heard her telling him that he was wrong.

Her features softened and her smile became even warmer than before. "It's all right. No need to be embarrassed. I did not come here to scold you."

This reassurance boosted his confidence. "I'm sorry. I don't know what's come over me. When I look at you, I feel…" His words trailed off, unable to express the tempest of emotions steadily growing inside him.

"You feel eager to please," she said, though without judgement in her tone. "You feel you know me. You feel inexplicable love."

Ethan nodded. "Yes, that's it! Exactly."

"All of our line who come to me feel this way at first. It's a consequence of my place in our history. It will pass."

Ethan looked at her more closely. *My place in our history.* These words echoed in his head. "You're Heather Dragonvein!" he exclaimed. "*You* were the first."

She nodded approvingly. "Very good. Most take a little longer to understand. I was the very first of our family to make a true connection with the dragons. Since then, all of my children, and their children's children down through the centuries have retained that connection because of what I did long ago."

"So you're not…alive?"

"If you are asking if I live as you do, then I suppose the answer is no. Did not Renald explain anything before he brought you here?"

Ethan glanced up the side of the canyon. "He hasn't said very much at all. I get the feeling he is somehow disappointed with me."

"Ah, poor Renald. I imagine he hoped for you to be a fully trained mage."

Heather glanced over to her left; a blue light flashed, out of which a pair of plush chairs materialized. She sat, and offered Ethan to do the same.

"You want to know what I really am?"

He nodded and took a seat.

"A spirit is the best way to put it, I suppose. All those of my bloodline, once they depart the mortal world, reside within the essence of the dragons. They have kept us with them for thousands of years."

"Are you trapped?" asked Ethan.

Heather laughed. "Of course not. We are not prisoners. Should any of us choose, we can be released and our spirits would scatter into the void."

"You mean you'd stop...existing?"

Heather shrugged. "Truthfully, I have no idea. I am contented though, and can see no reason to risk oblivion."

"How are you able to be here?"

"The power of the dragons created this place. Here, and only here, can I take on a physical form. Though I must admit, it is not something I enjoy. I prefer to dwell among my kin."

Seeing the confusion and doubt on Ethan's face, she paused for a moment. "One day you will join us. Then you will understand. But for now, there are things you must see. And much for you to learn. You are the last hope for Lumnia to survive."

Closing her eyes, she leaned her head back. The light in the canyon began to distort and ripple, much like heat rising from a sun baked earth. Ethan blinked in wonder as slowly the world around him melted away and he found himself gazing upon a vast expanse of rolling hills at the edge of a snow capped mountain range.

"Long ago, this was my home," Heather told him. A tiny smile lingered on her lips as she surveyed the scene.

Ethan rose from his chair and walked to the edge of the dais.

"Do not step off," she warned. "If you do, the spell will be broken."

He backed away a few paces. "How long ago exactly?"

Heather gave a wistful laugh. "My dear boy. Even *I* have lost count of the years. My people came here in search of game. The winters of the north had been increasingly brutal, and by the time we arrived there was only a small fraction of us still alive. It was a hard time."

Ethan continued studying the landscape. There was something eerily familiar about it. "Where is this?" he asked.

"Why Earth, of course," she replied.

Ethan's eyes went wide. But before he could speak, the sound of voices seized his attention. Over to his right, six people were approaching. The four men had thick, unkempt beards and wild hair. The two women were a bit more neatly groomed – but not by much. They all wore crudely fashioned pants and shirts made from animal hides and were wrapped in thick furs. The men carried long, flint-tipped spears, while the women had large woven baskets strapped across their backs.

As they drew near, Ethan recognized one of the women. It was Heather. He looked back. Her eyes were distant as she gazed nostalgically at her former self.

"Not exactly pretty, was I?" she said playfully. "But of course, we didn't have much time for beauty."

Ethan was speechless. The way they were dressed. And the weapons they carried. The implications were mind-blowing. He turned his attention back to the oncoming group.

A short man with thick shoulders and stumpy legs grunted disdainfully. "You go where you want. I don't trust them. Demons is what they are, I tell you."

A taller man with jet black hair sneered. "You'd rather die in the cold? I don't care if they are demons. They promise us food and safety. No more scavenging and stealing. No more running."

The short man waved his hand. "Go then. No one is stopping you."

Instead of replying, the tall man's eyes shifted across to Heather. This did not go unnoticed by his companion, who laughed scornfully.

"I think we should concentrate on getting home," Heather cut in quickly. "We're not supposed to be hunting here. If we're caught..."

"Hunting?" scoffed the short man. "We haven't seen a deer – or even a rabbit – in days."

"All the more reason to hurry," she countered. "There's food back home. And I'm hungry."

The tall man reached into a small leather satchel tied to his belt and retrieved a handful of blueberries. "I have these if you want them," he offered.

Heather smiled and shook her head. "No, thank you. Save them for later."

The other woman was not slow to react. Letting out a loud huff, she snatched the berries from his still outstretched hand. "I'll take them if you won't," she said, shoving the entire bunch unceremoniously into her mouth. Juices dripped sloppily from her lips as she moaned with delight.

"And I'll go with you to Lumnia if you want," she continued, even though her mouth was still full and her words muffled.

The tall man frowned. "You already have a mate."

She gave a shrug and sniffed contemptuously. "Since he hurt his leg he can't hunt. So what good is he? Besides, we have no children. He doesn't have any claim on me."

"He's my brother," the man snapped back with a flash of anger. "And you will watch what you say to me about him."

The woman looked at him impassively, wiping the juice from her chin. "I'm only speaking the truth. If he doesn't recover, what should I do? Stay with him and starve?"

"He'll be fine," he insisted. "You just keep your mind on helping him...and off anything else."

At this point, the scene became hazy.

"I never did like Kimma," Heather remarked.

Ethan turned, still awestruck by what he had witnessed and desperate to know more. "Did the brother die?"

Heather sighed and nodded. "Less than a week later. Tam – that's the tall one - had hoped the dwarves could help. It was rumored they could cure any illness and heal any wound. But there was no way to get his brother to them in time."

Ethan figured this must have been during the time the dwarves were recruiting humans to fight against the elves. "So you and Tam came to Lumnia after that?"

Her countenance darkened. "No. Tam wasn't with me."

The haze cleared.

Ethan could now see Heather climbing through an outcropping of rocks, a reed basket over her shoulder. She bent down and reached into a crevice, pulling out a small clutch of eggs one by one. She smiled as she placed them carefully in the basket.

"Another bribe for Tam?" called a voice from behind a gnarled oak. Kimma stepped out, a sinister grin etched on her face.

"What do you want?" Heather demanded, pulling the basket close to her chest.

"For you to leave Tam alone," she replied. "I'm the better choice, and you know it."

Heather sniffed. "I think he can decide *that* for himself. Now get the hell out of here. I'm not in the mood for your nonsense."

Kimma hopped nimbly over the rugged ground until only a few feet separated them. She peered into the basket. "A nice find. Surely you intend to share them."

"They're not for you," Heather told her sharply, taking a step back.

Undeterred, Kimma moved in closer. "Do you really think you can beat me? I have two brothers and a sister to help provide. What can you offer? Nothing. All of your family are dead. And you want to know why? Because they were weak. Weak and stupid, just like you. Why would Tam want anything to do with *you*?"

Tears welled up in Heather's eyes; her hands were trembling with fury. She wanted to strike the woman, but that would mean dropping her precious cargo of eggs.

Encouraged by this apparent reluctance to fight back, Kimma continued with her taunts. "You know that the others all want you to leave, don't you? Everyone knows that you're the one telling Tam he should go to the dwarves. In fact, I wouldn't be surprised if they forced you out before long."

Heather locked eyes with her tormentor, her tears suddenly gone. "I'm only going to say this one time, you bitch: Get the hell away from me."

This sudden injection of steel in her voice warned Kimma of the danger she would be in if she stayed around for very much longer. "What a pity," she remarked, looking again at the eggs. "I'm sure Tam would have really thanked you for those." Her hand then shot out, pulling hard at the edge of the basket. Without waiting to see the result of her attack, she spun around and ran for all she was worth.

Jerked sharply forward on the sloping and jagged ground, Heather struggled for several seconds to keep her footing. There was a sickening feeling in the pit of her stomach as she heard the crunch of eggshells striking stone. Though she had managed to hold on to the basket throughout, Kimma had ripped it almost completely apart.

After recovering her balance, she stared down hopelessly at the ruined eggs. Not a single one had survived. It was true she had intended them as a gift for Tam, though not as a bribe the way Kimma had suggested. He loved her, and she him. But now her surprise was ruined. She threw down the basket and let out a furious scream. Tears of frustration began falling.

Ethan glanced back. Heather appeared unemotional while watching herself - merely taking a long breath and leaning back in her chair.

"Is that why you left?" he asked.

She furled her brow. "I left because of Kimma. But not because she could ever take Tam away from me. He hated her and blamed her for the death of his brother. So even without me there, he would never have accepted her." She flicked a hand. "Anyway, watch on. You're about to see why I left."

Ethan returned his attention to the vision. Heather was still kneeling beside the shattered eggs, though she had now stopped weeping. She wiped her face on her sleeve and stood up straight, squaring her shoulders and forcing out a loud breath. With her resolve firmed, she set off over a high pile of rocks to renew her search.

After less than a quarter mile, she found her way barred by a sheer stone wall. The facing was smooth – unusually so for a natural formation – and she could find no hand or footholds to scale the obstruction. Just when she was about to give up and turn back, she spotted a small fissure at the base. It was just about wide enough to squeeze through.

Heather knelt to peer inside. The opening stretched back for at least ten feet, though a light at the far end told her she could make it all the way through if she wanted to. Pulling a flint knife from her belt, she crawled inside. It was a tight fit, and she could not avoid scraping against the surrounding rock faces. Dust and debris immediately began swirling around in the confined space, stinging her eyes and forcing a rapid succession of coughs and wheezes. But she had made her choice. There was now little option but to keep going.

Progress was slow, but at last she emerged at the other end, still coughing and spitting out mouthfuls of dirt. She tossed her knife aside to wipe furiously at her eyes and face. After blinking several times, she looked up to survey her surroundings.

At once, her jaw fell slack. She was inside a huge circular enclosure roughly one-hundred and fifty feet in diameter; its thirty-foot high walls were covered in millions of purple crystals. Caught by the sun shining down from directly overhead, their millions of brilliant facets rippled and twinkled like a sunset on a purple sea.

"Who could create such a thing?" she gasped.

A large object off to her left caught the corner of her eye. Instinctively, she scrambled for her knife, but her heart sank as she saw that it was now broken in half after hitting the ground. She looked up. Fear instantly seized her.

There lay a beast of such size that it could only be one thing. Her mind wanted to reject what she was seeing. Dragons were said to be long dead - cast into the realm of myth and legend. But her eyes were not mistaken. The creature's silver scales shimmered from the rays of purple light reflecting from the encompassing wall. Nearly forty feet long, and with onyx spines running down the length of its back, it was every bit the monster the ancient stories had described.

Terror stricken, she bolted blindly to the opposite side of the enclosure, slamming her back hard against it. Dozens of sharp crystals dug into her flesh, but this was barely felt. In an instant she realized that she had just made a grievous error. The fissure through which she'd entered had been right beside her. Now it was fifty or more yards away. She cursed herself for her stupidity.

It was then she noticed that the dragon had not made any movements. Its eyes were shut, and as far as she could tell, it was not even breathing. As silently as she could, she tiptoed back toward the opening. Once there, she wriggled inside, feet first, until only her head was poking out.

For a time Heather remained in this position, her eyes fixed on the great beast. But it never so much as flinched. Eventually, she crawled back out and took a few tentative steps forward.

"I must be insane," she whispered.

Ethan turned. "Why would you do that?"

Heather laughed. "Because I was a little fool. And in love with Tam. I thought that if I could bring back a tooth or a claw he would be pleased. And it would give him added status among our people. Dragon relics were quite valuable.

"So they were all dead?"

"Mostly," she replied. "There were rumors that some still lived in distant lands. But no one I had known had ever seen one."

"What killed them?"

She spread her hands. "Who knows? The world was changing. Perhaps they could not adapt. It's a secret they've kept...even from me."

Back in the crystal enclosure, Heather picked up the sharp end of her broken knife and approached the body of the dragon. For several minutes she simply stood there, scrutinizing the creature, then cautiously reached out to touch its scales with the tip of her finger. They were iron hard. She frowned. Even if she had an unbroken knife to use, cutting off any part of such a massive beast would seem impossible. The spines were far too thick, and she couldn't build up sufficient courage to touch anywhere near its mouth.

Unable to think of anything else, she bent down beside its front claw and dug her blade into the surrounding flesh. At first it was like trying to pierce stone. She pressed harder, and then her hand slipped, slicing a gash across her palm. The suddenness of the pain drew a loud hiss.

She clenched her fist as blood trickled through her fingers and onto the silver flesh of the dragon. She considered tearing a piece from her shirt to bind the wound with, but after a moment rejected the idea. Clothing was far too difficult to make just to damage it over a minor cut. Instead, she shook her hand loosely and then wiped the blood on her trousers until the worst of it was stemmed.

Still determined to claim her present for Tam if at all possible, she delved into the satchel attached to her belt and found another, much smaller knife, with which she continued digging into the dragon's hide.

Although this blade seemed even less suitable for the task than its big brother, at least it had a dull end and there was no risk of further injury.

"Just one scale, damn you," she grumbled.

Finally, through sheer perseverance, her efforts paid off and she felt the tip of the flint sink in slightly. Grinning with satisfaction, she began sawing and pulling to make the incision bigger. The creature's blood seeped out and was soon covering her hands. But then, just as she felt she was really getting somewhere, a terrible awareness dawned. Heather stopped short. She backed away, trembling and with eyes wide.

"You're...you're still alive," she stammered. She raised her palm and looked where the dragon's blood had entered her wound. "What did you do to me?"

The dragon's eyes peeled open, revealing two emerald green orbs. As it lifted its head to face her, a blast of hot breath issued from its nostrils, blowing her hair back and searing her face red.

She clenched shut her bloodied hand. "I can...hear you."

The creature let out a low gurgling growl.

"I'm sorry," Heather said. "I didn't mean to...I mean, I thought you were...dead."

In response, the dragon closed its eyes and, with an obviously supreme effort, rolled its massive bulk over to one side. Beneath her belly was a hole carved into the surface of the ground, inside which were a dozen, fist-sized, powder blue eggs.

In utter shock, Heather took a step back. Her hands shot up to cover her ears and she doubled over, screaming at the top of her voice. "No! It's too much! Stop! Please!" She fell to her knees, shaking her head violently. "Please!"

Heedless of her distress, the dragon lifted its head skyward to let out a tremendous roar. The sound reverberated back and forth within the confining walls with ear-splitting intensity. All Heather could do was squeeze her eyes tightly shut until the sound had fully dissipated. Only then did she slowly remove her hands from her ears and stand up. The dragon's eyes were closed and it was no longer moving.

After a few moments of hesitation, she walked up and touched it on its snout, bowing her head. Tears began to flow until her whole body was shuddering from the sobbing. Then, after a few minutes, the emotional release was complete. She wiped her eyes and knelt beside the eggs.

Ethan was transfixed. Only when the vision blurred did he turn back. "What did it say to you?"

"I wish I knew," she replied. "It was too confusing. When our blood mingled, a part of her went into me. But I wasn't ready for it. All I could understand was that she was desperate to protect her young and begging for my help."

"So did you help her?"

She looked at him with a guilty expression. "No. At least, not at first. After the dragon died, I ran home as fast as I could to tell Tam what had happened. He made me promise not to go back."

Ethan frowned. "Why? Didn't you say that dragon relics were valuable?"

"Indeed they were. But he was afraid for me. Dragons were looked upon as evil creatures and bad omens. It was said that to even dream about a dragon meant someone close to you would die. You see, Kimma was right about one thing. The people of my tribe didn't want me and Tam to be together. They saw her as a much better match. Tam feared that word of my encounter would give them an excuse to drive me away."

"So what did you do?"

"Nothing at first. But every night after that, my dreams were troubled. All I could hear was the spirit of the dragon calling for me to return and rescue her young. After a few days, I even began hearing her when I was awake."

Ethan nodded. "I know what that's like. I used to hear the same thing before I got here. It nearly drove me insane."

Heather laughed. "Yes, they are certainly persistent. And needless to say, I eventually did go back."

Again, the haze cleared. Heather emerged from the crack in the rock face and moved across the enclosure to where the dragon's body was still laying. In her right hand she held a leather bag. Her face was tortured, and there were dark circles under her eyes.

She half stumbled a couple of times before plopping herself down beside the eggs. For nearly half an hour she sat motionless, staring at them. Eventually, an exasperated grunt slipped out.

"What am I doing here?" she hissed angrily. "I should have listened to Tam."

Despite her self-recrimination and doubts, she reached down to pick up the first egg. The instant her fingers made contact, her back straightened and she let out a tiny gasp. It was amazing. She could feel the life dwelling within. Feel its tiny heart beating fiercely. Its very essence clinging to life - fighting for survival.

"I knew you were up to something," came a voice from behind.

Heather jumped with surprise and turned her head. So mesmerized had she been by what she was feeling, she hadn't noticed Kimma entering the enclosure. Her rival was now watching her every move with arms folded tightly across her chest and a smug grin on her face.

"You...you followed me?" Heather gasped. As quickly as she dared, she placed the egg back with the others and shifted her body, hoping to block them from view.

"They'll make you leave for sure now," Kimma said, venom dripping from each word.

Heather's hand slid to her belt where she kept her knife.

Kimma sneered. "You think I'm stupid? My brothers are waiting just outside."

A short, tense silence followed as Heather listened for any sound of the two men drifting in through the opening. None reached her. So there was a chance that Kimma might be lying. But if she wasn't, and something bad happened to her, Heather knew she would certainly be killed and the eggs destroyed. And now that she had felt the life inside them, there was no way she could allow such a thing to happen.

"What do you want?" she asked, trying hard to keep her tone steady.

Kimma gave a sarcastic laugh. "You know full well what I want. You...gone from our tribe." She leaned to one side to peer around Heather. "And I'll take those eggs."

Heather sprang to her feet. "You can't have them!"

"Is that right?"

Kimma strode confidently forward to collect her prize. But Heather blocked her path and shoved her hard back.

The furious woman glared at her. "Get out of my way," she demanded. "Or would you rather deal with my brothers?"

"You're not having them," Heather repeated, her voice hard as steel and her hands balled into tiny fists. "I'll leave. But you're not getting those eggs."

Once again Kimma tried to push her way past. This time, Heather's fist shot out, landing solidly on Kimma's jaw. She staggered back, holding her chin.

"You're possessed," she cried out, her voice trembling with fury. "The dragons...they've possessed you. You'll burn for this. I swear it." Spinning on her heels, she started back toward the opening.

With a feeling of desperation, Heather knew she was right. Kimma could easily convince the tribe that the dragon had possessed her. And if Tam came to her defense, they might easily kill him as well. The decision was made in an instant. Reaching for her knife, she chased after her.

Kimma heard the rapidly approaching footfalls and burst into a dead run. But the crack in the rock face was too low, forcing her to stop and drop almost flat. This gave Heather all the time she needed.

Grabbing Kimma by the ankle, she raised the knife. But Kimma wasn't going without a fight. Rolling quickly over onto her back, she kicked up with her free leg at Heather's face. Heather managed to shift her head out of the way, but the kick still caught her on the shoulder, sending her back and forcing her to release her grip.

Kimma again scrambled desperately for the opening, screaming out the names of her brothers as she went. But Heather was already resuming the attack. This time she didn't bother grabbing hold of her opponent. Instead, she simply fell forward with the knife outstretched. The flint blade sunk in just below Kimma's left buttock, causing her to jolt violently.

By now, the escaping woman had managed to get her head inside the opening. But it was too little, and much too late. Heather struck again, this time sinking the knife deep into the center of her back. At once, Kimma stopped struggling. Her shrill cries turned to weak whimpers as she lay face down and helpless.

Heather rose to her feet and pulled her fully back into the enclosure. "P…please…" was all Kimma could manage to choke out

Regret and fear seized Heather's heart. What had she done? Her hands were shaking so badly, she was barely able to retain her hold on the knife. But she had gone too far. There could be no turning back now.

Straddling her rival, she squeezed her eyes shut. Her heart was thundering in her ears; her breaths were coming in quick, panicky gasps. She tried to calm herself, but the reality of what she had done made such a feat impossible.

Raising the knife, she opened her eyes. Kimma had turned her head to one side and was now weeping uncontrollably. For just a moment, Heather weakened. Then she thought about the eggs; she must protect them at all costs. This firmed her resolve. With a swift decisive stroke, she plunged the tip of her blade into Kimma's exposed temple. There was a sickening crunch of skull being shattered, quickly followed by a spurt of blood. Heather grimaced at the sight, turning her head quickly away.

Getting to her feet, she hurried over to the eggs. Carefully, she gathered them into her sack and crawled into the opening.

Fearing that Kimma's brothers would be waiting by the entrance, she emerged cautiously. A loud sigh of relief slipped out on discovering that no one was there. Better still, it seemed they were obviously not anywhere within earshot. Had they been, the commotion of the fight would have carried clearly through the fissure and alerted them.

She eventually came across the pair sleeping under a birch tree about a quarter mile from the enclosure, the bones of a recent meal scattered on the ground between them. For now, they were completely oblivious that their sister had been murdered. And the entrance to the enclosure was not easy to spot, so finding Kimma's body would take time. Of course, it was possible she had shown it to them before entering, but even that possibility was not disastrous. Heather doubted very much that either of the two large men could fit through the narrow opening. This gave her precious time.

The light vanished, replaced by a swirling mass of fog. Looking back at Heather, Ethan could see from her expression that she had been deeply affected by the scene. He took a seat and waited patiently until she blinked several times and forced a smile.

"Forgive me," she said, bowing her head slightly. "I have not witnessed that in many years. It was the only time I have ever taken a life."

"I understand," he said. "If you'd rather not continue…"

She held up her hand. "I'm fine. But there's not much more to tell. I was unable to return home, and deeply afraid to tell Tam what had happened. So I ran. Eventually, I found the dwarves and brought the eggs to Lumnia. Soon after that, they hatched and thrived. And because of the power which resides here, our connection was made far stronger."

"Were there mages in Lumnia when you first arrived?" Ethan asked.

"No. Not yet. Humans were only just discovering magic. Our family was one of the first. And through our bond with the dragons, we were made quite powerful." She rose to her feet. "The Dragonvein family history is rich and filled with adventure. One day you may have the chance to hear it all – though the telling would take many years."

She walked to the edge of the dais. The fog lifted, revealing the six dragons – all of them staring at Ethan with severe intensity.

"I was given the gift through the transference of blood," she continued. "It has bound me to the dragons, and them to me, for thousands of years. When the first dragons were born in Lumnia, they formed a deep relationship with its spirit. Over time, they have become its guardians. Dragons feel the will of Lumnia every bit as much as the elves, and they live in harmony with its power. But now…Lumnia is dying. And with it, all who dwell here."

"How is Shinzan able to do this?" Ethan asked her.

Heather's expression dimmed. "He is not of this world. Shinzan – if that is the name you prefer to use – is a parasite. He seeks to drain

Lumnia of all its energy - to feed upon it. If he is not stopped soon then he will become too powerful for anyone to challenge."

A feeling of helplessness came over Ethan as the immensity of his task unfolded. "So how am I supposed to beat him? I'm not a mage yet. And it will take years for me to learn. Can't you fight him?"

"I cannot," she replied. "I have no power beyond this place. My spirit resides on another plane – within the souls of the dragons. Of course, should Shinzan prevail and the dragons are destroyed, I, along with our entire family, will be destroyed as well."

She leaned forward to touch his hand. Her flesh felt as silk, and was far warmer than he would have expected. "You are the last of us with the power to triumph. But you need not fight alone." With feline grace, she rose from her chair and walked to the edge of the dais.

Ethan followed and stood beside her. The magnificence of the dragons was spectacular. Raw power radiated from their bodies as if an inferno coursed through their blood. Their eyes were still fixed resolutely on him.

"What do they want me to do?" he asked.

"Simply put, they want you to save them." She lifted her arm in a grand sweeping motion. "They have sacrificed themselves in the hope that you can do as I did so long ago."

"Sacrificed themselves?"

Sorrow washed over her as she gave a slight nod. "Yes. Shinzan's seat of power is in his palace. It is from there that he infests the very core of Lumnia. The dragons have chosen to make a stand against him. Even now, they fight to halt his progress. This will force Shinzan to remain close to his source of power. But in doing so it will drain their lives... utterly."

A chill seized Ethan's heart. The thought of such marvelous creatures willingly giving up their own lives was almost more than he could bear. He wanted to cry out. To tell them to stop. To save themselves. But he knew they would not. Though the voice of the dragon no longer echoed in his mind, he could still feel their will.

He bowed his head, tears dropping onto the onyx floor. "What *is* the source?"

"We don't know," she admitted. "But to defeat Shinzan, it must be destroyed." She placed her hand on his shoulder. "But do not feel sorrow. The dragons have come here to ensure their kind lives on. They die so that others might live. And they do this gladly. Through you they will once again thrive. Just as I once saved them…so shall you."

Ethan looked up again to meet Heather's gaze. "Tell me what I have to do."

Barely had he finished speaking when there was a flash of light. From within this, a silver chalice and a small ivory handled dagger appeared at the feet of the black dragon Ethan had encountered on the mountain.

"You must acquire our strength," she explained. "And through the blood of the dragons you shall. Just as my blood once bonded me to them, they will now strengthen their bond with you beyond that of any Dragonvein before you."

A feeling of awe engulfed Ethan. "What will happen to me?" he asked.

Heather took a step back. "That is for you to find out."

In response to his searching look, she simply smiled and pointed to the dagger and chalice. He took a long breath and squared his shoulders. Courage, he told himself.

He jumped down from the dais. Heather's form had become misty, though her bright smile was still clearly visible. "Will I see you again?"

"Oh, I should say so," she replied, a hint of mirth in her tone.

Ethan approached the dragon, gazing into its penetrating blue eyes. After a minute or so, he picked up the dagger and chalice. At first, the idea of piercing the creature's flesh revolted him. But then he felt a great wave of reassurance which he knew instinctively that it was coming from the dragon. He closed his eyes and reached out with his thoughts.

"Raknifar," he said. "Your name is Raknifar." He opened his eyes and smiled.

The dragon lowered its head almost imperceptibly and raised its massive leg, offering it to Ethan. He pressed the blade down just above one of the dragon's talons, drawing it swiftly across. The scales slit apart easily, allowing deep crimson blood to pour from the wound, directly into the chalice he had positioned below. Just as the level was about to spill over, the wound sealed itself shut and the bleeding stopped.

After taking a few steps back, Ethan raised the chalice to his lips. The moment the hot liquid began pouring down his throat, all six dragons lifted their heads skyward. In unison, each one let out a tremendous roar, the combined volume of which shook the very ground.

Ethan drained the cup and dropped to his knees – the intensity of the dragon's call seeming a mere whisper in his ears. The world around him began to grow dark until he was in a complete void. Then, a distant pinprick of light pierced the darkness. He watched calmly as it moved closer. Eventually, he saw the face of Heather Dragonvein materialize. She was smiling warmly.

He returned her smile. "I understand now," he told her. "Thank you."

She gave no reply, only a faint nod of approval. Her aspect faded, to be replaced by another kindly face. Then another appeared, and another. He had seen them all before. It was the same as when he had touched the dragon for the first time. Only this time he understood. Now he knew who these people were – each and every one of them. They were his ancestors. Thousands of generations of Dragonvein's, living together and appearing with just one purpose in mind. To give him strength.

Their minds continued swirling around him in a tempest of pure thought until he could no longer distinguish one ancestor from another. Finally, with a rush, they merged together into one massive ball of spiritual power.

Ethan knew what he had to do. Reaching out, he embraced them all as a single entity, drawing their essence deep inside his own. He could feel their power - their immense knowledge. It was a combination of countless lifetimes: pain, joy, love and hate, all forming a barely contained maelstrom that was now living inside him.

He opened his eyes. The dragons were frozen in place, their heads lowered and their eyes shut. They would not move again…ever.

Ethan pushed himself to his feet. "I will not fail you," he promised the silent giants.

He then looked inside himself to where his family now dwelled.

"None of you," he added.

CHAPTER EIGHTEEN

IT WAS WELL past dusk by the time Ethan climbed back out of the canyon. The far distant howls and shrill cries of some unknown creature carried on the cool gentle breeze. He wondered what manner of beast could survive in this desolate land. Something terrible and vicious, he thought. But it made little difference. Whatever it was, it was not coming any closer. The idea of such danger might have unnerved him before. But not now. He was a completely changed person.

Renald was leaning against a large rock, humming softly while fiddling with his beard. He glanced up at Ethan and smiled. "You look... different."

He returned the smile before taking a seat beside the old man. "I *am* different."

Renald nodded with keen understanding. "What did she say?"

Ethan leaned back on his elbows and shut his eyes. "Nothing. Everything." He began to laugh softly. "I know what I must do. For the first time in my life, things are perfectly clear."

"In what way?"

"I finally know who I am." He opened his eyes and sat up straight. "I have a true purpose."

Renald's eyes narrowed. "And just what *is* your purpose?"

"To save them...and us." A rush of emotions coursed through Ethan's heart like a sudden gale. He gasped as visions of his destiny rushed uninvited through his mind. Slowly he forced them out. "*That* will take getting used to," he said quietly to himself.

Renald leaned in, regarding Ethan carefully. "What happened down there?"

He cocked his head. "Don't you know?" But the confused expression on the old man's face gave him his answer. "I'm sorry. I assumed that you...well...I assumed that when *you* came here you would have..." He stopped short for a moment, then burst into laughter, ridiculing his own stupidity. "Of course you wouldn't. Why would you?"

An ill-tempered frown formed on Renald's face. "I'm too old and tired for games and riddles. Just tell me what happened to you."

Ethan held up his hand. "Of course. I apologize."

He began unfurling his blankets, handing one to Renald while recounting his experience in detail. His uncle could only listen in sheer disbelief. Even when Ethan had finished, he was still unable to speak.

"And to think how long ago that was," Ethan said. "From what I remember at school, it must have been at least twenty thousand years ago...maybe more. Judging by their weapons and clothes, I'm guessing more."

Renald finally snapped out of his stupor. "You...drank their blood?"

"It was the only way," he explained. "It wasn't that bad. A bit salty."

"To hell with what it tasted like," Renald exclaimed. "You took their blood into you. No one has ever done that. No one."

Ethan turned his head and smiled. "Not true. Heather did. Though she didn't drink it. But it's how we are connected. Through blood."

"What does it feel like?" The old man was now sounding more like a curious child than a legendary mage.

"Strange. I can feel them. Our family, I mean. I can feel their thoughts. But it's like looking through a thick fog. Nothing is defined. It's all sort of out of focus."

"Do you possess their memories?"

"In a way," he replied. "Nothing specific. Just impressions really. But then I'm trying not to concentrate on it. It's too confusing."

"And the dragons?"

Ethan's face darkened. "There are no more dragons. Their voice is all but gone. Maytra is the last."

This had Renald instantly on his feet. He strode to the canyon edge and pointed down. "What do you mean, there are no more? I can see them right there."

"You may be able to see them, but they are dead to the world now," Ethan told him. "They are keeping Shinzan at bay. Forcing him to stay near the source of his power. Battling as we speak for the heart of Lumnia. And when Shinzan is gone, they will all die."

Renald shook his head violently, his long hair and beard flailing wildly. "No! This cannot be. I won't accept it."

"There's nothing we can do. They have made this sacrifice. It was their choice."

He watched as the old man paced back and forth, throwing his arms in the air and letting out incoherent screams. Ethan closed his eyes, allowing the vision of what he must do next to enter his mind. He wanted to tell Renald the truth. But there was too much at stake.

"You drank their blood," his uncle hissed accusingly. "You know how precious they are to our family...to this world."

Ethan nodded. "I know that more than anyone. Even you."

"Then you know we mustn't allow them to die."

The pleading, desperate expression on the old mage's face moved Ethan to give him at least a small measure of comfort. He considered his next words carefully. "They *will* die. Nothing can change that now. But I promise you that their deaths will not be the end of dragon kind."

The reaction was immediate. "What do you mean?" Renald demanded. "Tell me!"

Ethan shook his head. "I can't tell you more. You just have to trust me when I say that if we defeat Shinzan, the dragons *will* return."

The old man met his eyes silently for a full minute. "I believe you," he finally said, lowering his head. "What must we do now?"

"Sleep," he replied. "I'm tired."

Reluctantly, Renald settled down on his blanket. "Is there nothing more you say?"

"Only that I will need your help to succeed," Ethan replied.

He closed his eyes. He could still taste the dragon's blood on his tongue. And now he could hear the past generations of his family all speaking at once like a faint echo in the far corners of his mind. So many voices. All a part of him. And all would be silenced forever should he fail.

Such enormous weight of responsibility would have crushed the Ethan Martin of a short time ago. Even Airborne training and front line combat had not prepared him for anything like this. However, all that changed the moment the dragon's blood passed his lips. Any remnants of doubt had instantly vanished.

Yes, it was Ethan Martin, a raw kid from Brooklyn who had ventured into that canyon.

But it was Lord Ethan Dragonvein of Lumnia who had emerged.

CHAPTER NINETEEN

LORD VRAYLIC'S BREATH hung in the chill atmosphere as he stood at the threshold of the main Imperial throne room. Forewarned by others, he had thought to wrap himself in a thick winter cape before setting out. Large crimson pools of frozen blood were scattered haphazardly about the spacious chamber, a testament to the Emperor's foul and often unpredictable mood.

The throne was empty. Experience told him that this was not a good sign. It meant the Emperor could be anywhere. Even standing behind him. The hair on his neck prickled. When Shinzan played games, the loser usually died. And Shinzan *never* lost.

He took a step forward, his eyes darting from side to side. "Your Majesty?"

His voice reverberated from the walls for a split second before falling abruptly silent, as if the cold air had consumed the sound.

He continued toward the throne with slow, uneasy paces. He called out again, but still there was no reply. He could almost feel his death approaching. He had heard the stories. Shinzan liked to toy with those he deemed deserving of death. But what did I do wrong, he agonized? I'm just a supply officer. But he knew this was ridiculous. The Emperor didn't need a reason. If he decided you were to die, then you died. No explanation. No ceremony other than the hideous way in which he would toy with you first.

When he was less than twenty feet away from the base of the throne, from behind it, a great wall of black flames spanning the entire breadth of the hall suddenly erupted. The heat was unbearable. Vraylic instantly jumped back, throwing his cape over his head.

"Please, Your Majesty," he cried. "I have done nothing wrong. I swear it."

The roar from the inferno drowned out his words. Even through the protective cape, the heat was already scorching his flesh and he could smell the cloth starting to smolder. In an effort to make himself as small as possible, he began scampering away on his hands and knees.

A deep unnatural voice boomed out. "Where are you going, Lord Vraylic? I summoned you here."

Vraylic halted his retreat. "Please, Your Highness. Spare me."

"Uncover yourself, you silly man." This time the voice sounded quite human.

Shaking badly, Vraylic did as commanded. To his amazement and relief, the black flames were now gone. On the throne sat The Eternal Emperor, Shinzan. He was dressed in simple white cotton pants and a matching open-necked shirt. A pair of black silk slippers adorned his feet. He smiled warmly at Vraylic, gesturing for him to rise.

The terrified man struggled to his feet, sucking his teeth as pain shot through his body from blistered skin on his face and hands. Doing his best to ignore the discomfort, he bowed low. "Your Majesty. You wanted to see me?" There was something different about the Emperor. Something around the eyes. They looked weary.

"Indeed I do," Shinzan replied, his smile never fading. With a flick of his wrist, a stream of green smoke sprang from his hand and wrapped itself around Vraylic. The man staggered back, gasping. "That should make you feel better."

When the smoke vanished a moment later, all of Vraylic's burns were healed. He bowed again. "Thank you, Your Majesty."

"As of this moment, I'm promoting you to field commander," Shinzan told him.

Vraylic's eyes widened. "Field commander?" he repeated in disbelief. "But I'm just a supply officer. I have no real military experience."

Shinzan chuckled. "Nor do you need any. I do not expect you to lead an army. Unless I am misinformed, you are from a well-respected family in Ralmaria. Is this true?"

"I am, Your Majesty."

"Then I need you to journey to see all five kings of Lumnia. Tell them they are to prepare for war."

"Who shall I say we will be fighting?"

Shinzan threw a leg over the arm of his throne and leaned back. "You are a stupid one, aren't you? Many have died standing right where you are now for questioning me."

Vraylic began wringing his hands. "N...no, Your Majesty. I was not questioning –"

The Emperor's hand shot up. "You were chosen because you are familiar with the noble houses. So deliver the messages and be grateful that you will be permitted to live. Everything you need will be brought to your home within the hour. If you are still here ten minutes after that..." He cracked a wicked grin. "Then I shall summon you again."

No further warning was needed. After bowing low yet again, Vraylic scurried from the hall. While descending the long stairway leading to the main foyer, he had an unsettling feeling that the Emperor's eyes were still boring into the back of his skull. It was all he could do not to burst into a panicked run. Not that he would have been the first person to be seen fleeing from Shinzan's presence. But as the Emperor had rightly stated, he was a noble from Ralmaria. Such displays from people of his class were unbecoming.

As he left the palace, he couldn't help but notice that the guards positioned outside the massive doors were shifting nervously. This was most unusual for men of such fierce reputation. Rumors had spread that the Emperor was in a frazzled state of mind, even sending away most of his concubines. The iced blood spattered across the throne room floor and the ill-ease of the guards more or less confirmed these stories. Something had happened.

Perhaps the mages really are returning, he thought.

Beyond the palace grounds lay Noel, city of dreams. But to the locals it was secretly referred to as the city of nightmares. Though it was never spoken of openly, all those who resided there were known to experience terrible dreams of fire and death every single night.

The white stone used to build most of the structures was hewn from quarries deep within the desert wastes west of the city. Being so near to the desert of the Shadow Lands, one would never expect the lush gardens and mild climate that Noel possessed. Of course, everyone knew this was only an illusion created by the Emperor. The desert was expanding faster each year. And even beyond the sands, the soil was beginning to rot. One needed to travel for a week or more before seeing anything of substance growing.

In spite of this, the city appeared to be a veritable paradise. The buildings and streets were spotless, with not a single beggar or pauper found anywhere. Everyone had a place to call home as well as decent food and clothing. Though not large or densely populated when compared with the cities of the Five Kingdoms, Noel bustled with commerce. It wasn't until you entered the inns and taverns later in the day that the façade was removed. No revelry or merrymaking of any sort could be found. When the sun set, people hurried to their homes and did not emerge until daybreak.

Lord Vraylic lived on the outskirts of the city in an area called the *doldrums* – a place situated between the common dwellings of the lower ranking officers and the extravagant manors of the elite class. He quite liked it here. It kept him from being noticed. He didn't desire fame, or even fortune. Not anymore. These days he was content to keep his head down and simply live to see the sun rise again. In Noel, fame could easily be a death sentence.

While entering his home, he immediately heard the clattering of pots and dishes from the kitchen. Jassa was hard at work. The aroma of roast mutton and onions filled the house, making his mouth water. Not a king nor noble lord could match the fare that Jassa put on the table for him. He would miss it. And he would miss her too.

Careful not to alert her that he was home, he hurried to his bed chamber in order to change into clothing suitable for travel. He then packed as quickly as he could and placed his belongings next to the front door.

Jassa was still in the kitchen when a courier arrived with his new uniform and a bundle of five scrolls – one for each monarch he was to visit. Outside, an escort of ten soldiers waited, along with a magnificent black stallion for his use. Alerted by the commotion, Jassa hurried into the room, wiping her hands on her flour stained apron as she came. A cheerful smile formed when she saw Vraylic, and she immediately threw her arms around him in greeting.

Gently, he pushed her away and held her hands. Her honey blond hair was tied neatly in a bun, accentuating her delicate features and bright green eyes. She was young. Too young for Vraylic by most people's judgement. But she didn't seem to mind the twenty-five years that stood between them. And her affection for him appeared to be quite genuine. With her fetching appearance and household skills, Jassa could have gained employment with the wealthiest houses in Noel, and for far more money. But she chose to remain with him. As a servant, yes. But also as a companion.

She could see that something was troubling him, prompting a look of concern to come over her. "What is it, My Lord?" she asked.

She called him My Lord during sunlight hours. But after sunset, it was just plain Vraylic. Sometimes even Ray when she was feeling playful.

"I have to go," he told her, trying not to sound afraid.

She knitted her brow. "For how long?"

"I'm not sure. But there's something I need you to do for me after I'm gone."

"Of course."

He removed a small key from his pocket and pressed it into her hand. "There's a chest beneath the floorboard in the study behind my desk. Inside, you'll find enough gold to keep you comfortable for some time. Take it and go to my family home in Ralmaria. I've left a map and a letter for you to present to my cousin, Lyceane. She'll take care of you until I get there."

Jassa pulled away and stepped back. "You're scaring me. Please tell me what's going on."

He sighed heavily. "I can't. But I may be gone for some time. I'd feel better knowing you're with my family, far away from this place."

He stepped close to place his hands on her shoulders. "Will you do this for me?"

She touched his cheek and smiled. "Of course I will."

Just at that moment, a loud banging sounded at the front entrance. Jassa moved to answer it, but the door flew open before she was able to reach it and two grim-faced palace guards stepped inside.

"How dare you enter my home uninvited," Vraylic bellowed. "Who do you think you are?"

"We have orders from the Emperor," the first guard stated, unmoved by his anger. He held out a folded piece of parchment.

Vraylic snatched it away and read it carefully. At once, all the color drained from his face.

Jassa gripped his arm. "What does it say?"

He could barely speak the words. "It…it says that you are to go to the palace and serve as the Emperor's personal servant until I return."

The guards reached out to grab her, but she scampered behind Vraylic. "No! I won't go! You can't make me do this!"

"I'm afraid we can," the second guard told her. "You can either come willingly, or I will be forced to carry you through the streets over my shoulder."

She spun Vraylic around to face her. "You can't let them. Please. Don't let them do this." Her lips were trembling and tears were spilling down her cheeks.

He averted his eyes. "There's nothing I can do. You have to go with them. But I promise to return for you. You have my word on that."

Jassa collapsed to the floor, sobbing uncontrollably. Vraylic did not say another word as the two guards grabbed her arms and lifted her roughly to her feet. After they had led her away, he let out a feral cry. *I will be back for you*, he promised. *I'll save you from that monster.*

But it was a promise he dared not speak aloud.

*

Shinzan chuckled softly. The little cruelties were the best. And this one actually served a purpose. Loyalties were either bought, or gained through fear. An aspect of human predictability he relished. The wench would serve him well. And with any luck, he would completely break her long before Lord Vraylic returned.

His feeling of amusement did not last for very long. A sudden wave of nausea contorted his face, causing his anger to swell. Two women, part of the cleaning staff, were busy mopping up the now thawing blood. Neither of them dared to look up and notice his discomfort. Still…

A red light burst forth from his eyes, striking the floor just by the entrance to the room and causing a great serpent more than thirty feet long to materialize. Screaming at the top of their voices, the women raced to opposite walls. Not that this was going to help them. Within seconds the snake had cornered the woman to its left and struck, sinking rows of four inch razor-like teeth into her flesh. The second woman made a wild dash for the exit, howling in terror. But there was no escape from Shinzan's wrath.

With the first woman still dangling in its mouth, the snake raced across the floor to cut off the other one just as she reached the archway. Its sinewy body coiled around the helpless victim, stifling her screams and slowly crushing the life out of her.

Shinzan watched with a tiny smile on his lips until he was sure that both women were dead. Then, in a flash of brilliant light, the serpent vanished, leaving the mangled bodies in a heap.

That's what I'll do to young Dragonvein, he promised himself. *And when I'm done with him, I'll deal with the dragons.*

He regarded the macabre scene that had become his throne room. With a flick of his wrist, the carnage evaporated into puffs of black smoke. He leaned back and shut his eyes. He could feel the power of the dragons aligned against him. Fools. They only hastened their demise.

"Your Majesty."

Shinzan sighed and opened his eyes. Two guards stood just inside the room, a young, fair haired beauty standing between them.

He smiled broadly. A distraction. Yes. Time for a bit of sport.

CHAPTER TWENTY

AS RENALD'S HOUSE drew closer, both of them had a good view of the front porch. Ethan smiled to himself. Kat was sitting cross-legged on the boards, eyes closed and whispering a spell. Lylinora was standing a few feet away from her, looking on. Within moments, a flash of green light exploded near the door. When it faded, a tiny white mouse with pink eyes was looking inquisitively at them.

Kat opened her eyes, bouncing up and down and squealing with delight. Startled by the sudden noise, the mouse scuttled about the porch for a few seconds before disappearing in a puff of smoke.

"Very good," praised Lylinora. "And on your first attempt as well. I'm impressed."

Kat then spotted Ethan approaching and leapt to her feet, quickly spanning the distance between them. "Did you see that?" she asked, throwing her arms around his neck. "I made a mouse out of magic."

Ethan embraced her as she continued to dangle from her hold. "That was great!"

"Yes," grumbled Renald. "I'll be most glad to have you around should we ever be attacked by a group of savage cheeses."

Ignoring Renald's jibe, Kat finally released Ethan and bounded back onto the porch. Lylinora, however, was not prepared to let the insult go unchallenged.

"She did it on her first try," she stated. "And after only hearing the spell once. Were you so talented when you began?"

Renald stopped short and locked eyes with her. After a couple of seconds, he waved his hand in concession. "Yes, now that I think about it, I suppose it is impressive." He looked over to Kat. "But don't let such things go to your head, young lady. You can't become a *real* mage without hard work and dedication. You may have talent. But talent alone isn't enough. Understand?"

Kat beamed. "I do. I really do."

He nodded sharply. "Good. Now if you will excuse me, I must change and attend to Jonas."

The old man hobbled into the house, slamming the door behind him.

Lylinora sauntered over to Ethan with a devilish grin, draping her arms casually around his neck. "Did you miss me?" she asked, seduction dripping from each syllable.

He smiled. "Of course I did." Nonetheless, he gently but firmly removed her arms and headed for the door. "Where's Markus?"

Clearly surprised by this lack of affection, it took her a moment to respond. "At the shore," she replied. "He's decided to start sleeping on the boat."

Pausing only to give her a curt nod, Ethan stepped inside.

"What was *that*?" giggled Kat.

Lylinora was still stunned. "I...I don't know. But I most surely intend to find out."

Tight-lipped, she waited until Renald re-emerged. Only when he was on his way over to the building where Jonas was being held did she enter the house. Kat moved to follow her, but was halted by a fierce glance. Inside, she found Ethan sitting at the dining table, flipping through the pages of a thick, leather-bound book.

"Is something wrong?" she asked, taking a seat directly across from him.

Ethan closed the book and smiled. "No. Why?"

Lylinora puffed up. "Why? You push me away when I try to kiss you and you ask why?"

"Oh, that." He lowered his head as if in deep thought for several seconds before looking up again. "I'm not sure this is the right time to talk. Renald is trying to help Jonas and he might need you."

"I think this is the perfect time to talk," she countered stubbornly.

Ethan leaned in. His tone was level and commanding. "We will speak later. For now, there is nothing else to say."

She stiffened. "I don't know what has come over you, but we certainly *will* talk later."

His face softened. "Please don't be upset. It really is because of Jonas. Were it not for him, we'd be able to talk now."

Lylinora hesitated, clearly unsure how best to respond. Finally, she stood up and walked over to the door. "When we do, you can start by telling me what happened to you when you were with the dragons. Because whatever it is…I don't like it."

After she had left, Ethan leaned back and rubbed his brow. It was a good question. What *had* happened to him? He thought he knew. But even as the words he'd just spoken to Lylinora had come out of his mouth, he felt as if they weren't his own. It was as if someone else had control. He *did* need for Lylinora to wait, but had not intended to be so forceful about it. Still brooding on this, he rose from the table and left the house.

Lylinora was sitting in a chair, arms folded and sour faced. Kat, having obviously enjoyed the scene, was squatting on the grass with a tiny white mouse crawling across her lap.

"I'm going to get Markus," Ethan announced. "I'll be back soon."

Lylinora waved her hand indifferently.

"Can I come?" Kat quickly asked. The mouse puffed out of existence as she jumped to her feet.

"No," he replied. "Stay here in case Renald needs your help."

Though disappointed, she gave him a smile and sat back down on the grass to continue practicing her spell.

Ethan found Markus sitting on the dock, a bottle of wine in one hand while staring vacantly at the horizon. He sat down beside his friend.

After nodding a greeting, Markus handed the bottle over. "Did things go well?"

Ethan took a long drink, then wiped his mouth on his sleeve. "I suppose you could say that." He expected more questions, but Markus simply got to his feet and jumped aboard the boat. After disappearing below for a short time, he returned carrying another bottle.

"I came across a whole crate of these in the shack where Renald is keeping Jonas," he explained. "I guess I didn't feel much like sharing." He sat back down. "So you found the dragons?"

Ethan nodded. "I found them all right."

"Good."

He regarded his old friend closely. "You're struggling."

Markus raised an eyebrow. "I'm what?"

"I can see it when I look at you," he continued. "The darkness you're fighting keeps bubbling to the surface. Specter is still with you."

Markus sniffed and opened the bottle with his teeth. "What of it?"

"I just wanted you to know that I understand."

His remark raised a scornful laugh. "You do, do you? You understand? Then understand this: Mind your own fucking business. The last thing I need right now is a goddamn boy scout telling me that he understands what it's like being me."

Ethan felt a surge of anger well up – but Markus' words were not the cause. It took a moment for him to realize that it was the whirlwind of souls to which he was now bound that was influencing his emotions. He fought the anger down and forced a smile. "What I was, and what I am now, are two very different things," he stated.

His change of voice certainly caught Markus' attention. He studied Ethan's face for a short time, frowning heavily. "Yes. I can see that. Hell, I can hear it." His irritation was suddenly gone, replaced by curiosity. "What happened out there?"

Ethan looked to the setting sun before deciding there was time for a brief telling. He recounted the important aspects of his experience, glossing over the details.

"And you can hear them all talking in your head?" Markus asked, once he was finished.

"In a way, yes. And I'm learning that not all of them are very nice people."

This elicited a laugh from his friend. "Then I suppose you *do* understand."

Ethan's expression remained serious. "There is something I want to ask you." He drew a breath. "If you had the chance to return to Earth, would you want to stay there?"

Markus began to laugh again, but the sound faded away when he realized the seriousness of what Ethan was asking. He leaned his elbows on his knees and drooped his shoulders. "I really don't know."

"Think about it. And think about it carefully."

"Are you saying that's where we're going?"

"Yes."

Suddenly, Markus looked pale and anxious. "I…I lost all hope of going home a long time ago. I'm not sure I even belong there anymore."

Ethan gripped his shoulder fondly. "To be truthful, I don't know *where* you belong…other than at my side. I may have changed, but my friends are still important to me. Shinzan must be destroyed, and I can't do that alone. I'll need my friends with me. *You* in particular."

"What's so special about me?"

"Because of what you did on the ship," he answered flatly. "I need people with me who are willing to do what I cannot. I need you, Markus. But I need Specter too."

Markus shook his head and pulled away. "You don't know what you're saying."

"I know exactly what I'm saying," Ethan countered. "And I know what that might do to you. But even more importantly, I know that failure means death for every living creature on Lumnia."

There was a mixture of astonishment and revulsion on Markus' face as Ethan continued. "I hope you decide to return here with me. But I also admit that a part of me hopes you stay on Earth. Because if you return, what you did on the ship might be only a prelude of what's to come."

Markus blinked several times before speaking. "Who are you now? It's like you're not the Ethan I know anymore."

"Oh, I'm still him." He cracked a smile and pushed himself to his feet. "But I'm also something new. Something more than what I was before. And I'm learning more about who that is with every hour that passes." He offered a hand to pull Markus up. "But don't worry. In my heart, I'm still a lot like the boy scout you remember."

Markus was speechless. All he could do was nod in acceptance and then walk with Ethan back to the house. A cool salty breeze followed them from the shore, transporting Ethan's mind to unfamiliar places in the company of unfamiliar people. Memories not his own.

The stars were just beginning to peek through the twilight when they arrived. On stepping inside, they immediately saw that Jonas was there. Sitting at the table with his head hanging down and his body shuddering with sobs, he cut a sorry figure. Lylinora and Kat were seated on either side of him, Kat with a comforting arm draped around his shoulder. Across the room, Renald was at the stove preparing what smelled like fish.

Jonas looked up, his eyes red and face soaked in tears. "I'm so sorry," he wept. "I swear I had no idea what was happening to me."

Ethan smiled reassuringly. "I know you didn't. You shouldn't blame yourself."

"But it's my fault," he persisted. "Birger saved our lives, and he's dead because of my stupidity. I should have known. I should have told you everything."

"Told him what?" asked Markus.

"It doesn't matter now," Ethan said. "I already know. And it makes absolutely no difference."

A confused look came over Jonas. "How could you know?"

Ethan took a seat across from him. "I saw the dragons. And I saw the faces of my family: all of them throughout time. They live inside me now. But there was one notable exception."

Jonas' sobs renewed. "I'm so sorry. I was ashamed."

Ethan cast a quick glance over to Renald. But the old man did not appear interested in what he was about to say. He must have known... or at least suspected.

"Shinzan is my father," he revealed to the others.

A deathly silence fell over the room.

After a long pause, Lylinora spoke. "No. That's not possible."

"I'm afraid it is," Ethan told her. "As I said, I saw the faces of all my ancestors. All but one, that is. The face of Praxis Dragonvein."

"But that doesn't mean he's Shinzan," said Markus.

"No," agreed Ethan. "But later, when I arrived back at the house, I found a book. It was full of sketches that Renald had drawn long ago." He turned to Lylinora. "You saw me looking at it just before I went off to find Markus. One of those sketches was of my father. It was the same face I saw when Shinzan sent me a message through the *menax* crystal."

Markus turned to Jonas. "Is this true?"

He nodded weakly. "It is. I was there when Lord Dragonvein and the others fought Shinzan. I saw what happened."

Ethan reached out and took hold of his hand. "You don't have to..."

"No. It's all right," Jonas assured him.

He pulled his hand free to wipe his eyes with his sleeve. "The Council of Volnar was destroyed and Shinzan had already taken most of the north. Praxis wanted to flee to Elyfoss with you and your mother. But I...I shamed him into fighting. I convinced him that the only way to save you and Lady Illyrian was to gather as many of the remaining council members as he could find and confront Shinzan directly. But even then he resisted. I called him a coward. I said that his fear would doom us all. Finally, he gave in."

He paused to draw a long breath. "So sure was I that Praxis could defeat the Emperor that I even went with him to chronicle the events. Twenty mages set out. None returned. Shinzan killed half of them in the first minute of battle, unleashing magic I had never imagined possible. Only your father was strong enough to resist."

"Wait just a minute," said Kat. "I thought you told us that Shinzan *was* Praxis."

"He is," said Jonas. "In the end it came down to just Shinzan and Praxis Dragonvein. I can still remember my feelings of joy when Praxis stood over the shattered body of his enemy on that desolated field and claimed victory. I thought he had won, I really did. But my joy was still less than a minute old when the sky erupted into a maelstrom of black flames. Praxis was already severely weakened from the fight. There was nothing he could do to stop what happened next. The flames descended and enveloped him like a hellish fog. Had I been any closer, they would have consumed me as well."

There was another pause while Jonas steadied himself sufficiently to continue. "Slowly the flames died and all that remained was the body of Praxis. I ran to his side, praying to the spirits that he still lived. At first I thought he was dead. Then he opened his eyes and looked at me. It was in that moment I understood. Shinzan had...he had..."

Jonas stopped, unable to say the awful truth.

Ethan squeezed his arm. "I know. Shinzan had possessed my father's body." He turned to the others. "So in a sense, he *is* the Emperor."

Slowly, Jonas regained his composure. "He allowed me to live – though I have no idea why. I had hoped it was because some part of Praxis remained. But as the atrocities mounted, I knew that wasn't true. I never told Lady Illyrian. But I should have told you, Ethan. It's just that I was so ashamed. I am the reason why your father is dead, and why his body is now a vessel for evil."

"Nonsense, you old fool," snapped Renald, suddenly joining the conversation. He moved away from the stove and sat in the only unoccupied chair. "My brother was no puppet. Nor would he be shamed into fighting unless that was what he already wanted to do. It was Lady Illyrian who shamed him into fleeing. All you did was give him the reason he needed to change his mind."

Jonas shook his head. "No. Lady Illyrian was..."

"Was a wise and kind woman," Renald said, cutting him short. "And my brother loved her very much. But Praxis was a vain and arrogant man. He truly believed he could triumph, and hated that the other mages had fled. He *wanted* to challenge Shinzan. It was *his* decision."

The old mage's features softened and his tone became kindly. "Jonas, listen to me. If you hadn't said what you did, he would have simply found another reason to go. I promise you. I knew him better than anyone. It wasn't your fault."

Jonas nodded slowly. "Thank you. Though it's hard for me. I can still see him...his eyes...his face. It was Praxis, and yet it wasn't."

"Well, old friend," said Renald. "You'll have plenty of time here to heal your wounds." He leaned back to address the others. "Jonas cannot leave the boundary of my wards. When Praxis lived, he cast a spell on Jonas. It created a way to locate him should he ever be lost or captured. Though my brother is dead, the body lives, and with it the spell."

"You can't remove it?" asked Lylinora.

"No. I have to hand it to Praxis, he was one hell of a powerful mage. Removing the spell would almost certainly kill Jonas."

"How did I miss it?" she asked.

"You didn't know what you were looking for," he explained. "A weakness in your education I intend to remedy."

"That's all well and good," Kat interjected. "But I want to hear about what happened with the dragons. We've come all this way, so I think I deserve to know."

Renald nodded in agreement. Returning to the stove, he served a meal of grilled fish and vegetables while Ethan began his story. He was half way through this when Maytra entered through the open window and perched herself atop Renald's bedpost. Ethan paused speaking long enough to smile at her. Maytra gurgled a response and flapped her wings.

As he completed his tale, he could see that both Lylinora and Kat were deeply concerned.

"So you're…possessed?" asked Kat.

Ethan chuckled. "In a way, I guess I am. But it's not like they have control over me or anything like that. With the dragons forcing Shinzan to remain close to his source of power, I have shared the burden of my family with them, so to speak. Their spirits partially dwell inside me."

"Does it hurt?" she asked.

"No. But it does feel strange. I'm me. But it's like I've…I don't know how to put it."

"Aged," added Markus. "I can hear it in the way you speak."

Ethan shrugged. "I guess that's one way to put it. But I think it's more like I can benefit from their experience."

"Are you saying that you know everything they knew?" asked an incredulous Jonas.

Ethan shook his head. "I wish. It sure would save a lot of time.

But unfortunately, it doesn't work like that. I get impressions mostly. Feelings. And they're kind of foggy and distant."

"That may change with time," Renald noted. "Recalling what you told me about your encounters with Maytra's mate and the dragon on the mountain, there might be a way to tap into their knowledge."

For some reason, this was a disturbing thought to Ethan. It seemed somehow dangerous. Though he didn't know why he should feel that way.

"I'm worried," said Lylinora. "Without the dragons to fight with us, how can we possibly prevail?"

"Shinzan is powerful," Ethan replied. "But he's not invulnerable. There is a way. But first we must find the other children of the mages."

"You know where they are?" asked Lylinora.

Ethan nodded. "Earth."

She sat up straight. "You can't be serious."

Kat's reaction was entirely different. Bubbling with excitement, she clapped her hands enthusiastically. "I can't wait. When do we go?"

"*We* don't," Ethan told her, his expression uncharacteristically grim. "Markus and I will go. That's all. And there will be no argument over this. Am I understood?"

With the wind snatched out of her sails, Kat's bottom lip protruded. "But you promised to take me if you ever went home."

"I'm not going home," Ethan said. "I don't even know that I *can* go home. There's no telling where the other children who were sent to Earth ended up. For all I know, we might appear inside Nazi Germany or worse. I can't risk your life. I'm sorry."

She crossed her arms over her chest and glared angrily. "I can decide for myself if I want..."

"Enough!" Ethan snapped. "I said you aren't coming. And that's that."

Kat puffed up defiantly, but one look from Ethan told her that his mind was set. Throwing back her chair, she stormed out, spitting curses with each step.

Ethan sighed, regretting being so harsh. He promised himself to talk to her later.

Lylinora's voice brought him back to the matter in hand. "How will we do it?" she asked.

"Renald will teach you the spell," he explained. "Once you've learned it, we'll return to the dragons. I'm hoping they can help stabilize the portal long enough for us to enter and return safely."

This drew a laugh from Markus. "Hoping? Well, that sure sounds like a plan to me."

"Sounds like suicide," said Lylinora.

Ethan cocked his head. "Let's hope not."

They talked for a while longer, then Ethan left to find Kat. After searching near the house, he made his way to the boat, only to find she was not there either. Hiding, he thought. And with her ability to disappear, she would only be found if she wanted to be.

The sound of the waves crashing ashore was soothing. Once again, unfamiliar images flooded into his mind. This time it was a young girl, laughing as she took a moonlight stroll with him along the beach. Except, of course, it wasn't him.

Leaving the dock, he sat down on the sand just beyond where the oncoming tide reached before receding again. The image in his head was pleasant, and it certainly gave him a warm feeling inside. But again the feeling was not *his*.

"I have to learn to control this," he muttered under his breath.

"Control what?"

Lylinora was standing a few feet behind him, an intense look on her young face.

Ethan forced a smile. "Nothing." He gestured for her to sit beside him.

"So, can I assume you're ready to talk now?" she asked sarcastically.

"I'm ready."

She moved gracefully to his right and sat, hugging her knees to her chest. "So why did you push me away? Is it because of what happened when you were with the dragons?"

Ethan sighed, leaned back on his elbows, and looked directly into her eyes. "Why do you want to be with me, Lylinora?" His gaze intensified. "Or maybe, a better question might be: In your heart, do you really want to be with me at all?"

"Of course I do," she replied. A look of deep offense formed. "Do you seriously imagine I would pretend to have feelings for you? If so…"

"Then explain why you came to my bedroom in Elyfoss," he cut in. "Explain why you tried to erase it from my memory."

Lylinora shot to her feet. "What did Kat tell you?"

"Kat didn't tell me anything. It was after I drank the dragon's blood that the memory came back. But that's only a part of it. The truth is, you don't love me. And I don't think you ever will."

Lylinora knelt down and took his hands. "That's not true. I *do* love you. I want us to be together." She moved in to kiss him, but Ethan held her back. She lowered her head, stifling her sobs. "I'm sorry I deceived you. I should not have hidden what I'd done. I was confused at the time." She looked back up with pleading eyes. "But I'm not anymore. I know what I want now."

Ethan pulled his hands free and grasped her firmly by the shoulders. His eyes were fixed; his face a stone mask. "What you want is for the mages to return. Because of that, you think that I am the only choice for you. But you're wrong. You are free to choose anyone you want. And would you like to know why?"

Lylinora averted her eyes.

"Because the days of the old mages are *not* going to return," he said.

She grabbed his wrists and threw them back. "Don't say that. Yes they will."

"How? Through our children? How many do you imagine we can have?"

He gently lifted her chin with his finger and eased his tone. "Your duty isn't to be a breeding vessel. Your duty is to be a teacher. Once Shinzan is gone, you will be responsible for introducing a whole new generation of mages to the world. You are the only one who can do this."

"But there are no mages for me to teach," she countered, albeit weakly.

"Sure there are. They're just hiding. Kat is proof of that. And once people aren't afraid any longer, others will come. They'll come to learn about their gifts. They'll come to *you*."

Ethan could see the conflict and confusion raging inside her head. She had been desperately holding on to the idea that the world of her parents could live once again. The world she loved. A world of wonders and magic. To give this up and accept that there was nothing left of it but memories was a bitter pill.

Lylinora turned away from him and rested her head on her knees. "I need to be alone."

Ethan stood and touched her shoulder. "I'm sorry."

He started back in the direction of the dock.

"You're wrong, you know," Lylinora called after him.

Ethan paused.

"I *do* love you," she continued. "I didn't before. But I do now."

Ethan felt his pulse quicken as he looked back at her delicate silhouette curled up on the beach. He may have been changed by the dragon's blood, but he still found her incredibly beautiful. A rush of carnal desire stirred his passions. Her naked flesh pressed against his - the ecstasy he felt when he was inside her – these were memories impossible to erase. Beads of sweat formed on his brow and only with great effort was he able to continue on his way back to the house.

Kat was sitting on the porch when he arrived. A fist-sized ball of flame danced above her head – spinning and dipping as if to music. When she saw Ethan, it vanished.

"Not bad," he said, smiling.

"You're a liar," she sulked. "You promised to take me. I don't want to talk to you."

"Well *I* want to talk to *you*," he said, taking a seat beside her. "So you can just sit there and listen."

She pouted. "Just because all of a sudden you sound grown up, that doesn't mean you are. And it doesn't give you the right to talk to me like a child either."

"You're right," he agreed, giving a slight nod. "I shouldn't have spoken to you like that."

Kat gave him a sideways glance. "So does that mean I can go?"

"No. I'm sorry, I just can't let you. I'm not sure what's going to happen. If you got hurt…"

"But I won't," she jumped in quickly. "I'll be careful. I promise."

"No, it's bad enough I have to risk Markus' life. I won't risk yours too. Especially when there's no reason for it."

With her brief flicker of hope extinguished, Kat went back to sulking. "Like I said, you're a liar." She held out her palm and another ball of flame flashed into existence. "I bet if Lylinora asked to go, you'd let *her.*"

"No I wouldn't," he retorted. "Hell, *I* wouldn't go myself if I didn't have to."

The flame renewed its dance. "Then don't. Stay here. Be with Lylinora if that's what you want. But just stay here."

Ethan could see moonlight reflecting on a single tear as it rolled slowly down her cheek. He reached out and pulled her close. "I'm coming back," he said.

She extinguished the flame and buried her head in his chest. "But you can't promise me that, can you?"

"I promise I'll do my best."

"And what if you get trapped on Earth?" she argued. "Won't Shinzan win if that happens?" When Ethan offered no reply to this, she tilted her head up to him. "In that case, *you* shouldn't go either."

He kissed her forehead and smiled. "I know I shouldn't. But I can't send someone else in my place, can I? Who would go? Jonas?"

Kat tried not to laugh, but couldn't stop herself. "No. You sure couldn't send him. Markus would end up killing him."

She wrapped her arms around his body and squeezed. "Just make sure you come back. If you don't, I swear I'll find a way to Earth and fetch you myself."

Chapter Twenty-One

ETHAN HEAVED A sigh of frustration. "Half of these pages are too damn faded to read," he complained, pushing back his chair and twisting sharply. The stiffness in his muscles reminded him unkindly that he had been sitting in one position for far too long.

Kat sat down beside him. She crossed her arms on the table and laid her head sideways, blinking up at him playfully. "Lylinora says you're wasting your time with all that stuff anyway. She says wards are useless."

He looked to the window where Maytra was curled up. The sun had just passed its apex and the afternoon was fast approaching. He twisted again, this time letting out a loud groan. A harsh cracking of joints suggested that perhaps he had studied for long enough.

Smiling, he reached over to pinch Kat lightly on the nose. "What does Lylinora know?"

Kat giggled. "She knows more than you. Hell, *I* know more than you."

"Is that right?"

"Can you do this?" She sat up and held out her hands. "*Miora Vas Yetuli.*"

A light sparkled and flashed in the center of the table, then exploded with a loud pop. A black rabbit appeared and began scampering back and forth, eventually jumping to the floor and running around the table.

With a snap of her fingers, Kat made it vanish. She looked at Ethan, highly pleased with herself. "No one showed me how to make a rabbit."

He nodded with approval. "Very nice. But how did you do it if no one showed you?"

"It's the same spell I use to make mice," she explained. "All I do... well...I just think about rabbits instead. Later on, I'm going to try something even bigger. You can come watch if you want."

"I can't," he replied. "I have to work with Lylinora later."

During the past two weeks, Lylinora had taken on a tremendous amount of responsibility. Her heavy schedule of receiving lessons from Renald, and giving them to both Kat and Ethan, meant that she was now beginning to look more than a little weary.

Ethan's days were equally demanding. Renald had given him a book of wards to study, so when he wasn't under the tutelage of Lylinora, he was busy poring over the worn tome. Amazingly, he found the contents that were decipherable quite easy to understand. His lessons were going a lot better as well. Spells that he would have previously struggled to cast were now becoming second nature in minutes. An effect of the dragon's blood, he assumed.

"Do they still bother you?" Kat asked. "The voices, I mean."

Ethan shrugged. "They're more of a nuisance than anything else. It's hard to keep them out when I'm feeling tired."

Kat frowned. "I wouldn't want all those people rattling around inside me." She faked a dramatic shudder.

A minute later, Lylinora and Renald entered the house. Lylinora's eyes were burning and her face was a vivid crimson. Ethan chuckled. Yet another pleasant lesson, he thought.

"If your mother hadn't been so bloody proper, she would have taught you how to defend yourself against such things," Renald grumbled.

"What happened?" asked Ethan.

Lylinora stomped over to the table and sat heavily down. "I'll tell you what happened. That old pervert went too far."

Ethan cast Renald a questioning look. But the old man merely sneered and tottered over to his bed.

"Oh, come on," pressed Kat. "Do tell us."

"He stripped off all my clothes," Lylinora muttered, at the same time shooting Renald a hateful stare.

"He did what?" Ethan asked incredulously.

"You heard me," she snapped back.

By now, Renald was stretched out on his bed. "I did no such thing," he called over. "All I did was make her clothes invisible for a few seconds."

"You're joking," Kat giggled. But Lylinora's furious expression told her otherwise. "Oh, sweet spirits. I wish I could have seen it."

Ethan was trying hard to keep a straight face, but his mouth was twitching into a grin. He cleared his throat. "Can I ask why you did that?"

"You need to be prepared to defend yourself," Renald replied, with no hint of humor. "Distraction can get you killed. I've seen the tactic used before. And it's very effective."

Ethan considered this. "I guess it would be. If I found myself suddenly stripped naked in the middle of a fight, it would definitely distract me."

"You know what I think?" asked Kat, still laughing. "I think poor old Renald just wanted to see a pretty girl without her clothes on."

He sat up and huffed. "I've seen my fair share, child. Don't you worry about that."

Kat grinned impishly back at him. "Sure. But how long has it been? You can admit it. You liked what you saw, didn't you?"

Renald scowled. "One more word from you, and Lylinora won't be alone in her embarrassment."

Kat's mouth snapped shut. With a grunt of satisfaction, Renald laid back down.

"I think we should leave him alone for a while," Ethan suggested.

"Good idea," Renald growled, throwing his blanket up over his head and pulling it tight.

Ethan led them to a large apple tree a hundred yards or so away from the house. By the time they reached it, though a bit calmer, Lylinora was still clearly upset.

"He's right," Ethan said to her after they had all sat down on the soft turf. "You shouldn't let a thing like that distract you."

"If you're trying to make me feel better, it's not working," she snapped. "So just stop."

Ethan smirked. "All I'm saying is that you shouldn't let it rattle you."

"Very well. You asked for it," Lylinora growled. Her hands waved in a grand exaggerated circle. "*Onis Ona Lim.*"

Ethan sensed what was coming. Even so, this did not reduce his sense of alarm when he looked down to see that every stitch of his clothing was gone. Instantly, he scrambled to cover himself with his hands.

"Now *that's* what I call *magic*," remarked Kat, smiling broadly

Lylinora let out a satisfied sigh. "Indeed."

"Okay, that's enough," Ethan told her, his face now bright red.

"Oh, I don't know," she said. "I think Renald may be on to something now that I see it from his perspective." She looked him up and down, nodding appreciatively. "What do you think, Kat? Should I leave him like this?"

The young girl fell over backwards laughing. "Yes, please do. At least until Jonas and Markus get back."

"I said that's enough," Ethan repeated, this time more forcefully.

After taking one final, lingering look at him, Lylinora bowed her head. "As you wish…Lord Dragonvein." With a flick of her wrist, his clothes reappeared.

"Aw," whined Kat. "He was much cuter before. Now he's just plain Ethan again."

He tried to be angry, but soon found himself joining in with their laughter.

"So you'll be leaving tomorrow," Lylinora said, once they had settled down.

He nodded. "I should leave tonight, but Renald says it's too dangerous."

"I still don't understand," Kat said. "Where are you going?"

Ethan gave her a wink. "To fight Shinzan."

She frowned. "That's not funny."

He held up his hand. "I know. I'm sorry. The truth is, I have to do something for the dragons before I go to Earth."

"I get *that*," she countered. "But what?"

"I can't tell you."

Kat crossed her arms over her chest. "And why not?"

Lylinora answered for him. "Because if we know and are captured, we could reveal it. But you cannot reveal what you do not know."

"It's *that* important?" asked Kat, frowning.

Ethan nodded. "Yes, it is. Otherwise I'd tell you. But don't worry. I'll be back soon."

"I bet it has something to do with you studying those wards," she probed. "What are you trying to protect?"

"Kat!" snapped Lylinora. "If we needed to know, he'd tell us. Don't pester him about it."

"Don't tell me you haven't wondered too," she shot back. "And I don't think it's fair that he goes wandering off by himself while we sit here not knowing where he is, or if he's all right."

"I'll be fine," Ethan assured her.

"Kat is right about one thing," Lylinora remarked. "Isn't there a way you can take one of us with you? Even Renald would make me feel better. If you were hurt, no one would know to come."

"Renald is the only one I *could* possibly take," explained Ethan. "But being so far from his home would drain his strength. It's too dangerous for him." He gave them both a roguish grin. "You two worry about me too much. Shouldn't I be learning magic right now?"

Lylinora nodded. "I think we should go over the things you could use if you are attacked."

They made their way to an open field. Here, they spent the rest of the afternoon casting simple fireballs and other forms of elemental magic. This bored Kat no end, and she made no secret of her dissatisfaction.

"It's one thing to be able to cast a spell," Lylinora told her. "It's another to do it when someone is attacking you." Her arms shot forward and a pillar of fire instantly surrounded Kat.

Although taken by surprise, the young girl quickly recovered. She muttered a few words. The next instant, a gale wind lifted the fire and threw it straight back at Lylinora. Just before the flames reached her, they dissipated.

Lylinora smiled, almost clapping her hands with appreciation at first — then instinctively containing her enthusiasm at the last moment. "Yes! Very good. Very good indeed."

Kat beamed. Her eyes darted to Ethan, who was equally impressed.

"Better than I could do," he said.

Lylinora grinned viciously. "Let's find out, shall we?"

Again the pillar of fire sprang forth, this time surrounding Ethan. He could feel the intense heat bearing down relentlessly on his exposed face and arms. Concentrating as best he could, he focused on the same spell that Kat had used, but was only able to raise a light wind. In seconds, the heat had doubled. He could hear Kat pleading with Lylinora to stop, but the fire persisted. He tried repeating the spell, but with no better result.

He was just about to cry out, conceding defeat, when a brilliant flash shattered his senses. It was as if he had been struck hard in the center of his forehead. The light exploded and sparkled in front of his eyes, blinding him. Then it was gone…and so was the fire.

He felt a dull throbbing in his head, and for a minute his vision remained blurred. "What the hell happened?" he asked. But there was no reply.

As his sight cleared, he saw Kat and Lylinora huddled together against a fruit tree a short distance away, their eyes wide with fear. All around him for thirty yards, the ground was scorched and smoldering. He took a step forward, but Lylinora's hand shot out.

"Don't come any closer," she commanded. Her hand was trembling.

Ethan halted. "What's wrong?" he asked. He tried to recall how the earth had come to be so badly burned. Lylinora's spell couldn't possibly have done this much damage, and his own efforts to free himself had failed. He took another step.

A streak of lightning flew from Lylinora's palm, striking the ground right next to his feet. "I said don't come any closer," she warned.

Ethan held up his hands. "Hey. Wait a minute. What the hell is going on here? How did this happen?"

It was Kat who made the first move. Releasing her hold on Lylinora, she slowly approached him. He could see how badly shaken she was.

"Are you…still you?" she asked.

Ethan frowned. "What kind of question is that? Of course I'm me. Who else would I be?"

Lylinora had still not moved.

Kat stopped a few feet in front of him. "You really don't remember?"

"Remember what?"

"You almost killed us," she replied. "Not one minute ago, you almost killed me and Lylinora."

"What!" he exclaimed.

Lylinora finally decided that it was safe to approach. She positioned herself beside Kat and regarded him with a mixture of awe and suspicion. Ethan noticed that her hands were still glowing red – ready to strike if necessary.

"I've only seen magic like that used by the most powerful of mages," she said, wrapping a protective arm around Kat. "How did you do it?"

Ethan was at a complete loss. "I don't even know *what* I did, let alone *how* I did it. Why don't you just tell me what you saw?"

The tension on Lylinora's face remained. "I was about to release you from the fire," she began. "You'd already twice tried to use the same spell that Kat did and failed, and I'd held you as long as I dared without risking serious harm. But before I could free you, the ground began to shake and the fire swelled into a massive tower. It just went on climbing higher and higher, and spreading wider. Kat and I were forced to run away or be burned alive."

Ethan was dumbfounded. How did he not remember this?

"I cast a protection spell around us," she continued. Her lips were quivering. "But a wave of pure magic shot out from the fire and crushed my spell like parchment. Then you spoke. You said: *'Feeble child. You think you can trap me? You are nothing. A mere novice. Behold true power.'* Then the flames lifted into the clouds and formed a sphere at least five hundred feet in diameter. You were still standing there, laughing and with your arms spread wide. You looked…evil."

Evil? Ethan could hear a distant voice in his head. It was mocking her - saying that she didn't know what true evil was and spitting vile curses.

Lylinora was fighting hard not to weep as she continued. "Finally, the fire exploded with a force that knocked us both completely off our feet. What the hell has happened to you, Ethan?"

At this point, it all became too much for her. She lost the inner struggle and tears began falling freely down her face.

Guilt wracked him. He knew now what had happened, though the implications were terrifying. He wanted to comfort them - tell them that he would never allow such a thing to happen again. But that might well be a lie. All this had taken place without him even being aware of it. So how could he promise there would be no repeat? And next time...next time, he might seriously injure someone he loved. The mere thought of this horrified him. He felt his legs wobble and he dropped to his knees.

"I'm...I'm sorry," he said weakly. "You know I would never hurt either of you."

"I sure hope your family feels the same way," Kat told him, with a nervous laugh. "If not, we're in for one hell of a time."

Lylinora wiped her eyes. "Until you learn to control this thing, we should halt our lessons."

Ethan nodded, his face still guilt-stricken. "I'll fix it. I promise."

She forced a smile. "Understand that I don't blame you." Stepping forward, she offered him her hand. "It will be all right. I'm sure of it."

He allowed Lylinora to help him to his feet, though he far from shared her positive outlook.

Kat tried a touch of humor to help ease the tension. "If there are hundreds of your family wandering around inside you, let's hope that was just one drunk uncle who no one else likes."

Her ploy worked. The other two could not prevent themselves from laughing.

Ethan then saw Markus and Jonas hurrying toward them with worried looks. Each man held a small string of fish in one hand and a pole in the other.

"What the hell was that?" called Markus. "Are you sending signals to the bloody moon or something?"

"I'll explain when we're back in the house," Ethan told him.

On stepping inside, they found a highly irritated Renald sitting at the table.

"What did you think you were doing?" he demanded. "Are you insane? None of you are ready for such powerful magic. That you're not dead is amazing. Not to mention that you've now announced our location to anyone within five-hundred miles who might be looking. Shinzan may not be able to leave his source of power, but that doesn't prevent him from sending others out to find you."

His eyes settled on Lylinora. "I can only assume it was you responsible. What were you doing? Trying to impress Ethan?"

"It was me," Ethan cut in quickly, before she could reply.

Renald raised an eyebrow. "You? How did you manage such a thing? It's not possible."

Everyone gathered around the table while Ethan explained what had happened. At the conclusion, even Jonas, who in the past had always appeared most pleased when Ethan displayed great power, wore a worried expression.

As for Renald, he sat silently in thought for several minutes, scratching his beard. He then leaned back and threw up his hands. "Well, there is nothing we can do, I suppose. You must simply find a way to control yourself, and that is that."

"What do you mean, *that is that?*" cried Lylinora. "He nearly killed us. And that's the only bit of wisdom you can offer?"

"I don't know what you expect me to say," he retorted. "There is no precedent for this. Ethan has taken on a burden like no other Dragonvein before him. Why should I know what to do? I suppose you could try asking Heather. Perhaps she has the answer."

Ethan nodded. "Yes. I'll do that before I return."

"Speaking of which," said Renald. He got up and retrieved a cloth sling from a chest near his bed. "Maytra will be going with you. She likes to be carried in this sometimes."

Ethan had noticed her in the corner near the stove when first coming in. She was now circling an empty bowl and looking at the fish Markus and Jonas still held.

"It's coming, you old rat," snapped Renald.

The tiny dragon hissed and gurgled in reply.

Renald turned his attention back to Ethan. "I do think you should cease using magic until you've spoken to Heather. The power I witnessed would have impressed even Praxis. And not all of our family were good and noble. Some were, shall we say...not the type of mage one would want to encounter."

"That much we already guessed," Kat chipped in.

After dinner, Jonas raised the matter of sleeping arrangements. Given his age, and since he was not allowed to leave, he felt that Renald could either help him to build a proper bed, or offer to share his own. After a long and heated argument, the old mage eventually relented and made room.

Once this was settled, Ethan gathered his belongings and spent the rest of the night on the boat. Usually when he did this, Kat would come down and join him for a while, but this time only Markus cared to be there. And even his old friend kept mostly to himself that night.

Ethan had frightened them, and he knew it. More than that, he had frightened himself. How much darkness was now residing within him? He hadn't hurt Kat and Lylinora...this time. But could he really lose control to the point where that might happen? Was he even capable of such a thing? He prayed that Heather could somehow guide him to the answer before it was too late.

Sleep came slowly as he tried to keep his mind quiet. But no matter how hard he tried, the voices were always there. A distant call from a place he did not fully understand.

The morning offered a brief respite from his troubles. Markus had already left – probably fishing with Jonas again. The sun was barely over the horizon and the air was still cool as he strolled leisurely back to the house. Wild flowers and blossoms on the various fruit trees filled his nostrils with a wholesome aroma, bringing a smile to his face. Memories of upstate New York with his parents drifted through his mind...*his* memories. Not those of some long dead kin. This was enough to lift his spirits considerably.

As he had guessed, Markus and Jonas had already gone off fishing.

Lylinora and Kat were just sitting down to breakfast while Renald was settled on his plush sofa, reading.

"Off on your mysterious adventure, are you?" the old mage remarked casually, not bothering to look up from his book. "Mind that you pay attention to Maytra. She'll keep you out of trouble."

The dragon was perched atop a book shelf on the far wall. She let out a high-pitched growl in greeting. Ethan smiled. She had apparently forgiven him for the death of her mate, and over the past week had even seemed to grow a bit fond of him.

"You're not going anywhere on an empty stomach," Kat insisted.

Ethan sat at the table across from Lylinora, not knowing what kind of reception to expect. But she greeted him with a smile. He could tell she was still slightly unnerved, but not so much as to cause serious tension between them.

"I'll be loading rajni stones with the portal spell while you're gone," she told him, searching for conversation.

Kat, on the other hand, was completely at ease – as if nothing had happened. "How long *will* you be gone?" she asked.

"Four days." He had told her this several times already, but she still kept asking as if hoping the next time it would be shorter.

Kat frowned. "That's too long. And I'll tell you this: take one day longer and I'll come looking."

Ethan grinned. "I'll try not to drag my feet then."

With breakfast over, he donned his gear and said a final goodbye. Kat threw her arms around him so tightly, it was only after Lylinora pulled on her shoulders that she reluctantly let go.

Then it was Lylinora's turn. She kissed him lightly on the cheek. "Do be careful. And hurry back, or Kat won't be the only one coming to look for you."

Ethan stopped by the lake to have a word with Jonas and Markus. As he drew near, he could hear them arguing over what bait to use.

"I wish you wouldn't go alone," said Jonas.

As if in reply, Maytra screeched from high above.

"I'm not," Ethan replied with a wink.

Markus gave a good-natured laugh. "I'm not sure what use a cat-sized dragon will be. But at least she can lead us to your body."

Ethan chuckled. His friend's dark sense of humor never failed to make him smile. "Just get to me before I start stinking," he replied.

Jonas shook his head in disapproval of such talk. "Enough of this. Ethan has a long way to go – that's my guess anyway – and we still have fish to catch."

"Yes, and if you'd brought along some raw pork instead of fish guts, we'd already have caught some," Markus shot back.

Ethan left them to their argument.

It wasn't until he was several miles beyond Renald's grassy fields that Maytra swooped down to join him by landing on his shoulder. He winced as, for a brief moment, she dug her claws into his flesh to keep herself balanced. The sling Renald had provided was tucked into his belt, so he quickly put this on. With serpentine agility, Maytra crawled into the cradle and curled into a ball.

As the day progressed, Ethan began finding it easier to ignore the voices, particularly when Maytra was close by. It was then that he could once again hear the dragons' call clearly; they were directing him to his destination.

With only two short stops to eat and rest throughout the day, he was thoroughly tired by the time the sun began to set. After laying out his blanket and pillow, he found a large rock and placed it a few feet away. He muttered a short incantation that Renald had taught him, and the rock very quickly began to radiate heat. Ethan smiled. The old mage had assured him that this would last for several hours, and should be more than enough to keep away the night chill. As he closed his eyes, he heard the flapping of wings. This was followed by a short period of growling and gurgling as Maytra snuggled herself alongside him beneath the blanket.

He imagined what the next day would bring. It was crucial that he complete his task, and though it would certainly be trying, he was confident that he knew enough to succeed. Renald's book, along with his detailed instructions, would see to that.

Only a succession of hollow cries from the beasts of the Dragon

Wastes slowed Ethan's descent into slumber – from miles away they called out their lonely song to be carried on the wind. It was unsettling, yet at the same time somehow fitting in this desolate land. He could feel that Maytra was at ease. If whatever was out there was a threat, she would be aware of it.

He woke just a few minutes before the sun rose. After a quick meal, he hurried on, wanting to reach his destination as soon as possible. Maytra had taken to the air. She would have known where to go, even if he had not. And she knew the purpose of his trip.

As he'd been hoping, he located the entrance to the cave well before the morning was over. Disguised by angular boulders and an uneven rock face, it was almost impossible to spot unless you knew what to look for. The opening was narrow – three feet wide and ten feet high. Ethan held up his palm. In response, a tiny ball of white light hovered just in front of him, illuminating the way.

Once beyond the entrance, the path opened up wide enough for several men to walk abreast. Maytra landed a few feet ahead of him and sniffed the air. Ethan did the same. Unlike the dry dusty stench typical of the Dragon Wastes, the atmosphere here was moist and cool. It even carried a faint hint of lavender. Tiny multi-colored mushrooms and thick hanging moss littered the ceiling and walls: the only things that Ethan had ever seen growing in the Wastes outside of Renald's land.

Soon, the ground began to slope downward. It continued like this for several hundred feet before opening up into a spacious cavern, the interior of which was mostly unremarkable aside from the ground bearing a dull sheen that suggested it had once, long ago, been highly polished.

What really mattered though, was sitting atop a dense patch of emerald green moss growing in the very center - three dozen fist-sized, powder blue eggs.

Maytra immediately scrambled over to them, her talons scraping and clacking as she went. With motherly tenderness, she nudged them with her snout.

Ethan smiled. "You've been taking care of them, haven't you?"

He knelt down to touch one of the precious eggs. Just as Heather had described, he could feel the life raging within, fighting with every measure of its strength to survive. Though drinking the blood of the dragon had brought him close to their spirits, this was something different. Something far more.

"You'd better go," he told Maytra.

She looked at him, growling and thrashing her head. Ethan still couldn't hear her like Renald seemed to, but her emotions and intentions were crystal clear.

"I don't want you to get hurt," he said, trying his best to be firm.

His words had no effect. In a flurry of movement, she leapt into the air directly at Ethan, landing inside the sling. Hissing and sputtering, she glared at him defiantly. In a funny kind of way, it reminded him of Kat.

He sighed and bobbed his head in defeat. "Fine. I'll just go ahead then, shall I?"

He removed his pack and placed it at the entrance. He then knelt beside the eggs and began chanting softly, hands extended and fingers spread wide. For more than ten minutes he continued with this until a faint green light surrounded the moss on which the eggs lay. Once the chanting ceased, the light slowly dimmed and disappeared. Ethan then took a few steps back and repeated the process. This he did again and again until reaching the very edge of the cavern. He then returned to the center and started all over again. For six hours he labored on, each time growing ever more weary from the effort. Finally, when he was no longer able to stand, he crawled to his pack and collapsed into a dreamless slumber. The wards were in place. He had accomplished his task.

When he woke, it was pitch black. For a moment he couldn't remember where he was. Only the nudge of Maytra's snout on his ribcage urged him fully back to his senses.

"Are you ready to get out of here?" he asked, reaching down and gently stroking the tiny dragon's chin.

She cooed and growled in appreciation.

Ethan created another light to guide him out, grinning as it floated and bobbed in front of him. Despite everything he had seen, simple magic still filled him with wonder and delight.

Upon reaching the entrance, he set one final ward before starting back to the house. Thankfully, creating a single ward only drained him mildly. He'd been amazed at the sheer effort and strength it had taken to completely protect the dragon eggs. All the wards Renald had set around his home must have damn near killed him, Ethan found himself thinking.

Travel was pleasant – or at least as pleasant as it could be in a land as unwelcoming as the Dragon Wastes. Still fatigued from his labors, he stopped far more frequently than he had on the outward journey. Maytra didn't seem to care about what pace he moved, spending half her time in flight, and the rest curled up in the sling, sleeping.

By nightfall, the howling of the beasts returned. This time however, they were much closer. Even Maytra seemed ill at ease, frequently popping her head out of the blanket, craning her neck and hissing anxiously.

Early the next morning, Ethan had an uncomfortable feeling that he was being followed. Several times he thought he spotted shadows darting behind rocks. Maytra spent most of the day circling the sky above where he had recently passed. As he felt her anxiety growing, so did his own. Something was definitely stalking him, though no matter how many times he looked, it darted out of sight before he could get a clear view.

When he drew near to the dragons' canyon, the pursuit ceased and Maytra visibly relaxed. He felt a calm come over him as he descended. He took a moment to appreciate the magnificent creatures before him - frozen in place and locked in a desperate battle with a force of sheer evil. A tear spilled down his cheek when he thought of the unavoidable truth. They would never move again. And even the wards he had set would only delay their total destruction should he fail.

He mounted the dais. "Heather," he called out. His voice echoed from the walls, but there was no answer. "Heather. I need your help."

"So soon?"

The voice seem to come from everywhere at once.

"Where are you?" he asked.

"I am here," she replied. "Though until the dragons are restored, I can no longer take physical form."

"Something is happening to me," he said.

"Yes, I know. And I am sorry."

Ethan scowled. "You're sorry? I almost killed two of my friends. Why didn't you tell me what would happen?"

"Because I did not know," she answered. "Would you have refused if it had been otherwise?"

"No. But I don't understand how you couldn't know?"

There was a long pause before she spoke again. "What you did has never been done before. With the unknown there are always risks."

"Is there anything I can do?"

"Perhaps. But it is dangerous. And now is not the time. First you must find the children and bring them here."

"And once I do that, then what?"

"Then you must travel deep within your own spirit. You must take command of it. If you succeed, the spirits within you will be silent."

"What happens if I fail?"

"Then you will be trapped...forever. You will dwell here with us while another takes your place among the living."

One of his ancestors would possess his body, while he remained a spirit. The mere thought of this sent a chill up his spine.

He could feel Heather's presence fading. But she was right. Now was not the time. Somehow he would find a way to keep the voices at bay. At least long enough to finish what he must do.

He turned to the dragons. Though their eyes were closed, their essence was all around him, urging him to have courage. And for a moment, all other voices vanished. But only for a moment. He bowed low and started back up the canyon wall.

After a mile, the feeling of being stalked returned, and once again Maytra began circling nervously overhead. Relief only came when Ethan caught sight of the border to Renald's land. By this time, so tight was his grip on the hilt of his sword, his knuckles had turned pale white and his clenched jaw ached from the tension.

Maytra flew down to stand at the edge of the grass, glaring back and snarling. Ethan turned as well. There, just beyond a pile of loose boulders, were three creatures. He couldn't make out details, but they stood on all fours and were roughly the size of a large dog.

"What are they, girl?" he muttered.

Maytra hissed and screeched.

After remaining in sight for a few more seconds, the creatures darted off.

By the time he reached the house, the afternoon was turning to dusk. The pleasant tang of saltwater in the air was a welcome change to the barren wastes of the past four days, and the aroma of spiced ham soon had his mouth watering. His muscles longed for a soft pillow and a warm blanket, but such luxuries would have to wait for just a short while longer.

The instant his foot touched the porch, the door flew open and Kat raced outside, very nearly knocking Ethan off his feet as she wrapped her arms around him.

"I wasn't gone that long," he teased, lifting her up and returning the embrace.

"So you didn't miss me at all?" she said, feigning offense.

He put her down. "Of course I did."

The others were just preparing to eat supper.

"I see you made it back in one piece," remarked Markus, grinning.

Ethan responded with a wink. "Barely."

Lylinora gave a bright smile and rose to kiss him on the cheek. "I for one am certainly glad we don't have to listen to Kat complaining any longer," she said in a light-hearted tone.

Her welcome pleased Ethan. Outwardly at least, she had forgiven him for frightening her.

Renald's face remained solemn until he heard the sound of talons on wood. A moment later, Maytra scampered inside and jumped straight onto his lap. "There you are, you old rat." The old mage smiled, unable to hide his relief.

He switched his attention to Ethan. "She managed to keep you out of trouble, I see."

Ethan took a seat at the table. "Yes, she did."

Jonas passed him a pitcher of apple juice. "What is it like out there?"

He shrugged. "Desolate. From what I saw, Shinzan did his job well when he destroyed this place." He went on to tell Renald about the creatures he had encountered.

Renald sighed heavily. "They can sense the dragons are no longer a threat to them. But don't worry. They won't come here."

"What are they?"

"Cursed beasts. The few creatures who survived Shinzan's wrath were transformed. The dragons kept them far from here. But now..." Renald cleared his throat. "Well, now they only have my wards to fear."

"Will they attack us when we leave?" asked Jonas.

"I doubt it," he replied. "And if they do, Lylinora should be able to handle them easily enough."

This helped to ease Ethan's concerns. He decided to leave out any mention of his encounter with Heather for a more private talk with Renald. Renewed mention of the spirits dwelling within him might upset Lylinora or Kat, and he was already feeling guilty enough over the incident. Instead, the others spoke to him of Kat's lessons, as well as the preparations they had made for his and Markus' perilous journey.

After dinner, Ethan returned to the boat with Markus. While trying to sleep, he pondered on what they would encounter once they stepped through the portal.

How many years might have passed? And where exactly would they end up?

Since drinking the dragon's blood, fear had been something he could easily overcome. But now, with what he was about to do, it was becoming far more difficult to ignore.

Chapter Twenty-Two

ETHAN SMILED. "I felt the same way the first time I saw them."
Jonas, Lylinora, Kat and Markus were standing slack-jawed
and speechless as they gazed up at the six enormous dragons.

"Are they...alive?" Kat asked in a half-whisper.

Ethan stood beside her. "Of course they are."

"Can I touch one?"

"Sure."

She took a tiny step closer. "Come *with* me."

After taking her by the hand, they approached one of the white
dragons side by side. Ethan glanced over his shoulder and saw that
Renald had stepped up onto the dais and was giving them a disapprov-
ing scowl.

"It's not moving," remarked Kat. "Not even breathing."

"They've bound themselves to the core of Lumnia," he explained.
"Their bodies are slowly dying. But for now they're still alive, I promise."

She pressed her palm against its front haunch and gasped. "It's so
warm. I've never felt anything like it. It's hard and soft all at the same
time." She turned to the others. "You have to feel this. It's amazing."

"That's enough," barked Renald. "Leave them alone."

Ignoring his protest, Kat pressed her cheek to the dragon's scales.
"I wish I could hear their thoughts like you do, Ethan. How wonderful
that must be."

He touched her shoulder. "It is."

"I said that's enough," Renald repeated, this time more harshly. "We didn't come here to engage in nonsense."

Ethan nodded and took a deep cleansing breath. It was time. He and the others joined Renald on the dais. In preparation, he had done his best to dress in a manner that would not draw too much attention.

"That's assuming we end up in our own time," Markus had said. "If we end up in medieval times, we'll fit right in."

Lylinora selected a spot and unfurled a small round rug. While she was doing this, Renald dug into a satchel and retrieved two pendants and a thin golden rope.

He handed the rope to Lylinora. "Put this on. It will help you retain your strength."

"Is this a Rope of Making?" she asked, eyes wide.

Renald nodded. "A gift from my brother. He was one of only three mages who were able to craft them."

After admiring the rope for a moment, she wrapped it around her waist. "Thank you."

Renald then handed Markus and Ethan each a pendant. They were plain and unremarkable, aside from the blue rajni stone set at the end. "These will help guide you," he said. "Lylinora used Jonas' description of the one given to him to make them. And she cast a spell so they would be attracted to anyone from Lumnia born in her time. It should ignore Ethan as long as he wears one. When you're ready to return, smash the stone and a portal will open. Lylinora will be keeping it open at this end."

"You've told us this ten times already," complained Markus.

"And I'm telling you again," he snapped back. "Remember. Once the stone is smashed, you will have only a few seconds to enter. So don't use it until you're sure."

"Are you ready?" asked Lylinora.

Ethan nodded. Each of them was carrying only a small pouch containing a few gold coins and a handful of precious stones. It had been decided to leave behind any weapons aside from a dagger they kept hidden beneath their shirts.

Ethan closed his eyes and reached out to the dragons. *We are ready.*

Help us. He could feel their power instantly envelop the dais. He knew it would weaken them further. But there was no choice. Without their help, the portal could not remain stable. They could easily end up returning a thousand years into the future.

He looked back. Jonas was wringing his hands. Kat had been standing beside him, but was now nowhere to be seen. Unable to watch, Ethan guessed.

"Be careful," Jonas called out.

Ethan smiled and winked. "Unless I'm wrong, it will only seem like a few seconds to you."

Lylinora kissed them both on the cheek before taking her place on the rug. Once in position, she began chanting the incantation and swaying rhythmically from side to side. After about five minutes, a small disk of swirling blue and black light appeared in the center of the dais.

Ethan glanced over to Markus, noticing the tension building on his face. "Are you all right?" he asked.

His friend gave a sharp nod. "It just brings back bad memories, that's all. I'll be fine."

By now, Lylinora was dripping with sweat – hair clinging to her face and neck as the ritual grew to a fever pitch. Slowly but steadily the portal continued to expand until it was over six feet in diameter.

Cautiously, the pair positioned themselves close enough to enter in one short leap. Ethan wrapped his arms around Markus and counted down.

"Three. Two. One."

At the very instant they jumped, Ethan felt another pair of arms suddenly encircle his waist. He looked down to see Kat smiling impishly up at him.

*

"Get up!"

The voice sounded muffled and distant, like someone shouting through a pillow. Ethan struggled to regain his senses, but his muscles wouldn't cooperate – not even his eyelids.

"Get up," the voice repeated.

He felt himself being lifted to his feet and dragged for several yards. For a few moments he could hear his boots scraping against what sounded like stone. The soft crunching of leaves and the musty odor of earth then told him that he was lying down again.

"Is he all right?" asked an unfamiliar voice in English. It had a distinctive southern twang.

"He...um...fainted." This time it was Markus speaking.

Finally, Ethan managed to peel open his eyes. His mouth was dry and his head was pounding. As his vision slowly cleared, he could see that he was beneath a large oak tree.

"I'm fine," he croaked.

Markus was kneeling beside him, looking confused and a little bit angry. He helped Ethan into a seated position.

"We need to get out of here," he said, his eyes darting nervously from side to side.

Ethan tried to clear his head. They were in a small park – no more than two-hundred yards square. Off to his left at the park's center, a circular fountain featuring several white marble cherubs spewed a continuous gush of water. A number of paths leading to the outlying city streets radiated out from this like spokes on a wheel.

The surrounding buildings were mostly two stories high, with wrought iron railings encircling a second floor balcony. Scattered randomly amongst these were a few larger, four or five story buildings, which to Ethan's eyes had a more modern appearance than their smaller neighbors.

A few people were about the park, some sitting on benches and others strolling casually. One man, dressed in a pair of overalls and wearing a red cap, was standing a few feet away, a suspicious look on his weathered face.

Taking hold of Markus' hand, he got to his feet, his mind at last getting back to something like normal working order. "Where's Kat?" he asked, suddenly remembering her last second intervention.

"I'm right here," she replied, appearing from the other side of the oak. There was nothing guilty or apologetic about her. In fact, she looked quite pleased that she had managed to come with them in spite of Ethan's objections.

"What the hell!" he shouted. "I told you –"

"This isn't the time or the place," Markus cut in quickly. "We need to get moving."

"That boy on drugs or somethin'," asked the onlooker.

The thick southern accent suggested that they were at least in the United States.

"No, sir," Markus replied. "Just not feeling good."

Ethan waved his hand dismissively. "I feel better now."

He could see the man frowning. *English*, he warned himself. *I must speak English.* "Sorry, sir. I think I ate something bad."

"Ate something, did ya?" he said with obvious disbelief. "Well, you boys better skedaddle. Ain't no loiterin' 'round here."

Ethan gave him a sharp nod and set off on unsteady legs toward the nearest street. Markus and Kat were at his side at once. When they reached the street, they turned into an area that looked to be commercial.

"I should fucking strangle you," hissed Ethan. "Now what are we supposed to do?"

Kat sniffed. "I told you I didn't want to be left behind."

"And I said we can talk about this later," Markus told them both. "First of all, let's find out where the hell we are and what year it is."

They continued walking for a few blocks, glancing in windows they passed, all the time searching for a clue as to their location.

"One thing is for sure," said Markus as a red sports car raced by. "It's definitely not nineteen forty-four."

Two young men wearing denim jackets, ripped jeans and black leather boots passed by. Their hair was all the way down their backs, and in their left ears hung gaudy silver earrings – one in the design of a skull, the other a cross. Chain belts were fastened around their waists, and both had an assortment of silver bracelets on each wrist. Their eyes showed clear signs of eyeliner, while their cheeks were heavily smeared with blush. Black lipstick completed the 'look'.

Ethan nearly burst out laughing. "Men sure have changed."

Markus cracked a smile. "Are you sure they *were* men?"

Along the next block, Ethan spotted a police car parked on the curb. "We're in Mobile, Alabama," he announced.

Markus groaned. "That's just great. Two New Yorkers and a girl from another planet wandering aimlessly in the Deep South."

"It could be worse," Ethan countered. "It could have been Berlin."

His friend chuckled. "You have a point, I guess. And at least we speak the language." He looked over at Kat. "Well two of us do, anyhow."

Kat simply cocked her head and smirked. "Then it's a good thing I've got you with me."

A few buildings further down they came to a corner store. Alongside the front door was a box containing the local newspaper.

Markus bent down to examine it closely. A moment later he stood up straight, eyes wide. "Would you believe it? It's nineteen eighty-eight."

Ethan gave a soft whistle. "Forty-four years!"

"You look pretty good for your age," quipped Kat.

He shot her a furious glance. "I don't want to hear from you right now."

She shrugged and took a long, slow look around. "It's not how I pictured it." Just then, a blue car whizzed by. "Those things are amazing though. What are they?"

"They're called *be quiet!*" Ethan snapped. "We're not here for a bloody tour."

Kat puffed up, but made no further comment.

He turned to Markus. "At least it's cars and not panzers rolling down the street. And I don't see any SS goons strutting about."

Markus grinned. "So it seems like the good guys did win the war."

"It looks that way. But I'd sure like to know how it ended, and what happened to Hitler. The Japs too after what they did to Pearl Harbor. Are we occupying Tokyo these days?"

"That's not exactly the kind of questions we can just ask someone," Markus pointed out. "Not unless you want us branded as a bunch of crazies."

Ethan nodded. "I know. But I'm real curious, all the same.

"We'll need some money," Markus said, changing the subject. He jangled the pouch on his belt. "I sure hope they still have pawn shops around here."

Ethan was only half paying attention. He had already removed the pendant and was holding it out as far as the chain would allow. A dim pulse of light emanated from the heart of the rajni stone. He turned slowly, pointing it in every direction. When he was facing the way they were already going, the rate of the pulse increased slightly.

"Well, at least we know the damn thing works," said Markus. "Wait here."

He ducked inside the store, returning in less than a minute wearing a broad smile. "The lady inside says there's a pawn shop a mile further down." He chuckled softly. "I must say, it feels a bit odd talking in English again."

Ethan turned to glare at Kat. "That reminds me. Don't speak unless we're alone. We need to do what we came here to do and then get back."

She crossed her arms. "I'm not stupid, Ethan."

He snorted. "Really? Then why are you here?"

"Ease off," Markus scolded. "She's here, and that's that. So don't be an asshole." He placed an arm around the young girl's shoulder. "But he *is* right. You need to keep quiet when other people are around."

She smiled up at him, pretending to lock her lips with an invisible key. "I promise. Not a word."

As they moved on, Kat lingered every now and then to take in her surroundings, clearly impressed by the many bright lights and fancy looking goods for sale in the shop windows. While a fuming Ethan remained a few steps behind, Markus stayed by her side, doing his best to answer her questions about what the various items were. When an airplane streaked across the sky, she nearly toppled over from shock.

"You told me about those things," she gasped. "But I don't think I really believed it. Why would you want to go back to Lumnia?"

"Now *that's* a good question," agreed Markus.

"Stay if you want," snapped Ethan. "Both of you."

A few moments later he spotted the pawn shop on the other side of the street and stalked off toward it.

"What's wrong with him?" asked Kat.

Markus shrugged. "I don't know. Ever since he came back from the dragons, something about him is different."

"And it's not just that he seems older," she said, nodding in agreement. "He's...I don't know..."

"Darker," Markus completed for her.

The single word hung heavily in the air. Ethan had already reached the front entrance to the shop and was waiting for them with arms crossed, tapping his foot impatiently.

The moment they stepped inside, Kat's eyes began darting everywhere. The place was packed with hundreds of various items: everything from bicycles to farm tools, and water skis to lawn mowers. Off to their left, a long, glass-topped counter displayed jewelry at one end and hand guns at the other, while behind the counter, a variety of rifles and assault weapons were set against the wall. In the corner sat an old man wearing jeans and a check-patterned button down shirt. He scarcely bothered to look up from his newspaper as the trio approached.

"Ya'll buyin' or sellin'?" he asked in a rough baritone.

Markus stepped up to the counter and pulled out a diamond from his pouch. "What can you give me for this?"

The old man glanced over the top of his paper, a frown quickly forming. "Where'd you steal that, boy?"

"It's not stolen." Markus replied, trying to look offended.

With a deep sigh, he folded his paper and heaved himself up. "Let me see that."

He took the gem from Markus, rolling it around in his palm for a moment or two. "If this is real, you need to get your ass outta here."

Markus creased his brow. "I don't understand."

"'Cause if it's real, it's worth a damn fortune." Reaching to a shelf behind him, he produced a jeweler's eyepiece and turned on a lamp beside the cash register. After examining the diamond for a full minute, he tossed it onto the counter as if it had suddenly burned his fingers. "Get that thing outta here. Right now, boy. Before I call the law."

"I promise you, it's not stolen," insisted Markus. "It belonged to my mother."

"I don't care if it belonged to your grandmother's mother," he shot back.

His hand eased over to a telephone hanging on the wall just within reach.

"Please, sir," Markus hastily continued. "All we need is enough money to get some food and a place to stay for the night. I just lost my house. This is all I have left." He gestured to Ethan and Kat. "I can't let my children sleep on the streets tonight."

Ethan struggled to keep a straight face. His children?

The man eyed Markus closely, then did the same to Ethan and Kat. "Five-hundred," he eventually said. "That's all I'll give you."

Markus pretended to be disappointed. "I guess I don't have much choice."

Without another word, the man opened the register and placed five, one-hundred dollar bills on the counter. With a show of reluctance, Markus pushed the diamond across, then quickly snatched up the money.

"Thank you," he said, but received no response. The old man merely sat back down and continued reading his paper. The deal was done and that was the end of it.

Once outside, Markus' attitude instantly changed. A broad smile formed. "Five hundred dollars. And you heard what he said. That diamond was worth a bloody fortune. Hell, we have at least ten of them between us."

"So let me see if I understand this," Kat cut in. "You gave him a diamond, and he gave you five pieces of green paper." She shook her head. "That doesn't sound much like a good deal to me."

Ethan's foul mood finally broke. Unable to help himself, he burst into laughter. "Come on. Let's go find whoever the hell it is we're looking for." He pulled out the pendant and pointed it around until the pulse once again quickened.

As they walked, a few people glanced curiously at them, to which Ethan put down to their odd clothing. But after encountering several more of the long haired young men, as well as a few young women wearing so much make-up that Ethan remarked that they belonged in the circus, his anxiety lessened.

"Well *I* think it's pretty," said Kat. "Women in Kytain paint their faces like that."

Occasionally, a car passed them with its radio blaring. Ethan and Markus frowned, clearly not appreciating the new style of music.

"Sounds like old pots being banged together," sniffed Markus.

Kat laughed. "How can you say that? It's wonderful."

A mile or so further on, the modern buildings gave way to a series of large houses dating back to before the Civil War. Their manicured yards and well-tended flowerbeds stated that people of means lived here. The main avenue was lined with massive oak trees on both sides, trimmed so that they formed a majestic half-canopy above the road.

At another store they passed, Markus stopped to buy them each a chocolate bar and a cola. Ethan sighed with pleasure as the cold liquid poured down his throat. Markus had an even stronger reaction – after the first sip, gulping down half of the bottle in almost two seconds flat.

"I never thought I'd taste that again," he gasped, out of breath from such rapid swallowing.

Kat looked curiously at her bottle. "What is this? Why is it bubbling?"

Grinning, Markus reached out a hand to snatch it away. "If you don't want it…"

She jumped back, holding the drink close. "Oh, no you don't." She took a sip. "It's…good. How is it made?"

Ethan shrugged. "It's supposed to be a secret recipe, so I guess you'd need to ask the cola people. And if you liked that, wait until you try the chocolate."

She unwrapped the bar, took a small bite and smiled. "It reminds me of *sweet pods*. My mother used to give them to me as a child when I'd been good."

"I bet that wasn't very often," teased Ethan.

Kat pretended to be hurt. "I'll have you know that I was a very good girl when I was little."

"Well you weren't being so good when you decided to come here," he scolded, albeit not nearly so harshly as before.

She reached over to take his arm. "I'm sorry I upset you. But I just had to see Earth for myself."

Markus poked her playfully in the ribs. "You just didn't want him out of your sight."

Kat batted his hand away. "He actually *did* promise to take me if he ever went back."

Ethan let out an exasperated sigh. "Fine. You're here. Be happy about it."

She gave him a light squeeze. "I *am* happy."

They continued on for a time, with Ethan checking the pendant every so often to be sure they were still heading in the right direction. Eventually, the houses gave way to a series of small businesses and the occasional empty lot.

The sun was beginning to set when the rajni stone's pulses suddenly became far more rapid and urgent. As they passed a single-story cinder block building, Ethan felt the stone tugging him toward it. A shabby sign above the door read: 'Shotgun Harry's'. Even from the street he could catch the stench of stale beer and moldy carpet.

Ethan and Markus looked at one another doubtfully.

"So here it is," said Markus, shaking his head. "We travel through time to find a mage who will help to save Lumnia. And where do we end up? At some lousy, rundown bar."

Ethan sighed and spread his hands. "Well, at least we found it."

"I suppose so."

Inside, it was dimly lit, forcing Ethan to squint for a few seconds until his eyes adjusted. He then saw a long bar at the far end. To his right were four pool tables, and to his left a few dozen booths and small tables surrounding a dance floor and crudely built stage. Decorating the walls were a number of posters advertising upcoming entertainment, along with an assortment of bright neon liquor and beer signs.

The churning sound of unfamiliar music blared out from speakers hanging from the ceiling. A young, red-haired girl in a short black skirt and white cotton top tied into a knot at the midriff was busy wiping down tables.

Behind the bar stood a young man in a black tee-shirt. He had shaggy, shoulder length brown hair and was chatting with the bar's solitary customer while swigging from a bottle of beer.

He looked up at the newcomers. "She can't be in here," he shouted over the music.

Ethan glanced at his pendant. It was now pulsing so quickly, it almost appeared as one continuous light.

Markus' own pendant was reacting in an identical manner. "It's got to be one of these three," he said quietly

As they approached the bar, the bartender put down his beer and placed both hands flat on the bar top. "I said she can't be in here. No kids allowed." He took a long look at Ethan. "And I'll need to see your I.D."

The lone patron sniggered drunkenly, nearly falling off his stool. "Aw, let them stay, Jake. They ain't hurtin' nobody."

"We won't be staying," said Markus. "I'm looking for a friend, that's all."

Jake's arm swung in an exaggerated sweep of the room. "And do you see him?"

"No. But maybe you wouldn't mind if I asked you a few questions? It might help me find him." In one deft movement, Markus reached into his pocket and tossed a twenty dollar bill onto the bar.

"You a cop?"

He huffed a laugh. "Do I look like one?"

Jake eyed him suspiciously. "What kind of questions?"

"Where were you born?"

The bill was snatched up and disappeared into Jake's pocket. "Right here in Mobile," he said. Grabbing his beer, he took a long drink.

"Are you sure?" pressed Markus.

"Yeah, of course I'm sure. Why do you want to know?"

"Were you adopted?" Ethan cut in.

Jake paused in mid-swallow and sat the bottle down. "How the hell do you know that?"

Ethan and Markus grinned at each other.

"How old were you at the time?" asked Ethan.

"Three. Maybe four."

"What do you remember?" asked Markus.

"About what…my childhood? Nothing really. My parents abandoned us and we got adopted."

Ethan cocked his head. "We?"

"Yeah, we. Me and my sister."

"Where is she now?" asked Ethan.

Jake's eyes narrowed. "Don't worry about where she is. Tell me what the fuck you want or get out."

Ethan looked at Markus in an unspoken question.

Markus shrugged. "Just tell him, I guess."

It seemed like there was little choice. "We are from…well…another world," Ethan began. "And so are you and your sister. We're here to take you back."

Jake stared at him blankly for moment. Slowly his face twisted into an angry scowl. "Did Val put you up to this? Because it's not funny."

"I don't know who Val is," said Ethan. "And I promise you, I'm not trying to be funny."

Jake finished the beer in one gulp. "Val!" he called out. "What the hell is going on here?"

The girl cleaning the tables looked up. "What is it now, Jake?"

"Did you send these guys?" he demanded.

Tossing her cleaning supplies aside, the girl called Val walked over to the bar. In spite of her red hair, her skin was well-tanned. Her features were long and angular, with dark blue eyes and full lips. And though a bit shorter than Lylinora, she was just as well proportioned.

"I don't know what you're talking about," she insisted irritably. She looked at the trio one by one. "Sorry. Never seen them before."

"Bullshit," said Jake.

"She's not lying," said Markus. "And Ethan is telling you the truth too."

"What truth?" asked Val.

Ethan repeated what he had told Jake. With each word, her eyes widened and her hands began to tremble more noticeably. In seconds, tears were running down her face.

Jake's anger instantly changed to concern. Rounding the bar, he gently touched her arms. "Are you okay?" he asked, his tone tender.

Val nodded. "I...I just need a minute. That's all." With that, she turned and ran toward the stage, disappearing through a door on the right hand side.

"I'm sorry we upset her," said Markus.

Jake's fists clenched. "Look, I don't know who you are or why you're here. But my sister has been through enough. So tell whoever put you up to this to stay the fuck away from us."

Ethan held up his hands. "If you'll just calm down and let me explain..."

Jake took a menacing step forward. "I don't want to hear your explanations. It took a long time for Val to stop thinking about all this *other world* shit. I'm not going to let you come in here and start fucking with her head." He poked Ethan hard in the chest.

He was taller by about two inches, and broader in the shoulder. But this did not concern Ethan. He knew he was facing someone untrained in hand-to-hand combat. He could tell simply by the way the guy moved. If he wanted, he could have him flat on his back in an instant. But he was hoping it wouldn't come to that. Out of the corner of his eye he saw the drunk patron slowly get to his feet, holding his beer bottle by the neck like a club.

"Somebody better tell me what's happening here," said Kat.

The drunk coughed a stupid laugh. "What the hell language is that?"

This gave Ethan an idea. He took a step back and held up his hands. "All right, Jake. We'll leave. We don't want any trouble." Reaching inside his shirt, he pulled the pendant over his head. It was still pulsing wildly. "Here, take this so there's no hard feelings."

"I don't want shit from you," he replied. "Just get out."

Ethan stepped forward. "Please. Take it."

But Jake was in no mood for further talk. Leaning back, he threw a wild roundhouse punch. Ethan easily ducked beneath it, then countered with a straight left to the tip of Jake's jaw that was intended to stun rather than injure. He staggered back a few steps, but recovered quickly. It was clear from the look on his face that the admonishing blow had only fed his anger.

At that moment, the drunk charged at Ethan with his beer bottle raised. Not that he was ever going to get very far. After only two paces, the tip of Markus' elbow slammed into his mouth, sending him stumbling back again, knocking over two bar stools on his way before hitting the floor.

Snarling furiously, Jake lowered his shoulder and ran headlong at Ethan's waist in an attempt to use his size advantage. Ethan stepped nimbly out of the way. But the time for playing nice was obviously over. He rammed his knee hard up into Jake's solar plexus. The dull thump of contact was followed by a loud whooshing sound as Jake, with face contorted and arms clutching his stomach, gasped desperately for air.

"Grab him," Ethan shouted.

Markus reacted immediately. Stepping behind the stricken barman, he held him firmly while Ethan moved close to touch the pendant to Jake's cheek. The effect was instantaneous. His eyes flew wide and he became absolutely rigid, as if suddenly hit by a powerful electrical current. Then, after only a few seconds, he went totally limp. Only Markus' grip prevented him from collapsing completely.

Even after a full minute had passed, Jake was still struggling to breathe. "What the hell?" he gasped. "What did you touch me with?"

Ethan looked over to Kat. "Why don't you introduce yourself?"

She smiled broadly. "It's a pleasure to meet you. You can call me Kat. And your name is?"

Markus finally released his hold, allowing Jake to stumble back against the bar. At the same time, the drunk was just managing to get to his knees. When he saw Markus moving toward him, he quickly held up a defensive hand and shook his head.

"I've had enough," he sputtered through the considerable amount of blood still running from his mouth.

Markus backed off.

Jake's eyes were fixed squarely on Kat, his mouth hanging slightly open. "I...I understand what you're saying," he stammered. "How can…?" The truth then dawned on him with a rush. Once again, his legs began to wobble.

Ethan chuckled, remembering his own confused reaction when Jonas had first touched him with a rajni stone. "Like I said. We're here to take you and your sister home."

After letting out a loud groan, Jake dropped to one knee and began rubbing his temple. Kat moved closer to place a hand on his shoulder.

"It will be all right," she assured him. "You can trust us."

The door near the stage opened and Val reappeared, wiping her eyes. When she saw her brother kneeling, she raced over.

"What did you do to him?" she demanded.

Her eyes then moved to the drunk, who by now had climbed back on his bar stool and was dabbing at his bloody mouth with a napkin. "I'm calling the cops."

"Wait," Jake told her, struggling to his feet. "They're not lying. At least, I don't think they are."

Val stiffened. "Jake. You're not speaking English. That's…"

She couldn't finish her sentence.

Jake nodded, his expression grave. "I know. You were right all along."

Her tears returned. "Don't do this, Jake. It's not funny."

"He's telling you the truth," said Ethan.

When she heard him speaking the language of Lumnia as well, it all became too much and she burst into uncontrollable sobs. Jake wrapped his arms protectively around her.

He kissed his sister's brow. "I'm so sorry that I never believed you. I really am." His eyes shifted over to Ethan. "When we were little, the doctors said she was traumatized from being abandoned. They said she had made up a language as a defense mechanism so she didn't have to communicate with the outside world. She didn't speak anything else until she was eleven years old."

"What about you?" Ethan asked.

"I don't remember much of anything before we were adopted. Sometimes I thought I understood her. Maybe I was too young, or maybe I just blocked it out. I was only three or four at the time. Val was eight. We use the birthdays the state gave us, so I really don't know exactly how old we are."

"So, Val, do you still remember the language enough to speak it fluently?" Ethan asked.

She nodded. Her red and swollen eyes flicked from him to her brother, then back to him again. "You really are from...Lumnia?"

He smiled warmly. "We sure are. And we're here to take you back."

Val moved a little away from Jake. "Why now? Why after all these years?"

"That's a long story. But it's important that you come with us."

She shook her head. "No. I can't accept this. It isn't real."

Kat stepped forward. "It's real," she assured her. Her tone was gentle and sisterly. "And they can prove it."

Val hesitated a moment. "Okay. Show me."

"I'll need something heavy," said Ethan.

"Wait," Markus warned. "Remember what Renald told us. Be sure we're ready to return."

Ethan groaned. "All right."

"What's wrong?" asked Jake.

Ethan forced a smile. "Nothing. But if there is anything you want to bring with you, you need to get it now."

"Wait a minute," said Val. "Are you telling us we can't come back?"

"It may be some time," he admitted.

She turned to her brother. "What do you think?"

He took a long look around the dingy bar. "It couldn't be much worse than this."

His remark brought a smile to her lips. "Okay. I just need to go home and grab a few things."

Jake walked over to the drunk who was still sitting there with a perplexed expression. "I need you to watch the bar for a while, Larry."

Larry gave him a slack-jawed nod.

"You're leaving *him* in charge?" Kat giggled.

Jake grinned back at her. "Why not? He owns the place."

CHAPTER TWENTY-THREE

JUST AS THEY left the bar, a ragged pick-up truck towing a tarp covered trailer squeaked and sputtered its way into the parking lot. Jake ran over and spoke to the four, long-haired young men inside for a couple of minutes.

"Who was that?" asked Markus when he returned.

"The band," he replied.

Markus raised an eyebrow. "*Those* were musicians?"

Ethan laughed. "Things have really changed."

"What do you mean?" asked Val.

He shook his head. "Nothing. Just a private joke."

"How far away do you live?" asked Markus.

"About ten miles," Val told him.

Kat's shoulders sagged. "We have to walk ten more miles?"

Val crinkled her nose. "Walk? In these heels? Are you kidding?"

She led them to the rear of the building where a white, four door sedan was parked. The dents and rust on the body clearly showed it had seen much better days. Not that Kat seemed to notice the damage. She ran her hands over the hood and door as if it was a priceless sculpture.

"Get in," said Val after unlocking the doors.

Kat jumped up and down, clapping her hands. "We get to ride in this?"

Val gave her a sideways glance. "How else would we get there?"

"She's never ridden in a car before," Ethan explained.

She eyed him suspiciously. "But *you* have?"

He nodded. "A long time ago."

Jake huffed a laugh. "It can't have been that long. How old are you anyway? Eighteen?"

"It's hard to explain," he replied.

"Try," Jake insisted.

Ethan gave him a reassuring smile. "Look, don't worry. You'll have all the answers you want very soon. That's a promise."

He saw Markus frown, obviously not understanding his evasion.

"Can I ride in the front?" asked Kat, still bubbling with excitement.

Jake smiled and mussed her hair. "Sure you can."

With everyone inside, Val started the car. The engine shuddered and clanked for a short time, then leveled off to a low growl.

Val gave an embarrassed grin. "She needs some work, but it gets me around."

"Are you kidding?" said Markus. "I never even owned a car."

"So you've been here before?" asked Jake. "Earth, I mean."

"We're *from* Earth originally," he replied. "Well, *I* am anyway."

Ethan shot him a warning glance. "It's a long and boring story," he said.

Markus gave him another questioning frown in response, but Ethan simply smiled and began asking Jake about his life in Mobile. Throughout all of this, Kat sat with her head poking out of the window, giggling and laughing one minute, and firing a stream of questions at Val about anything that happened to catch her eye the next.

They wound their way through a series of residential neighborhoods before eventually pulling into the shell driveway of a small, single story house. Its chipped and dingy paint, together with numerous patches of rotted wood, made the property a good match for the car they had arrived in. A narrow flight of five steps led up to a small covered porch with a swing dangling precariously from rusted chains.

"Be it ever so crumbled," said Jake.

But Kat wasn't interested in the condition of the house. "Can we go for another ride?" she begged. "Just a quick one before we leave?"

"That's up to your father I suppose." Val replied with a wink.

Kat burst into laughter. "Markus? He's not my father. *My* father's a king."

This made Val smile. "So you're a princess? That's good to know."

Kat sighed heavily. "Markus and Ethan don't believe me either."

They all went up the steps together. Val had just unlocked the front door when the throaty roar of a motorcycle thundering up the street reached them. Kat jumped to Ethan's side, gripping his arm.

The rider turned in and pulled up behind Val's car, revving his engine as loudly as possible several times before shutting it off and dismounting.

"What's *he* doing here?" asked Jake, his mouth twisting into a grimace.

Val brushed past the others and went down to meet the newcomer. As she did so, he removed his helmet, revealing a mop of dark wavy hair crowning a square-featured, clean-shaven face. Of muscular build and standing several inches over six foot, he was wearing a black leather jacket over a white tee-shirt, together with a pair of blue jeans with rips and tears along both legs.

"Get the hell out of here, Mike," Val said when a few yards away. "I told you. We're through."

He tossed his helmet carelessly over the rear view mirror. With long confident strides, he swaggered up close to her, a roguish grin on his face. "I heard you. Don't worry. I'm not here for trouble." He looked up at the porch. "Who are your friends?"

"None of your damn business," she snapped.

Mike held up his hands. "Okay, okay. No need to get your panties in a wad. I just came by to tell you that Roscoe wants to see you. You and little Jake there."

Val stiffened. "What for?"

"I think you know 'what for'. He's not too happy about you stealing his shit."

"It was your goddamn idea," she shot back.

"My idea?" he scoffed. "That's not the way I see it. Not the way Roscoe sees it either. And he's plenty pissed. Of course, I could talk to him…if we could work something out." He moved even closer to place a hand on her hip and give it a firm squeeze.

With a roar of anger, Jake came charging down from the porch. "Get your hands off her!" he shouted, shoving Mike hard in the shoulder.

Mike's smile vanished. "Better watch yourself, junior." The heel of his hand thudded into the center of Jake's chest, the sheer force sending him stumbling back several paces.

Val was instantly beside her brother. "Are you okay?"

He nodded, though the pained look on his face clearly showed how much the blow had hurt him.

Ethan started to move, but Markus pulled him back. "I'll deal with this," he said.

He stepped down from the porch, eyes firmly fixed on Mike. His face was like stone as he placed himself in front of Val and Jake.

"Time to go, fella," he said.

After looking him up and down, Mike let out a scornful laugh. "And what the hell are you supposed to be?"

A vicious grin formed. "I'm the man who is telling you to leave… while you still can."

Mike tilted his head to one side and spat on the ground. "Is that right? Well, asshole, here's a newsflash. You've just bitten off more than you can chew."

Baring his teeth, he threw a wild right at Markus' head.

For a fighter of Markus' experience and ability, the punch was laughably easy to avoid. So was the straight left that followed. He then countered with a bone crushing right hand of his own to Mike's jaw. His opponent staggered back a step, throwing up both arms to prevent another strike to the head. But Markus simply switched the attack, landing a rapid series of punches to the body, forcing him to double over.

He snorted with contempt. "I thought you were tough. You *act* like you are. But you fight like a girl."

Mike was still crouched over, groaning and gasping for air, when Markus jerked up a knee, smashing it into his nose. He landed hard on his back, a horizontal fountain of blood erupting from both nostrils. Yet even now, Markus was not finished. Reaching down, he grabbed Mike by the collar, pulling him up into a half-sitting position. Again and again he pummeled punches into the man's face, not stopping until he was totally unconscious.

"That's how to handle guys like that," he told Val and Jake, disdainfully allowing the blood-soaked mess that was Mike to slump back down. The couple were staring at him, wide-eyed and terrified. Ethan and Kat, however, were smiling broadly.

"Val, take Kat and Jake inside," Markus continued. "Ethan, stay out here with me."

Val blinked several times before pulling herself together sufficiently to do as Markus told her. Kat objected at first, but Ethan had a quick word with her.

"You should take care of them," he said. "They need to get ready."

With the others inside, he joined Markus beside the still unconscious Mike.

"There something I need to tell you," Markus began. "I'm not sure you'll like it."

Ethan had already sensed what he was about to say. He'd been watching Markus carefully since they'd arrived, and he recalled his friend's evasive reaction during their talk by the dock when he'd asked if Markus might want to stay on Earth. When he spoke, it was with an air of inevitability.

"You're not coming back with me, are you?"

Markus blew out his cheeks, obviously relieved that his decision was being accepted so calmly. "No, I'm not," he confirmed. "Ever since we've been back, it's just kind of hit me. I want to try and make a new start here. Maybe I can leave Specter behind in Lumnia where he belongs." He reached down and jingled his pouch. "And this is going to help a lot."

"I wish I could change your mind," Ethan told him. "And I sure will miss you. But I do understand." He removed his own pouch and handed it over to Markus. "Take this one too. I don't have any use for it."

His friend smiled and shoved it into his pocket. "Thanks, Ethan.

And at least I know you don't need me anymore. Whatever those bloody dragons did to you made sure of that. One thing though. Be careful. There are some dark places you can take yourself that are hard to come back from. Trust me on that."

Ethan slapped him fondly on the shoulder. "I'll watch myself. And you do the same."

Just then, Mike began to moan and roll from side to side. When he opened his eyes, the mere sight of Markus had him crawling hastily backwards down the driveway.

"Well, I did tell you to leave while you had the chance," Markus said with a smile. "Maybe you'd like to go now?"

Mike did not need telling again. Scrambling to his feet, he made for his bike as quickly as he was able to. Blood had stained the front of his white tee-shirt almost completely red, and his still dripping broken nose was laid over to one side below a half-closed left eye. A moment later the motorcycle rumbled to life. After throwing on his helmet, he pushed himself back into the street.

"This ain't finished," he shouted over the engine noise. "Tell that bitch Val that Roscoe will be seeing her real soon."

With these final words, he roared off into the distance.

The two friends started toward the house. When they reached the door, Markus paused.

"One more thing. Why are you avoiding talking about Lumnia to Val and Jake?"

"Because I need them," Ethan replied. "You think they would come if I told them about Shinzan, or what it is I need them for?"

Markus shook his head. "You *have* changed."

He shrugged. "I had to, didn't I?"

Ethan opened the door. Directly inside was a small living room, its main feature being a green couch with torn and heavily stained cushions. To the right of this, a matching love seat was in similarly poor condition. Aside from these, the only other objects in the room that could even vaguely claim the title of 'furniture' were two stacked milk crates, upon which stood a portable television with a bent coat hanger protruding from the antennae socket. Two doors, one to the left of the couch and another in the opposite corner, led to the bedrooms, bathroom and kitchen.

Kat was sitting cross-legged in the center of the room on a ratty beige carpet. Val and Jake were huddled together on the love seat, still looking nervous and afraid.

"So which one of you is going to tell me what that was all about?" Markus asked them.

Brother and sister looked at one another. Finally, Val spoke.

"Mike used to be my boyfriend," she began. "Last week he told me and Jake about a stash of weed hidden in an abandoned house a few miles from here."

Markus cocked his head. "Weed?"

"You know," Jake cut in. "Pot. Marijuana."

Markus nodded. "*That* I've heard of."

"Anyway," Val continued. "It belonged to a biker in the Devil's Priests named Roscoe. The plan was for me and Jake to take the weed and sell it, then the three of us would split the money. Mike was supposed to tell Roscoe that someone in another bike club had taken it."

"Looks like Roscoe figured your plan out," said Markus.

Val lowered her head. "It was stupid. But I was just so damn broke. I should have never trusted that asshole."

"It doesn't matter now," Ethan said. "You and Jake will be far away from here very soon. You'll never need to worry about him again."

Jake pushed himself up from the seat. "Then let's get a move on. How much stuff can we take with us?"

"Just what you can carry," Ethan replied. "The portal is not very big."

Val knitted her brow. "Portal?"

"You'll see," said Ethan. "But you should hurry."

The pair disappeared through the door next to the couch.

"And if you have a hammer it would be nice," Ethan called out after them. "Or even a big rock," he added much more quietly. "I have to break the pendant with something."

He then noticed Kat staring at the television. He turned it on, as much to satisfy his own curiosity as to please her. For most people in New York City when he'd left, TV was still a new and amazing thing;

only a small number of the very affluent were actually able to own a set. And even if you could afford one, all you got for your money was a few hours of transmissions every week in poor quality black and white. The televisions back then were big too. Great bulky things that would need two men to carry them. Their screens though, were small. Much smaller than the one he was looking at now. And this TV was so compact, it even had a handle on the top which meant he could pick it up with one hand if he wanted to.

With a sharp pop and crackle of electricity, the set came to life. Ethan stared in wonder as the images of a football game appeared.

"Markus," he whispered. "You see that? It's in color."

A wide grin split his friend's face. "Yeah! A lot has changed all right."

Kat was mesmerized. "It's like magic," she sighed.

Ethan sat down on the floor beside her. "Listen, Kat. There's something you need to know. Markus is not coming back with us. He's staying here on Earth."

Her eyebrows shot up and the television was immediately forgotten. "What? Why?"

"He wants to make a fresh start. The gold and diamonds we brought will see that he has everything he needs. And I was thinking…"

He paused to look up at Markus, who nodded knowingly. "I was thinking you might want to stay here too. Markus will take care of you. You'd be safe here."

Kat leapt to her feet, her face crimson. "No! You are not leaving me behind! You can't do that."

Ethan rose quickly and took hold of her hands. "Calm down. I won't stop you if you want to return. But think about it for a minute. There's no war here. No Shinzan…"

"And no *you*," she said, cutting him short. She looked over to Markus. "I understand why you'd want to stay. Well, I think I do. And I'm going to miss you, Markus. A lot more than you can imagine." She met Ethan's eyes. "But I'm going back to Lumnia. There's nothing more to talk about."

Ethan gave her a lopsided smile. "As you wish, Princess."

Another twenty minutes passed while Jake and Val changed their clothes and rummaged through their belongings, trying to decide what to take and what to leave behind. Ethan was growing impatient. He was just about to go through and hurry them along when the ominous rumble of approaching motorcycle engines reached him.

He ran to the window. Six bikers were pulling into the drive; Mike was amongst them. The others were all burly, wore full beards, and had dozens of tattoos on their bare arms. One tattoo in particular sent Ethan's blood boiling.

"They've got Kraut swastikas on their damn skin," he spat. "What kind of asshole does that? Maybe we didn't win the war after all."

The largest member of the bunch rode almost to the bottom of the steps, then pointed for the others to spread out. The sheer volume of their combined engines was rattling all the windows and had Kat covering her ears.

Markus stood beside Ethan, assessing the situation. "You know what they remind me of?"

"Ugly Nazis?"

Markus squeezed his shoulder. "No. Dwarves."

Ethan couldn't help but laugh.

Jake and Val came hurrying in from the back. Val had changed into a pair of jeans and a tee-shirt; she'd also shed her heels in favor of running shoes. She shoved past Ethan to see out of the window.

"It's Roscoe," she said. "Hurry. Let's go out the back."

Markus pulled his dagger from under his shirt. "There's no need to run from these bums." He glanced at Ethan. "Right?"

Ethan grinned and drew his own blade. "Right. But you get to fight the big guy. Okay?"

As the engines went silent, Markus looked out again. His confident expression faded. All six men were pulling pistols from their belts.

"*Now* there's a need to run," he said. "Where's the back way out?"

Val pointed to the door beside the couch. "Straight down the hall."

Markus glanced across at Ethan. "Stay with Kat. Val and Jake, get behind me."

Brother and sister followed Markus while Ethan positioned Kat in front of him and brought up the rear. On reaching the back door,

Markus kicked it open and stopped just beyond the threshold, forcing the others to wait inside.

After checking the corners of the back yard, he waved the others toward a chain linked fence that separated them from the house on the next block. Jake paused to help Val over. Ethan offered to do the same for Kat, but she hopped easily over the top without assistance. Just moments after Ethan and Markus followed her, the first shot came.

Ethan gasped with relief on realizing that the bullet had missed everyone. He glanced back to see one of the bikers at the corner of the house, weapon leveled. Another was rounding the opposite corner.

Two more shots were fired as they ran for their lives, with one round passing just over his and Markus' head. But no more followed. A few seconds later they had made it beyond the effective range of most hand-guns. Ethan risked another rapid glance back. It was as he suspected. No one had climbed the fence to pursue them. In fact, there was no longer a sign of any biker at the back of the house. It was a breathing space, but it was sure to be a short one.

Just as they reached the next street, the combined roar of bike engines firing up confirmed Ethan's fears. They had no hope of outrun-ning a bunch of motorcycles. He needed to find somewhere out of sight to open the portal damn quick – and something to shatter the rajni stone with.

They crossed over and ducked between two more houses.

"Is there an empty building somewhere around here we can hide in?" he asked Jake.

A wide-eyed Jake gave a stuttering shake of the head. Both he and Val appeared far too frightened and breathless to offer any information of use. Ethan and Markus groaned in unison.

They continued through the next set of yards and crept around the side of the house, all the time crouching low. By now, the street lights were starting to come on. Very soon they would have the cover of dark-ness. But the roar of the engines circling the area warned they may not have that long.

"There," said Markus all of a sudden, pointing down the street to a pair of three-story, red-brick buildings a hundred yards away on the other side. "We can open the portal in the alley between those two."

He listened carefully. For now, the motorcycles sounded like they were at least a block behind them. With a wave, he urged the group to run as fast as they could.

Recalling the day he'd been transported to Lumnia, Ethan could not resist an ironic chuckle. At least these Nazis didn't have panzers, he thought.

When they drew closer, it was clear that the space between the two buildings was much wider than Markus had anticipated - roughly thirty feet across, and it was blocked off at the far end by a brick wall that reached all the way to the top floor. Should the bikers pass by, they would almost certainly be spotted, *and* they would be trapped. But it was too late now. He waited at the corner until the others were well inside.

The brick beside Markus' left arm exploded before he even heard the shot, sending shards of debris digging painfully into his flesh.

"Damn it," he snarled, covering the wound with his other hand. "Open the portal, Ethan!"

Looking back the way they had come, he saw the silhouettes of two bikers advancing. The street light directly over his head had made him a perfect target. Cursing his stupidity, he ducked down the alley just as another shot was fired.

Ethan was still searching desperately for something with which to smash the pendant. But cardboard and general household trash were the only things littering nearly every inch of the alley.

"They're coming," shouted Markus. He pointed to a collection of crates piled up against the wall at the far end. "Get behind those."

Though trembling with sheer terror, Val and Jake did as they were told. Kat, however, ignored the order and continued helping Ethan in his search for something heavy and hard.

With no time to argue, Markus gripped her arm and shoved her roughly behind the crates a bit further along from Val and Jake. "Stay there!" he ordered. She glared at him, but did not move.

"They're down here," called a gruff voice from the street. "They're trapped."

Several shots were immediately fired, echoing loudly and whining as they ricocheted off the paving stones. Someone gave a brutal laugh. They were toying with them now. Ethan ducked down beside Kat, while Markus put his back against Val and Jake, pressing them to the wall.

The rumble of more motorcycles arriving sent chills down Ethan's spine. But at least the gunfire had temporarily stopped. A pair of dim lights fastened to the rain gutters high above was all that illuminated the alley. Good for cover, but it was making it harder than ever for him to spot something he might use to open the portal.

A minute later, the engines stopped. A deep, intimidating voice rolled down to them.

"Come on out, girl. You know you got this coming. No one steals from me and gets away with it."

Ethan could only assume this was Roscoe.

Val looked at her brother, tears dripping down her cheeks. "I'm so sorry I got you into this."

"Calm down," said Markus. "We're not dead yet."

"I'll count to three," Roscoe continued. "Then we're gonna light ya'll up. One…."

As Markus shifted his weight, he felt something touch his foot. Something hard. He pushed aside the remnants of a cardboard box. Beneath this was a brick.

"Two…"

Ripping off his pendant, he held up the brick so that Ethan could see.

"Do it!" Ethan immediately shouted back.

"Three!"

Markus tossed the pendant to his feet and brought the brick down with all the strength he could muster. At literally the same moment, the bikers opened fire.

Amongst the volley of bullets and flying debris, a flash of pure white light exploded, for a split second transforming the deep gloom to brilliant daylight. A sigh of relief slipped from Ethan when he saw a portal appear about ten or twelve feet to the far side of Markus.

The shots ceased for a moment, and they could hear confused shouts and curses coming from the bikers. Seizing this opportunity,

Markus shoved Val and Jake toward the portal, but they resisted furiously, looking even more terrified than before.

"You'd rather stay here?" he growled at them angrily.

Val was the first to move toward the swirling disk. After hesitating for a second, Jake then followed her.

Seeing this, Ethan took Kat's hand and moved into the open, hurrying over to join them. But two more shots rang out before he was even halfway there. One bullet zipped into the ground right beside his feet. Instinctively, he jumped back, knocking Kat down.

As Markus turned to face him, a fearful Jake clutched hold of his arm. Val was already at the very edge of the portal, and the sound of renewed gunfire startled her further forward. Just as she fell inside, her trailing hand shot out to grip Jake's shirt collar, dragging her brother along with her. Markus, off balance and unable to stop his momentum, was forced into the swirling light as well.

Terror and panic gripped Ethan's heart as he saw the three of them vanish. He knew the portal would only remain open for a few seconds longer. Rapidly, he jerked Kat to her feet and started once more toward it. He could hear the sound of heavy boots pounding their way down the alley. Another shot came, this one grazing his left leg, causing him to stumble sideways. His shoulder and head banged into the back wall, leaving him momentarily stunned.

Forcing his way through the fog and pain, he realized that he was no longer holding Kat's hand. He started to call out her name, but the air was driven from out of his lungs as something struck him hard in the center of his back. The impact sent him lurching forward and tumbling directly into the portal. Desperately, he tried to turn and reach out for her, but to his horror saw that she was already in the arms of one of the bikers, kicking and fighting furiously.

Realization hit him like a punch to the stomach. *She* was the one who had struck him; she'd been pushing him to safety.

The last thing he saw as he completed his backward fall into the portal was Kat's loving eyes looking straight into his own. They were crying tears of farewell.

CHAPTER TWENTY-FOUR

THE POWERFUL IMAGE of a tearful Kat battling in the clutches of the biker was enough to all but eliminate any after effects of traveling through the portal. Ethan pushed himself up from the cold hard stone of the dais, but before he could gain his feet a pair of arms lifted him the rest of the way. He blinked hard to fully clear his vision. There it was. The portal was still open.

"Don't close it!" he shouted.

But it was too late. The disk began shrinking rapidly. He clutched at the pendant still hanging around his neck. He would not abandon her. He tried to reach the portal and dive through before it was gone, but the same arms held him back.

"It's too late," he heard Jonas say.

Enraged at being restrained, Ethan twisted and brought his elbow around, connecting sharply with Jonas' left ear. The impact sent the old servant sprawling. But none of this made a difference. The portal was already gone. Ignoring Jonas' plight, he looked to where Lylinora was still kneeling. But even as he ran over to her, she collapsed on the rug.

He desperately tried to shake her awake. "Please! I need you. Don't do this." But no matter how hard he shook, she did not stir.

Out of the corner of his eye he caught sight of Renald. His aged face was stricken with sorrow.

"Help me," Ethan begged. "You can open another portal. You have to."

Renald averted his eyes. "I'm sorry. I don't have the strength. I'd be dead before it opened."

"You have to try!" he insisted, but the old man sadly shook his head.

Markus was sitting a few feet away, still recovering. He dragged himself up and regarded Ethan. "Where's Kat?" he asked.

"I...I couldn't save her," he replied, unable to look his friend in the eye.

"You mean you left her there?" Sudden fury contorted Markus' face. In a flash, he grabbed Ethan by the collar. "You son-of-a-bitch." His fist raised to strike, but a now partly recovered Jonas grabbed his arm.

Ethan made no move to get away. He deserved it. He had failed her. Left her to die. He could still feel her hand clutching his. Why had he not realized she let go?

I can help you.

A voice in his head echoed from the depths. The spirits of his ancestors had been virtually silent on Earth. Now they were back.

I can save her.

All at once, the anger on Markus' face faded and he released his grip. Ethan fell to his knees, holding his head in his hands.

"I'm sorry," said Markus. "I know you wouldn't have left her if you could have helped it." Pulling his arm free of Jonas, he sat on the edge of the dais facing away from the others to hide his tears.

Jonas knelt beside Ethan. "I'm sure it wasn't your fault."

This only made him feel worse. "It *was* my fault!" he shouted.

I can help you bring her back.

"How?" he whispered.

Just let me in and all will be set to rights.

"You can save her?"

"Who are you talking to?" asked Jonas. He tried to look into Ethan's eyes, but they were shut tight.

Of course I can. Just let me in and all will be well. I have the knowledge...and the power.

"What must I do?"

Just let me in. Give up your will. I will see to everything.

"I'll do anything you ask. Just save her." He could feel himself surrendering; his grip on his mind lessening. Then a face appeared from the darkness. Strong and confident, it regarded him for a moment.

Very good. Now sleep. Sleep and I will do what you cannot.

An incredible sense of well-being came over Ethan. He felt as if his body was light as air and drifting on a warm spring breeze. All sorrow and doubt was gone - washed away and replaced by a sense of utter contentment and calm. *All will be set to rights.* The words wrapped around him like a mother's loving arms. No longer did he care for the troubles of the world. This is where he belonged. Safe and at peace....forever.

*

The aching in his joints was surpassed only by the dull throbbing in his head. He tried to sit up, but every muscle in his body felt paralyzed. Even his eyes refused to open.

A cool rag was pressed against his forehead. "Don't try to move," said a soft feminine voice. "You've been through a lot. Just be still."

He tried to place who was speaking. Lylinora had a slightly higher timbre. And as for Kat...just thinking of her made him want to weep. He would never forget her final desperate expression as he'd fallen into the portal.

"Is he awake?" This time it was Markus.

Ethan wanted to answer, but was only able to moan.

"I think so," the unfamiliar voice replied. "But he's too weak to move."

He heard a door open, then weary footsteps dragging across a wooden floor.

"How are they?" asked Markus.

It was Renald who answered him. "Angry. Afraid. Confused. As one would expect. Jonas and Lylinora are still trying to calm them down. You really should have told them more before you brought them here."

"That was Ethan's decision."

"And what about you?" Renald asked. "Were you honestly planning to stay behind?"

"Yes, I wanted to. I thought I could make a new start of it. But it just didn't work out that way."

Ethan could feel his entire body tingling each time the cool rag touched his head. After a few minutes he found himself able to open his eyes. The dim light of the room didn't reveal much at first. A shadowy figure was sitting beside him. He guessed it was the female voice he had heard earlier, but the darkness hid her features.

He turned his head slightly and caught sight of Markus and Renald sitting on a sofa. Things were becoming a little clearer now. They were back at Renald's house. But how did they get here? The throbbing in his head increased as he attempted to recall what had happened. He let out another soft moan.

The woman on the bed reached down and produced a cup. Tenderly, she slid her hand beneath his head and tilted it. "Drink this," she told him.

Holding the cup to Ethan's lips, she poured a small amount of sweet tasting liquid into his mouth. It felt soothing to his tongue and throat.

"Thank you," he said, though his voice was a mere whisper. "Mar… Markus."

The woman rose and Markus sat in her place. Ethan tried to get a better look at her as she moved away, but she was across the room in an instant and out of sight.

"What…what happened?" he asked.

Markus smiled down at him. "I think you should wait until you're rested."

"Kat," he pressed. "He told me he'd help her."

Even though he was smiling, Markus' expression still looked strained. "*Who* told you?"

"I don't know. But is she safe?"

"She's safe," Markus assured him.

Renald got up and made his way over. His eyes betrayed his fatigue and concern. "That's enough for now," he said. "All this can wait until morning."

He placed a hand on Ethan's brow.

The effect was instant. Ethan felt his body relax and the darkness of sleep rapidly took him.

When his eyes opened again, the sun was shining through the

windows. The soreness in his muscles and joints was still quite intense, but the throbbing in his head was completely gone.

He shifted his body up toward the headboard until he could see the interior of the house. At the table sat Markus and Jonas, along with an unfamiliar young girl. Her raven hair was tied into a tight ponytail that fell down to the middle of her back. Her features were delicate, though not fragile, and her ample bosom was made even more apparent by a form fitting, short-sleeved shirt. Ethan was immediately taken by her beauty.

Markus noticed him watching and shot a welcoming smile. "Back from the dead, I see. How are you feeling now?"

Ethan returned the smile and sat up a bit more. "Sore as hell. What happened?" He nodded toward the girl. "And who's this?"

Markus shifted in his seat and cleared his throat. "Come on, Jonas. We should go."

Jonas chuckled softly. "I think you're right."

They started to the door, both with amused smirks on their faces.

"Hey! Where are you going?" Ethan called out. He tried to rise, but the pain shooting through him was too much. Wincing, he collapsed back against the headboard. By the time he recovered, they were gone. Only the girl was still there.

Once again it occurred to him how attractive she was. "Hello," he said.

She folded her hands and kept her eyes fixed on the table.

"I'm sorry," he said in his friendliest tone. "But I'm a bit confused. How did you get here?"

"I came with Markus," she replied, without looking up.

So Markus *had* gone back. The voice had told him the truth. He remembered Markus telling him that Kat was safe. But safe where? Here, or on Earth? And why would Markus bring someone else to Lumnia? But one look at this gorgeous girl suggested the obvious reason.

"Did Kat make it back as well?"

The girl nodded.

Relief flooded through him. "Where is she? Is she coming to see me?" A chastening thought then stabbed at his heart. She must hate him. God only knows what those bikers had done to her. More than ever, he needed to see Kat. To beg her for forgiveness.

The girl rose from the table and moved toward the bed. Even the way she walked was attractive – each step casual yet perfect. Her clothes reminded him of those he had seen on Earth in nineteen eighty-eight. Tee-shirt, jeans, and ankle high suede boots.

She sat beside him on the bed and smiled. At that moment, now much closer, her face became strangely familiar.

"I *did* come to see you," she replied.

For an instant, her words did not make any sense. But after a few seconds realization struck him and his eyes shot wide. With an almighty rush, the strangely familiar face, although older, became clearly recognizable. How could he have not seen it before?

"Kat?" he gasped. "How?" No other words would come.

She smiled sweetly and touched his cheek. "I've missed you."

Ethan could only stare, mouth agape. As the truth of what had happened flooded through him, tears began to fall. "How long has it been?"

She wiped his tears away with her thumb. "Five years."

He looked down, shame burning intensely. "I'm so sorry, Kat. I didn't mean for this to happen."

Her laughter had a musical quality to it as she lifted his chin until their eyes met. "You didn't do anything. I was the one who sneaked through to Earth when you told me not to. And it wasn't *you* who sent those bikers after us. Besides, I pushed you into the portal. So it's not like you deserted me or anything."

"Why? Why did you do that?"

"Because I knew you would never leave me, and I thought those bikers were going to kill you. It was the only thing I could think of to get you out of there." Her mouth twisted slightly. "Of course, I didn't know at the time that the cops were only about ten seconds away from showing up."

She shrugged and her smile returned. "Oh, well. Nothing I can do about it now."

Ethan's sense of relief on hearing that the bikers hadn't harmed her was enormous. "So what happened after I went through?"

Kat rolled her eyes. "*That* was not fun. They had no idea who I was, or what to do with me. I didn't speak English. And even if I could, what would I have told them? That I'm from another world?" She grinned. "Oh, and by the way. English is a real pain in the ass to learn. One word has fifty different meanings, and fifty words have the same meaning."

She drew a breath. "Anyway, the police eventually took me to a youth home. But after a few weeks they sent me to a foster home north of Mobile." She saw the pained expression in Ethan's eyes at the mention of foster parents and held up her hand. "It wasn't that bad. Well… it was at first. I kept worrying that I'd be too far away for you to find me. But after a while I settled in."

The memory of this time was obviously causing her some pain, in spite of her effort to hide it. "Were they kind?" Ethan asked.

"Oh yes," she replied, quickly back in her stride. "The Pollard's were wonderful people. Simple folks, but good-hearted. They owned a soybean farm and took in hard-to-place children. You know, older kids, and those with drug problems or learning disabilities. They used the farm as a sort of rehabilitation facility. The whole southern *'hard work builds character'* thing. I didn't mind it at all. Hell, compared to being a thief, it was an easy life. Sure the work was hard, but at least no one was trying to kill me. And once I started getting the hang of your language, I ended up getting pretty close to Mr. and Mrs. Pollard."

Kat spread her hands. "That's about all there is to tell, unless you want to hear about day to day life on a soybean farm. So you see? Nothing horrible happened to me. Well…aside from waiting five long years for you or Markus to show up. Took him a week to find me, poor guy. He looked terrible by the time he wandered up to the farm. And *he* didn't recognize me at first either."

Ethan regarded her with enthusiastic approval. "Well, you've certainly grown up."

She gave him a wink. "You bet I have."

"But I need to know something. Why did you come back? If you were doing okay there, why not stay? You knew Shinzan would still be here. And you know the danger we're facing."

"I came because of a promise."

"What promise?"

Kat's smile suddenly took on a hint of seduction. "The one I made to myself."

She leaned forward gradually. "I promised I'd be patient until I was old enough. Through everything, I never stopped loving you, Ethan. And now you can love me back...if you want to."

As she eased closer, Ethan's heart began pounding. His mind was torn two ways. This was Kat after all - the little girl who had been just thirteen years old yesterday. Of course, there was no mistaking her for a little girl now. She had indeed grown up. And when her lips touched his, he could not help but respond.

He felt her tongue searching for his. Gently at first, then more passionately. Closer still she moved, until he could feel her breasts pressing against his chest. The heat of her body sent his desires into a frenzy. All of his uncertainty was now gone; as was the little girl who was once Kat.

"Ahem."

Their lips parted and Kat sat up. In the doorway stood Lylinora, her hands planted firmly on her hips.

"I see you two are getting reacquainted," she said with undisguised anger.

"You might say that," replied Kat, giving her a tiny smile.

Lylinora fixed her gaze on Ethan. "Renald wants to speak to you before you see Val and Jake," she told him. "He's waiting for you under an apple tree about halfway to the boat."

Ethan was unsure how to handle the situation. Nothing the voices of his ancestors whispered into his mind had prepared him for this. He smiled inwardly. Though as problems go, this wasn't the worst one he could think of.

He tried to sit up, but the pain had him hissing and groaning with each attempt.

Lylinora crossed the room. After roughly moving Kat aside with her body, she sat on the bed and placed her hands on his chest. He had felt the power of her healing magic before. Usually, it was pleasant. Or at least, not painful. This time, however, it felt as if she was touching him with hot coals rather than warm flesh. He sucked his teeth, trying to mask his discomfort. After a few seconds, she stood up and took several steps back.

"You should be able to walk now," she told him curtly.

Ethan tried again to move. This time the pain was nearly gone, with only a bit of stiffness remaining. "Thank you," he said. "I feel much better."

Lylinora sniffed. "I bet you do." She glared at Kat, who once again smiled in return.

After finding his boots near the door, Ethan quickly put them on and took one more look at the two women.

"You do realize that she was just a child when you last saw her," Lylinora said.

Kat jumped in before Ethan could respond. "I think he knows what I was," she said, giving Lylinora a dismissive flick of her wrist. "And I'm *sure* that he knows what I am now."

Her smile became almost spiteful as the two women locked eyes.

Ethan hurried out, not bothering to close the door behind him. This was one argument of which he most surely did not want to be caught in the middle.

With the sun halfway to its apex, the familiar taste of salty air and the scent of blossoms produced a contented sigh. He paused just beyond the porch. Lumnia - this was his true home. Even the ground beneath his feet felt right. Earth was now an alien land to him. As he walked on to meet Renald, he wondered what had made him feel this way. Was it due to all the adventures he had experienced since arriving? Or perhaps the people he had met and befriended? Of course, it could simply be the fact that generations of his family now resided within him that had produced this sense of belonging. Whatever the reason. He was happy to be back.

Renald was waiting for him as promised, sitting beneath an apple tree just off the path. He had Maytra curled up in his lap and was stroking her snout with his fingertip.

The little dragon growled a welcome when Ethan sat down, though she was not about to move while receiving affection. "You want to speak to me?" Ethan said.

Renald nodded. "Does the name Martok mean anything to you?"

Ethan shook his head. "Not that I can remember. Why? Does it have something to do with how Kat came back?"

"Indeed it does," he affirmed. "I take it you have no memory of what transpired after you returned from Earth. Am I right?"

"Nothing," he replied. "I was hoping you'd tell me."

"I will, very soon." He pulled a sealed parchment from his pocket and handed it to Ethan. "But first I would like you to read this."

"What is it?"

"A message," he answered.

"From who?"

Renald's expression darkened. "That is what I need to find out."

"Why didn't you just open it yourself?" Ethan asked. He turned the parchment over in his hand. Aside from the wax seal, there seemed to be nothing especially remarkable about it.

"I couldn't," explained Renald. "It is sealed with far more than just wax."

"And you think *I* can open it?"

"I am certain of it," he replied.

Ethan traced his finger around the wax before easily breaking the seal. From the way Renald had been eyeing the parchment, he'd half expected it to erupt into some sort of magical flame. But nothing happened. From all appearances, it was merely a letter. It read:

Ethan,

I bid you warm greetings. My name is Martok. The power I have used to rescue your companion has shortened my time, so I must be brief.

You will hear things, terrible things, connected to my name that you must judge for yourself to be either true or false. That doddering old fool Renald will certainly want you to think the worst of me. But what little he actually knows will have been passed down by those who murdered me long ago. So I would ask only that you reserve judgement until I have my say. I hope the help that I have provided you with has earned me this courtesy.

But until we meet again, I must give you this warning. Do not rush to challenge Shinzan. If you do, you will be destroyed. I have looked into this demon's spirit and seen the truth behind who and what he really is. His power is far greater than you realize. Only with my help can you succeed. Only I know the creature's vulnerabilities. Without me, you, our family, and all the peoples of Lumnia are doomed.

When you are ready, I will be waiting. Simply call for me, and I will come. I can be the teacher and the friend you will need. Together we can find victory. We can save this world and all who dwell here.

Martok

Ethan handed the letter to Renald, who read it carefully several times before passing it back.

"Who is Martok?" Ethan asked.

"You mean, who *was* Martok," Renald corrected. "He lived thousands of years ago. His name is rarely spoken. He was the most powerful mage who ever lived, as well as the greatest shame our family bears."

"Shame?"

Renald nodded. "Yes. Before Shinzan, only one evil had ever threatened to consume this world. And that evil was Martok. His power made him arrogant and cruel. He sought to rule all lands and all races. And those who resisted were slaughtered. Entire cities were reduced to ashes as his armies spread across the land like locusts. Whole populations were wiped out completely."

"So how was he defeated?" asked Ethan.

"The great mages of that time formed the Council of Volnar. How they overcame his power, I don't know. Only a few rare texts tell the actual account, and I've never read them. What I do know was told to me by your father. He studied the life of Martok in great detail."

Maytra was now asleep in his lap. "I know he was able to command the dragons, and that he used them to terrible purpose. If he is offering you his help, I would strongly urge you to decline."

"What if he's telling the truth?" countered Ethan. "What if your history has misjudged him?"

"I don't see how it could have," he replied. "Not completely."

Ethan considered this for a long moment before speaking again. "Suppose it *is* true. All of it. If he can help me, shouldn't I accept it anyway? I mean, it's not like he's here in the flesh. He's just a spirit, after all."

Renald locked eyes with him. "What I witnessed you do tells me there is more danger than you may understand. And I fear where it may lead. When you came back through the portal, I had never been so relieved in my life. Markus, Val, and Jake came through first, as you already know. Only Markus was conscious, and he was too disoriented to tell us what had happened. None of us knew if you were coming or not, and Lylinora was growing weaker by the second."

Ethan recalled the desperation he'd felt knowing that Kat had been left behind. Then the voice came. It promised to help. Then…after that, everything seemed distant and strange. It was like a dream at the edge of his memories, teasingly just out of reach.

"After the portal vanished," Renald continued. "I could feel the power of the dragons receding. Even with their power to aid me, I could have opened the portal for only a second or two, and the effort would have almost certainly killed me. But without their help, I didn't even have the strength to do that much."

Ethan could hear the frustration in his voice. Renald was not a man who dealt well with helplessness. "I didn't blame you," he said.

Renald chuckled. "Of course you did. Not as much as you blamed yourself. But you were distraught, and your reaction was perfectly normal. Don't dwell on it. What came next should be your concern."

Ethan leaned forward.

"I saw you weeping. You were talking – at the time I thought to Jonas. But I was wrong. As if transformed, you stiffened and stood up. Your tears had vanished, and your face…I've seen that look before: the confidence that only great and terrible power affords. You pushed Jonas aside and commanded him to carry Lylinora from the dais. I wasn't sure what was happening at first. You walked straight toward me, looked me up and down, and spoke the words: 'Yul et amon'. It means weak and feeble in the old language. You then turned to the dragons and raised your arms high, as if in greeting. To my utter astonishment, the ground trembled in response."

"The dragons moved?" asked Ethan, stunned.

"Their bodies, no," he replied. "But I'm sure they caused the ground to shake. That was when I first suspected I was looking at Martok and not you. Next, you called Markus over. He said you were courteous, albeit direct, when requesting that he return for Kat. You'll need to ask him yourself if you want to know exactly what he said in reply.

"Once Markus was ready, you began chanting the spell. I could feel the power of the dragons flood over the entire dais like a tidal surge. It was so strong that it took my breath away. Where Lylinora had labored for many minutes, you opened the portal with ease within seconds. What's more, when Markus returned with Kat and the portal vanished, I expected you - or Martok - to be showing signs of fatigue. But you stood there as if it had taken no more effort than a flick of your finger. Of course, neither Markus nor Kat were in any condition to walk very far. And as for Jake and Val, they were in an even worse state."

He paused to take a breath. "*That they brought horses for themselves would be too much to hope for*, you said. But before I could respond to this, you smiled at me and a black cloud began swirling around the dais. Lylinora and the others were all lifted from the ground and placed beside me. You didn't utter a single word or move a muscle. You simply willed the spell to happen. In time, you'll realize just how impressive that was." He shook his head and whispered: "Fearsome power."

Ethan remained silent, eager to hear the rest of the old mage's story.

"Suddenly, we were all consumed within the black vortex," he continued. "And there we stayed, immobile for several minutes. Throughout, you just stood there as if nothing was happening, completely unconcern with your surroundings. I swear I never felt my feet leave the dais for an instant. But when the cloud dissipated, I saw that we had all somehow been transported to within just a few feet of my own house."

No matter how eager he was to hear everything, this time Ethan could not prevent himself from making a comment. "You mean, he carried everyone an entire day's walk in just a few minutes?"

Renald nodded. "Like I told you, Martok was the most powerful mage to have ever been born. There are legends about him conjuring one-hundred horses for his men to ride into battle."

He could see that this claim had only mildly impressed Ethan, so added: "Your father, who was a truly great mage, could not conjure more than three or four. And even those few would disappear very quickly if you tried to mount them."

Renald waited for a more enthusiastic reaction. But after a moment he shrugged and continued with the story. "Once we were all inside the house you asked me - no, asked is not the right word - you *commanded* me, to find some parchment and a quill."

Ethan glanced down at Martok's message. Suddenly, it felt heavier in his hand. With great care, he placed it on the ground beside him.

His action drew a laugh from Renald. "There is nothing to be afraid of now. Once opened, it became nothing but a piece of parchment. The ward used to seal it was spent the moment you broke the wax." He picked it up, waved it back and forth, and then tossed it into Ethan's lap. "See? It's harmless."

For an instant, Ethan looked sheepish. But this rapidly faded. "Please continue," he said.

Renald shifted his old bones slightly. "Very well. By the time you finished writing, Val and Jake were regaining their senses. You removed your boots, stretched out on the bed, and beckoned me over. *Do not fill his head with useless nonsense and wild stories*, you told me. *Your fear of my name and the power I wield will only become an instrument of your doom. I am not your enemy. After all...we are family, are we not?* Having said that, you smiled and laughed softly. I could see Martok's hold on you was fading. Within a minute or so you had fallen into a deep sleep.

"After that, when everyone was fully recovered from the effects of the portal, Lylinora, Jonas and I spent most of the time trying to explain things to Val and Jake." He wagged an admonishing finger. "You really should have explained things to them more fully. Don't expect a warm greeting when they see you."

"I did what I felt I had to," Ethan responded. "I need them here in Lumnia, and couldn't risk them being too afraid to come."

Maytra growled unhappily as Renald shook her awake and lifted her from his lap. "But shouldn't they have been given the choice?" he asked.

Ethan stood and helped the old man to his feet. "No," he replied, with absolute conviction in his voice. "What do I care about their right to choose when the fate of an entire world is at stake? I'll live with my decision. And if they're upset about it…" He spread his hands and shrugged.

Renald gave him a sideways look. "Markus is right. There is something much darker about you since you drank the dragon's blood."

"What's your point?"

"Just that if I can see it, Martok can too. Be careful not to lose yourself."

Normally, Ethan would dismiss this particular brand of advice as nothing more than a casual warning. But now …

There is no need to fear me.

The voice echoed in his mind, bleeding out from the tempest of souls within. It was Martok. Ethan could feel him watching. Waiting.

They walked on together in silence until the dock came into sight. Ethan spotted Val and Jake sitting on the edge of the boards at the far end, both of them staring out at the horizon. Val was leaning against her brother's shoulder, clutching his arm for comfort.

Markus and Jonas were talking on the deck of the boat, passing a bottle back and forth. On seeing them approach, Markus leapt onto the dock to meet them midway. "How did it go with Kat?" he asked, grinning boyishly.

Ethan cocked his head and blew out a breath. "She's changed a lot."

"You can say *that* again. When I first saw her at that soybean farm, I didn't recognize her at all. But hey, didn't I tell you she'd grow up to be a beauty?" He threw an arm around Ethan's neck to whisper in his ear. "And she still carries a torch for you, buddy. That's why she came back."

Ethan laughed. The boy he used to be would have turned red with embarrassment, but not any longer. "That's what I call *good* news," he said. "But I keep wondering why *you* came back with her. I thought you wanted to make a new start for yourself on Earth."

Markus shrugged. "I figured you might need my help after all. Besides, once Shinzan is dead, I'll be able to make a new start here." He withdrew his arm. "By the way. Whoever that guy is who possessed you…I suppose that's the best way to put it…he's all right in my book."

This caught Ethan by surprise. "What did Martok say?" he asked.

"Martok? Is that his name? Nothing much. He just promised to help us. He said he was your relative and that you had let him take control of your body so we could save Kat. That's true, right?"

Ethan nodded. "That's true."

The pounding of footsteps on deck planks then drew his attention. Jake was storming toward him, eyes ablaze with anger.

"Before you say anything…" Ethan began.

That was as far as he got. Jake's fist shot out and connected solidly with his jaw.

Ethan stumbled back, bumping into Renald and very nearly sending them both to the ground. Markus reacted quickly, grabbing the infuriated youth and putting him in a restraining hold.

"You son-of-a-bitch!" Jake shouted, struggling ineffectively to free himself. "You bring us here and don't tell us what we're getting into? Who the hell do you think you are?"

After rubbing his jaw for a couple of seconds, Ethan widened his stance and extended both arms sideways. A bright ball of flame erupted from each palm.

Jake's eyes shot wide. All his struggling ceased. "*What* the hell are you?"

"I am Ethan Dragonvein, and I brought you here because you and your sister are needed. If you think what I did was wrong, I honestly don't care. But if you do not listen…" Ethan closed his hands and the flames vanished. "Then we will wait here until you do." A smirk crept upon his lips.

Renald shook his head with disapproval, but Markus gave him a slight nod.

Val ran up, followed closely by Jonas. "Please don't hurt him," she pleaded.

"I just wanted his attention," said Ethan.

"Well you've damn sure got it now," Jake muttered.

"That's good," said Ethan. "I'm sorry you feel you've been deceived, but there is an entire world at stake here. I couldn't risk you and your sister refusing to come. If it meant tricking you or withholding information, that's what I was ready to do. So you can be as angry with me as you want. I would still do it again."

Jake glared. "You had no right."

"I had every right."

Val placed a hand on her brother's arm. "Jake. Did you really want to keep living the god awful way we were? At least here we have a second chance."

"Are you kidding?" he shot back. "Didn't you hear what the old man said about that Shinzan guy? This asshole has brought us here to die."

"You were just about to die anyway, if you remember," Markus pointed out.

With a growl of frustrated anger, Jake spun out of his now much relaxed hold and stomped back to the end of the dock.

"Give him a few minutes," said Val. "This is a lot for him to take in."

"And what about you?" asked Ethan.

She smiled. "Yeah, I was angry at first...and a little scared. But I'm finally where I belong. And if I've come home to die, so be it." She looked over her shoulder at Jake, who was now sitting at the far end of the dock. "Let me talk to him. We'll meet you back up at Renald's place."

While Val joined her brother, the rest of them headed back to the house.

"I'd like to hear what happened when you went back," Ethan told Markus.

His friend chuckled. "It was one headache after another. The pendant I had wasn't made to find Kat, so it kept sending me in the wrong direction. Because of that, it took me a while to figure out where she actually was. I'll tell you all about it later." He slapped Ethan on the shoulder. "I did discover one thing you'll be happy about though. We won the war. That nice Mister Hitler shot himself in the head, and Japan surrendered a few months later. From what I managed to find out, we paid them back a thousand times over for Pearl Harbor."

This news drew a big thumbs up from Ethan. "One tyrant down, and one to go," he grinned.

When they reached the house, they saw Kat sitting on the porch. She was munching on an apple and humming an unfamiliar tune. Ethan thought that even her voice was beautiful.

"Lylinora's inside," she told them before anyone could ask. "But be careful. She's in a pretty bad mood."

Markus smiled. "I'm not surprised. I'm sure you had nothing to do with that."

Kat held up her hands and gave an elaborate wink.

"Let's get inside," said Renald. "We have matters to discuss."

Lylinora was seated at the table with a thick, leather bound book in front of her. But at the rate she was flipping through the pages, it was clear she wasn't actually reading anything.

Markus sucked a breath through his teeth. "A bit tense I see."

"I'll do without your comments," she snapped, slamming the book shut and shoving it across the table.

"I think you should sit next to me," Markus whispered into Ethan's ear.

He nodded in wholehearted agreement and was just about to take a chair when a sharp pinch on his backside made him jump. Before he could turn, Kat rounded the table, winking at him as she passed. She sat down right beside Lylinora – obviously with the aim of antagonizing her.

Ethan positioned himself so as not to be sitting directly across from either woman.

Once they were settled, Renald banged on the table to get everyone's attention. "Now that two more of the children are with us, I think we need to decide on our next move."

"What's to discuss?" asked Jonas. "They must be taught. That falls to either you or Lylinora."

"You were in my brother's service for far too long," Renald told him sourly. "Nothing is ever that simple when it comes to magic. There is a reason why mages choose their students so carefully."

"I understand all this," remarked Jonas. "But unless you know of another trained mage…"

"You don't understand at all, you old fool," Renald snapped. "Numbers is not the problem. One mage can train dozens if the need arises. It wasn't done in Praxis' time because of arrogance, and even more than that, sloth. Mages are a lazy breed. To teach more than one at a time involves hard work. And hard work was not exactly a quality for which mages were renowned."

The door opened and Val and Jake stepped inside.

Jake looked directly at Ethan. At first he was silent. Then Val poked him sharply in the ribs.

"I'm sorry I hit you," he said.

When he didn't say anything else, Val poked him again, prompting him to continue. "Now that I've thought about it some more, I'm glad you brought us here. Markus was right. We would have been killed anyway." He glanced back at Val. "And she was right about our life back in Mobile. It sucked."

Ethan rose up and shook his hand. "No apologies necessary. I'm just happy you're here."

With no more chairs inside, they retrieved two from the porch and squeezed in at the table.

"Did we miss anything?" asked Val.

"No," Renald told her. "In fact, you're just in time. Lylinora will be instructing Jake in the use of magic. *I* will be handling your lessons."

"What about me and Ethan," Kat jumped in quickly.

Renald sighed. "Your instruction is not so important, I'm afraid, Kat. But Ethan's is."

She crossed her arms firmly over her chest. "I don't see how leaving me out is fair."

"You are not being left out," Renald said. "I will instruct you as far as my endurance will allow. But Lylinora should really be the one to teach you. And I can see quite clearly that this may be a problem."

Lylinora flashed her a spiteful grin. "We'll see just how much of a problem it is."

"Bitch," Kat muttered under her breath. But her look of irritation was soon gone as a tiny smile grew from the corners of her mouth. "If you don't have the time, Lylinora, maybe I'll just have Ethan teach me what he learns. I'm sure he won't mind giving me...you know...a few private lessons."

Renald spoke quickly to quell the storm that was obviously brewing. "And therein lies the problem. As I was trying to explain, mages take on an apprentice according to their different abilities. Most often a child will have talents similar to one of the parents. This is the case with Ethan. Though he has some of his mother in him, his abilities far more closely favor his father. Unfortunately, neither I nor Lylinora are suited to teach him in the way that he really needs to be taught."

"So what does this mean?" asked Ethan, suddenly alarmed. "That I don't learn anymore?"

"No, it just means that you will not learn enough for our purpose," he was told flatly. "Not from either of us. We simply don't have the skill. I could never teach you to be as powerful as your father. And it is *this* type of power that we will need."

"So what can we do?" asked Lylinora.

I can teach you.

Martok's voice crept to the fore of Ethan's thoughts.

I can show you things you have never dreamed of.

"We continue on with what we have," Renald answered. "And hope that a solution presents itself."

"There is still the matter of the final child," Jonas pointed out.

"There is nothing we can do about that for now," Ethan told him. "The dragons were greatly weakened by helping us."

"Will they recover?" asked Lylinora.

"In time. But I don't know how long it will take. And until they do, we can't go back to Earth."

Renald turned to Jake and Val. "Then we will begin your lessons tomorrow. Assuming that the two of you are agreeable with this."

They looked at one another. Jake then burst out laughing. "I'm sorry. But are you serious? We're actually going to be learning...*magic*?"

Ethan recalled his own similar reaction. "You'll see soon enough."

"Then I suppose we're in. Right, Val?"

She hugged her brother's arm. "Most definitely."

"Then it's all settled," Renald declared. Standing up, he hobbled over to the stove. With a flick of his wrist, the wood inside ignited. "Now, if Jonas would be so kind as to get off his rear and help, I'd like to eat some time before dawn."

*

Lylinora listened to the waves crashing onto the beach. The sea was rough and the stars were partially hidden by scattered patches of clouds. Hugging her knees, she curled her toes into the sand. Were the *sirean* near, she wondered? Were they watching her?

The sound of Ethan, Kat and Val's laughter carried over from the boat. With the two newcomers swelling their numbers, it had been decided that the women would sleep on board, and the men at the house. Kat, however, had insisted that Ethan join them for a while before turning in.

She didn't notice Markus until he plopped himself down beside her.

"What are you doing here all alone?" he asked.

Lylinora forced a smile. "They're talking about Earth. It seems Kat and Val have that in common now."

"You don't want to hear about it?"

She shrugged. "I'll never see it. So why bother?" She glanced over at Markus. He was leaning back on his hands with head tilted and eyes closed. "Anyway, what are *you* doing here?"

"I came to see you, of course," he replied, his tone good natured and warm.

Lylinora huffed. "I'd rather be alone, if you don't mind."

"Is that because of Ethan?"

She shot him a warning glance. "That's none of your business. Why don't you just go?"

"Kat sure did grow up beautifully," he remarked, ignoring her rebuff. "But I'm sure you've noticed that. And so did Ethan, apparently."

"Did you just come here to gloat?" she snapped. "Or perhaps you think my feelings don't matter." She turned her back to him. "Maybe you want to know if I'm jealous and angry. Will hearing that make you happy? Very well. Yes - I am both of these things. Now go away."

Markus chuckled. "Why would you be jealous? Do you think Kat's beauty surpasses your own? Because it doesn't. Or do you think Ethan will choose her over you?" He sat up. "Is that it? Do you even love him enough to care?"

She spun around, eyes glistening with tears on the verge of falling. "I *do* love him. I didn't before. I admit that. But now…" She picked up a handful of sand and threw it angrily into the ocean. "And now, just when I realize the truth. Just when I finally know what I want…"

"Kat comes along and steals it all away," he said, finishing her sentence. He looked into her eyes. "I know the feeling. I really do. But what I'm not understanding is why you are here on the beach instead of on the boat fighting for what you want."

The tears finally began to fall. "Because I have already lost. I love Ethan. I can see a future for us. And in time, I know that love would grow and blossom. But Kat…" She averted her eyes. "She loves him in a way I cannot match. It is something so powerful and pure, I could never challenge her." She paused to wipe her cheeks. "And in truth, even if I were able to, I shouldn't. No one should stand in the way of what she feels. She has the same love in her eyes that my father had every time he looked at my mother. I…just can't."

"Would you like to know why I came back to Lumnia?" Markus asked.

She gave a fragile shrug.

"I had enough wealth with me to live a life of luxury, the like of which you can't begin to imagine. But when I saw Kat…when I heard her speaking about Ethan, I realized the same thing you did. I knew her feelings for him would not be denied. And seeing that made me ashamed."

This caught Lylinora's attention. She looked up questioningly. "Ashamed? Ashamed of what?"

"Of myself. I gave up on the one I love far too easily. Here was a girl who was willing to risk everything for one chance to be with the person she loves. And what did *I* do? I abandoned hope almost at the first sign of a problem."

He leaned in. At first she jerked away, but Markus would not be deterred. He kissed her lightly on the lips, allowing the contact to linger for a few moments before backing away. "I don't know how you feel about me, Nora. But I do know what I felt back in Elyfoss." He got to his feet and offered her his hand. "And I know that this time, I won't be giving up."

She stared at him, stunned and speechless. Then, slowly, she reached out and took his hand.

"Why don't we go join them on the boat?" Markus suggested. "It sounds like they're having fun."

Lylinora listened for a moment to their laughter and happy chatter. "No. I think I'd rather it just be the two of us for a while." She smiled. "That is, if you don't mind."

CHAPTER TWENTY-FIVE

KING GANIX WIPED the sweat and grime from his brow. Dozens of slain Imperial soldiers littered the ground, but it had come at great cost. Of the fifty dwarves left behind to protect him, little more than half remained standing. Each one who had fallen had given every last measure of strength to guard their king. Never before had Ganix witnessed such valor.

The clamor of battle filtered through the trees in the near distance. Though out of sight, the field beyond these was where the real fighting still raged. Even from where he stood, the stench of burning flesh filled his nostrils and he could see the towers of smoke rising above the treetops. The Imperials were using weapons made by his own people. Dwarf weapons being used to kill dwarves. The thought of it made his blood boil.

He looked over his shoulder. The elderly, the infirm, and the children - all of those who could not fight - were huddled in great masses not two hundred yards to his back. Behind them lay the ocean cliffs, hundreds of feet high and spanning for miles. There would be no retreat; no surrender. And should the enemy be victorious, every last one of his people would meet a brutal end.

So far, the main dwarf battle lines had faltered four times. And four times, Ganix and his guards had fought off the enemy soldiers who had made it through to them. The human commander was clever; striking hard and decisively, then pulling back before the dwarves could recover and adapt. This was the human's ground, and they were seeing to it that the dwarves understood this clearly.

A dwarf horn blew three times, causing Ganix's guards to shift nervously. Another wave of soldiers had broken through. Within moments they would be repelling a fifth attack.

"Steady," called Ganix. "You can do this."

He drew a small axe with his right hand, and with the other retrieved a thin green rod from his belt. He held it up and frowned. This was his last one. There were more back with the elderly and the children, but there was no time to get them. Besides, one rod should be enough...at least, that's what he hoped.

The guards spread out, various dwarf rods in their hands. Earlier, the first wave had been simple to repel. The humans foolishly formed ranks at the tree line and marched in a neat and orderly fashion across the field — straight into the slaughter. But it didn't take them long to learn their lesson.

This time, just like their previous three attacks, the first few to emerge from the trees had shields in front and swords held high. Immediately they began running in irregular patterns — veering left to right, right to left, slowing down and then speeding up again — anything to confuse the defenders' aim. More and more poured out until almost one hundred soldiers were charging erratically toward Ganix and his surviving men.

The dwarves let loose the power of their weapons. Balls of fire, bolts of lightning, and beams of deadly energy crisscrossed the field. And though the humans had adjusted their tactics, the dwarves had adapted as well. No longer confused by the unpredictable approach, they had quickly become far more skilled at picking off their targets.

One by one the soldiers fell. Ganix himself struck two. Most died instantly, but some were left screaming in agony, their flesh seared from their bodies. After a few seconds, Ganix found himself almost smiling. This group would be easier to handle than the last.

The still forming smile then froze, and the hairs on the back of his neck stood up.

At the edge of the trees, a line of twenty archers had formed. Ganix bellowed a warning just as the deadly missiles came arcing across the sky. The guard to his left dashed across to wrap his thick powerful arms protectively around his king.

The act was brave, but unnecessary. Only three arrows found a home in dwarf flesh. And none of these wounds were fatal. But then, as Ganix quickly realized, that had not been the purpose of the aerial attack.

The arrows had forced his guards to cease firing just long enough for the humans to span the rest of the field. Ganix could see the archers now dropping their bows and drawing swords. Soon the dwarfs around him would be outnumbered by at least four to one. And if their main battle lines had not been able to reform, even more attackers would come.

The guard shoved him back. "Go, Your Highness!"

Ganix did not enjoy the idea of allowing his people to die for him. But the fact remained, he was not a warrior, and age had weakened him. The axe he carried would be virtually useless against a trained soldier.

The combined clashing of steel and battle cries was deafening. And though outnumbered, the dwarf fighters were fierce and determined – made even more so by the defense of their king. After only a brief spell of vicious, hand-to-hand fighting, they had gained ground and had slain more than a dozen soldiers. Gradually, a protective circle was being formed around Ganix, though this did not sit well with the old king. It meant that both the left and right flanks had to fall back, thereby allowing themselves to become virtually surrounded. The screams of pain tore at Ganix's ears as both human and dwarf alike suffered terrible wounds. This was not a story in a book, or a tale told by an elder. This was real war, and real blood was being spilled.

At length, a lone soldier managed to force his way through the ring of dwarf defenders, his eyes fixed resolutely on the king. As he charged forward to claim the head of his prize, Ganix lifted his rod and took aim. Lightning leapt from the tip, leaving behind a distinctively metallic smell in the air. The bolt struck the soldier in the right thigh – though the point of impact was of little consequence. Anywhere the power of the dwarf weapon touched was lethal.

But no matter how bravely and ferociously they fought, the defenders were gradually being worn down by sheer weight of numbers. The defensive circle around Ganix was becoming ever thinner and weaker. Two new soldiers pushed their way through on the left. Just as the king turned to point his rod at these, another two burst through from the opposite side. He heaved a defeated sigh. This is it, he thought. Not a bad death for an old dwarf I suppose.

He struck down the first two men in rapid succession, and was just able to turn in time to fell a third. But the last soldier was on him, hacking down with his blade.

Just as the strike was about to split his skull, Ganix raised the head of his axe in a desperate, last-ditch defense. The violent contact sent massive vibrations running up his arm, almost dislodging the weapon from his grasp. He tried to point the rod, but a swift blow split his forearm guard in two and sent the precious rod flying several feet away. Pain shot up his arm to his shoulder. The soldier swung again, this time in a low sweeping arc. The tip of the sword struck the king's breastplate, sending him stumbling backwards. Ganix swung his axe wildly, but his defense was clumsy and useless against such a seasoned warrior.

He was still trying to regain his balance when his foe's boot thudded into the center of his chest, sending him hard down onto the turf. The heavy impact drove almost every bit of air from his lungs, and shook the axe from his grasp. He was helpless. Still, he was a king, and would not die cowering. As the soldier stalked toward him, sword held high with deadly intent, he looked his killer squarely in the eyes.

The flash of lightning that came next was so close that, for a moment, Ganix thought he had been blinded. But when his vision cleared, a loud gasp of relief slipped out. His enemy lay dead just in front of him, a smoldering hole burned deep into his chest.

The king scrambled to his feet, eyes searching the area for his benefactor. When he finally saw who it was, he could not prevent himself from bursting into laughter. Two dwarves, both so old and infirm that they could only walk a few steps unaided before needing to rest, were looking at him disapprovingly.

"You shouldn't be out here, Your Highness," said the dwarf on the left. "Let the young do the fighting. Come back to the rear with us."

They beckoned him to follow, then turned without bothering to see if he would obey.

Ganix looked to his remaining guard. The near death of their king had enraged them beyond reckoning. So much so, that against all his expectations, they were now steadily pushing the enemy back. Though still outnumbered, the odds were swiftly becoming more even.

A trumpet blast echoed three times through the trees, and at once the soldiers began to fall back. The guard gave pursuit, but Ganix shouted for them to halt.

"Let them go," he commanded. "Your duty is here." He looked over his shoulder and saw the two elders still tottering along at a painfully slow pace. "Two of you men, help them back to the others. And see to it you afford them the highest respect. They saved my life."

Two guards hurried to do his bidding.

The soldiers had vanished into the trees, and so far there was no sign of them returning. "What do you think has happened, Your Highness?" asked a young dwarf.

"Let's hope they've given up," he responded. This statement was met with no small measure of enthusiasm.

After half an hour had passed with no further developments, Ganix was on the verge of making his way to the front, in spite of having given his word to his commanders that he would not do so. He could hear his guards growing restless - their fear of not knowing outpacing their fear of their enemy.

He threw up his hands and let out a curse. "Damn those Imperials!"

Barely had he spoken when three dwarves appeared from out of the trees. As they drew closer, Ganix could see that their faces and hands were soaked in blood, and that their armor was damaged to the point of uselessness. The dwarf in the center was Fulgur, his third-in-command. He was limping heavily and clutching a deep gash on his right shoulder.

On reaching the king they bowed, though the wounded dwarf was only able to lower himself slightly. He hobbled another step forward and met the king's eyes. Ganix could see his confusion and concern.

"The enemy has fled, Your Highness," Fulgur announced in a deep rumbling voice. "We have won the day."

He let out a heavy sigh of relief. "Thank the spirits. How many have been killed?"

"Our losses were great, I'm afraid. But theirs were far worse. Without counting, I would guess we have lost more than two-thousand men today."

Ganix felt his chest tighten. A two-thousand men! The number seemed unreal. For a moment he felt as if he would vomit. Had he made a mistake in fleeing to Elyfoss? Had he doomed his people?

Fulgur could see the distress in his king's eyes and forced a reassuring smile. "But as I said, they have lost far more."

This did little to salve Ganix's wound. "Do you anticipate another attack?" he asked.

"I can't say, Your Highness. But I've spoken to the other commanders and we are all in agreement. The retreat of the Imperial forces was odd. They had broken through several times, and in spite of their high losses, they were far from defeated. As far as we can tell, there was no apparent reason for their withdrawal."

Ganix pondered on this for a moment. "What do you suggest we do?"

"That depends, Your Highness. We should definitely move on as quickly as possible. But there are the dead and wounded to consider. Some will not be able to travel."

This cut deep into the king's heart. He knew what must happen. There was only one decision to make. "Take me to the lines," he ordered. "I will at least face those who we shall be forced to abandon."

Fulgur nodded solemnly. He too shared his king's deep sorrow over what must be done, and waited quietly while the guards set about gathering medicine and bandages before leaving.

The forest which separated the dwarf front lines from the rear party was less than a quarter mile wide. The humans had been planning to ambush them from the east as they passed by. Not that this was ever going to be successful. The dwarves knew much better than to travel above ground without sending scouts far ahead. This had enabled them to ready their forces and fight on a battlefield of their own choosing.

But as they emerged from the trees, Ganix could see that even with these preparations, it had not been enough to stay the carnage.

Thousands of dwarves were still lined up in formation, staring out over what had only a short time ago been a field of death. The wounded were being taken to an area just inside the tree line. The dead were being carried further in, out of sight of their comrades.

A messenger ran up and gave a low sweeping bow. "Your Highness. Lord Anwair has requested your presence. He says there is something you must see." He bowed once again, then beckoned for them to follow.

They were led north along the rear of the formations. Cheers swelled from the ranks as the people saw their monarch passing, filling Ganix's soul with an even deeper sense of guilt. Yet no matter how badly he felt, he knew he could not allow it to show. With steely control, he kept a stern confident look plastered on his face and frequently shouted out words of appreciation and encouragement.

Lord Anwair awaited them at the very center of the line. He was a stout dwarf with a jovial nature and a keen mind. Though from a family of serious scholars, he had chosen a life dedicated to art and music – which in Ganix's estimation was far better suited to his personality.

He waved his arm high in greeting as they approached. His blond beard was stained red with blood: his armor dented and broken in numerous places. Even so, he had not lost the sparkle in his eye that always brought a smile to the old king's face.

"Your Highness," roared Anwair, laughing. "I see you're still with us - unkilled by the Imperial swine. Though I hear, not from their lack of trying."

Ganix struggled to maintain his kingly demeanor. "They did indeed give it their best effort. But thanks to the bravery of our people, we live to fight another day."

Anwair strode up close to place a hand firmly on the king's shoulder. Suddenly his face grew more serious and his eyes looked upon his monarch with sympathy. "I know this is difficult to bear," he told him in a low whisper. "And I know you well enough to see the doubt in your face. But you have made the right choice in evacuating our home. Not a single dwarf believes otherwise."

Ganix was touched by these words. Of all the lords, Anwair knew him best. And of all dwarves, he trusted no one more. If he said the people supported his decision, then it was undoubtedly true. That, at least, was some small comfort.

Anwair's confident smile returned. "Come, Your Highness, there is something you should see. Perhaps your eyes will be able to unravel what mine cannot."

The moment they stepped into the battlefield, Ganix's face turned deathly pale. Thousands of bodies – both human and dwarf – were scattered about like so much refuse. Some were mangled beyond recognition, others burned nearly to charcoal. Many dwarves had been literally turned into pin cushions by the human archers. Severed limbs and discarded weapons were so numerous that they were forced to hop every few steps in order to continue forward. Time and again Ganix's foot landed in a deep pool of blood, splattering it over his trousers and soaking it into his boots.

"A hell of a thing, is it not, Your Highness?" remarked Anwair, frowning. "How the peoples of this world continue to do this is beyond understanding."

"Indeed," agreed Ganix grimly. "Perhaps we will live to see the end of such madness."

"Perhaps," said Anwair, but with more than a small hint of doubt.

When they had walked a hundred yards away from the dwarf lines, Anwair swept his hand over the field. "This is where we were when they began to pull back." He looked to Fulgur, who nodded his agreement. "We decided it was best to withdraw as well. Our lines had reformed, but we were still disorganized and feared it was a ruse to lure us further out."

Ganix nodded. "Yes, a wise decision." He noticed that for a while, as they moved further on, that fewer bodies lay on the ground. But after another hundred yards, the number of dead sharply increased once again. He looked up. "This must be where you first engaged them."

"No, Your Highness," said Anwair. "We never made it this far." He could see the king's confusion, so quickly added: "Anyone reading the field would think exactly the same. That's why I hope you can reason out what we cannot."

Ganix furled his brow. "I am not an expert on war."

Anwair laughed. "What dwarf is? It's been five-hundred years since our last battle. I have studied war strategy, as have some of the other nobles. My father insisted on it. But we have never actually seen or fought in one before."

"I regret my studies were focused on other subjects," said Ganix. "Though now I wish it were otherwise."

"I fear that if Shinzan has his way," Anwair continued, "there will be plenty of opportunities for us all to learn the ways of war very quickly." He pointed off to his right where a thinly forested area ran along the entire north end of the field. "Ah. Here we are. This is what I want you to see."

Ganix looked to where Anwair had indicated. At once, he saw the reason for his confusion. Strewn among the human bodies were the bodies of several dozen elves.

"So far, none of our people claim to have killed an elf," Anwair added.

"Do you think the elves are fighting on the side of the Emperor?" asked Fulgur.

Ganix approached the bodies and looked at them closely, careful not to touch them. After several minutes, he stepped back and looked over the battlefield.

"If the elves are with Shinzan…" Anwair began.

"The elves are not with Shinzan," Ganix quickly told him. "At least, *these* elves were not. They were killed by long blades swung by someone much taller than a dwarf. Human swords killed them. And look." He pointed out several human bodies that had arrows protruding from their flesh. "We do not use bows."

Both Anwair and Fulgur came to the same conclusion at once.

"Then it was elves who drove them away," the two of them said together.

"But why would the elves care if we are slaughtered?" asked Anwair.

Ganix stiffened. "I think we are about to find out."

From behind a pine tree stepped a large elf. Taller than a typical human by at least six inches, his muscular limbs, narrow waist and broad shoulders gave him the look of someone even taller. Dressed in a thin leather shirt and trousers, his black hair was tied into rows of tight braids. A long bow and quiver full of white fletched arrows were strapped across his back. His keen, penetrating blue eyes were fixed on Ganix. Without saying a word, he drew a short sword from his belt and tossed it to the ground. He then removed his bow and did the same.

The dwarves began to draw their weapons, but Ganix ordered them to stop.

"If he wanted blood, he could have fired his bow from the trees," he pointed out.

This did not sit well with the others, but they obeyed their king.

"Have any of you ever seen an elf before?" asked Anwair nervously.

"Only in drawings," replied Fulgur. He gave a smirk. "And the ears were not quite so long as they are in real life."

"Long, yes," called the elf. His voice was clear and commanding. "And they can hear the slightest whisper."

"We meant no offence," Ganix called back. He shot a reprimanding look in Anwair and Fulgur's direction. "Did we?"

"No," responded Anwair quickly. "You have my apologies."

"And mine" added Fulgur.

The elf sniffed contemptuously. "Save your courtesy for when it is needed. I did not come here to exchange pleasantries."

"Perhaps not," said Ganix. "But one need not be friends to extend courtesy." He bowed low. "I am King Ganix…"

"I know who you are," said the elf, cutting him off. "And I know why you dare to cross our land."

Ganix's calm demeanor remained. "Then you are aware that we bear you no ill will."

"We know that you were fools to attempt such a crossing with so many," he shot back.

"We had no choice."

"There are always choices. Yours was made through ignorance."

"And what should we have done?" asked Ganix, trying to mask his now rising irritation.

"You should have remained in your mountain," the elf replied.

"And waited for Shinzan to annihilate us?"

"It is unclear what Shinzan plans," said the elf. He paused for a while, as if in deep thought, then gave a sigh. "But what's done, is done. And perhaps this can work to our advantage. We know the time is nearly at hand for all peoples to gather together. And when all fates shall be decided."

"Is that why you drove the Imperials away?" Ganix asked.

"We drove them away because *you* may hold the key to our survival," he stated flatly.

"I take it you are speaking of Ethan Dragonvein."

The elf nodded in affirmation. "We know he was with your people."

"He was," agreed Ganix. "But he has since left us to seek the dragons."

"He has already found them," the elf told him. "And for now, Shinzan cannot leave his lands. He can only send out his armies and minions to do his bidding."

This was welcome news indeed for the king, but he masked his feelings by only nodding stoically. "So what is it that you need from my people?"

"You must summon Ethan Dragonvein to us. We wish to speak with him."

Ganix lowered his head in thought. Finally, he met the elf's eyes and nodded. "I will fetch him on one condition."

The elf raised an eyebrow. "And what would that be?"

"Bring your leader to me," Ganix told him. "I would have a lasting peace between our people. What good is victory if it does not end the war?" He pointed to the battlefield. "The day Shinzan dies, that should be the last day anyone need ever witness such horror as this."

The elf sneered. "And what of the humans? You think such a peace would be honored by them? You dream of things that can never be, Dwarf King."

"Perhaps you are right. In fact, you probably are. But when in our long history did the elves ever come to the aid of the dwarves? Yesterday, I would have said that such a thing was impossible. And yet I was wrong. Do as I ask, and let us hope that we can continue being wrong about what is and is not possible."

The elf stared at the king, his expression unreadable. Slowly, the corners of his mouth upturned. "You are indeed a fool. But were your ancestors such fools as you, our history might well be very different." He bowed his head. "You need look no further. I am Lotheri, ruler of the elven tribes. I am endowed with the authority to speak for all of my people. And there will be a peace between us. No elf will harm you or your kind so long as this peace lasts."

A combination of satisfaction and relief rushed through Ganix. "Is there a ceremony or ritual we should perform?" he asked.

"If you would wish it that way," Lotheri replied. "But for an elf, our word is enough."

Ganix nodded. "Then I swear that no dwarf will raise arms against your people so long as the peace lasts." He could see doubts and reservations on the faces of the others. It probably *was* a fool's wish. But for today, the wish had come true.

"Leave your wounded behind," said Lotheri. "We will tend to them and deliver them to your mountain in the south when they are well enough to travel. As for your dead, if you will allow it, we will bury them with all reverence."

Fulgur leaned into the king's ear. "This will not sit well with our people."

"If you do not hurry," Lotheri continued, "The humans will return. We can hold them at bay long enough for you to escape. The choice is yours."

Despite Fulgur's warning, it was not a difficult decision for Ganix to make. Especially with time being so precious. Their badly wounded were going to be left behind anyway, so this arrangement would ensure they had the best possible chance of survival. As for the dead, he firmly believed Lotheri when he promised that they would be buried with full honor.

He drew a deep breath and nodded. "We thank you. Your help is received in the spirit in which it is given."

"I also offer to an escort anyone you send to summon Ethan Dragonvein," Lotheri added. "My people can traverse this land unseen and unheard. We can ensure the message is received."

"Then you will be escorting me," Ganix told him. He pulled a stone from his pocket. "I gave the other one of these to Ethan should he need to find me, and only I can use it."

"No, Your Highness," snapped Fulgur. "*This* I will not allow."

Lotheri frowned. "I see your wisdom may take time to spread amongst your people."

"And I suppose all of the elves will start loving dwarves simply because you say so," Fulgur countered.

"No," he admitted. "Many will resist and think me a fool. But they *will* respect my decision. Will you not afford the same respect to your own king?"

The words struck home. Fulgur's anger and embarrassment was painted clearly on his face.

"A valid question," said Ganix.

The dwarf grumbled and lowered his head. "You will always have my undying respect and obedience, Your Highness."

Apparently satisfied with this, Lotheri pursed his lips and let out a rapid series of high-pitched chirps. From behind another pine tree stepped a younger, female elf. Though not as tall or as muscular as Lotheri, she was far from fragile. Her hair was a deep brown and tied in a single braid that fell to the center of her back. She was wearing similar clothing to Lotheri, though her shirt was cut short at the midriff.

She stepped behind him and bowed to the dwarves.

"My daughter, Keira, will be your escort," he said. "When you are ready, return to this spot and the two of you will depart."

He turned briefly to whisper into his daughter's ear. She smiled and nodded in return.

"Until we meet again…King Ganix," Lotheri said. "Tell your people they have nothing to fear between here and the mountains. We will guard them well."

"Thank you…" Ganix paused. "I'm sorry, but I am unsure how to address you."

Lotheri smiled. "My title is Suldani. But I am simply referred to by my name."

"Then I look forward to our next meeting, Lotheri. With your permission I would like to leave a few of my people behind to aid with our burial rites and to help with our wounded."

Lotheri nodded. "That is acceptable. They will be returned when your wounded can travel."

Without another word, he picked up his weapons and strode off into the forest, his daughter at his side.

"I don't like this, Your Highness," said Fulgur, once they had disappeared.

"I have to agree," added Anwair. "How do we know we can trust them?"

Ganix slapped him fondly on the shoulder. "We don't, my friend. But that's how trust is built. One step at a time. And the first step is often the most difficult to take."

End Book Two

CPSIA information can be obtained at www.ICGtesting.com
Printed in the USA
BVOW05s0251211215

430709BV00026B/761/P